C0-AJQ-862

The Shadow of God

By the same author

The Bride of Suleiman

The Shadow of God

AILEEN CRAWLEY

St. Martin's Press • New York

For information, address St. Martin's Press, 175 Fifth Avenue, New York, N.Y. 10010.

Library of Congress Cataloging in Publication Data

Crawley, Aileen.
The shadow of God.

1. Suleiman I, Sultan of the Turks, 1495-1566—
Fiction. I. Title.
PR6053.R3758S5 1983 823'.914 83-2874
ISBN 0-312-71406-8

First U.S. Edition

10 9 8 7 6 5 4 3 2 1

First published in Great Britain by Hutchinson & Co.
(Publishers) Ltd.

Contents

BOOK ONE
Rhodes

1

On a spring evening in the year 1522 two ageing men had climbed to the battlements of a tower on the north side of the city of Rhodes. They looked out across the sea, empty now of shipping, over which they might soon expect to see the Turkish fleet sailing to attack them. Their meeting was purely accidental; they were not close friends, and although they respected each other, had little in common. They had merely shared an impulse, predictable in experienced soldiers at that time and place, to find somewhere quiet from which to see what was to be seen and wonder about the future. Both wore the sombre but dramatic habit of the Knights Hospitallers of St John of Jerusalem, and both ranked high in that Order.

At first neither had much to say, but Thomas Dockwra, Prior of the Knights of the English Language, and commander of the Order's light cavalry (Turcopilier was his title, and the rough-hewn word expressed his personality to a T) was uncomfortable with his companion and could not keep quiet in his presence.

'How goes the work, then?' he asked abruptly, looking down at ant-like figures labouring over enormous stone blocks.

There was a long silence, then the other man smiled and said, 'Oh, well enough. We don't lack willing hands but some materials are growing short and we have not the money to buy more. Even if we have the time, eh, Thomas?'

Dockwra cleared his throat and said gruffly, 'No doubt we'll survive.' He was ashamed of the platitude at once and wished again that he could resist the urge to talk nonsense in the presence of the new Grand Master. It was certainly not hostility on his part, even though he had himself been a candidate for the office, nor that he did not admire him – indeed, who could fail to honour his splendid achievements as soldier and diplomat? It was simply that Thomas wished he would just once betray a weakness and prove himself human.

Philippe de l'Isle Adam raised his head and looked at him with the faint smile that Thomas always found disconcerting. He seemed to speak seriously enough. 'Oh, we will,' he said softly. 'At the worst, nothing is ever quite destroyed and we are survivors above all else.'

Eight months before, Philippe de l'Isle Adam had been elected Grand Master of the Knights Hospitallers. At the time of his election he had been in France and had returned immediately to Rhodes, there to be greeted with all the ceremony and congratulations which went with the office. The most momentous message had come from the new Sultan of Turkey, Suleiman. This young man had himself just returned from a victorious campaign against the Hungarians, his first, and his letter of congratulation mixed an unmistakable threat of invasion and conquest with its good wishes.

Diplomat as he was, de l'Isle Adam was also a realist. He wrote in reply that he had 'right well comprehended the meaning' of the Sultan's message, as well as the fact that a serious attempt had been made to wreck his ship and take him prisoner on the voyage from France. There had been no more correspondence, but the new Grand Master had set about defence preparations immediately. He had called the Council and put the letter before them. Then he had sent envoys to the Pope and all the principal courts of Europe asking for support and practical help – which latter had been singularly unavailable. He had called home all the Knights who were abroad, rallied the town and city folk to their support, repaired the sea defences and collected arms and ammunition. But never until this moment had anyone heard him say a word to suggest that the Turkish threat might not be withstood, or that the Knights could possibly be seriously at risk.

The Prior could hardly believe his ears. He was an intelligent man and had frequently questioned their chances himself. For instance he knew, none better, that his own king, Henry VIII, far from proffering support was casting greedy eyes at the Order's English properties, and that his response was typical of Europe's as a whole. But still, he was a buoyant man, and self-reliant, and so he did not look to hear this sort of talk from his Grand Master. He was disconcerted. He said, 'We've been here two hundred years or more, and even we couldn't get it by conquest alone. If it wasn't impregnable before, we've made it so – and even Chancellor D'Amaral says we've got powder and supplies for more than a year –'

De l'Isle Adam interrupted him. 'Ah, yes,' he said. 'The Chancellor.' It seemed to the Prior that at that moment he and the Grand Master moved a little closer together in spirit. Perhaps it was his use of the word 'even' that had done it. Chancellor D'Amaral had been the third contestant for the office of Grand Master and had been unwise enough to feel himself entitled to it. His own pride and arrogance had denied it to him, but of course he was unable to concede this. The silence that fell between the two men was, it seemed to Dockwra, different in quality from the earlier one. He, certainly, no longer felt a need to say something for the sake of speaking but waited calmly for the Grand Master to come to the point. When he did, he spoke obliquely, but Thomas felt he understood him pretty well.

'It never does to leave anything to chance, especially at a time like this. We must have a commission to watch over the dispersal of our supplies, particularly of powder, ammunition and the like. The Chancellor must be one, of course, and perhaps you, Thomas, will also serve. There should be a third, I will think of someone –' His hand on the Prior's arm urged him forward, so that Thomas thought he had grown tired of the conversation or had something else to do, but if so he changed his mind, for instead of descending the narrow stairs, he stopped and looked once more across the sun-sequinned sea. 'Beautiful, isn't it?' he murmured, and leant his arms on the rough stone.

'Beautiful, indeed,' agreed Thomas, slightly taken aback by this change of direction. However, he was pleased by the Grand Master's mark of confidence in him and the late afternoon sun was making him drowsy.

'When I first came here as a young knight I could think of nothing but the loveliness of the place and the – the purity, the perfection of what I had been called here to do.' He leaned his chin on his clasped hands and went on, almost dreamily, 'To care for the sick and the poor, to carry God's war to the infidel – what, I thought, could be nobler or a better way to spend one's life? Eh, Thomas?'

'To be sure.' Now that he thought of it Dockwra could not remember that he had ever been possessed by any enthusiasm to care for either the poor or the sick although he had served his stint conscientiously enough. But fighting the infidel, or any other legitimate enemy, that had been something he understood. He hadn't been able to wait to get into the galleys! It was still the same. Except for the genuinely religious, young Knights served in the Hospital because they had to and reserved their enthusiasm for the fighting.

The Grand Master went on, 'I have been thinking about us, my friend, our achievement over the centuries, and the Christians of Europe and the rest of the world, wherever they may be, and – and –' He turned his face to Dockwra, who saw to his amazement that there were tears in his eyes. 'I realized how we have declined.'

The Prior broke this silence with a little sound between a chirp and a grunt. He cleared his throat, and said gruffly, 'Declined, have we? I'll swear the Turk doesn't think so, or any other of the infidel brood. We command these seas and take their trade goods and their treasure – their merchants hardly dare set sail! After all, that's why he's coming after us, isn't it?'

The other gave his gentle laugh but didn't answer the question. 'As you say, we take the infidel's property and drive him from the sea. We are pirates, Thomas.'

Dockwra stared at him for a moment while a slow smile crept across his heavily bearded mouth. 'Well,' he said, 'if that's the way the Lord wants His work done, so be it.'

But the Grand Master looked at him seriously and shook his head. 'Oh, I know we all serve Him according to our talents, but do we have to enjoy it quite so much? We take their gold because we want it, and kill them because we hate them.'

'Well,' expostulated the Prior, 'what I say is, if a man puts his life at risk to serve Him, he's entitled to enjoy it if he can!'

'Thomas,' said his superior sternly, 'this is a serious matter; we must not descend to scoring off each other in a war of words. Though I am bound to admit,' the sweet smile reappeared momentarily, 'that you are better at it than I am.' Although he was the shorter of the two, Thomas had a momentary sense that the Grand Master was looking seriously down at him. 'Answer me this: how many of the younger knights have women in the city?'

Dockwra's broad face flushed purple.

'Don't misunderstand me – I'm not seeking a literal answer, or even any answer. What I am saying is that as we have become a powerful and complex organization, so we have gradually lost sight of our pristine purpose. We have become worldly – we eat rich food and wear fine clothes. Too much of our business is bloody and violent, too much of it is conducted in the midst of the temptations of courts. We do the Lord's work for its own sake not for His, and this is what frightens me.'

The Prior rubbed a great hand over his prickly beard. 'After we've dealt with your Sultan Solomon, or whatever his name is,' he said, 'perhaps we should see about reform.'

'Yes.' De l'Isle Adam's reply was incisive, so that Dockwra flushed again, but no reproof seemed intended. The Grand Master withdrew from the battlements and sat down on a block of stone, folding his arms around his knees. 'So we shall. But does it not occur to you, my dear sir, that if the sickness or inertia that is the spirit of this age were confined to ourselves, we would not have been working and worrying ourselves to death to meet this threat alone? That harbour down there would have been full of the ships of every country in Europe and the city crammed with their soldiers. And very possibly, the Turk might have thought better of it. As it is,' he shrugged, 'France cannot help us because of her war with Italy, the Emperor is frightened by a renegade monk who stirs up the people to something like revolution, and as for your King Henry –'

'The less said the better,' Thomas finished for him. 'I know. But with respect, sir, if it were not one thing it would be another, and the last Crusade was abortive. The world's moved on, and away.'

'That is precisely my point. The Turk has not moved on, he still believes in a holy war, while our friends believe only in power. This is what disturbs me. Our friends have deserted us, but the enemy believes in the virtue of what he does.' He looked up at Dockwra, his face intent. 'I don't think the battle's lost before it's begun. It is simply that we should know exactly where we stand. No one is coming to rescue us. We shall depend entirely on our own efforts. What was the number at the last count?'

'Four thousand or so, I believe,' responded the Prior. 'Five hundred knights, give or take a few, and the rest are mercenaries and Rhodians.' The Grand Master nodded. 'Four thousand, our faith in God, and such determination and ability as we possess.'

2

Suleiman, Sultan of all Turkey, sat at his ease in a small room in the harem of the Old Palace in Istanbul, and watched his wife of five months, Sultana Hasseki Khurrem, as she played with their little son. Presently he extended his forefinger towards the baby who promptly leaned out of his mother's arms to grab it.

'Oh, careful now, baby, I'll drop you!' exclaimed Khurrem, laughing and clasping him firmly to her small bosom. She went on, 'Who's a big, strong boy, then? Who's getting almost too much for me to manage?'

Suleiman laughed too, quietly, but with immense enjoyment. He came to the harem every day to visit his wife and baby. He accepted without reservation that they were the heart of his life, but it had not always been so. Not for the first time, especially on that day, he reflected on the fact. It was only just over a year since he had made Khurrem his own, but during that time, eight months of which he had spent away from her on campaign, she had become essential to him in a way he could not explain and had at first resented. Now he was content to accept it as a piece of superb good fortune, vouchsafed to him by God's will (he was a religious man), but not to be taken for granted or probed too deeply. Now he had to tell her news which he knew would distress her and he did not know how to go about it.

Searching for the right words, he found something else to say, anything to preserve the cocoon of security and happiness which held them. Something about the child had caught his attention. 'His hair seems to be changing colour,' he said; 'should that be?'

Khurrem looked at her offspring unmoved and said, 'Most babies' hair changes colour. Mehmed looks as though he's going to have dark red hair like mine.'

She glanced at her husband, slightly puzzled, detecting an air of constraint about him. But perhaps she was wrong, for now he smiled again and held out his finger for the baby to clutch.

The little boy, however, had lost interest in that game. His attention had been caught by shining objects standing on a low shelf near his mother's pile of cushions: a gold box, an enamel vase and an enormous ruby, as big as a fist, which Suleiman had brought back from his successful campaign against the Hungarians the previous year and given to Khurrem. Little Mehmed wanted them all, but especially the ruby. He gazed at it wide-eyed for a moment and then held out his arms to it, crowing with delight.

'No!' cried Khurrem, restraining him with difficulty, 'Not for little boys. Stop it, I say!' She began to clamber to her feet.

At that moment, Suleiman, who had been looking at the ruby and following his own train of thought, said abruptly, 'What would you like me to bring you back from Rhodes?'

She had her back to him, and he saw her stop suddenly while a tremor passed over her whole body. Then she disappeared through the door into the sleeping room beyond. Suleiman cursed himself for his clumsiness. After a moment he heard her talking soothing nonsense to the little boy who had begun to cry. In a very few moments she came back, half-smiling, her expression one of bright and intelligent interest. Suleiman rose to his feet in one quick movement and seized both her hands in his, crying, 'That was not well done! I am sorry, I wanted only to tell you as gently as possible without making it too important. I see now that that is impossible. Forgive me.'

Khurrem clung to his hands, saying only, 'How long will it take to get there? When do you go?'

He pushed her gently down among her cushions, sat beside her and took her hands again. He answered the question he judged to be the more important.

'Not until June.'

'June,' repeated Khurrem softly. It was now only the beginning of February and she had thought he meant to go away almost immediately after telling her, as he had last year. The reprieve eased her and she smiled.

Suleiman, watching her intently, saw the change and continued less urgently, 'You know how it must be. Every year, or nearly every year, there must be war. Otherwise the army will not be paid and they will be discontented. But this year –' he broke off. The pressing need for this year's campaign could not possibly be of interest to her and in any case did not concern her. He heard her take a deep breath, but when she spoke again her voice was tranquil.

'You still have not told me how long the journey will take.'

'About four weeks if I travel overland. I have not yet decided the details.' He looked at her affectionately. She had never failed him, he thought. He would have been bitterly hurt had she been indifferent to his going, but now that the worst was over and the difficult news broached she would not make him feel guilty by tears or reproaches.

She said hesitantly, as if she thought he might not approve, 'I know where it is. Once, after I heard talk about one of our ships being sunk by these people, I found it on a map.'

Suleiman smiled, reflecting what an extraordinary girl she was. Most women had no curiosity beyond the kitchen wisdom taught them by their mothers, or, in the case of harem girls, the little store of knowledge necessary to get and keep their place in a harem such as his – how to play a musical instrument, dance, prepare a water-pipe or make sprightly conversation, but Khurrem had taught herself to write and read fluent Osmanlija Turkish. She was ready-witted, interested in everything. He was sure that as soon as he left her she would turn once again to her few precious books for information about Rhodes, and if she could not find out all she wanted by herself some unfortunate teacher or mullah would be sent for and cross-questioned. It behoved him to be very careful what he said to her about this dangerous mission to which he was committed. He did not want her to worry too much about his safety. The Sultan considered this for a moment, a little surprised at himself. He had never previously given a thought to the reactions of his women to his comings and goings; but he perceived, not for the first time, that his feelings for his wife were involving him in emotional exchanges he would not previously have believed possible.

He went on carefully, 'If you know about these Hospitallers it is easier for me to explain why I must destroy them.' But now he had embarked on the task he hesitated again. How could he describe these ferocious warrior monks and their achievements without terrifying her? Moreover, his own emotional commitment to this campaign was deeper and stronger than he cared for her to see. He began again, saying calmly, 'They have a formidable reputation which they deserve, but it was gained in the past. Now there are fewer of them but still enough for them to be a thorn in the flesh. On Rhodes they are strategically placed to attack any shipping in the Mediterranean, and they are dedicated to fighting Islam on land or sea.'

Khurrem's eyes were dark with worry. 'Why were they not turned out of Rhodes long ago?' she demanded quietly.

'No one ever tried hard enough, it seems. After all, we are used to pirates in those waters. But since my father conquered Egypt our traffic there has increased, and their pillage and rapine proportionately.' His face set into lines so grim that Khurrem was abashed and had nothing to say.

After a moment he noticed her silence, and leaned forward and took her hand. 'I'm not angry, my love, except perhaps with ourselves because this was not foreseen and dealt with long ago.'

'I have never understood this,' said Khurrem. 'Monks are men of peace, holy men! How can they bring themselves to fight and kill so viciously?'

He shook his head. 'I don't pretend to read their motives, but I see it as a sacred duty to carry war to the infidel.' He stopped and looked at her anxiously. After all, up to a little over a year ago she had been a devout Christian, the daughter of a Russian priest. She had been carried off by Krim Tartars and sold eventually to a Turkish slave-dealer. Like all slaves entering Ottoman service she had been compelled to profess Islam. Suleiman knew she had had doubts, and had consequently been careful to avoid the subject of religion with her, hoping always that her conversion would prove to be total.

He said now, 'There are some orders of monks who have been fighting men almost from the start. They were in Palestine hundreds of years ago when the Crusades began. The Hospitallers are one of the oldest of their orders and certainly the most diabolical of them. I am sworn to destroy them however long it may take.'

Khurrem shivered suddenly. She wondered why none of his powerful forebears had succeeded in the task that he, a young man of twenty-eight, newly girded Sultan and comparatively inexperienced in war, had taken upon himself, and she felt sick with fear for him.

'My father, I know, intended to make war on the place but did not live long enough. Now I must!' He seized her hands and drew her to her feet, saying, 'You have been good to me; you have been patient and made no fuss. In particular, you have not asked the question I know must be in your mind. Why must *I* go, and why now?' His grip on her hands was painful. 'My father was a great soldier. He never questioned what he should do, or failed in the doing of it once he had made up his mind. Such a man is very hard to follow.' He stopped abruptly, realizing that what had been meant to be a simple explanation of his intentions had developed into a confession of his inmost doubts. It was not what he had meant to say at all.

But the last few months had been testing in the extreme. Many of his most trusted advisers, in particular Piri Pasha, his Grand Vizier and old friend, feared this expedition to Rhodes and said so. Not of course bluntly and in so many words, but counselling delay on pretexts so flimsy that he had laughed at them. He knew that they would have followed Selim there without question. So it had become his task to persuade them to follow Selim's son. By dint of reason, persuasion and sheer weight of personality he had succeeded, but he had found the necessity humiliating and the emotional effort well-nigh intolerable. So he needed an outlet, and who more understanding, more loving than Khurrem? She had made his interest hers and proved herself beyond a doubt. She would not despise him and she would understand.

'Therefore,' he said, 'I must show myself able.' He swallowed and finished, 'I must take Rhodes.'

She did not answer him at first, and when she did not speak or move he looked down at her. She was staring beyond him into space. He could not gauge from her expression, as he usually could, what she was thinking.

Then she looked up at him, her eyes shining. For once she took the initiative and kissed him, saying simply, 'Yes, of course you must. And you will, I know it.'

Now that he had got the reassurance he sought, contrarily he must needs wonder how she, a girl, protected and confined as she was, could say so confidently that she understood his feelings in the face of the necessity to make war, to condemn thousands of Ottomans to death and destruction. But, unwontedly humble as he felt at that moment, he remembered instead what he knew of her past history: a girl little more than a child, snatched away from home and family, subjected to cruelty and humiliation and yet maintaining a cheerful integrity in spite of it all. These things, he saw, were relative. Who was to say that what he faced was worse than what she had survived?

Immediately, Suleiman felt lighter in spirits, more confident than he had felt for months. He had always known that what he planned to do was right and just; now he felt a surge of strength and self-reliance in his ability to carry it through to victory. He was, quite simply, totally happy.

He would have liked to tell Khurrem something of how he felt, but understood that his feelings were beyond mere words. Instead, he kissed her hands and said, 'I must leave you. There is work to do. But I will come back tonight.'

3

The work which Suleiman had in mind for that day was a ceremonial visit to the imperial cannon-foundry at Tophane on the northern, European shore of the Golden Horn. The Grand Vizier was to be present, together with the Sheikh-ul-Islam and lesser sheikhs and viziers to the number of forty; also, because he willed it, the Sultan, his commanders-in-chief, his Master of the Horse and various lesser dignitaries. Thus Suleiman intended to make clear to all those whose doubts and objections over the past few months had incensed him that the project of Rhodes was finally launched and that his will was paramount.

He rode in a blaze of gold and colour, of precious stones and precious stuffs, wearing a caftan of brocade over a vest of embroidered satin, the imperial 'phoenix feather' of gold and enamel displayed in his turban. One of Piri's earliest lessons to his young master had concerned the importance of splendour to the mystique of the Sultan. Suleiman hoped that he might today notice that the lesson had been well learned.

Apart from his escort of egret-plumed janissary halberdiers and the gold-tissue-clad pages, his retinue was small. The viziers who would normally have accompanied him had a part to play in the ceremony and had travelled ahead. Only his Master of the Horse, Ibrahim, the oldest and closest friend of his own generation, rode with him. Suleiman was amused but also pleased to see that Ibrahim, whose taste for finery amounted to a passion, was also splendidly arrayed.

His mood was buoyant. He was now prepared to admit to himself that he had been bitterly hurt by Piri Pasha's failure to support him when he had first mooted the question of Rhodes in the Divan. Piri had risen to his feet and mildly and regretfully brought out once again the old standard objections to the expedition against Rhodes, its general impregnability, the high cost in lives, and the unreliability of the new methods of warfare. To Suleiman it had seemed plain that he was really saying that the new Sultan was not equal to the task. He had been enraged. Now he saw it for what it was: the eternal contest between age and youth. Piri was old and tired, even ill. He had been a good, even a great soldier, but his time was past. The gusto with which the junior viziers and the Kapudan, the Lord High Admiral, had rallied to their Sultan's support demonstrated this.

Suleiman was still thinking earnestly about all this when his short procession reached the point opposite Galata where they would embark for the crossing of the Golden Horn. He hardly noticed the mob of citizens who appeared from nowhere to fling themselves at his feet and cry to Allah to preserve him.

Suleiman loved the water, and wasted no time in leading the way aboard the royal barge and giving the order to cast off. In the prow of the vessel a gilded throne had been set up beneath a jewelled canopy. He ignored it, dropping carelessly on to the wooden seating which ran the length of the barge. His escort looked at him curiously, and Ibrahim, always more concerned with state and status than his master, indicated the proper place for a Sultan in vain.

'We'll talk here,' said Suleiman firmly. He raised his face to the breeze, leaned over to dip a hand in the water, and smiled at last. 'It's a splendid morning,' he said gaily, adding, 'What's been happening to you, Ibrahim? It's two days since I saw you.'

Ibrahim was prepared for this, as he was prepared for most things where his master was concerned. He had, he said, put all the imperial horses out to grass at Kiaghitkhane, on the European side, and was in process of installing himself in the pavilion there. 'Soon,' he said seriously, for one of Ibrahim's virtues was his readiness to adapt to new jobs and do them to the best of his ability, 'I'll be able to invite your majesty to the customary dinner and present you with two thoroughbreds. Julfi, I should think, or perhaps a couple of Mahmudi.' Then, as Suleiman did not answer, he added anxiously, 'That is right, sir, isn't it? Two Arab thoroughbreds of the finest quality?'

The honouring of time-hallowed and often meaningless customs which owed their existence to the whims of past Sultans was a mild joke between them, but this morning Suleiman could think of one thing only. He smiled however in acknowledgement of the question, and then said, 'You will have to think seriously about selecting the animals we'll need on Rhodes. That'll have to take precedence over your other arrangements, my friend!'

Ibrahim smiled, but before he could make any comment, his master rose to his feet and stared across to Galata. He took a deep breath and said, 'Well, there'll be plenty of bustle on the other side. The area is being scoured for experienced seamen. A pity we haven't time to go to Kasimpasha to see the new galleys.' He was referring to the huge new shipyard Selim had built on the Golden Horn, where as well as at Gallipoli and Kadirga, a whole new fleet had been born. Suleiman's father had foreseen the need to expand into the Mediterranean against the Hapsburgs, as well as the problem of getting an army to Rhodes.

Ibrahim watched him sympathetically and said, 'There are hardly enough hours in the day for you now, sir.'

Suleiman laughed excitedly, and then moved to the prow and looked out across the sparkling water. He clapped his hand heavily on Ibrahim's shoulder and squeezed it, so that his friend felt the blood pulse painfully for moments afterwards. 'Two, perhaps three months on Rhodes and we'll have settled our account with the sons of Sheitan,' he said. 'Then the real business will start here at home. And your opportunity will come. Together we'll have put this empire on a sounder basis than it's ever known, consolidated all the gains and put an end to the everlasting struggle for power. In the meantime, get yourself ready for Rhodes.'

The rest of the journey passed pleasantly and swiftly enough, Suleiman doing most of the talking. As they approached the European side of the Golden Horn his attention was attracted as always by the crowds and bustle. The people here were different, noisier, more excitable and independent. Many of them were foreigners, and most of them craftsmen or sailors. Suleiman and Ibrahim talked on sporadically. Nothing of any great moment was said, there wasn't time for confidences and the occasion hardly allowed for serious talk. But Suleiman valued such exchanges and did not take them lightly. Indeed, in their way they were unique.

As Sultan he occupied an extremely lonely eminence. The Ottoman Ruling Institution was largely based on slavery, but slavery with a difference. Most state offices were occupied by men who had once been Christian slave boys. Forcibly taken from their home villages in the conquered countries of the now far-flung Turkish empire, they were examined for intelligence, special gifts and physical stamina and beauty. The run of the mill went into the army, becoming the Sultan's dreaded janissaries. The best went to the Pages' Schools, there to be trained and educated. A boy could begin life at the ploughtail and end up as Grand Vizier. All that was required of him was a show of ability in any field. This periodic collection of slave boys was known as the Devshirme and came to give its name to the system. Thus many of the Sultan's officers of state and his soldiers were his slaves and he, at the head of the Institution, was the only free man and the only one who achieved his office by birth. This in itself was enough to cut him off from his fellows. His power was total, he was head and centre of the whole state. Such a responsibility required immense strength of character and intelligence in the man who wielded it, but while the system provided him with the best possible servants to help in his task it also denied him friends.

Ibrahim had not come to him through the usual channels. He was not a graduate of the Pages' School nor a born Turkish gentleman, but a slave purchased at the age of sixteen as a companion for the seventeen-year-old Crown Prince, then governor of the state of Sarukhan. He was a superb musician, which was his principal attraction for the lonely Suleiman, but he was also handsome and witty, and had been carefully educated by his previous owner, a wealthy widow. The friendship between the sympathetic Greek boy and the prince was immediate. Soon they were inseparable, riding and swimming together, reading and talking far into the night.

Suleiman's mother, the Sultana Hafise, and his tutors looked on with tolerant eyes. If two gifted young men in the process of exploring each other's minds also explored each other's bodies, it hardly mattered. Many princes, and rulers for that matter, had had their boon companions, and no doubt the Crown Prince would grow out of it. Suleiman had grown out of it and had taken the lovely Gulbehar as his concubine, but he had not abandoned Ibrahim. He knew an able man when he met one, and Ibrahim was able. When Selim died and Suleiman was summoned to Istanbul to assume the Sword of Osman, Ibrahim went with him. Suleiman made him first Chief Falconer and then Master of the Horse, and Ibrahim repaid him by carrying out the duties of these comparatively humble posts with seriousness and distinction. But there was talk among the ministers and senior officers of state, and Hafise, now Sultana Valideh and the most powerful woman in the state, was worried. No doubt Ibrahim was gifted, but he had not come up the right way. By now he should have sunk into comfortable obscurity, retired with a grant of money or land, a robe of honour and the Sultan's thanks.

It was hardly a crisis. It was simply that some of the younger, promising men felt that their noses might be put out of joint, and some of the older, starchier men looked down theirs. No one took into consideration the Sultan's character. It was not easy for him to make friends, but when he made them he was loyal to them. Also he was quietly determined to have his own way; so, on most occasions, Ibrahim was in attendance. He was tactful, knowledgeable, and careful not to give offence. Some of the court quite liked him.

The great arsenal at Tophane had been built by Mehmed II and was the largest in Turkey. Here the greatest cannon were made for the army, and it was to see the casting of one of these great monsters - an occasion of high seriousness and danger - that they had come there today.

A full twenty-four hours previously the heating of the enormous wood furnaces had begun. The Grand Master of the Arsenal, the Chief Overseer and all the foremen and founders had assembled in the vast main hall of the foundry. To assure the approval and assistance of Allah in the work, an Imam and muezzin led the cries of 'Allah! Allah!' to the rhythm of which hundreds of tons of wood had been fed into the furnaces. Timing therefore was critical, and the moment he dismounted Suleiman's first question, addressed to the Grand Vizier who awaited him on the steps with hands clasped in the attitude of respect, was 'Am I early?'

Piri bowed, and answered tranquilly, 'The fires burn well, your majesty. It will not be long before we are summoned. In the meantime we can wait in the Grand Master's room. Or if you prefer, in the garden.'

Suleiman nodded and elected to wait in the garden. The heat of the building could be felt even on the steps outside, and he could smell the reek of burning timber.

'What is the procedure?' he demanded, excitement beginning to rise in him. He began striding up and down on the grass, so that Piri had difficulty in keeping up with him.

'I have the Grand Master of Artillery in attendance, sir. He will explain everything. Also –' he turned to indicate the Second and Third Viziers who were waiting on the terrace. Plainly, as always with Piri, things were to be done in due order, and as always Suleiman, although impatient, perceived the wisdom of his arrangements and fell in with them. He paused to greet Mustafa Pasha, the Second Vizier and his own brother-in-law, a great bull of a man no longer in his first youth whom he had named commander of the expedition against Rhodes; and then Ahmed Pasha, the Third Vizier, also a soldier of dash and distinction.

A most remarkable apparition now appeared. Suleiman took in the great height, the disproportionate leanness, the reddened face and equally red eyes. What with his height and enormous turban, the Grand Master of Artillery appeared to be twelve feet high at least, and even dwarfed the grizzled janissary NCOs who guarded the foundry. Suleiman, himself an unusually tall man, was obliged to look up at one of his subjects, even when the Grand Master bowed stiffly before him. All this appealed to his sense of humour and a smile played briefly round his mouth as he asked, 'Is everything prepared? Are the omens good?'

A booming voice, not unlike that of a cannon itself, Suleiman thought, assured him that everything was as it should be. 'The viziers, the sheikhs and the Grand Mufti await us,' the Grand Master continued. 'If your majesty is ready I will conduct you into the foundry, where you will please to sit on the divans provided, and, above all, refrain from walking about.' He paused and the red eyes dwelt on the Sultan's face briefly before he addressed them all as a group, 'Once you are seated, you will be good enough to join with the other gentlemen in repeating the phrase, "There is no power and strength save in Allah!" over and over again. Then my men will begin to throw in the tin. When the brass is running, the head foundryman will ask you to throw in some gold and silver coins as alms in the name of the Faith.'

'It is all understood,' said Suleiman. 'We are in your hands.' And indeed he did understand, for did not the Ottoman Institution place professional competence above all?

The place was vast and the heat appalling. In the semi-darkness huge furnaces glowed in the distance like the flames of hell. Suleiman stopped dead at the sight and the Grand Master said urgently, 'I beg your majesty to move ahead. The door should be closed as soon as possible –' He even dared to lay a hand on Suleiman's sleeve, so that Piri muttered an exclamation.

Suleiman checked him. 'We must do as he says,' and added calmly to the Grand Master, 'Lead the way. We are blind in this darkness.'

Once seated they were able to see better. They were on the perimeter of an enormous chamber, for safety's sake at the greatest possible distance from the furnaces. In the glare of the flames they were able to see the figures of the founders as they moved urgently about their business. Because of the heat they were stark naked, wearing only slippers, heavy felt sleeves which completely covered hands and arms, and hoodlike caps which concealed the entire face except for the eyes. They looked like lost souls.

All the time the Grand Master continued a meticulous explanation in his harsh, booming voice. Ibrahim, whose sense of humour was untrammelled by any religious sense of the solemnity of the occasion, soon settled down to enjoy it as pure spectacle. He was careful to keep his thoughts to himself; he had only to look at his master's rapt, serious face to know that levity would be entirely out of place. That the viziers and sheikhs who constituted the rest of the company were also enthralled was evident as the light of the flames illumined the serious, bearded faces.

Ibrahim grimaced. He appreciated the scene for its dramatic value, but one could have too much of a good thing and this, he knew, would last a long time. It was also dangerous. Hadn't Suleiman told him during the journey of the dreadful explosion here in his grandfather's time on just such an occasion as this when thousands of people had been killed? He had to admire his master's courage and devotion to duty, but for himself he could think of many other things he would rather be doing. At the same time, this continual intoning of the name of Allah was both impressive and unnerving.

In the meantime great trolleys were being drawn up to the furnace with much nerve-wracking clattering and squeaking. Ibrahim's head began to ache and he gave up the effort to see. But suddenly one of the weird figures gave a signal and shouted hoarsely. The Grand Master's voice took over urgently. Hundredweights of tin were about to be thrown into the great cauldrons of already molten copper, and now was the time to cast their coins into the glowing mass. Feeling a fool but impressed in spite of himself, Ibrahim rose with the rest and hurled a handful of coins as far as he could. He saw the foundrymen struggling to stir the enormous cauldrons with poles as long as the yards of ships.

The Grand Master's voice went on. When the brass began to bubble they would know that the tin had dissolved. Now more timber was to be piled on to the furnace, and the moment of greatest danger would have come. He cleared his throat. His majesty's presence was an inspiration to them all, but half an hour must now elapse until the mouth of the furnace could be opened. Would the Sultan care to accept the hospitality of the Arsenal while he waited? the heat, the darkness . . .?

Ibrahim held his breath, but Suleiman had taken the point. He rose.

4

Once outside in the blessed fresh air, they were conducted to a charming little garden pavilion, a *kushk*, where light refreshments had been provided. The Sultan looked about him appreciatively. 'They preferred my room to my company at that point. At that, I suppose I am a liability.'

Piri said seriously, 'They are honoured by your majesty's interest, but your safety is a heavy responsibility in addition to the work itself.'

Suleiman smiled and sat down. Truth to tell, he was glad enough to escape from the Arsenal. The heat and the continual chanting had created an atmosphere of tension within him which he found very disturbing. He saw, too, that he was not alone in this. Ibrahim, Mustafa and Ahmed, all of whom had accompanied him outside, looked pale, and each in his own way agitated or confused. Piri alone, perhaps because of his greater experience - he had seen several great guns cast - remained comparatively unmoved.

Mustafa indeed was sweating heavily and mopped his wide forehead unabashed. 'I'm not built for this sort of work,' he growled, but at least seemed able to laugh at himself. Ahmed, an irritable man, merely frowned. Suleiman looked from one to the other, and on an impulse signalled to Ibrahim.

'Refresh yourselves, gentlemen. You see that there is sherbet here and fresh spring water. For myself, I intend to walk in these grounds which I have not seen since I was a boy, and perhaps look at the rebuilding work which was completed last year. Come with me, Ibrahim.'

The grounds surrounding the Arsenal had all the rather melancholy charm of such places, which are maintained in good order from duty rather than from enthusiasm. The grass had been freshly sickled, in his honour Suleiman supposed, and there were a few Persian rosebushes and beds of narcissi.

They took a path which led them away from the building and afforded an excellent view of the roof, which had been repaired after the main dome had been blown into the sea by the explosion he had earlier described to Ibrahim. Now Suleiman stopped abruptly, for an unusual scene was taking place in front of them. Ahead of them were two janissaries in engineer uniform. The smaller of the two, who was also plainly the younger, was bent over, hands braced on thighs, presenting his flat young back to his fellow. On his back was balanced a drawing-board, and the other man, oblivious to all about him, was engaged in drawing on the block, the tip of his tongue protruding in concentration from the corner of his mouth.

Suleiman's eyes sparkled. This was the sort of unexpected opportunity he loved, when he could talk directly to simple people like these, his soldiers, without formality or strain.

He raised his hand to silence Ibrahim and advanced, his soft leather boots making no sound on the powdery gravel.

'What are you drawing?' he asked gently.

For a moment there was no response. The young man's concentration was so perfect that it took a few seconds for the sound of a human voice to penetrate to him. Suleiman, understanding this perfectly, waited unconcerned, looking him over curiously. He was certainly an outstanding physical specimen, well over six feet in height and broad in proportion. The hair beneath the grey felt cap was tawny, the features regular except for a beak of a nose. The hand working away so dextrously was as large as a joint of meat, but the fingers were long and delicate.

Unfortunately the youth acting as the giant's table had less to think about than his friend. He could see little but the imperial boots and the lower part of the imperial caftan, but it was enough. Visitors to the foundry did not normally wear gold brocade.

There ensued what, but for the quickness of wits and physical co-ordination of the two men involved, could have been an untidy couple of seconds, at the end of which the two splendid young representatives of the Zemberekji Regiment stood to attention, eyes front, before their Sultan. The larger clutched a drawing-board in his fist. At no time had it been out of his control.

Suleiman smiled appreciatively, and said, 'That was well done. But you have not yet told me what you are drawing.'

'Dome, sir.' The tone was colourless, maddeningly unforthcoming. Suleiman cleared his throat and looked up to where a dome so plainly was not to be seen. He murmured, 'At ease,' and held out his hand insistently for the block, which was handed over a shade reluctantly, Ibrahim thought, as he watched curiously.

The man had drawn a dome, a splendid dome, most suitable for an arsenal. He had drawn it meticulously and in detail. He had also sketched around and beyond it a building which could have been an arsenal, but not the present one. Suleiman looked at him questioningly. Noting in passing that he was looking up at a subject for the second time that day, he said appreciatively, 'It is certainly a most excellent dome. Am I also to understand from this that you feel we need a new Arsenal?'

The giant flushed. 'It would all depend on what you had in mind, sir.' Suleiman noted that he spoke thoughtfully and without embarrassment, and a vast thumb lightly touched the drawing. 'This, now, is just an exercise. It's not worked out, but I've seen chimneys that'd be an improvement on what we've got here – and no question, that's the sort of dome you want for an arsenal. You see –' he went on in detail for a moment or two, leaving both Suleiman and Ibrahim behind. 'Of course,' he added, coming to the end of his disquisition, 'this building's safe enough for years yet, that's not the problem.'

'That's a relief,' interjected Ibrahim drily.

'Yes, well, all the repairs have been well done. But it doesn't look good and never could.'

'You think we've grown out of it?' Suleiman pressed him. The young man cleared his throat. 'Yes, sir, since you put the question. Everything always does grow. Anything you build, the next one always has to be bigger, especially if it's a practical thing like a caravanserai or a dockyard or –'

'Or an Arsenal?' suggested Suleiman thoughtfully. He added, 'What's your name?'

'Sinan abdur Mennan, sir.'

'Spearhead,' said Suleiman, 'a very splendid name, and

most suitable. Where do you get your interest in this sort of work?'

'My father is a stonemason, sir. Of Aghirnas in Anatolia. He was training me. He taught me to cut the stone and I helped him to build anything the village needed.'

'I see. And then the Devshirme came and you were drafted into the army. Is that how it was?'

'Yes, sir. Seven years ago.'

'And since you have served with the Zemberekji you have learned more about building?'

'Bridges and an aqueduct, sir, and some work on this Arsenal.'

'Thank you, Sinan.' Suleiman would have liked to prolong the conversation, but his inborn sense of timing told him that enough was enough. The day's programme must go on. 'I wish you well,' he said, bowed, and went on his way.

To Ibrahim he said, his eyes shining, 'That was a pleasure. But surely so promising a fellow should have been sent to the Pages' School, not into the rough and tumble of the army?'

'Well, he made the Zemberekji, sir,' pointed out Ibrahim. He thought it possible they had not heard the last of Sinan abdur Mennan, but how his master did worry about trifles!

As they returned to the pavilion, Suleiman looked regretfully around. 'We must go back into the heat and darkness now. But that was a most encouraging interlude and this has been a good day.'

Pleasant interlude as the incident had been, it was memorable. Suleiman had just met for the first time the man who was to become the greatest of Turkish architects: Sinan, who built for his royal master some of the loveliest buildings of all time.

It had not been a good day, however, for everyone. They were not visible to the occupants of the *kushk*, and since Suleiman had elected to stroll in the grounds unattended their approach was soundless too. A voice, not loud but quivering with rage, broke in upon his tranquil mood. 'You dare address me in such terms? You whom I took from the ranks? Be very sure I can unmake you too!'

There was no mistaking Piri's voice. Suleiman stopped dead in amazement. The Grand Vizier was not a man to give way easily to anger. The Sultan raised his hand automatically to restrain Ibrahim, who was already stepping forward, alert for trouble. The Greek in him loved a row, be it anybody's.

Mustafa spoke, half-laughing. 'Oh, come, sir, why this heat? To be sure, Ahmed was a little over-positive, but we're all soldiers and all love our craft – and, sir, if you become so angry, you will make yourself ill . . . again.' He paused before the last word and when he spoke it, accented it insultingly.

Suleiman's face darkened. He was not himself best pleased with Piri at the moment, but Piri was an old man and was entitled to respect. He made as if to move to his defence and then stopped. Piri was, he remembered, well able to take care of himself. Also, before he intervened – if he intervened – he wanted to know what they were quarrelling about.

'My health will outlast your care and this ill-fated campaign that you will mismanage between you,' snarled Piri.

'You would not dare to say so before the Sultan! Any more than you have been able to answer my arguments. You would not even see me demonstrate the manoeuvres I proposed.' Ahmed's voice was low but shook with rage. Of the three he was the least able to control himself, the most intransigent and perhaps the most dangerous.

'I have said it before the Sultan, and you were there to hear me,' said Piri cuttingly, and added with a certain gusto, 'As for your little demonstration of mining techniques, it was nothing new. I learned all that as a recruit.'

'Well, perhaps we are at one on that,' Mustafa laughed again, 'but, to be sure, sir, you are much older than my young friend here and have seen everything!'

There came a muffled exclamation from Ahmed. Suleiman waited no longer. 'Enough of this,' he snapped, his nostrils white and pinched. He stopped in the doorway of the *kushk*, looking at each contorted face in turn. Such was the power of his presence and his anger that all three, even Piri, remained silent before him. When he was sure that none of them was prepared to make an issue of it, he said curtly, 'I'm waiting, gentlemen,' and turned on his heel.

They got out of it pretty well, considering everything, thought Ibrahim a few minutes later as he followed Suleiman's quick strides back to the Arsenal. He looked at his master's stiff back curiously, sensing the rage that possessed him, although he had said little.

In truth Suleiman was very angry indeed. With Piri because of the implied criticism, with all three of them for behaving like schoolboys, and most of all with himself, because he had waited too long and had not been sure what to do. It was in his mind to cut short his part in the ceremony and return to the Topkapi immediately. But that, he soon saw, was impossible. The ceremony must go on for the gun must be cast, and possibly his leaving, in mid-flight as it were, could bring bad luck to the operation.

He took his seat, therefore, once more guided through the murk by the attentive Grand Master. Now he was grateful for the darkness. No one could see how furious and restless he was and he could think, undisturbed by anything except the hollow roar of the Grand Master's interminable explanations.

Mustafa's feline bullying and Ahmed's ill-nature should not be allowed to cost him Rhodes, as the incompetence of Paleologus had denied it to his great-grandfather Mehmed II. But there was a difference: Mehmed had not himself gone to Rhodes. He, Suleiman, intended to be at the head of his forces and to approve everything that was done.

He sat on, frowning in the gloom, while the dangerous, ceremonious work went on. In fact he only roused when the Grand Master came to tell him with appropriate fervour that because of his presence and the will of Allah the operation had been a success. The gun was cast. Then he recovered himself with a graceful speech of thanks, and, rescuing Ibrahim, who had found himself included unwillingly among the guests at the Master's dinner, returned to Istanbul. His happiness of the morning had gone, but he had a more realistic idea of the problems before him.

5

Khurrem, left to herself, sat among her cushions. She wanted to cry, but found she couldn't. Besides, what good would tears do? They solved nothing. And in any case she didn't need tears. He loved her, more than ever. The way he had taken care to tell her about this new campaign, belittling its dangers and simplifying what she sensed was a very complex story, proved that. So she ought to rejoice. Her mind told her all these things, but all she could feel was apprehension and loss.

She made herself small, folding her arms around the knees drawn up to her chest. I'll have to get used to these partings, she thought. I ought to be used to it already. After all, it's more than a year since it happened the first time and I'm sure I didn't feel so bad then. She sniffed and passed the back of her hand across her nose. That's no way for a Sultana Hasseki to behave, she reproved herself. But last time it was all new and I didn't love him so much or have his child to care for. And I don't care what he says, it's going to be dangerous, I know it.

Having identified her ultimate fear, she felt marginally better but still didn't want to move.

Someone scratched at the door and Hulefa, one of her two slaves, came in carrying a length of velvet. She looked searchingly at her mistress, who was moved to sit up against her cushions and push back the dark red hair which tumbled about her face. She knows, she thought, but then Hulefa always does know. There were few secrets in the harem, and a slave who used the system effectively was valuable.

Hulefa, tall, strong, uncompromisingly plain and independent, proffered the velvet and said briefly, 'Fatma sent this.' Fatma was the Keeper of the Silk Room. 'It's just come from

Bursa. She says it's special and would make you a caftan. Do you want it?'

Khurrem looked at the offering without interest. 'Not my colour,' she said dully.

'Well, perhaps not this morning.'

'I've got all the clothes I need,' sighed Khurrem.

'It's a really beautiful heavy velvet. It would be very useful for the winter,' suggested Hulefa.

'The winter's nearly over.' Khurrem sighed again. But even she was beginning to find her performance a little excessive. She sat up. 'I'll have it,' she decided, 'but I don't want to be bothered about anything. Tell Fatma to choose the style. And – and Hulefa –'

'Yes, mistress?'

'Go and find out if the Sultana Valideh can receive me, any time at all.'

The smallest possible smile lit Hulefa's impassive face. 'Not this morning, mistress. I know for a fact she's receiving the wife of a Western ambassador. I saw her arrive, in the oddest clothes.'

'Well, after the midday meal, then,' snapped Khurrem, getting a little short-tempered, which Hulefa considered a good sign.

Suleiman's mother, Hafise, the Queen Mother, was Khurrem's refuge in time of trouble and her inspiration when things were going well. A Tartar princess, she was fitted by birth, character and ability to occupy the great position she held as the most powerful person in the empire next to her son, the Sultan. And if this were not enough, she had humanity and humour as well. Khurrem knew there was no one she could turn to for comfort and help who was more able to deal with her problem than Hafise. The trouble was, she did not quite know what she wanted to do. But at least, she thought, she'll be able to tell me more about this dreadful place.

Having decided to do something she felt able to get up and busy herself. She wasn't quite ready, as Suleiman had thought, to start reading or enquiring about Rhodes, for it is one thing to have fears and quite another to have them confirmed, but she spent a profitable half-hour deciding what she should wear that afternoon, for Hafise was a stickler for good appearance and good manners. She also allowed Meylisah, her other slave and oldest friend, to braid her hair in the latest style.

Except for a face a little paler than usual, it was an elegant figure which, attended by the nurse carrying little Mehmed, made its way to Hafise's reception room in the Old Palace early that afternoon. A caftan of the palest lilac allowed a glimpse of a yellow gauze shift, and a draped turban of deeper violet crowned the glorious hair. There were those who claimed it was her only beauty and that she was a witch who had caught the Sultan in its tresses. Certainly he had plenty of more conventional beauties to grace his harem, but since the advent of this slight, graceful girl he took no interest in them.

The Sultana Valideh's eye rested on her with approval as she entered the presence chamber and made the obligatory curtseys.

'And you have brought little Mehmed,' said Hafise affectionately, extending her arms. 'Bring him to me, nurse. How he's growing!' She took the little boy on her lap where he obligingly settled himself to blow bubbles and play with her rings.

'The little love!' cooed a lady ensconced in a bower of cushions beside Hafise's divan. This was Suleiman's elder sister, Ayse, married to Mustafa Pasha, the Second Vizier. Khurrem looked at her without enthusiasm. She had nothing against her, indeed hardly knew her, but would have preferred Hafise's undivided attention today of all days.

Indeed, for a good ten minutes the two ladies gave all their attention to the baby, exclaiming over his evident health, the growth of his hair (his father had not been alone in noticing the change in its colour) and his winning ways. Mehmed certainly was a charming child and quite willing to bask in the warmth of their evident approval, especially when it took the form of a sugar-plum popped into his mouth by his aunt. She had a basket of sweetmeats on her plump lap and was working her way through them at a steady rate.

Khurrem eyed her askance, now a little disapproving. I only hope he doesn't choke on that, she thought, alarmed. She's got a child of her own, she ought to know better. She noticed Ayse's creased satin caftan and her rumpled hair, over which a headdress was pinned askew, with disapproval. At the same time, she was so unaffectedly friendly and her dark eyes so merry that Khurrem, an outgoing girl herself, found it difficult to go on being angry with her. If she would only go, Khurrem concluded, I believe I could quite like her.

Hafise's shrewd grey eyes rested on them thoughtfully. She had a pretty good idea of her daughter-in-law's feelings and mentally approved her good manners and self-restraint. Nevertheless she was unwilling to hasten Ayse's departure. All her children were welcome whenever they chose to come and were free to stay as long as they wished, provided they did not interfere with official business. Moreover she was rather dreading the forthcoming interview with Khurrem. The child was deeply distressed although she was concealing it well, and Hafise shared her feelings too deeply to be able to give her much comfort. So they sat, three highly-bred Ottoman ladies making agreeable conversation, each one busy with her private thoughts. Only Ayse chattered away with real gusto.

'My dear, you never saw such a creature! Skirts down to the floor and all held out with – horsehair, she told me! Can you imagine such a thing? And a thing on her head like the roof of a house. No veil at all, these foreigners have no modesty –'

'She was a pleasant woman and very well-educated,' interrupted Hafise gently. 'We are talking of the wife of the envoy from the Low Countries,' she explained to Khurrem. 'Her husband has been received by the Sultan and I had her brought to visit me. I have never seen a Flemish lady before. She had very good manners,' she concluded, looking thoughtfully at her daughter, who, fingers once more picking over the sweetmeats on her lap, was lolling against the cushions.

Khurrem looked at Hafise affectionately. So have you, she thought, admiring the Sultana's upright carriage. Hafise had been beautiful in youth and remained impressive in late middle age. Her husband's death had aged her, and there was now ample grey in her dark hair, but the demands of her new status as Sultana Valideh seemed to have enhanced her vitality and enthusiasm. Despite her state she was quite unself-conscious, and when, as his mother had foreseen, Mehmed choked on his sugar-plum, she hooked it out of his mouth in a most businesslike and efficient fashion.

Mehmed, deprived and a little frightened, began to whimper. 'Now, now,' said Hafise with authority, rocking him comfortably, 'You're all right now.' She patted his back, crooning over him, and the little boy decided to cut his losses. This lap was one of the most comfortable he had ever occupied. He yawned and went to sleep.

Ayse said, 'The pet!' but said it automatically. Their low-keyed response to her chatter had not been lost on her. Lazy and easy-going she might be, but she was not a fool. In any case she had finished her sweetmeats and the day was wearing on.

'I should be at home,' she said. 'I have a husband to look after.' She looked at her mother expectantly, and remembering her manners, belatedly added, 'If I may be excused, madam?'

'To be sure, if you really feel you must,' replied Hafise.

Ayse rose untidily to her feet, looking from one politely smiling face to the other. Want to talk about this war, I suppose, she thought. Both worried about my brother. Well, I'm prepared to worry about him, but I shan't mind seeing the back of my old man for a while. She kissed her mother warmly, curtseyed with surprising dignity, and waddled out, draperies trailing.

She left silence behind her. They smiled at each other, Khurrem tremulously, Hafise encouragingly, but at first neither had anything to say. The baby sighed and stuffed a small thumb into his mouth in lieu of the sugar-plum. He slept on. Hafise looked down at him. So like Suleiman at his age, and yet unlike, with his round face and red hair. But Suleiman's child unmistakably. She rocked him gently and said the first thing that came into her mind.

'Ayse can be careless, but she is kind and without malice. Also perhaps not very happy.'

'Yes, madam,' said Khurrem dutifully. Hafise sighed and came to the point. 'You've heard, of course.'

'Yes, madam,' repeated Khurrem.

'And you are unhappy?'

Khurrem looked up at her with huge eyes which suddenly brimmed over with tears.

'Oh, my child!' said Hafise, and in a moment Khurrem was on her knees before her.

'It's not the going to war I mind,' she was saying. 'It's this place, Rhodes, it frightens me, I don't know why –'

Hafise withdrew a hand from the sleeping child and drew

Khurrem's head against her breast. Rhodes, she thought, again. It filled me with terror, years ago, when Selim first talked of it. All the places he talked of frightened me, but none so much as Rhodes. But time went on and there was always something more urgent and at last I forgot Rhodes. I should have known better, for now my son is under the same compulsion and must try to do what neither the great Mehmed or even Selim could do. . . . She could think of nothing to say, and held Khurrem in a grip so fierce that eventually the girl broke free and looked up at her, crying, 'Oh, my dear madam, I have distressed you! I didn't mean to, truly I didn't!'

She sniffed frankly, and Hafise, touched, said, 'Khurrem, you must not upset yourself so. How will you go on during the next few months if you begin like this?'

This had the necessary effect. After a moment or two, the Hasseki Sultana sat back on her heels and brought a handkerchief out of her sleeve. Then she said in an almost natural voice, 'There, I'm better now. I wouldn't mind if it were anywhere else, at least I don't think so. But Rhodes sounds so dreadful.' She stopped and looked expectantly at Hafise, but the Sultana had nothing comforting to say. Who, she asked herself angrily, has told you so much about Rhodes and caused all this distress?

Pushing the girl gently but firmly against the cushions, Hafise said firmly, 'Come, we are in danger of becoming hysterical. It may be that Rhodes's reputation is its greatest defence. We are not soldiers after all, and Ayse tells me that her husband is very confident. You must remember that you are a soldier's wife,' Hafise went on bracingly. 'The Ottomans live by conquest and the booty they win. In this case there is the matter of self-defence as well, for you may be very sure that if we do not destroy the infidels on Rhodes they and their fellows will destroy us.'

Khurrem said soberly, 'I do remember it, but it doesn't help me very much.' She hesitated, then added baldly, 'I shall ask him not to go.'

She saw the Sultana Valideh stiffen, but was quite unprepared for the violence of her reaction. Her eyes blazing, she seized the girl's shoulder and turned her round, saying, 'What did you say? Are you mad?'

Khurrem stared but held her ground. 'I shall ask him not to

go,' she repeated. And as Hafise did not speak she plucked up her courage and went on, 'How can I do otherwise? If Suleiman were to die, you know what would happen to him –' her trembling finger pointed to the sleeping baby and her voice broke.

Both were silent, contemplating something which dominated all their lives but which was never mentioned, which indeed all strove to forget.

Sultan Mehmed the Conqueror had been a great ruler who placed the well-being of the state above all else. Perhaps also there had been a deficiency in his make-up of normal human warmth or perhaps he had been disappointed in his sons. However he had arrived at the decision, he had promulgated a law which shadowed and poisoned the lives of his successors for nearly two hundred years. It was called the Law of Fratricide, and stated simply that a Sultan on accession must put to death his surviving brothers, nephews and any other male relatives who might, by laying claim to the throne, weaken the state by civil war or revolution. Suleiman had been fortunate: his three younger brothers had died before his accession. But he himself had one other son, Mustafa, a child born to him by his early concubine, Gulbehar.

Silence lay between the two ladies while Hafise contemplated the nightmare which Khurrem had placed before her. Eventually she said crisply, 'I will not have this, Khurrem. Rhodes is a dreadful undertaking, I admit it, but that it will bring my son to his death is a remote possibility which neither you nor I can dwell on. To do so would be to paralyse the whole of life. Have you considered what would happen if we allowed this – this thing to tyrannize over all our thought and action?' She swallowed, then went on more gently, 'Khurrem, you are greatly loved. Do not presume on that love. Do you understand me?'

Khurrem, the tears once more streaming down her face, buried her face in her hands. Presently she controlled herself again and raised her head to say, 'I'm not thinking of myself. You do believe that, don't you, dear madam? Oh, you do, you must!'

'I think you should stop crying and control yourself,' replied Hafise drily. Silence once more fell coldly between them as Khurrem raised a wan shocked face to look at her. At length the bright colour rose in her cheeks and her crying stopped.

'That's better,' said the Sultana Valideh. Although she had judged it necessary to pour cold water on Khurrem's misery, she was by no means so unsympathetic as she forced herself to appear. Only, she thought, tears and lamentations won't help.

'My dear child, I do understand how hard this is for you to bear, but since I've known you you have usually borne your troubles with more courage than you're showing now. I believe you when you say you think only of little Mehmed. But should you not also be thinking of your husband?' She held up her hand to stop Khurrem's interruption and swept on, 'You should be thinking of him not only as the man you love and the father of your child, but also as the Sultan to whom you are subject, who must do things, not because he wants to, but because he must.'

Her last words echoed in Khurrem's unhappy mind. They echoed what Suleiman himself had said to her only that morning, and perhaps they would have carried more weight, caused Khurrem to stop and weigh their meaning, if only Hafise had stopped there, kissed her and sent her away.

Unfortunately her own anxiety was such that she talked on, enlarging on the Sultan's duty to lead his people to war, on duty and acceptance and other chilling virtues in which Khurrem could find no meaning, harried as she was by her own more pressing emotions of love and fear.

She listened dutifully of course, dully accepting the implied criticism that she had allowed herself to be carried away by grief and that her behaviour was that of a peasant wife rather than a Sultan's consort. But nothing Hafise said was enough to deflect her from her purpose.

In the large beautiful room with its carved beams and softly splashing fountain they took affectionate leave of each other, Hafise holding Khurrem warmly in her arms for a moment or two. But for the first time there was constraint between them, each thinking of the other, 'She doesn't understand.'

6

That evening Khurrem sat alone in her room, Mehmed on her knee, her mind in turmoil. It was only when the tired child's fretful crying stopped at last that common sense reminded her that she had not dressed or prepared herself to receive her husband, let alone made any preparation for his entertainment. For lately, as they had become intimate and used to each other's ways, he had got into the habit of eating a simple evening meal with her while they talked warmly and easily about whatever caught their fancy.

Khurrem shivered. There seemed little likelihood of warmth or intimacy tonight, but at least there should be the appearance of normality. Khurrem carried her son back to his cradle and hastily changed into a robe of dark silk. At that point Meylisah returned from her supper, all innocent eagerness to serve and to comment. In short, to chatter. Khurrem suppressed a sigh. She would have preferred the silent common sense of Hulefa tonight, but at least Meylisah was docile. Khurrem issued a series of crisp orders and Meylisah took one look at her old friend's closed expression and silently did as she was told.

The pomp and display which necessarily accompanied the Sultan throughout most of his day stopped short at the Guard Room of the Old Palace except on great family occasions. There he left his escort of pages and janissaries, and when he entered the harem to visit his wife he came alone and unannounced. Tonight was no exception. Khurrem, huddled against her cushions, heard a movement and looked up to see the tall figure at the door. His face seemed tense and stern and Khurrem, hurrying to greet him, felt a sinking at her heart.

He greeted her, it seemed, even more warmly than usual,

holding her in his arms for a moment before stripping off the heavy caftan and turban and tossing them aside. He sat down on his usual low divan, sighed, and said simply, 'How good it is to be here. I'm ravenous.'

Khurrem found herself making an elaborate business of serving the simple vegetable stew and pilaff which was the sort of food he preferred, but Suleiman seemed not to notice anything unusual. Only once, as she silently placed green figs and yoghurt before him, he took her trembling fingers in his for a moment. But he began to eat the fruit without any comment, and Khurrem, seating herself opposite him, thought, 'Now is your chance, why wait? But no, he is tired. Let him eat in peace and when the slaves have gone, then I will see.'

The moment came when the maids were dismissed and husband and wife were left alone. Suleiman, used from birth to the presence of slaves, hardly noticed any change, but to Khurrem their going was an unwelcome signal that she no longer had any excuse for delaying what she dreaded. An older, more experienced woman might have realized that something she dreaded doing so much must inevitably be done badly, and that it would be better to wait for another opportunity. To Khurrem in her feverish state it seemed merely that she had issued a challenge to herself and must keep it.

At that moment, however, Suleiman raised his head, smiled, and said, 'Tonight is a night for music. Send for that woman who sings to my mother sometimes.'

'Oh!' cried Khurrem, taken aback, 'I hadn't thought –' She stopped, not knowing what she intended to say.

'No?' asked Suleiman gently. 'I thought that since you seem a little restless tonight it might please you.' He continued to look at her thoughtfully, no more than puzzled by her troubled face and restless manner.

'My Khurrem!' said Suleiman. He sat up and pulled her to him. 'What is it? Surely you are not thinking about the campaign already? I shall not leave you for four months yet, at least.' He held her tightly, remembering what a bad business he had made of breaking the news to her that morning and determined to be patient with her feminine fears.

Khurrem clung to him, making a mighty effort not to cry. To be fair to her, she had cried more during that day than ever in her life before. But she could not restrain herself, and burst into tears. Suleiman, holding her, was himself distressed, for this storm of weeping was unlike her. But he soothed her and stared into space over her shoulder, wondering what he could possibly do or say to restore her to her normal balance. He was also conscious of disappointment that the evening was not going the way he would have liked; and was ashamed of the disappointment.

Eventually the flow of tears lessened somewhat and Suleiman relieved, took her handkerchief out of her unresisting hand and began to dry her eyes. He noticed that it was very damp and had obviously been used quite a lot.

Unfortunately Khurrem, conscious that she was doing everything wrong but unable to help herself, chose this moment to find her tongue and say quite clearly, 'Don't go, please don't go. Not for me, but think of Mehmed –' The rest of her appeal, if there was any more, was lost in another great flood of tears.

At first Suleiman did not fully grasp the implications of what she was saying. He loved her, although perhaps he was unaware of the depth of his feeling, and he had made her unhappy. But it did not take more than a moment for the full meaning of this tearful outburst to penetrate. When it did, he was overcome by a sense of betrayal so poignant that he knew no way to deal with it except at the level of violence. He struck her across the face and hardly realized he'd done it. He stood looking down at her, conscious only of the great bursting flood of anger which swept over him and the painful tangle of emotions – distrust, disappointment – which came with it. At that moment he hated her and had nothing he could bear to say to her.

Khurrem cowered before him. The blow and the anger were as nothing when she looked into his face and saw the hatred there. She had wronged him and lost him. The tears stopped, but in the face of such withdrawal there was nothing she could say. But she tried, grasping the folds of his robe, crying out, 'No, no, don't leave me! Oh, don't, please –' She hardly knew or cared what she said, only so long as she might establish some link, some communication between them.

He would have none of it. It was as if he had shown her his soft underbelly and she had chosen to claw at it. He snarled, 'Get away from me! You humiliate me!'

He turned and blindly found the door and Khurrem, paralysed, could only watch him go.

Suleiman walked slowly in the direction of the Guard Room. He was still cold with anger, and his temper, he knew, was violent like his father's. He felt grateful for the quiet, the darkness, for the flaming torches in the wall-holders only allowed enough light to walk by. Soon he was in a part of the harem he hardly knew, dedicated to the use of humbler slaves.

Suddenly from behind a shut door he heard a whimper and after a moment a baby began to howl. There were always children in a royal harem who had come there indirectly, orphans fostered by Hafise whose heart was notoriously soft, or the offspring of slaves, maybe of a woman sold after she had lost her man. Certainly it was not his business and of no interest to him. But immediately a door at the end of the corridor opened and a woman hurried out. He even saw her face momentarily as she came towards him, eyes wide and anxious, mouth half open. The next moment she had seen him, realized who he was and dropped perfunctorily to the floor. Then she scrambled to her feet and scuttled into the room from which the crying came.

He stood still and looked after her.

That a female slave had just treated him to an exhibition of gross discourtesy hardly touched him, and after a moment he walked on. But as he passed the open door he looked in, his eye drawn by the light of the lamp. The woman was lifting the child, and he was struck by the sweetness of her expression and the tenderness of her movements as she cradled it against her breast and murmured soothingly to it.

He went soundlessly by. It seemed important not to frighten or disturb her.

A woman and her child. It had been there all the time and in his blind anger and pain he had refused to see it. Because it was so important to him he attempted and successfully made the imaginative leap between himself and Khurrem. Her world of emotion, of love for child and man, was different from his. He could not enter it but at least he could perceive that the difference existed, and understand too that her world was as valid as his.

He understood also that all this emotion had been too dramatic, too much. The likelihood that he would meet his death on Rhodes, or any other battlefield for that matter, was slight indeed. No one was guarded like a Sultan. Yet Khurrem in her inexperience, her ignorance and her fear had created a situation which had nearly torn them apart. This was the crux, the thing which had made him so angry. She had behaved mindlessly, unlike the girl he knew her to be, because she feared for him and loved her child. At last he understood all this, but still knew that she must learn not to do it again. The future would hold many bitter partings such as they faced now, the great threat lay always over his sons, and one day he would have to face it and deal with it as best he could, but the immediate problem was Khurrem's. She must learn the painful lesson his mother had learned many years before, to look past fear and be silent. But he could not help her, no one could. This was something she must teach herself.

At the next intersection of silent corridors he started back to Khurrem's rooms. He began to hurry. Suddenly he wanted her abominably, without love.

In her misery Khurrem had not been able to face the darkness, and a small lamp burned on the shelf over her mattress where she was curled up. As soon as she heard him she half-rose and he saw her eyes gleam, and perhaps the glint of tears on her cheeks. He seized her wrist without a word, threw her back, heard her gasp, and mounted her. He took her hard, and did not know or care whether he hurt her. But after it was over his anger had gone, too. He lay beside her, sated and at peace. Presently he took her hand and felt the immediate answering pressure of her fingers. He sighed and felt sleep begin to steal over him, knowing that she had understood at least something of what he had tried to tell her without words.

7

The following morning Khurrem sat beneath an enamelled pavilion in the garden of the Old Palace and took stock of herself. It was not a pleasurable experience and she did not enjoy it. She had come into the garden to be alone. In her rooms in the harem the maids were at work, plumping up cushions, arranging flowers, rolling up and stowing away her mattress, while the nurse bathed little Mehmed and played with him. Normally she loved this domestic bustle and played her full part in it, but this morning she could not bear it, any more than she could bear to look about her and see the many gifts Suleiman had brought her, the things that beautified her two rather small rooms and made her never want to leave them. Hafise had more than once reminded her gently that as Sultana Hasseki she was entitled to a much grander apartment with more rooms, more slaves too if she wished. But she, Khurrem, who knew everything, had always replied airily that she was happier where she was.

Technically she was alone, but the garden of the Old Palace was not large and all the women who lived there were free to use it. Even now, early as it was, she could see from her arbour one of the kiayas, those dignified, well-trained ladies who controlled the household under the direction of the Chief Black Eunuch, walking purposefully back and forth, ticking off items on an important-looking list she carried. Getting a breath of air while she works, thought Khurrem, and smiled a little as she remembered that there had been a time when to achieve the status of kiaya had been the limit of her ambition. But then Suleiman had seen her. . . . And I won't cry, she told herself fiercely, I won't. Look at those tulips, already in bud, standing up straight like janissaries on parade. And over there, the young cypresses, their green as dark and soft as velvet.

She thought of their parting that morning. He had gone early, for it was a Divan day. They had had little to say to each other, worn out as they were by emotion, but at least she had done one thing right. She had not plagued him with apologies and tearful self-reproach. He did not need to be told she was sorry, and indeed there were no words to express the depth of her remorse. So they had parted tenderly, saying little, and Khurrem knew that when they met again everything would be as it was before. Except to her, who would never take Suleiman for granted again.

She looked over to where, playing at ball on the grass, was a bevy of young girls of no more than fifteen or sixteen, each one chosen for her beauty and accomplishments, each one fit to grace the bed of a sultan. Khurrem stared at them stony-eyed. These were the future ikbals, or at least they hoped they were, the girls from whom Suleiman would, if or when he wished, select his bedmates, the mothers of his children. Only up to now he had never looked at them because he loved only her. Only a few days ago she had discussed the future of these very girls with Hafise, had expressed concern for the waste of their youth and charm, and had felt relief when Hafise had explained that presently the eldest of them would be married off, quite advantageously.

Now she hated them and could not bear to sit still and watch them. She got up, a restless little figure in trousers of figured silk beneath a very heavy caftan of rose and gold brocade, her beautiful hair carefully dressed in the latest style. She had not known why, this particular morning, she had allowed her maids to dress her in this elaborate fashion, as it was certainly not her usual style; she knew they did not understand why one who had the resources of a sultan's harem at her command should normally throw on the first thing that came to hand because she was so happy and life was so precious that she had not time to waste on such inessentials as clothes.

The nurse, Leila, had brought little Mehmed into the garden and was walking up and down the paths in the warm sun of the forenoon. Khurrem smiled involuntarily as she watched them stop before a bed of early spring bulbs and saw the little boy stretching out his hands to the starry flowers. She was suddenly at peace, relaxed, content to sit and watch.

The ikbals had spotted the baby and there they went, streaming across the grass like so many gaily-coloured butterflies to admire him, to beg Leila to let them hold him for a moment, or to try to give him the indigestible sweetmeats they themselves were so fond of. Their excited chatter and laughter fell sweetly on her ears. Of course she didn't hate them. They were little girls such as she had been herself a little more than a year ago, and she had nothing to fear from them unless she betrayed herself and Suleiman again. And that she would not do.

For the first time she made a conscious effort to understand the well-springs of her husband's life. Hands folded in her lap, she sat still and thought about what she knew of his days and how they were filled. Quite a lot, really, for of an evening he would often talk to her about the day's events. She knew his opinion of some of the things he had to do. The Divan, for instance. 'The time is coming,' he had said, 'when I shall no longer have the time to give four days a week to a body which has no power and only gives advice.' And again, 'The world is changing and the empire grows ever bigger. I hold all the power in my hands. It is too much for one man.'

All this and much more he had told her and she had listened, fascinated but only in an idle way, never really reflecting on what he said but accepting the fact that he talked to her about his work as further evidence of his trust in her. Seeing everything in relation to myself, as usual, she thought wearily. I never questioned his attitude to all this responsibility. Knowing that he was trained to it from childhood I assumed he must enjoy it, and do as he likes without questioning too much whether what he does is right. And yet I know that he is not that sort of man at all and that sometimes it must weigh heavy on him. Now I realize he no more wants to go to Rhodes than I want him to go. Only he must!

A sharp little wind had sprung up, bringing a salty tang from the Bosphorus, and fur-trimmed velvet caftans offered little protection from it. Even Leila, a hardy peasant girl from Rumelia, began to feel the chill. Only Khurrem, pensive in her pavilion, was protected from it. Indeed, with the sun shining in on her she was pleasantly warm, almost drowsy with heat. Sensible Leila appeared suddenly in front of her. 'It's growing cold, mistress. Shall I take the baby inside?' Khurrem roused and sat up. 'It's warm here. I'll take him,' she said willingly, extending her arms, 'You go indoors, Leila.'

Left alone, she held the warm bundle tightly. Mehmed, cheeks red from the wind, looked up in momentary reproof, giving her a straight glance from serious grey eyes. He had had an enjoyable morning but now he was tired and wanted to sleep. His mother held him close, savouring his warmth and softness. 'Oh, baby,' she whispered against the dimpled neck, 'I've got to look after you, too.'

She remembered what Suleiman had often said, 'I love both my sons.' Yes, and she was sure it was true, and that when the terrible time of choice came he could be relied upon to make it well and fairly. But what mother, she asked herself, could care about fairness in a situation such as this? Instinctively she brought up a hand to shield the child's head, as if he were already threatened. You, she promised him grimly, shall have more than fairness. You shall have certainty. One way or another, I'll manage it. The picture of another little boy rose, unbidden and unwelcome, in her mind's eye. Mustafa, as she had first seen him in the harem at Manissa. So handsome a little boy he had been in his apple-green caftan. And she had held out her arms to him because she loved children, all children. She crushed the thought. I mustn't think about him, she told herself stonily, and I won't. It's all I can do now. That, and take one step at a time.

A couple of weeks later, she found she was pregnant again.

8

The Knights Hospitallers of St John of Jerusalem came to Rhodes at the beginning of the fourteenth century. By then they had fought the Muslim for two centuries in the Holy Land, dying gloriously at Jerusalem, Kum Hatun and Acre. But when the Christians were finally defeated at Acre for the second time it was time for them to go home, and the Muslim star was in the ascendant. Only seven Knights of St John escaped from Acre to Cyprus in 1291, but the Order still survived. Other Orders, like the Teutonic Knights, might find another role, or, like the Templars, come to a shameful end through carelessness or sheer inanition; the Knights Hospitallers fought on. If they could not fight the infidel on the land they would fight him on the sea. Rhodes was a very good place from which to do it.

It took two years of patient negotiation, hard fighting and dirty tricks to win Rhodes from its nominal owner, the empire of Constantinople. Once there they thought they had come to paradise, but it was not only beautiful, it was strategically important as well, sitting astride one of the principal sea routes of the eastern Mediterranean. And, as the Hospitallers had reason to know, it was a natural fortress.

For the next two hundred years the Hospitallers stayed on Rhodes and made themselves a terror to the Muslim on the sea. Along with Rhodes they had acquired most of the neighbouring islands of the Dodecanese, as well as Budrum on mainland Turkey opposite Kos and Castellorizon near to the mainland of Caramania. Thus they commanded the Gulfs of Kos, Doris and Symi and the approaches to Syria and Egypt. They built themselves a modest navy and took to the sea with the same efficiency with which the original simple monks had taken to the sword. After all, sea warfare was only land warfare transferred to ships and they had a head start over the Turks and Egyptians who had not yet learned to be seamen.

It did not take the Hospitallers long to prove themselves; three years after establishing themselves on Rhodes they destroyed a Turkish fleet of twenty-three ships off Amorgos and, in alliance with the Cypriots, another one off Ephesus. Later, allied with the Holy League, they captured Smyrna, and later still sacked the Syrian littoral from Tripoli to Alexandretta. By the middle of the fifteenth century they had become such a thorn in the flesh of the Muslim that the Egyptians were stimulated to attack Rhodes itself. Their siege lasted forty-four days and ended when the Knights came out and beat them in a sea-battle.

In 1480 came the first Turkish siege. This was a much more serious business. Mehmed the Conqueror could afford a force of something like 100,000 men and over fifty ships. Perhaps if he had led his army himself he might have been victorious, but he did not. As it was, the Ottomans reduced much of the city to rubble and nearly killed the Knights' legendary Grand Master, D'Aubusson. But after more than two months they had had enough and went away.

Over the years the Knights Hospitallers had acquired sophistication. When they had become an order of chivalry back in the twelfth century it meant that humble monkish fighting men gave place to knights conscious of rank. The highest class within the Order, the Knights of Justice, were aristocrats whom no young man could aspire to join unless he could show untarnished lineage for four generations back. The second class was reserved for the truly religious, the Chaplains of Obedience, and there was a third class of Servants-at-Arms who were not required to prove nobility so long as they were gentlemen.

Their vows spoke unequivocally of chastity, poverty and humility. Poor and humble they now certainly were not, nor were they notably chaste. What they most emphatically were was a body of first-class fighting men dedicated to the destruction of Islam, and as such, they and the Turks understood each other. By the sixteenth century they were also an anachronism and something of an embarrassment to the great powers of the West.

But they were not such singleminded warriors that they ever

forgot their rule of chastity and obedience or the original purpose of their existence; the care of the sick and the poor. They still looked after the pilgrims to the Holy Places, but they probably enjoyed it most when it entailed fighting. Led by a series of outstanding Grand Masters they streamlined their administration, took care of their defences and their ships and did not neglect the interests of the native Rhodians when these did not conflict with their own. Rhodian merchants especially, who were usually not native-born Rhodians, flourished under their rule.

Socially they divided themselves into eight sections, roughly according to language. These they called the Langues, and each Langue maintained a house where its Knights lived well on the whole, if not always peaceably. For instance, the English Langue included the Scots and the Irish as well as the English. It was not to be expected therefore that the English Langue could be at any time a nest of cooing doves. The other Langues were those of France, Italy, Auvergne, Aragon, Provence, Germany and Castile. Each Langue was also responsible for the maintenance of a particular section of the city's defences. This had a disadvantage: there was a tendency for Grand Masters to favour the defences of the particular Langues from which they came. Hence the Ports of France and Auvergne, from which Langues so many of the Grand Masters had been drawn, were, for instance, rather better maintained than some of the others.

As de l'Isle Adam went about the city overseeing the preparations for its defence it seemed to him sometimes that he was only the instrument by which history would repeat itself. He was not a fanciful man: he simply knew that every decision taken by himself and his Council echoed a similar one taken in the past at a like moment of crisis. This fateful feeling comforted him obscurely, but he did not allow himself to be carried away by it.

He knew Rhodes well and had loved the place from his earliest years, when, a boy in his teens and already a Knight, he had come there to serve his apprenticeship in the Hospital and the galleys. Evidence of the destruction inflicted by the Turks in 1480 was all around for him to see. The Tower of St Nicholas had been destroyed, many of the walls and watchtowers reduced to rubble, and the Ghetto wiped out.

This had appalled him. It had never occurred to his naive young mind that victory could wear scars indistinguishable from those of defeat. He had never forgotten the lesson.

Over the years they had rebuilt the city, stronger and finer than ever. The Great Powers, who had been no readier in 1480 than they were now to help resist the Turk, had been impressed by the victory they had done nothing to win and had poured out money and materials for the work. Now, thought de l'Isle Adam wryly, it was all about to happen again. Win or lose, these splendid new bastions and fortifications would see just as much destruction, and his little army just as much death and agony as before.

By the end of April all the obvious things had been done; food and munitions bought from Italy, wine in great quantities from Candia, not only for drinking but also for medical use. The island's rich countryside had been robbed of such crops as could be garnered so early, and then scorched. The two harbours on which the city was built were closed. The galley port to the north, where lay the precious fleet of galleys and the Great Ship, the magnificant carrack of 2000 tons which was their supply ship and their special pride and joy, was blocked by sunken hulks weighted with stones. Heavy chains across its mouth shut the commercial port.

The Grand Master now made it his business to go about the city, not only in the splendid streets of the citadel behind the galley port where lay his own palace, the Hospital and the various lodgings of the Langues, but also the Merchants' Quarter and even the Ghetto to the south of it. He did not particularly enjoy these excursions but believed them to be necessary. He would walk, tall, upright, an aristocratic figure in his black peacetime surcoat with its eight-pointed cross on breast and back, hands clasped behind him, apparently at random about the streets. With him would come Gabriel de Pommeroys, his lieutenant, squat, rugged and watchful. He did not altogether understand, and certainly did not approve, his superior's suddenly-acquired habit of stopping to talk to all and sundry, particularly when humbler citizens took the opportunity to speak their minds.

'If it weren't for you lot, the Turks wouldn't bother us,' said one man roundly. He was as broad as a barrel, with grizzled hair and beard, and having spoken he spat, so that de

Pommeroys' hand flew to his sword-hilt and he jerked his head at the bodyguard.

De l'Isle Adam, however, shook his head at them and spoke the man fair, which certainly had not always been his way.

'That's not quite true, you know. Before we came here the Turk was always sending out his raiding parties to attack you, burn your boats, steal your crops. Now we're all Christians together and will fight together, isn't that so?'

He smiled his particularly sweet smile and went on his way, and the man, who had had it in mind to say something sharp about the seizure of his harvest and the subsequent burning of his market-garden, was left, if not convinced, at least mollified and flattered that his words had been taken seriously.

De Pommeroys drew abreast of the Grand Master to express outrage. 'You can't trust these islanders, riff-raff the lot of them,' he declared.

The Grand Master shrugged. He felt no particular sympathy with the Rhodians either, if the truth was told. All the emotion of which he was capable was reserved for the Order and the glory of God. But he had responsibility for these people and knew their importance in the scheme of things. At the moment he was not very pleased with what he had said to the man, thinking it fatuous. Still, he told himself, the will is everything. The fact of speaking is what matters.

He said, 'You're unjust, Gabriel. They fought well in 1480 and will again. At a time like this, it is the poor and weak who are most at risk.' He meant this sincerely although he was already beyond feeling it.

He walked on, finding something to say to an old man sitting in a shop doorway, a matron trudging across the Piazza with her basket, and a sober citizen who told him that his soldiers had destroyed his summer villa outside the walls.

'There was no sense in that, your reverence,' the man complained. 'It was only a tiny place. We used to go there for a breath of fresh air in the summer heat. The military are all the same.'

De l'Isle Adam listened courteously. 'Were you here in 1480?' he asked.

The man's chest swelled. 'Was I here? Aye, I rather think I was here! Fought with the sailors, I did, and a likely lad I was too.'

'Then,' the Grand Master interrupted gently, 'you will remember that all the villas and farms outside the walls became a menace, for the Turk used them as cover when he didn't destroy them. Now our cannon will be able to rake the whole countryside and he won't be able to hide from us. But I am sorry about your villa.' He bowed and moved on unhurriedly.

As the weeks passed, the Grand Master's visits to the outer city came to be welcomed by the native Rhodians; he was greeted with smiles instead of complaints, and sometimes as he passed something like a cheer went up. The first time this happened de Pommeroys looked back in amazement, but de l'Isle Adam, walking on, murmured, 'They are our friends now and that is all we can, or have the right to, hope for.' He added abruptly, 'Let us go on to the ramparts. I am happier among my own kind.'

His lieutenant shook his head over this seeming inconsistency, but in fact his superior's attitude was not illogical. He knew that if things went badly for them the local people would be the first to cry for surrender. He did not blame them for this, but knew that it was not the way the Holy Religion fought. So he turned his steps towards the Post of Auvergne, from whose fine new bastion he could look seaward across the whole city of Rhodes, breathe the salt-fresh air that was also laden with the scent of myrtle and thyme, and listen to enthusiastic young Knights who talked wisely about trajectories and escarpments and who would, he knew, never give in.

At the end of May the Grand Master held a great review of all his forces. It was great in everything except numbers, he thought as they passed. They were well-armed, they had arquebus and matchlock as well as pike, bow and axe. Their spirits were high and the Knights, wearing now the wartime surcoats, white with the crimson cross, over their armour stirred his own weary spirit as nothing else could. He only wished there were more of them than the five hundred who now marched past him, each Langue displaying its banners. With them he computed he had some five thousand men-at-arms, including the citizens' militia and the sailors and mercenaries, those stout-hearted adventurers who had trickled in, mostly from Italy and France, because they sympathized with the Hospitallers' cause or even simply because they liked to fight. He watched the effect of the review on the watching crowds in the Piazza, and risked marching some detachments past again. They deserved to have their spirits kept up.

The beginning of June brought the first piece of hard news of how the enemy intended to fight. A Turkish brig was captured off Kos by Brother Jean Beauluoys. Brother Jean was rough with the crew, and they spilled out a lot of hearsay and gossip which included one gem: Sultan Suleiman hoped to overcome Rhodes by mining its walls and had sent for a force of expert sappers from the garrison in Bosnia. The Grand Master took thought and sent to Candia for a military engineer and mining expert called Gabriele Tadini da Martinengo. He was just in time. On 26 June, the lookouts saw the first Turkish ships on the horizon.

9

Sultan Suleiman arrived on the island of Rhodes on 28 July 1522. It took him over a month to get there, for he had marched the Asiatic army of some 15,000 men down the western rim of Turkey to Marmarice, whence they would be transported the short distance to Rhodes by sea. Mustafa Pasha, the Seraskier, Arnavut Ahmed Pasha, his deputy, and Piri Pasha, who was acting as Chief of Staff, had already arrived by sea over a month before, with the main body of the army. Thus by the time the Sultan arrived, all the hard mechanical business of transporting men, cannon and munitions, siege-engines, pack-animals, food on the hoof, and stores of every kind to their final positions before the city would have been accomplished, the camps would have been set up, and the Seraskier and his aides would have decided their final strategy. Also the fleet, under the command of that rogue Cortuglu, the corsair whom Suleiman had taken under his wing, would have taken up their positions to blockade the city. No time was to be wasted, Suleiman thought, and the siege would be over and the men well on their way home before the end of September.

He was happy. In the face of all opposition he had forged his own way. Of Khurrem's opposition he no longer thought; her reasons had all been emotional, rooted in her love for him. For this he had every reason to be grateful. He promised to bring her some of the roses from which Rhodes traditionally took its name and lovingly put her to the back of his mind. He had dealt with Mustafa and Ahmed, too. He matched his brother-in-law's catlike bluster with a little flexing of his own claws within a velvet glove. He was by no means certain, he suggested, that the new artillery, excellent as it was, would suffice to reduce Rhodes in the first instance. How fortunate, he added, that Mustafa had, in the person of Ahmed, an engineer officer of such experience to support him. Mustafa's eyes had narrowed at this. He talked rather fast of the improvement in fire power, of the new mortars which, he was sure, would be able to lob balls right over the walls into the city and much else, but he took the point.

With Ahmed, a blunt man of few words himself, it was possible to be more direct; do not harry the Seraskier, you are there to support him and not supplant him. Both methods seemed to work. The Pashas, after circling round each other for a few days like a couple of dogs growling in their throats, settled down to a working arrangement which if not cordial, at least allowed things to get done.

Suleiman had learned much during the previous year's campaign against Belgrade; he was no longer the untried commander, supported at every turn by his senior men. The decisions were now his to make and he had indeed given strict instructions to Mustafa that the main bombardment of Rhodes was not to start until he himself should arrive. So now he allowed himself to relax and enjoy the long journey westward. This was largely due to the men who accompanied him. Ibrahim, of course, travelled with him in his official capacity, for it was the Turkish rule that the business of the state must accompany the Sultan, even to war, so that all the high officers of the court made the journey as well. But at Kutahia, an ancient town situated on the edge of a well-watered plain, he was joined by old military friends from the previous year who brought a breath of fresh air into the proceedings. Bali Aga, the Aga of the Janissaries, vigorous, cheerful, easy-going when things were going well and a lion when they were not; Ali Bey, the Commander of the Azabs; and Qasim Pasha, Beylerbey of Anatolia. Suleiman was very well aware that these were good commanders of the second rank whom he could and easily did dominate. At the moment this suited him. He felt he was held in check until the time came when his utmost energy and ability would be demanded of him.

On the fourth day of Ramadan, Suleiman came ashore at Kalitheas Bay at the head of the picked janissary troops who had travelled with him. It was a splendid day. Although so late in the summer, there was a breeze to stir the crystal air and as yet the sun had not grown too hot. Mustafa was on the beach to greet his royal brother-in-law. He was enormous in his chain-mail, with a turban wound around a damascened steel cap, but also somehow splendid in his ebullience. His broad face sweated and beamed with enthusiasm and emotion. Everything had gone splendidly, he proclaimed, his majesty had but to look around him!

His majesty did look, and had to admit, willingly as it happened, that there had been an enormous achievement in just over a month. Already, as they rode away from the beach, they passed through a small market which had grown up as such places do because there was a need and because it was a suitable spot. There were rough stalls set up by tradesmen who had followed the janissaries from Istanbul, cobblers, barbers, saddlers and bowmakers. A coppersmith was repairing one of the huge cauldrons in which the janissaries prepared their supper soup; there was the smell of boiling sheeps' heads, that favourite delicacy of soldiers, and everywhere little knots of men in sleevecaps and turbans were going about their business, some serious, some swaggering, but all intent.

Mustafa, mopping his face, apologized for what he called the disorder, but Suleiman looked about him with pleasure as he always did when he had the opportunity of seeing ordinary men doing ordinary things. Besides, some of them had spotted him; there were cries of 'The Sultan! The Sultan! Our father has come!' And lithe young men in blue uniforms flocked to press round him, touch his stirrup and raise a cheer, among them a well set-up corporal of the sixty-seventh orta, who gazed at the Sultan with rather more curiosity than his fellows. This was Kasim, brother to Hulefa, and because of this connection, slight as it was, he felt an almost proprietary interest in this Sultan whom he had never seen before. He took a long comprehensive stare at Suleiman and decided in his unemotional way that he would do. Managed his horse well, and when he looked at a man, really looked at him, not just a quick glance sliding over him like quicksilver. For his part Suleiman was already pleased and relaxed when they reached the outskirts of the enormous camp which had been sited behind the Turkish lines, south of the city walls.

As far as the eye could see stood the orderly rows of tents. In front of the largest, which were the barracks of the janissary regiments, Suleiman saw the familiar divisional symbols, here a fish, there an anchor or a key. Here were the tents of the medical orderlies. Over there, with becoming deferencce to rank, the green tents of senior officers. All was quiet, neat and clean. Suleiman took a deep breath and turned his head to look at the Turkish lines. Here was the same order and precision. The great cannon of the batteries gleamed from elbow-grease and balls were piled symmetrically. Already an enormous bank of earth was rising against the city wall in one place, and Azabs, the lowest form of Ottoman military life, were busy with shovels and baskets, moving the stony soil.

There was so much to see, to take in, that he would have been content to be left here for the rest of the day admiring their achievement. But he had to remember what was expected of him. Even so, finding adequate words was difficult. He said, 'Nothing could have been better done, brother. I am delighted.'

Mustafa nodded seriously. A complex man, he had taken Suleiman's implied rebukes to heart not because he felt he merited them but because there was nothing else to do. He had wanted this command desperately. After all, he was the Sultan's brother. He deserved something! He intended to make a success of it, but the Sultan's words had rankled and he had determined to show the young puppy what a really seasoned commander like himself could do. Now he smoothed his moustache and pointed to the cavalier, the great earthwork being built against the Bulwark of Auvergne. 'You will see the purpose of this erection, sir, when I tell you that this is the bastion of Auvergne. See those walls, their thickness, and the gun emplacements immediately behind? Even our new bombards and mortars would be hard put to it to make much impression on that lot! But the cavalier is to be built up above the top level of the wall with a ramp to this side up which cannon will be dragged. Then we shall be in a position to fire down into the city.'

Suleiman looked at the walls. The midday sun was turning them to gold but not even that mellifluous colour could mask their frowning strength. Beautiful or not, the place was a fortress. And the newer parts, like this bastion of Auvergne, had all the advantages of the latest military design. His eyes narrowed. It was as well, he thought, that he had listened to Ahmed and sent for additional sappers. But at the same time gunnery had improved too, and they had enough artillery, God knew. Not for the first time he was grateful for his experience at Belgrade. But still, not even Selim had come up against anything like Rhodes. He asked, 'Whose sector is this?'

'Ahmed's, sir.' Mustafa spoke a little abruptly and Suleiman, who had been on the point of turning to Ahmed with a question or two, changed his mind. He knew Mustafa's insecure and jealous nature but was determined today to placate him. He had done well and deserved his hour in the sun. He said instead, therefore, 'Tell me how many divisions there are and how they are disposed. I can see that we are drawn up in a crescent to command the city from all sides.'

Mustafa smoothed his moustache again. He said, 'Ahmed threatens the Bulwark of Auvergne and that of Aragon. That tower,' his stubby finger stabbed the air, 'is the Tower of Aragon and marks the boundary between them. On his left flank Ayas Pasha confronts the Bulwark of Germany and the Tower of St George, and the Amboise Gate. Between Ayas Pasha and the sea Bali Aga and the janissaries are even now moving into the positions prepared for them facing the Bulwark of France.' He hesitated, then added, 'They are menaced by the battery in the Tower of St Nicholas and we shall attempt to do something about that, but I am advised that after 1480 it was rebuilt with such strength that it is impregnable.' He sniffed, and once more his finger jabbed the air as he added, 'You see it, sir.' Looking obediently, Suleiman had difficulty in believing that the tiny toy at the end of the long mole enclosing the Hospitallers' Galley Port was indeed the famous tower that had cost so many lives. He said only, 'Continue.'

Mustafa took a deep breath and swung about. 'Now, sir, to Ahmed's right Qasim Pasha is now moving into his position against the Post of England, where, you will remember, we received the information that the walls are in bad repair. Certainly no new work seems to have been done on them. My position lies on his right flank menacing the Bulwark of Provence. Piri Pasha lies between me and the sea, facing the Post of Italy. That completes our major dispositions, sir.' He allowed himself a moment to twist one end of the enormous moustache and continued, 'In addition, there are three major batteries directed against key points: one on the hill called Saints Cosmas and Damian is directed against the Post of England, another threatens Provence, and a third the Tower of Aragon. Also, of course, sixty heavy cannon have been deployed, most heavily in this area but also against Italy. Also, my mortars –' He spoke lovingly, and paused for effect. When Suleiman remained silent he finished triumphantly, 'Once they feel those nine-foot balls inside their walls, then we shall see something!' He talked on.

'What I do not understand,' said Suleiman, at last asking the question which had been in his mind ever since he had first realized the completeness of the Ottoman preparations, 'is why the enemy has allowed us to get so far and do so much. Has there been no opposition at all?'

'Nothing of any account. A few sorties, sporadic artillery fire, that sort of thing.' Mustafa waved a fat hand. Suleiman, looking at Ahmed who stood silent in the Seraskier's rear, saw a frown cross the Third Vizier's face and asked pointedly, 'You were about to say, Ahmed?'

'With respect, sir, we know the enemy is short of men and therefore he must conserve them until the siege starts in earnest. We have thousands to his hundreds and that's all about it. Nevertheless, I am bound to say that where sorties have occurred they have been uniformly successful, costing us men by the dozen –'

('By the *dozen*,' interjected Mustafa contemptuously, but growing red in the face.)

'Dozens, which, if they are allowed to continue, will grow into hundreds and then into thousands,' continued Ahmed, unmoved. 'As to their cannon fire, it is prompt and accurate and has cost us already many casualties.'

'To be sure,' said Suleiman, looking at him curiously. 'But what of our own artillery fire, how effective has that been?'

'It is too soon to tell,' said Mustafa smoothly, regaining the initiative. 'You will remember, sir, that you yourself directed that there should be no full-scale bombardment until your arrival. Tomorrow will see a different story, I think. By your leave, sir, I have prepared to conduct your majesty on a tour of the positions tomorrow morning at dawn, if that is satisfactory to you. In the meantime we are ready to conduct your majesty to your headquarters, a short distance away, where Piri Pasha is waiting to receive you.'

He talked steadily as they rode the few miles to the villa which had been prepared for the Sultan. Beyond noting that the place was too far from the city and that he would move nearer at the earliest opportunity, Suleiman gave himself up to the enjoyment of the scene about him. He was not worried by the eternal push-pull of personality between Mustafa and Ahmed as it had been displayed to him yet again. Ahmed was a realist and inspired confidence; but he knew Mustafa pretty well, too. Sanguine, even slightly ridiculous he might be, but he still had a gift for getting things done and inspired confidence in his men. In the prevailing mood of high spirits he thought it a good thing that Ahmed's caution should qualify his brother-in-law's enthusiasm, while the latter's dash and optimism was a spur to Ahmed's eternal prudence. In any case, he thought, I am not their prisoner; I have something to contribute as well.

He turned his face to the sea and the mountains. It had never occurred to him that Rhodes might be so beautiful. He looked at mountain silhouetted against mountain, at mountain silhouetted against cloud, and wondered, not for the first time, about these strange, arrogant men who had come to such a place for no other purpose than to wage war. He turned to smile at Ibrahim riding beside him, and saw that he too was obviously moved by what he saw. Then he remembered that Ibrahim was himself a Greek and that this was for him some kind of homecoming.

He was shocked at Piri's appearance. Never a big man, he had always carried himself erect. Now he seemed shrunken, and his eyes, which had ever been direct, fierce and alert, were dull and listless.

Suleiman automatically acknowledged the old man's affectionate greeting, and allowed himself to be conducted on a tour of the villa which was to be their headquarters. It had previously belonged to a high-ranking officer in the Order of St John, and had been overlooked in the general burning and destruction the Order had indulged in before locking themselves into their city. There he waited impatiently for the Seraskier, Ahmed, and the other high-ranking officers who had accompanied him to take their reluctant leave.

When they were alone he sat down on a divan and smiled at

Piri, wondering what he could say to break down the reserve which suddenly seemed to have grown between them. Anything would do, he decided. If it was bland nonsense, Piri would soon let him know he recognized it as such and then tell him what was on his mind. Accordingly Suleiman said, 'How long did we take at Belgrade?'

Piri shook his head uncertainly. 'A few weeks. I no longer remember. I fear, majesty, that my memory is no longer what it was. But I know this: we shall be longer here. Those miserable peasants will not see this year's harvest.'

Suleiman stared at him, suddenly daunted by the facts of old age. Belgrade had been only last year and he could not remember! And it was not like the Piri he knew to concern himself about the misfortunes of Bessarabian pioneers. He said gently, 'A few weeks here or there makes no matter. We will stay as long as necessary. You know that.'

Piri straightened himself and said bluntly, 'Sir, I am about to tell you what you will not want to hear.' He took a deep breath. 'This campaign has never had the support of the janissaries. For several reasons they fear and dislike it and had begun murmuring even before we left Turkey. Since they have come here and seen what they are up against they like it still less.'

Suleiman's eyes narrowed. 'Forget their reasons for the moment. What have they done or not done?'

The old man shrugged. 'Nothing. Nothing dramatic has happened, but I know these men. They murmur. They spit, and say they do not like long campaigns, and already they know it will be long. After all, they are experienced men too. They see the tunnelling begun and know we are using mines. They talk about new-fangled methods. Also –' he hesitated.

'Go on,' said Suleiman.

'The reputation of the Sons of Sheitan loses nothing in the telling. They know what happened in 1480.'

'But,' said Suleiman, 'the methods of warfare in which they place so much faith were used in 1480. And got us nowhere.'

Piri nodded. 'They are not amenable to reason, as you know, sir.' He hesitated again, and added, 'Now that you are here, majesty –' He stopped, noting that the Sultan was thinking deeply. A year ago, he thought, he would have reacted immediately and probably violently.

Suleiman was thinking about the janissaries, the core of his army. Slave soldiers made out of boys selected with care from the Christian peasant families of his vast empire. Trained to think of only one way of life, to know no other and certainly to want no other, they had their own traditions and knew their own worth to their Sultan. As time went on, it seemed, their sense of their own value was making them ever more independent and unruly. As against that, their life was rigid and dangerous, and their lives themselves were sold for a pittance, their pay amounting to only a few aspers a day. A flash of insight told him that what they asked above all was a romantic notion they could believe in to make their existence endurable. Then they would fight to the death. But the slow, dangerous and meticulous methods of modern siege warfare did not provide that. He said as much.

Piri nodded. 'Undoubtedly that is so. They like instant glory and instant plunder.'

'The plunder they shall have. I will order that everything movable in the city shall be theirs. I cannot do more.'

'With respect, sir, yes, you can.' Piri's smile made him look his old self again. 'Do not forget you are one of them as well as their Sultan.'

This was true. The Sultan held rank as a non-commissioned officer in the corps of janissaries, and they never forgot the fact. 'Very well then,' said Suleiman slowly, 'my first act before Rhodes must be to – what? Address them, reason with them? Those I saw on the beach this morning greeted me with apparent rapture. What do they want of me?'

'Of course, sir,' said Piri, tranquil now that he saw he had succeeded in his purpose, 'their dislike of this undertaking has nothing to do with you personally – yet. When they see you ride amongst them and learn that they were your first thought, they will be content. Then, if the campaign goes well, they will forget they ever had a grievance. I will arrange that tomorrow morning –'

'No,' said Suleiman flatly; 'tomorrow at dawn I will be there to see the bombardment and the tunnelling begin in Ahmed's sector. If the janissaries are my first thought, so be it. I will come now.'

He only stayed long enough to assume chain-link armour and a brilliant robe. He wore a lofty helmet adorned with the ceremonial feather, refusing the splendid parade helmet with the diamonds. The time for that would be a victory parade. Then he rode back to the city with his bodyguard of peiks and solaks and accompanied by Piri Pasha and Ibrahim. For three hours he rode along the lines in the glare of the afternoon sun, stopping often to talk to his janissaries, as well as the occasional militiaman or Piyade or gunner. The din was frightful, for a janissary band materialized as if from nowhere to accompany him wherever he went with its elephant drums and flutes, and this with the noise of artillery salutes and the cheering of the men made the Rhodians and the Hospitallers, listening behind their walls, wonder if the bombardment was about to start. Both Ibrahim and Piri noticed that although Suleiman gave his full attention to the men who crowded around him, sometimes having to be dislodged by the watchful escort, he often raised his eyes thoughtfully to the massive golden walls and bastions towering above them.

10

At midday on 29 July one of Ahmed's aides, a young sapper captain, rode up to his Sultan where he watched the bombardment from a small hill to the south-west of the city, saluted, and told him briefly that the Seraskier had called off the attack until dusk. The loss of Azabs and pioneers was proving too great. Suleiman thanked him courteously, and, summoning his escort, returned to his headquarters.

The plan was straightforward and simple. A bombardment involving all the artillery in Ahmed's sector was mounted against the Bulwark of Auvergne with the purpose of silencing the enemy's guns and covering the men working on the cavalier and digging the ditches for Ahmed's mines. It did not work out that way. The artillery fire was murderous, but so was that from inside the city. It raked the men straining and sweating in the ditches and on the earthworks and they fell in their hundreds and lay where they fell, blocking the escape of their luckier fellows and the advance of those who followed them. So far as anyone could tell the Turkish fire had no effect at all, either on the city's cannon or on the walls themselves. For hours Suleiman had watched it all happen as if pre-ordained, and had no complaint to make when the attack was called off. All that he had ever heard about the Hospitallers was proving to be true.

Later, Ahmed, red-eyed, his face black-streaked, rode out to tell him what they now planned to do. He said in effect what Piri had said the day before. It would be a long job and they would have to rely on the miners, but the bombardment, although less effective than they had hoped, must continue, and they would also direct it against the Bulwark of Germany in the hope of making a break-through there. They would throw in everything they had, mortars, bombards and basilisks as well as cannon. In effect, there was no better plan than the one they had. It must work eventually if not immediately. Suleiman agreed with him. He was here, he had seen the place for himself and had nothing better to suggest. Besides, Ahmed in his laconic way inspired confidence.

So throughout August the crashing of the cannon, the screams of the wounded and dying, the curses of the non-commissioned officers as they drove the hapless peasants and Azabs into the ditches and tunnels, were ceaseless. Mustafa had boasted that he was taking as many men to Rhodes as there were stones in her walls. But if those same men muttered to each other that the men would all be dead before the stones toppled, they were careful to keep their voices low and their eyes front, for discipline was tighter than ever.

The Hospitallers had other surprises in store for them apart from their skill as gunners. Tadini da Martinengo, the engineer and master gunner, had responded without hesitation to the Grand Master's invitation to throw in his lot with them and leave his safe and lucrative post in Crete. Now he was there, this gifted son of the Renaissance used all his superb skill to catch and destroy the luckless Turkish sappers in their own tunnels as they inched forward towards and under the walls of Rhodes. He devised a listening apparatus, the top half of a drum whose sensitive membrane registered any movement below ground and set a series of little bells tinkling round its edges. The Turkish miners, sweating and suffocating in their tunnels, knew nothing of him or his methods. All they knew before they died was that someone allied to the devil always knew where they were as soon as they knew themselves.

Nevertheless, the ditches and tunnels in the stony soil crawled forward relentlessly and the earthworks (there was one fronting the Bulwark of Aragon now, as well as Auvergne) rose inch by inch. If after ten fruitless days the guns had to be withdrawn from the Bulwark of Germany and massed against Auvergne and Aragon, they had battered down most of their new ravelins and ramparts and the Post of England was so badly damaged that it held open breaches in the walls. Provence was nearly as bad. And if the Rhodian masons built them up at night, next morning's cannonade sent them toppling once more.

There were spectacular successes, too. On 14 August a mortar shot from Piri's sector landed fairly and squarely on a Genoese carrack in the commercial port and sank her. This cheered everybody up. The new mortars had really proved a disappointment up till then, and if Piri, grey with fatigue and suffering agonies with rheumatism, said it was only a chance shot, no one wanted to hear. Then their most reliable agent within the city walls, Apello Renato, a Jewish doctor planted in the city by Selim years ago, warned that the enemy had a battery in St John's Church and were using the tower as a lookout, ringing its bells to warn of Turkish attacks. So the Turks destroyed the tower, silencing the battery and the bells.

Kasim the artilleryman took part in this action and it inspired him as nothing before had done. The atmosphere in the orta had worsened considerably since the campaign started. It was not to be wondered at, but Kasim, brighter and more responsible than his fellows, had to work hard with his tongue and sometimes with cane and fists to keep order in the ranks. He understood very well why Rhodes must be taken, and why it would be a long job, but even he wondered sometimes about the outcome. Nevertheless the toppling of this tower, while it didn't win the war, put heart into them all.

During August the Turkish cannon fired 1713 stone balls against the walls of Rhodes, and the mortars 1721. Piri said most of it was wasted effort.

The naval blockade was not very thorough. Cortuglu was a corsair, and this was not his kind of fighting. At the end of August two vessels slipped insolently out of the Mercantile Port under the navy's very nose. It was anybody's guess where they were going – in fact, one was making for France and the other for Rome – but their purpose was not difficult to imagine: to ask yet again for help from Europe. Perhaps this time it would be forthcoming. Suleiman, when he heard about it, was furious. Remembering how Cortuglu had told him of the ease with which Rhodes could be taken, he had him bastinadoed on the quarter-deck of his own flagship.

Now it was September, two months since the undertaking had begun, and he told himself grimly that now he expected to see results. He was not unsatisfied, for he had only to raise his eyes to the walls to see the Turkish achievement. There were great breaches in the walls and bastions of Germany and

England, and the masonry from the shattered walls of Provence filled the ditch in front of them. Soon the first mine would be sprung. Ahmed's sappers had the worst of it perhaps. Tadini never let them rest. In addition to his listening devices he found other means of killing them, building traverses on each side of the breaches in the walls of Italy and mounting batteries of cannon and 'murdering pieces' to cover the approach trenches. Then when the miners emerged, mole-like and blinking from their covered ways, they were mown down. Still, if less spectacular, Ahmed was resourceful. He had tentlike screens of rawhide erected against the bases of the walls, so that those of his pioneers and sappers who survived could go on tunnelling unseen; and despite the appalling loss of life, their burrows lay under four-fifths of the enceinte by the end of August.

Suleiman could not rest. He knew the Turkish achievement, so tedious, so prodigal of life, was considerable, but now he wanted a conclusion. He waited grimly, time hanging heavy on his hands. He was only a spectator at these slow, dangerous exercises, and although he expressed impatience with the janissaries' idea of war as instant death or instant glory he began to feel more sympathy with them, though his real admiration was reserved for the anonymous men in mud-coloured rags who inched their way forward through the dirt and darkness and might disappear for ever in one of those echoing, rumbling explosions below the ground.

Ibrahim tried to divert him, sensing, though not entirely understanding, his distress. Why not visit other parts of the island, relieve his mind by seeing its beauty spots and the sites of its ancient towns and temples? There were long hours when there was nothing a Sultan could do, so why not enjoy himself a little? Suleiman refused briefly but in terms that discouraged argument, and Ibrahim was disappointed. This place was part of his heritage. It spoke directly to him as the men labouring and dying beneath its walls did not. He felt no kinship with them. But when Suleiman told him he was free to go on such expeditions by himself if he wished, he refused, sitting his horse behind his Sultan, straining his eyes to see he knew not what, and carefully suppressing his yawns.

The first mine exploded under the Bulwark of England on 4 September. It shook the city to its foundations and broke open a six-yard gap in the bastion. Kasim, who had been sent by his Pasha with a message to the commander-in-chief, saw it all and never knew thereafter whether to count himself lucky to have been there or not. He had barely presented himself, smart and alert as usual, to Mustafa's aide-de-camp when there was a roar that nearly burst his ear-drums and the landscape around him shook as if in an earthquake. When the noise and the dust and the smoke had cleared a little, he looked up at the bastion and saw the great hole in it. He heard another roar, this time from men's throats, and found himself borne forward in the press of men and weapons as the janissaries, screaming their war-cry, flooded out of the trenches. Even while he was pushed forward helplessly, he saw seven horsetail standards appear on the ramparts, quivering from the force with which they had been implanted. Kasim found himself roaring with his fellows and groping at his belt for his knife. He wasn't supposed to stay here, but by Allah, if this was the breakthrough it seemed to be, nothing was going to move him – they'd even got a foothold on the bastion itself!

But even in this wonderful moment as the men surged forward, drunk with the smell of victory, he saw something more and was shocked back to reality. Inside the bastion there were retrenchments; and behind them were the English Hospitallers, solid, immovable, the red crosses on their surcoats gleaming like blood, their faces immovable too so that they all seemed to be replicas of the same iron man, waiting there, clutching sword and pike, to kill or be killed but not to be moved. Kasim hesitated momentarily. He had never seen anything like them, but his brain told him that if they were men they were for killing. He screamed out the battle-cry and thrust himself forward, only to feel an iron hand descend on his wrist and a furious voice rage at him – 'What are you doing here? Get back to your Pasha, tell him –' The aide-de-camp had spotted him. Kasim stopped, hesitating, and the officer, scimitar raised, screamed at him again, 'Get out of here or I'll have you broken!'

There was nothing for it; he had to turn away and begin to push through the press of jubilant men behind him. When the situation changed he did not need to be told. Suddenly it was easier to push forward, for suddenly the crowd of onward surging janissaries began to hesitate as they took in what they were up against. There was the crack of bullets and the dull thud of crossbow bolts ramming home into flesh, there were groans and screams where before there had been only victorious shouts. Kasim slipped to one side and looked back. There was a melee on the ramparts now and where he had seen only sleevecaps and turbans and chain-mail there was now an inextricable mixture of struggling bodies. He saw broadswords held aloft in mailed fists, saw Christian musketeers firing into Turkish ranks, and knew the initiative was lost, at least for the moment. Even while he watched, dismayed, he heard a low growling cheer from beyond the ramparts, and then an exultant shout. A figure had appeared in the midst of turmoil, enormous, commanding, white hair streaming, right arm raised and clutching a half-pike. Behind and beyond it Kasim had an impression of a banner. He did not need to be told that here was one of the Christian commanders and that his presence had put heart into his men. Where Kasim had been carried inexorably forward he was now being borne backwards towards the ditch. He had to look to himself too. A bullet whistled unhealthily close and he had a job to do, to carry the commander-in-chief's demand to his Pasha for small cannon to be brought up to support the Turkish advance. He slipped into the ditch in time to see Mustafa, roaring like a bull and laying about him with his scimitar, rush to rally his men and thrust them back into the fray.

When he returned, straining with his fellows, at the ropes which pulled a falconet, he was amazed to see that the battle still raged and that the situation was much what it had been when he had hurled himself panting into the ditch. That was his first thought; then he saw the piles of dead, saw the earth slippery with blood and the glazed eyes of men who still pushed themselves exhausted into the press, there to be mown down. The cannon were useless by now, they couldn't get near enough to the ramparts; if they fired them now they'd only hit their own men, what was left of them. His Pasha took one look and shook his head. But Mustafa was still there, cajoling and roaring by turns, driving the wretched infantry into the gap with the flat of his scimitar when all else failed. That day the battle swayed back and forth for two hours before the Turks broke, panicked by their apparent inability to make any headway against these steel Christians. Appalled by the carnage they fled for the last time, leaving hundreds of dead and wounded, including three Sanjak Beys. Kasim saw it all, including the commander-in-chief being pulled bodily away from the awful scene by his bodyguard; the tears were streaming down Mustafa's face. Kasim could understand it. This was the most savage fighting he had ever seen. Later, he heard that the Christians said that the Turkish losses were ten times their own and felt, however unwillingly, that it was probably true. Still, the Christians had lost plenty of men too and could ill spare them. But they had not lost the imposing old man he had seen on the ramparts – that, from what he could learn from camp gossip, had been their commander-in-chief himself, de l'Isle Adam. He was glad to have seen him.

Suleiman, watching from his usual vantage-point, did not know what to make of it. He was enraged at his Turks' early loss of the initiative, but at the same time their terrible losses told him how much they had endured before they broke. Mustafa's bewildered shame told him the rest. What more could they do against these madmen within their broken walls? He thought that now they had got the measure of the Hospitallers, had met the first shock of their ferocious resistance, they would do better, and would be prepared for what they had to face. Turkish soldiers did not break and run. The janissary was any man's equal and better. This was an article of faith.

He soon learned that this assessment was wrong. As the month progressed and Ahmed's men burrowed even further into the city, and mine after mine breached the crumbling bastions, his commanders mounted attacks which always had the same result: defeat and heavy loss. Something decisive must be done before the men lost heart altogether. Mustafa had nothing to suggest beyond the everlasting costly assaults in which he placed all his faith. Suleiman consulted Ahmed and Piri and decided on a general attack. They knew that the losses within the city had been great, including many of the senior Knights. Certainly the Hospitallers had long since stopped their sorties, which suggested that they needed to conserve their men. None of his spies had been able to tell him what their original strength had been, but now he thought they must be seriously depleted. By rushing such men as they had to the scene of an isolated attack they had succeeded brilliantly, but he thought a general attack would be too much for them. From his own point of view there was nothing to be lost. It would put heart into the men, and if they succeeded they could still be home before the winter. He determined on 24 September as the fateful day and sent the heralds to proclaim it through the camp. He also repeated what he had said before. The city and its buildings were to be his, but everything that grew or moved above ground should belong to his victorious army.

He believed he had thought of everything. Certainly the prospect of battle and plunder had wrought their old magic and now wherever he rode he saw confident, smiling faces. Never vainglorious, he nevertheless had a raised platform set up on the high ground from which he usually watched events, so that he would be easily visible and his men should know that their Sultan was with them.

Certainly the attack began well for the Turks. The heavy artillery put up the heaviest bombardment of the whole siege against the Posts of Aragon, England, Italy and Provence. Kasim, sweating and filthy, crouched beside his cannon and watched, as the smoke cleared away, the whole front come alive. Allah, it was wonderful! Everywhere he looked on both sides the massed power of the janissaries swept forward in irresistible, orderly waves of red, blue and grey. Even as he looked he saw thirty or forty horsetail standards and banners quivering on the ramparts of Aragon to his left, as Bali Aga, scimitar aloft in one enormous paw, led them in a headlong rush into the bastion itself. No Azabs today, to be flung into the ditches to take the first enemy attack. Who needed them? Today was to be the janissaries' day! And he could see up ahead that it was the same in his own sector. Well, naturally, for the Post of England and its ill-repaired and ill-maintained walls had taken the worst of the battering he and his chaps had been directing against it for the past three months. They were no longer walls but piles of rubble, and today would – must – see the end of them.

But it was not to be. Kasim and his fellow-gunners watched, at first unbelieving and then in dismay, as the battle swayed back and forth beyond them. They saw the infantry beaten back beyond the ramparts, and then had no more time for thought or emotion as their Pasha descended on them cursing and they stood to their guns again to lay another barrage, and then another, to give the battered infantry yet another chance to get beyond the golden walls and stay there.

The battle raged back and forth for six hours. The piles of Turkish dead grew wider and higher, but still they came on. Now the enemy could be seen on the bastion, the scarlet crosses clearly visible against tattered white surcoats. The watching Kasim felt despair rise in him at last. It was to be the same story over again after all. Although his eyes told him that these people were at the end of their tether, staggering with exhaustion and worse, they still pressed forward, driven by something harsher than the promise of booty or the sergeant's cane. Then, towards the end of that awful morning, he saw something that made his blood run cold.

Among the armour-clad figures draped in red and white rags, one, smaller and slighter than the others, drew his attention, with such clumsy fury did it hurl itself again and again against the mass of blue-clad janissaries in the breach. Suddenly a blue arm ending in a scimitar flashed and the slim figure staggered and fell back. Kasim, caught up in the drama, shouted exultantly, and then had the cry strangled in his throat by what he saw next. As the figure fell to the ground its helmet rolled off and a mass of black hair streamed over its shoulders. The next moment it had disappeared in the press. Kasim, staring fruitlessly, heard the man next to him cry, 'By Allah - even their women fight! What creatures are these?'

Weeks later, when they at last got into the city, he heard the whole story. The Rhodians were full of it, and no wonder.

The woman had been the mistress of an English Knight. Like the rest of the women of the city she had been on the ramparts, helping with the wounded or bringing up ammunition. Seeing her man killed, she had not hesitated. Believing their world destroyed she had rushed home carrying his sword and had put her three children to death. Then she had returned soberly and purposefully to the ramparts, donned her lover's shattered armour and thrust herself into the thick of the battle. What Kasim had seen was the end of her story. Incomplete as it was, it filled him with horror. He could not believe that such people could ever be defeated.

The unyielding, furious face of Rhodes was at last too much for the Turks. They believed in paradise after death and feared the Sultan and his officers, but they had looked death in the face all that day and were sickened by it. Yet they had no cause for shame. When the Brother chosen to regain the Bulwark of Aragon entered the bastion at the head of a body of picked men-at-arms he found the Turkish banners still flying over piles of Ottoman dead. Only two or three remained alive but they had not fled. He did not spare them. They joined the rest of the 2000 who died that day.

Suleiman had the retreat sounded. He was shocked and humiliated. In all his confident young life he had never seen anything like this. He did not understand it and needed time to come to grips with it. But one thing he did understand. His men in their thousands had been outmatched by the Hospitallers in their hundreds and he did not know who to blame. He went to his pavilion and summoned his Pashas to report on the battle. When he heard the details of the dreadful losses, the emotions which had been seething beneath the surface of his mind at last found relief in a burst of fury against them all, these men who had so confidently advised him that victory would be his, but particularly against Ayas Pasha, whose losses against the key posts of Germany and Auvergne had been the highest of all. He could hardly speak for rage but he found the few words necessary to condemn Ayas to death and order him to be put in chains.

The silence which succeeded was almost tangible as the commanders, weary and dispirited, stared first at their Sultan and then blankly at each other. They had done their utmost. True, they had not carried out his orders, but what if they could never be carried out? Suddenly, Piri stepped forward. He had been astounded at Suleiman's performance, for while he knew him capable of rages as formidable as those of his redoubtable father, injustice was out of character. Ayas was a devoted and capable officer and the fighting in his sector had been fiercer than anywhere else. Briefly and clearly Piri begged for his life. But Suleiman had taken refuge in his anger. Piri, standing there, humble, calm, and, worst of all, always obstinately and implacably right, seemed at that moment the worst enemy of all. He stared at him with his face contorted and roared that Piri could join Ayas in death.

His voice screaming this unthinkable sentence rang in Suleiman's own ears. He heard it and momentarily wondered who this madman could be before he came to his senses. He gazed into the stricken faces of his Pashas and was appalled. Then rage deserted him and he set his jaw, not knowing if he wished, or even how, to retreat.

They got him out of it eventually, these hardbitten, unsubtle men. After the first shock a murmur broke out like a buzzing of bees at the back of their ranks as they stood before him. No one ever remembered who first produced the formula, but eventually Ferhad Pasha, who had not so far been called upon to play a leading role in this campaign, stepped forward, threw himself at his Sultan's feet in the required fashion, and implored him not to do this thing, which could only bring comfort to the enemy. Suleiman saw with relief that he could accede to this request with honour. He said curtly, 'So be it,' and dismissed them.

Burning with shame, Suleiman sat down to consider what to do next. He needed no one to tell him the meaning of the scene through which they had just passed. His had not been the justifiable rage of a sovereign whose wishes had been flouted, but that of a spoiled and vainglorious young fool who gave orders which could not be carried out. Ayas and Piri were blameless, had simply been the first objects on which his eye had lighted in his senseless rage. Mustafa certainly was culpable and must go, but not in abject disgrace, for the ultimate blame was not his. No, he would kick him upstairs somewhere, where his facile optimism could do little harm.

Suleiman now realized that it takes a special kind of courage to tell an absolute ruler that his dearest ambition is not feasible; Mustafa did not have it, and Suleiman should have known he did not. Few men have it, he realized, and those that have are worth their weight in gold. A lesson for the future, he told himself; and wondered how many more bitter lessons Rhodes had in store for him.

He rose, and went to stare through the door of the tent with unseeing eyes at the hard blue sky and burnt grass. Perhaps he should throw his hand in now, go off with his tail between his legs, get these miserable peasants back to their harvesting and the janissaries back to their barracks before the autumn rains came on. But he found he could not face such a thing. He did not know whether it proceeded from weakness or strength and did not greatly care. He only knew that there was a core of obduracy within him which would not allow it. Too many lives had been lost, too much pain and thought and agony expended. Here they would all stay until they took Rhodes or died.

The next morning he made it clear what the future had in store for him and his army. Mustafa was demoted and Ahmed promoted to be Seraskier. Piri must go home. Not in disgrace, but because his Sultan, not knowing how long they would have to sit before Rhodes, thought him now too ill to stand the pace. He knew that he would be relieved when Piri had gone, and knew too that the relief proceeded from shame.

October came, and the first warm rains began to fall. They refreshed, but were followed by an ominous chill in the night air. Then came the frosts and the first snow on the mountains. Ahmed and Ferhad the Slav, patient, impervious and watchful, went on with the mining. Bali Aga and Ayas the Albanian caught their janissaries in a tight ring of discipline and continued the eternal bombardment by night and day. And it was plain they were having their effect. Most of the city's guns, except for those of Auvergne and the Koskino Gate, were silenced.

Suleiman consulted with Ahmed and did what only he could do. He sent to Syria and Anatolia for fresh troops from the janissary garrisons to make good his losses; he ordered munitions and fresh food, and, to make his own position plain, he had his flimsy pavilion torn down and replaced by one of stone so that his men should know he intended to stay. Soon the camps were awash with mud which got into the miners' tunnels, drowning and suffocating some of them but not stopping the work. The cold and the snow brought sickness in their wake and men began to die from something other than wounds. Despite the sergeants' lashes and canes, the men once more began to gather in muttering groups. Now when their Sultan rode through their midst they eyed him sullenly and kept their distance. Suleiman tightened his lip and as October drew into November ordered the fleet to leave the island anchorages and stand off the Anatolian mainland. No one was leaving.

The Turkish suffering was relieved a little when spies brought news of famine in the city, of murmuring among the inhabitants, and finally that the devil Tadini da Martinengo had been wounded. But still when they stormed the breaches the patient Ahmed made for them they were beaten back.

Now Suleiman allowed Ibrahim to take him on expeditions about the island, to visit Ialysus and Mount Fileremos and other places nearer the city where there were ruined villas and houses which he thought might make winter quarters for the troops if they could be repaired. He worried Ibrahim by his withdrawn quietness; but he certainly seemed to benefit from getting away from the camp, away from the noise of the cannon and the sick and weary eyes of his men.

11

In the city it was discovered that powder and shot and ball were unexpectedly low. No one could believe this was the result of bad judgement or unforeseen heavy use. No, it had to be the result of treachery! The place was full of rumours, of ominous messages sent by crossbow from the Turkish lines, of spying, of treason in high places. How could it be otherwise? The walls were half-destroyed, the Turks had even got a foothold on the bastions in two places. The people saw their city crumbling before their eyes. They were half-hysterical with exhaustion and lack of food. Then, as if this were not enough, a Spaniard, a woman of great reputed piety who had made the pilgrimage to Jerusalem, suddenly felt the call to prophesy. She took to roaming the streets barefoot, hair streaming and clothes dishevelled, screaming that the wrath of God had fallen on Rhodes as a punishment for the sins of their leaders. She named no names, she was after all only a poor crazy woman, but nothing more was needed.

Even the most level-headed of the Rhodians felt their blood run cold. They had suffered so much, had even become a little larger than life in their efforts to save their city. It could not go on for ever and only needed some little thing to make the spirit of heroism and self-sacrifice waver. They questioned themselves and each other. Could it be true, and if so, who was guilty?

Disastrously, an answer was forthcoming almost immediately.

On the morning of 27 October the look-out on the Tower of St George in the Bulwark of Auvergne was looking down over the battlements towards the Turkish trenches and the lower slopes of Mount St Stephen. It was near the end of the morning watch. A fog had rolled up from the sea and it was raining steadily and hopelessly as it had been raining for two days. The man huddled deeper into his cloak, reflecting that it was an ill wind that blew nobody any good. That very rain which had drenched him and his comrades and had robbed them of hot food since they came on duty, he could not remember when, had also made a mess of the Turkish earthworks in front of the bastion of England. It had washed them half away, so that they'd had to get their batteries off the top of them before they got bogged down. Now it seemed that the infidel were having to pull back from their advance positions too!

He craned carefully over the battlements to get a better view. Something moved on the ramparts below. He looked again, and the next moment went hurtling down the steps. He caught the fellow red-handed just as he raised a loaded crossbow to his shoulder, and knocked him down. Then the sentry turned his attention to the quarrel. Sure enough, there was a letter attached to it. All hell broke loose then. What with holding on to the miscreant in his wet, slippery cloak (and he struggled like a seal), keeping tight hold of the crossbow and its telltale bolt, *and* yelling for help at the top of his lungs, he had his hands full for a while. But help soon came. The alert sentry told his tale to the captain of the guard and went back to his post and out of history, but he had caught, indirectly, a very big fish indeed.

Several things were self-evidently true. The villain with the crossbow was a Portuguese Jewish convert to Christianity named Blasco Diaz and he had been, for some years, valet and confidential servant to Andrea d'Amaral, Chancellor to the Knights Hospitallers. The letter he had been about to fire into the Turkish lines was addressed to Ayas Pasha and contained a summary of the Rhodian shortages of food and war supplies and suggested that if the Sultan offered suitable terms they might be accepted. These were facts. It is also a fact that after preliminary questioning, to which he made no response, they put Diaz on the rack. They did not have to exert themselves much before he came out with the information that the letter was from his master the Chancellor and that this was not the first time he had fired, or attempted to fire, messages to the enemy. This may or may not have been true but everybody was prepared to believe that it was. No more perfect scapegoat could have been found, for the Chancellor had no friends. The Knights of the Spanish Langue were an arrogant lot and d'Amaral was the most arrogant of them. He had other qualities as well: he was proud, impetuous and courageous, and his performance when put to the question (which was done summarily as soon as they had listened to the many witnesses who came forward against him) was very different from that of his servant. He confessed nothing and made it plain that he had nothing to confess. 'Am I now to tell a lie and sell my honour in order to save my old limbs from the pain of the rack?' he asked, and reminded his judges of his lifetime of service to the Order and the wounds and other hardships he had suffered for it.

The evidence against d'Amaral, or what passed for evidence in the prevailing atmosphere of shock, war-hysteria and personal dislike, seemed very heavy. Apart from Diaz, there was a Greek priest who averred that a few weeks previously he had seen d'Amaral and Diaz on the walls of Auvergne, that Diaz was holding a crossbow and that the Chancellor had placed himself so as to screen his servant from view, asking the priest roughly what he was doing in such a place at such an hour and telling him to go away at once. There was a woman from Candia who said that Diaz had told her that the Chancellor had been plotting with the Turks for a long time, that he had stolen stocks of gunpowder and had misinformed the Council about the amount of munitions originally held. This was hearsay, and the priest was a drunkard who only remembered the incident on the walk-way once d'Amaral was accused, but other accusations were to come from the ranks of the Knights themselves. Some Spanish and Portuguese Knights remembered that when de l'Isle Adam was elected Grand Master, d'Amaral had burst out, 'He will be the last Grand Master of Rhodes!' If these depositions were evidence of anything at all it was that d'Amaral's judgement was sometimes faulty and that he had gone on disliking and envying de l'Isle Adam over the years ever since they had quarrelled before the Battle of Laiazzo twelve years before. But his greatest fault was that of making himself hated, and it was his undoing. A military tribunal summarily condemned him to death. On 7 November he was taken to the church of St John and stripped of his habit and all his honours and on the following day he was beheaded. His body was quartered and displayed on the ramparts.

The Order and the people of the city were appalled.

Treachery had come out of their midst and destroyed them. All this time the Chancellor had, they believed, been telling the enemy what was going on and how badly off they were. De l'Isle Adam believed it, too. He was deeply shocked, but unlike the Rhodians he was buoyed up by his faith in God and the Order. The very day after the Chancellor's execution two brigantines brought reinforcements. Only twelve Knights and a hundred men-at-arms with some food and powder and shot, but six days later another vessel got through from Lindos with another twelve Knights and more powder. It was all precious and it gave him heart. Other pitiful little cargoes of men and powder got through and he sent a French brother off to Naples to make one last plea for help. He was determined to fight to the end of his life. He and his Knights and the people of Rhodes would go out in a tremendous holocaust that would revive faith in Christianity all through Europe. Then they would not have died in vain.

Meanwhile Suleiman, having taken his stand, recovered his balance. He had forbidden any more general attacks, so wasteful of life and so ineffective, but Ahmed's burrows spread like arteries ever deeper under the enceinte. They were beyond the retrenchments now, and even if Tadini's minewatchers were still effective he must surely by now be short of slaves and timber for the making of shores and props. His spies told him of the dreadful conditions in the city, and messages were starting to come from sources they knew nothing about – ordinary people, he supposed, who fired crossbows over the walls – for pitiful notes attached to crossbow bolts were being picked up in the Turkish lines, all telling the same story of death and shortage and a desire for peace.

At the end of November he sent for Ahmed. They understood each other pretty well by now, and the interview was short. Ahmed was always a man of few words, and Suleiman in no mood to waste any. Had the time come, he asked, to call for surrender? Ahmed considered carefully and said cautiously, 'Terms, sir?'

Suleiman sighed. 'Only the best available will tempt such people, I am sure.' He thought for a moment and added, 'And they deserve no less. I will respect their faith and they may live in peace under Islam, or if they prefer they may go elsewhere unharmed. As to the Grand Master and his Knights, they must leave Rhodes, but they may take with them all their property and any of its citizens who wish to go with them.'

Ahmed digested this in silence. He was not, and he would have been the first to admit it, so large-minded as his Sultan. Gestures, whether of generosity or admiration, meant little to him. He was also a soldier and he liked to win. He thought he still could. He said, 'I would like your permission for one more general assault, sir. They are near their end.'

Suleiman frowned. His impulse was to say that enough was enough. He looked at Ahmed's tired, lined face and the dogged faces of the Seraskier's little escort of sapper officers. They were young men like himself, and even if they did not carry his weight of responsibility they deserved something of him, and so did Ahmed. He nodded, therefore, and said, 'If that is your wish, so be it.'

So they made one more general assault on 30 November.

The fighting was desperate and the end predictable, particularly as it was raining and Tadini, recovered from his wound (he had lost an eye), was back in the thick of the fighting along with the Grand Master. The Turkish ramps were again reduced to their constituent mud and their powder was soaked. Their casualties were as heavy as ever. Suleiman did not complain when he heard the inevitable, but said simply that now they would proceed to the next step. He would offer the terms he had outlined, but there was an addition to the message. 'Tell them,' he said, 'that if my terms are rejected, I will destroy every soul in Rhodes.'

They proceeded cautiously, sending an Italian merchant who happened to be in the Turkish camp to the Koskino Gate to offer terms under a flag of truce. The commander of the guard shouted to him that 'Brethren of St John only do business with their swords,' and sent him off. Suleiman and Ahmed were well prepared to believe this but thought it possible that the Rhodians themselves by now might have other views. So they tried again, several times. Eventually the news that terms were being offered became general knowledge. It became plain that if the Grand Master would not negotiate with the Sultan, there was a real danger that the people would take matters into their own hands. De l'Isle Adam called the Council. His own views on what should be done had not changed, but some of the more influential brethren believed that the work of the Order could go on elsewhere. Perhaps they did not share his belief in the influence of martyrs. De l'Isle Adam for his part was inclined to doubt Suleiman's good faith, but it hardly mattered. Tadini and others pointed out that the city could not be saved anyway, the enemy was already inside, above and below ground, and there was no more labour for moving cannon or anything else as all the slaves were dead, sick or wounded, and there was no more ammunition. All of them, the Grand Master included, were living in holes in the ground like animals. They had only bread and water for food. A deputation from the townspeople broke into the Council's desperate deliberations. They had made up their minds what they wanted, and they were prepared to believe that Suleiman meant what he said. De l'Isle Adam saw that he had no choice. Death might be the best way out for an elderly and exhausted warrior of God, but young and simpler folk had other ideas as he had known they would. He agreed to the views of the majority and then collapsed at their feet, worn out with emotion.

Two days later Suleiman heard that his terms were accepted, but that was not by any means the end of the matter. Negotiations dragged on for three weeks. Truces were made and broken, during one of which Ahmed generously entertained a hostage Brother and discussed the fighting with him, telling him that the Turks had lost 64,000 men in battle and nearly as many again from sickness. There is no doubt that Brother Antoine de Grollée inflated the figures when he told the story later, but even at half the number it would have been bad enough.

Now that the end was in sight, Suleiman, relieved, was patient for a while with the shilly-shallying. At one stage the Rhodians, who were Greeks after all, completely reversed their standpoint, claiming that they were not satisfied entirely that the Sultan's terms adequately protected their families. They might trust Suleiman, but what about Ahmed and the janissaries? They might massacre them all once the Brethren had left! Perhaps it would be better to die fighting. The Grand Master agreed readily. He temporized, asking for an extension of the current truce so that he could consult all the Langues, the Frankish settlers, and everyone in sight.

Suleiman ordered the resumption of hostilities and the guns opened up all along the line. Not ill-pleased, the Grand Master told the Rhodians to get back to the barricades, and so they did for a day or two.

Eventually, on Christmas Day, Suleiman repeated his promises, adding that if the Hospitallers had not enough shipping he would furnish what was needed. He added further that Rhodian citizens might be free to leave the island at any time for three years to come, and that taxes would be remitted them for five years. Within twelve days the remnants of the Order must be prepared to leave. This time no one doubted what he said. Twenty-five Knights and twenty-five citizens were despatched as hostages to the Turkish camp, and four hundred janissaries under Bali Aga entered the city as guards. The rest of the Turkish force was withdrawn to a line one mile from the counter-scarp.

Two days later, de l'Isle Adam went to Suleiman's pavilion to make his formal submission. It was as usual pouring with rain. A Divan was being held and the Grand Master had to wait outside for it to end. He waited for two hours. The Sultan's attendants did their best for him, bringing the obligatory robe of honour of padded silk and fur and putting it on him. De l'Isle Adam hardly cared, for the worst that could happen to him had already happened and a little rain was hardly here or there.

So eventually they met face to face and summed each other up. Seated on a golden throne between two golden lions and robed in white and gold, at first Suleiman appeared to the Grand Master, who had seen no one but grim-faced armoured men for the last six months, like a being from another world. But while the first formal exchanges were being made and interpreted (by Ibrahim among others), he had the opportunity to attempt to assess the Sultan's character, weighing up the firm mouth, heavy grey eyes, and arrogant expression. He was not, truth to tell, any longer very interested. He had known this young man for over a year now even though he had never seen him before, and had devoted a great deal of thought to him. All he wanted to know now was whether or not he could be trusted.

Suleiman, for his part, was deeply interested. He had often wondered what sort of being could have inspired the resistance of both Hospitallers and Rhodians. At first sight he was disappointed. He saw only a wet, tired old man with red-rimmed eyes, hardly a vision to spur men to die for him. But he too watched and listened when it came to de l'Isle Adam's turn to speak, and gradually, through the stilted exchange of compliments, the speeches of submission and acceptance, they grew used to each other's looks and manner and began to grow towards an understanding of each other's quality. In the nature of things it was bound to be an anti-climax, for the meeting was short and its terms prescribed, but equally neither party was interested in making any sort of impression on the other. Each appeared in his normal guise.

When the preliminaries were over a silence fell. Suleiman broke it at last, sympathizing with the Grand Master in his misfortunes and reminding him that it was the lot of all rulers to lose cities and realms and praising his gallant defence. So the encounter ended.

Its success could be gauged from Suleiman's performance the following day when he returned the visit. He rode through the Gate of St John, leaving his escort outside the city and saying, 'My safety is guaranteed by the word of a Grand Master of the Hospitallers, which is more sure than all the armies in the world.'

They could be more informal with each other now. Suleiman, as the apparent victor in the almost equal contest, had not only said all the right things but had meant them. Despite the differences of faith and culture and the discrepancy of age, they edged from respect to liking. De l'Isle Adam took the Sultan on a tour of the bastions and showed him what was left of the barricades. Suleiman, thoughtfully looking him over as he talked, suddenly asked him if he would care to enter Turkish service. It was a bit of a shock, but the Grand Master was equal to it. He declined, adding with a touch of humour that 'A grand prince would be dishonoured by employing such a renegade.'

They met for the last time on New Year's Eve when de l'Isle Adam came to kiss the Sultan's hand on departure and make him a gift of four golden vessels. He received a safe-conduct for himself and his companions. There was a certain amount of emotion in the air but no point in expressing it. After the Grand Master had gone, Suleiman turned to Ibrahim and said, 'It distresses me to have to turn that fine old man out of his home.' He meant it; of all the things about Rhodes that had distressed him this was not the least. As for the 'fine old man', he was only fifty-eight but was feeling and looking much older. Still, his career was no means over.

The Hospitallers left Rhodes the next day, going to Cyprus in the first instance. They marched out of their citadel to the beating of their drums, one hundred and eighty of them - all that were left - their armour burnished and their banners flying. The Sultan, for his part, went the following day to say his prayers in the new Turkish mosque which had been the Church of St John.

12

Once Suleiman had gone Khurrem let herself fall into despair. She had tried so hard to remain calm and smiling during the last few weeks, which seemed to her to pass like a flash, and succeeded so well that when at last the morning came when he kissed her farewell she hardly knew what to do with herself. She had stood at her window to watch him ride away from the Old Palace in a state of benumbed misery such as she had never experienced before. When the great gates closed on him she stood there still, unable to move and unable to think.

Eventually it occurred to her to walk into the sleeping-room and pick up little Mehmed. Even this did not help; she looked down at the little boy as if he were someone else's baby and found she could not bear to look into the unformed little face which did not resemble his father's. Finally she walked back into her sitting-room, sober, sensible, aware of all that went on around her, and totally at a loss. Hulefa and Meylisah watched her covertly. Both would have liked to comfort her, and Hulefa had her own reasons for feeling particularly sympathetic to her mistress at this moment, but Khurrem's closed face and stiff back warned them off. They took counsel with each other without words and went silently on with their morning tasks.

She remained courteous and aloof for the rest of that day and most of the next. She did everything required of her, even to the extent of visiting Hafise, and while with her contrived to talk with her usual animation on a variety of subjects. If Hafise looked at her daughter-in-law a little thoughtfully she had no comment to make and was careful not to mention Suleiman.

However, all emotion must have something to feed on, even misery. By the late afternoon of the second day Khurrem was heartily sick of herself. The trembling knot of fear at the pit of her stomach was still there and would be there until Suleiman came home again, but it was not only possible but necessary to think of other things and she could if she tried hard enough. Fear can sometimes heighten sensitivity, and the first person her eye fell on when she raised her head and looked around her was Hulefa, who was arranging a bowl of flowers. She was not doing it very well. Even in her own lacklustre state of mind Khurrem could see that. Marigolds, roses and lilies were being jammed anyhow into the great copper vase with irritable dabbing motions of Hulefa's usually capable hands.

Khurrem watched her for a moment or two and then turned her attention to Meylisah who was sitting in a corner looking at nothing. She felt a small twinge of irritation. If I'm low-spirited, she thought, everybody else is the same. Why must they rely on me all the time? This was unfair but she was too miserable to perceive it. Indeed it was almost with the purpose of finding something to grumble about that she took the opportunity of Hulefa's leaving the room to say to Meylisah, 'What's wrong with Hulefa?'

Meylisah jumped. 'Oh, you're – I mean – oh, Hulefa? Her brother's gone to Rhodes. She's upset,' she finished unnecessarily; 'he's all she's got.'

Khurrem sat up. 'I didn't know she had a brother!' she said. 'Nobody told me.'

'Well, no,' said Meylisah, staring. 'I mean, we wouldn't, unless it came up, would we? After all, janissaries aren't supposed to have anything to do with their families, are they? Anyway, he went yesterday, the same as his majesty.'

But with considerably less fuss on the part of his nearest and dearest, thought Khurrem, shame washing over her. True, a brother is not a husband, but when he is your only family he is still very precious. Khurrem pushed her hair out of her eyes and considered. The feeling of shame had blotted out all her irritation and even blunted the edge of her fear. I must do something, she thought, to lift us out of this. Poor Hulefa, she never said a word, just went on with her work getting crosser and crosser because that's the only outlet she has! I wonder . . . Aloud, she said, 'Meylisah, do you like the water?'

'The water?' said Meylisah, who always repeated what was said to her to give herself time to think. 'Why, yes, I think so. I was never on it except when I was brought here from Egypt when I was a baby and I don't remember that.'

Hulefa came back to be greeted by the news that they were all going on a water-party the very next day.

'The Sultana Valideh will lend us her barge, and we'll take the baby and Leila. We'll go on the Bosphorus to the gardens at Beshiktash or somewhere like that, and take lots of lovely food and fruit and think of nothing the whole day,' proclaimed Khurrem. She added firmly, 'We shall feel all the better for it.'

She was right, they did. The expedition gave them a breathing space in unusual surroundings while they adapted themselves to their fear for their loved ones and sadness at parting from them.

Meanwhile Hafise had also been giving thought to Khurrem's peace of mind. She was delighted to know that she was to have another grandchild but also knew that preparing to bear his child was not necessarily the best or easiest way to await the return of a husband from the wars. She took thought therefore and sent for Khurrem who came looking as if she had not a care in the world.

Hafise came straight to the point. 'Khurrem, you will admit that so far I have never interfered with the way you arrange your household or conduct your life. You obviously make my son very happy –' She paused and was rewarded by a dreamy smile, and went on, 'But, with the joyous news you brought me recently the time has come to think again. You must have a larger establishment of your own.'

'I have been very happy as I am,' replied Khurrem, a shade wistfully. Hafise nodded understandingly, noting the use of the past tense, and waited.

'But,' continued Khurrem, 'I suppose there won't be room for us all much longer in my present rooms.' She sighed and added, 'So I suppose I shall have to move. I wish –' she stopped, wondering if she dared confide her most private desire to Hafise, decided that she could, and hurried on, 'I just wish that the Sultan and I could live together – I mean, at least under the same roof. The present arrangement just doesn't seem natural to me.'

Hafise had wished the same thing throughout her married life but she knew that there was no point in saying so. Besides, Khurrem was already rather too prone to rebellion against the natural order of things. She said drily, 'It is the Ottoman way, my child,' and changed the subject. 'I have been thinking about proper quarters for you. The suite of rooms occupied by Sultana Ayse has been empty these last ten years. I will speak to the Aga of the Girls and he will arrange for their cleaning and re-decoration for you.'

Khurrem stared in apparent disbelief. 'Sultana Ayse's rooms? For *me*? But –' She stopped and shook her head.

'Why not?' demanded Hafise robustly. 'When I have gone to my fathers and it is your turn to be Sultana Valideh, as we all hope, you will occupy these rooms. Will you find something in that to wonder at? What is the difference?'

Khurrem thought about it. Eventually she said seriously, 'The difference is that I know you and love you, but the Sultana Ayse is a great personage from the past and she doesn't seem to have anything to do with me. Although I suppose you remember her and she doesn't seem a great personage to you?'

'Exactly so,' said Hafise drily. She remembered her own mother-in-law only too well and would under no circumstances have called her a great personage. She tried however to enter into Khurrem's difficulty. At last she said gently, 'You feel inferior to these past Sultanas because you know nothing about them and dwell on the wrong things about yourself, that you were a slave and not well-born. This is false modesty. Rather you should remember that you are the wife of the Padishah, who chose you because of the qualities you possess as much as for the love he bears you. Now, will you consent to occupy the rooms I have chosen for you?'

It seemed she would. 'Very well, then, that's settled.' Hafise cleared her throat, trying to remember what she wanted to say next. It was sometimes difficult not to be sidetracked by Khurrem. Of course! The whole purpose of this exchange was to keep the girl engrossed and contented until Suleiman returned from Rhodes. She said abruptly, 'Splendid! I shall send for the Aga of the Girls.'

Four days later, as instructed, the Aga of the Girls presented himself at Khurrem's quarters and announced that the suite of rooms selected by the Sultana Valideh for the use of the Sultana Hasseki Khurrem had been cleaned and garnished and was ready for her inspection.

Khurrem's eyes sparkled. She had not by any means lost sight of her ambition to educate herself in statecraft and fit herself to become Suleiman's confidante. How could she do that in her present two small rooms, happy as she had been in them? And she had taken Hafise's words to heart as well, but the thing that weighed most heavily with her was the thought that Suleiman would approve. So she greeted the Aga of the Girls with her customary unaffected friendliness and energetically insisted on being conducted to see her suite immediately.

'Now, lady?' he asked, taken aback. He was a black eunuch, tall and splendid in appearance and more than a little rigid in mind. He fitted admirably into the Ottoman system with its sober insistence on convention. The arrival of the Sultana Valideh at the Old Palace on the death of her husband, the Sultan Selim, rather more than a year before, had shaken him to the depths of his being. But she was a great lady, one had only to look at her! If she wished to subject the harem to a complete re-organization, then her wishes must be complied with. Khurrem he could not begin to understand. Look at her now, standing there in a plain robe of dark green silk, not a jewel in sight, and her hair in two simple plaits. It was almost indecent. And now it became plain that not only was the lady coming to see these rooms at once, without any seemly preparation or making of appointments, but her two maids were coming too. His high yellow turban and one of his chins wobbled. That's another thing, he told himself grimly, willy-nilly leading the way while the three girls pattered briskly behind him, she treats those two slaves more like friends than maids. He shook his head in genuine bewilderment because, being a fair-minded man, it now occurred to him that despite their preferential treatment, Hulefa and Meylisah were among the best-behaved and most discreet of the slaves under his care. He took refuge in a platitude, something he had found himself doing increasingly over the last year. It was the one about things being different in his younger days.

'But this is lovely!' cried Khurrem when she saw her reception-room. She was right. The Old Palace was inconvenient, draughty in winter, hot in summer, and too small, but its principal rooms were beautiful. Built mainly of timber, it was tightly wrapped in its gardens and high stone walls which protected sultans' women from intruders and the gaze of the commonalty and gave little promise of the splendours within. She stared at the delicately carved wooden screens and doors, at the fairy-like lattices and the blue-painted ceiling, and could find nothing more to say for the moment.

The Aga preened himself. He wondered briefly why it was that, although he did not particularly care for the Sultana Hasseki Khurrem, he always extended himself to please her, and could find no satisfactory answer. Certainly she was never rude to him as were some ladies he could remember, but he was uncomfortably aware that on occasion her courtesy could be more cutting than their lack of it.

However, the slaves of the Intendent of Buildings had certainly done their work well in the short time allotted them. There wasn't a speck of dust in sight and the woodwork and tiles gleamed with polishing. They had even found a magnificent Seljuk carpet for the floor. That brought him to another cause for grievance. The Sultana Valideh had told him specifically that Sultana Hasseki Khurrem would select her own furnishings and draperies and he, the Aga of the Girls, had had to pass on this unwelcome piece of news to the Intendent of Buildings who was, unlike himself, touchy. There had been a little coolness. Fortunately they had been able to unite in condemning the levity and freedom of behaviour in the young. For, as the Intendent said, if even his majesty visited the Treasury and gave instructions that certain green Chinese porcelain, which had been safely stored there for years, should be used at his table, where would it end?

He waited now while Khurrem's brilliant eyes turned from one delight to the next. When a few moments passed and she still had not spoken, he was at first affronted and then apprehensive, wondering what could have been forgotten.

Her thoughts were far away. Over a year ago she had stood, a newly purchased slave, in Hafise's exquisite reception-room in Manissa and had looked around her in wonder just as she was doing now. She had been carefree, had she known it, heart-whole and happy. She was no longer heart-whole or carefree, and the happiness she had now was of so different a quality, so precious and in a way so precarious, that it hardly seemed the same sort of emotion. She could not resist one backward glance at the heedless creature she had been. But already her quick mind had grasped that something in the present demanded her attention. She read accurately the assortment of expressions which succeeded each other on the Aga's face. Almost before she knew it she heard her own voice thanking him gracefully for his kindness and care. Placated, he led her and the maids through the rest of the rooms. Practical questions, such as the nearest source of water, were of course asked by Hulefa. Meylisah stared with eyes as bright as a cat's and murmured over the beauty of everything.

At last they paused in a small room opening off the sleeping-room, its walls fitted with broad shelves and cupboards with airily carved doors. 'Not room to swing a cat. What's it for?' demanded Hulefa.

'A wardrobe for your clothes and jewels, lady,' replied the Aga, addressing Khurrem. He never spoke directly to slaves except to give them instructions or to reprove them.

'Clothes? A whole room for clothes?' demanded Khurrem, before she could stop herself. 'I couldn't possibly –' She stopped, suddenly thoughtful, and added, 'It will do splendidly for my books.'

'Books,' repeated the Aga in a flat, uncomprehending tone. He fell silent, looking helpless, so that Khurrem and the maids were able to flit rapidly from room to room, discussing what was needed and progressing rather more quickly than they would have done had courtesy compelled them to defer to his ideas of what was and what was not proper and possible. Nevertheless, when they were ready to leave and Khurrem thanked him once more, something, perhaps the unaffected friendliness of her manner, impelled him to say, as he had known all along that he would, that there was in the Treasury an elegant divan of state, inlaid with precious woods and mother-of-pearl, which in his humble opinion would suit her reception-room excellently. 'Divan of state?' repeated Khurrem, and if her voice contained the same note of total lack of comprehension with which he had repeated the word 'books' he did not notice it. She blinked and recovered quickly. 'Anything you select, Aga, will, I'm sure, be superb,' she stated, and went off with her head held high.

Later that day Hafise had the opportunity to congratulate herself on the success of her plan to divert Khurrem. Her daughter-in-law sat on a cushion beside her divan, eyes sparkling, and described with zest and in detail the beauties of her new apartments. Hafise, whose days were full of administrative problems, formal visits from great ladies of one sort or another and other tiresome duties, did not listen very carefully to the details; it was enough for her at the moment to observe the play of expression over the girl's face while she turned over in her mind the best way of approaching the next subject she wished to discuss with Khurrem. It was not going to be so easy this time. Not only might she be hurt, she might also be discouraged or even - unthinkable! - crushed. Hafise observed her carefully. She was beautifully dressed as always when she visited her mother-in-law, or indeed (it was very necessary to be fair) on any formal occasion. This afternoon a caftan of ultramarine brocade covered a long robe of dark green silk and emeralds glittered at her throat and in her turban.

Hafise rested her chin on her hand and thought carefully about her problem - if indeed I have one and am not merely imagining things, she thought wearily. Her manners are always perfect, her judgement is excellent and she seems to be beloved in the harem as well as by my son, who does not see her with the senior slaves but nearly always informally. She pounced on the word. This was the crux. Khurrem's strength was in her close and loving relationships, with her husband, her child and certainly, thought Hafise, with me. She is more to me than my daughters, who sometimes seem like strangers. She sighed over this, but since it was true, accepted it.

She roused herself from her reverie to hear Khurrem say happily, '- and the poor Aga seemed quite dumbfounded!'

It seemed as good an opportunity as any. Hafise said gravely, 'My child, he is not there to be dumbfounded. He is a good, painstaking man and even you admit that he has gone to a great deal of trouble to please you. Now, don't look so cast down. You haven't offended him, but you have caused him to wonder at you, as you admit yourself.'

Khurrem raised her hand to her mouth and stared in honest bewilderment. 'But I wasn't unkind or rude. I - I didn't laugh at him! I don't understand, truly I don't!'

Hafise raised her own hand to her head and rubbed it as she was prone to do when she was at a loss for words. To be fair, this seldom happened. Now she seemed to have overstated the case and the poor child was worried. How difficult matters of decorum can be, she thought, and began again. 'I repeat, child, he was not offended, nor has he any right to be, if it comes to that!' She added downrightly, 'Where was I? Khurrem, a royal court is a very serious place, full of conventions and devoted to tradition.'

'Yes, madam,' agreed Khurrem with feeling.

Hafise glanced at her. 'Well, there are good reasons for it, as you will see. A Sultan's splendour and the good behaviour of those around him represent him and his family to the outside world. If their conduct is in any way unbecoming it will eventually reflect on him and his.' She glanced at Khurrem's face and hurried on, 'I am not for one moment suggesting that your conduct is in any way unbecoming. It is simply sometimes a little – unusual. You are much cleverer and quicker than most of the people in this harem. Even among the senior officials –' she paused, and then corrected herself, 'particularly among the senior officials, there are some to whom the customs and conventions are articles of faith. They don't ever look behind them to see what originally inspired them, they simply accept them and live by them, so that small things which more independently minded people would not even notice cause them wonder or even distress.' She paused, wondering if she had expressed herself clearly, or even, she thought, if I have said what I really mean!

Khurrem considered this and said in a clear voice, 'Then I don't think they should be encouraged.' She had not asked, and did not need to, how Hafise had come to hear about the morning's work. Gossip was the harem's favourite recreation and a few indiscreet words uttered in the heat of the moment in the hearing of a junior slave would be all over the place in no time, with accretions. Guzul, one of Hafise's two maids, was an enthusiastic gossip and mimic, and although in theory the Sultana Valideh set her face against such weakness she was both too human and too shrewd not to enjoy a little tattle for its own sake, as well as for the insight it gave her into what was going on.

Hafise gave vent to a little sound, indicative of being at a loss for words, and rested her head on her hand. She suddenly found she had a headache. After a moment's thought she said, 'It doesn't matter whether you encourage them or not, they are as they are and they can't change! Khurrem, I'm not scolding you, please believe me. But when you run about the harem at a moment's notice, with your hair streaming down your back, like – like a housewife, with no veil, no turban – Why, the Aga of the Girls can only think that that's not the way he expects to see a Sultana Hasseki behave, and the younger slaves think that if you go about like that then they can too! Now do you understand? Khurrem, Khurrem! What are you laughing at?'

Khurrem wiped her eyes and took another moment to control herself. 'I'm so sorry, indeed I am. Now that you put it so clearly I understand. That poor man! I made him do something in a hurry for once, didn't I? No wonder he gobbled like a goose! It's just that I get so interested and want to do everything at once. In future I will be grave and dignified and think before I speak, at least to the Aga of the Girls!'

'I'm sure you will. There is something else. I propose now to increase the number of your slaves. Perhaps two more?'

'Whatever will I do with them?' Khurrem rested her chin on her hand and stared at her mother-in-law.

'Your family is about to increase by one,' pointed out Hafise with a certain asperity. 'Really, Khurrem, this – this cosiness,' she found the word and brought it out triumphantly, 'must cease! Or rather, be confined to your most intimate hours. You are, after all, very young. Dignity and decorum will seem natural to you as you grow in years. Yet one more thing: I notice that you do not receive the wives of court officials nor make many visits. Why is this?'

'They bore me. They can only talk about their clothes and each other,' responded Khurrem crisply. She was growing apprehensive, seeing her privacy and freedom threatened.

'They bore me, too,' admitted the Sultana Valideh before she could stop herself, and hurried on, 'Nevertheless, I have to receive them and you should do the same. Some of them are very well-born ladies whose manners are worth observing, and who have, as far as women can have, considerable knowledge of the world. Besides, it is not good for either of us to give way to the sin of intellectual pride. I mean it, Khurrem,' she went on, seeing the girl's obstinate expression. 'You can learn a great deal from some of these ladies. Some even are very well educated.'

Without knowing it she had found the key. Khurrem's eyes

opened wide. 'I suppose I do need polish,' she admitted; 'indeed, I know I do. And I should like to meet some of the Western ladies who come here with their husbands. I should like to learn all I can about other countries.'

Hafise looked at her curiously. She knew the girl's passion for knowledge, and had noticed that it had grown in intensity since her marriage. She would have expected the opposite to happen. Now she remembered from Guzul's vivid account of the Aga of the Girls' bewilderment, the matter of the books which were to occupy the wardrobe. She said gently, 'I have never found you deficient, my dear, and I don't want you to overtax your strength.'

Khurrem hesitated. She would have liked to take the Sultana Valideh into her confidence, but how could she say boldly, 'I want to learn all I can so that I can help my husband to govern'? It was an unheard-of idea, impertinent, and probably impossible to realize. And without intending it she had already given Hafise enough problems to cope with for one day. Her strong, handsome face looked quite tired! When she considered how easily she gave offence and disturbed people without knowing she was doing it, it was the grossest impudence on her part to think that she could ever gain her husband's confidence to the extent of being allowed to discuss matters of state. Not that she wanted to, for she wasn't personally ambitious. All she wanted was to protect her son, and everything else followed from that.

She remembered how, when she and Suleiman had first become lovers, Hafise had talked to her much as she had done today about her new responsibilities, and how she had seen a new world full of exciting possibilities opening out before her. Now it was happening again.

A less sensitive girl might have seen in the Sultana Valideh's reproof no more than a fussy regard for the conventions of the harem and the court. Khurrem, soberly taking stock of herself, realized that it was much more. It was a warning to prepare for a future more complex and perhaps more frightening than she could yet foresee. Its beginnings might lie in the pleasurable and trivial business of ordering her apartments and extending her social life, but who knew where they could lead?

In the meantime her pregnancy followed its course, keeping

her still and quiet and giving her time to think and read, activities she found all the more enjoyable when her normal boundless energy was in abeyance. This time there were no complications, emotional or otherwise, to frighten Hafise and the midwives, and on a dark November night a dark-eyed little girl slipped into the world without too much fuss. She was received with the restrained joy that always greeted the arrival of a girl in a Turkish family; by everyone except her mother, that is. Khurrem was delighted with her, sure that she would grow up to have as much energy and self-reliance as she had herself. We'll be great friends, you and I, she promised the solemn little scrap of dimpled flesh lying in her lap. It'll be nice to have another woman in the family.

They named the new princess Mihrimah, which meant Moon of the Suns, and Khurrem chuckled at the contrast between the high-falutin name and its small, not to say passive owner, but she was careful to keep her thoughts to herself in front of Hafise who had suggested the name.

Now, too, the news from Rhodes was cautiously optimistic, and surely Suleiman must at last be coming home. And he was delighted to have a daughter; his real joy was patent, even through the stiff wording of his letters. So Khurrem, with nothing more to worry about, recovered rapidly and completely – so completely indeed that she was soon at a loss for something to absorb her new-found vigour. With Suleiman away the days were so long, and she soon tired of the ordinary pursuits open to her – visits to the bath, gossip with her friends and trying on clothes. She could take a carriage and go calling, of course, but when she reached her journey's end what was there but more gossip, more sherbet, more indigestible sweetmeats to be eaten?

So she took longer and longer drives into the city simply for the pleasure of being out and about, of seeing people going about their business. She got to know the city quite well, to absorb its flavour and understand its geography. Soon she went further afield, even borrowing Hafise's barge and crossing the Golden Horn. Hulefa and Meylisah were less enthusiastic about these chilly expeditions on the water in winter, but Khurrem, child of the plains as she was, merely wrapped her velvets and furs more closely about her and gazed out over the choppy water with delight.

One day she had herself taken to Kiaghitkhane; a friend had told her that there was a Hindu convent near the village, so Khurrem, always alert for the strange and unusual, had to go and see it. It proved rather a disappointment. It was there, certainly, but none of its inmates were visible. 'What a bore,' said Khurrem, peering from the inadequate little window of the carriage. 'I suppose we'd better go back. I should have known better, nobody's likely to be out in this weather.'

'Except us,' murmured Meylisah, huddling deeper into her cloak.

'It's a nice, crisp day,' her mistress defended herself. 'If I could, I'd get out and walk a bit.'

Meylisah, horrified, said nothing and took refuge in staring out of the window. Which was why she said, after a long pause during which the chilly landscape slid past the window at a satisfyingly fast pace, 'Why! What funny horses!'

Khurrem, occupied with her own thoughts, asked a little sleepily, 'What's funny about them?'

'They've got little beards, and –'

What else they had she never had a chance to say, for her mistress rapped out, 'Stop the carriage!', slithered down to the door at the end and began knocking on it urgently.

'Whatever –' began Meylisah, gathering her wits, but Khurrem was already sliding in a most undignified manner out of the carriage door and down on to the road, to the manifest amazement of the Spahi escort.

By the time Meylisah got herself and her flowing garments out of the carriage her mistress was already at the roadside, standing on tiptoe to look over the hedge and exclaiming, 'Oh, aren't they wonderful? Oh, I never thought I'd see them again! Look, Meylisah, aren't they beautiful?'

Meylisah looked obediently. All this fuss about a lot of undersized, odd little animals, she grumbled to herself, more like mules than horses, not a patch on his majesty's lovely Arabs or Cappadocians with their long, silky manes! Whatever will she do next?

The captain of the escort had approached, a slight smile visible beneath his heavy moustache. Meylisah saw the smile and interpreted it in her own way, thinking, she doesn't care what sort of exhibition she makes of herself! This man must think she's mad! Whatever he thought, however, the captain saluted Khurrem and said, 'These are wild horses, lady. Part of a gift to his majesty from the Czar of Russia.'

Khurrem looked up at him, adjusted her veil and allowed her caftan, which she had been holding up with both hands to allow herself to move freely, to fall in dignified folds about her. Then she said in her usual friendly fashion, 'I know! I do hope I didn't alarm you, stopping the carriage like that, but I simply had to see them more closely. When I was a girl in Galicia, I used to ride horses like these.'

Meylisah saw the captain blink. He coughed, and Khurrem rattled on, 'It was very reprehensible of us, I know, and we might have been killed, I suppose, but you don't think of things like that at fifteen. You see, after they'd been broken in, we children would catch them and ride them bareback. In my part of Galicia they use horses quite a lot on the farms. They even use them for ploughing instead of oxen.' She smiled happily up at him while the captain blinked, trying to reconcile this elegant lady, his Sultan's wife, with the picture that she had evoked for him of a wild, red-haired girl galloping bareback on one of these tough little horses. He smiled again and asked if she would like to see more of the horses, because if so he would try to find one of the grooms.

'What is this place then?' demanded Khurrem.

'His majesty's stud farm,' he told her. 'Perhaps I should inform the Acting Master of the Horse that you are here, lady.'

'Good gracious, no!' said Khurrem, to Meylisah's relief. 'I only stopped to look because – because –' she faltered, and Meylisah saw that there were actually tears in her eyes. But the next moment she cleared her throat and said briskly, 'They reminded me of my childhood, you know.' Still she did not move, but gazed wistfully over the hedge at the sturdy animals with their neat hooves and short, thick manes. Presently she shook her head and said matter-of-factly, 'Whatever am I thinking about? You're cold, Meylisah, and time's passing. We'll come back another day.'

Alas for the shivering Meylisah. A man had appeared suddenly beyond the hedge and addressed them sharply in a language neither the captain nor she could understand. He was a very exotic character indeed, even in that land of mixed nationalities. Meylisah had an impression of flat features and high cheekbones under a round fur cap, and a stocky, muscular body clad in a heavy tunic.

'Oh, dear,' said her mistress, not turning a hair, 'I'm afraid he thinks we're up to no good. He wants to know what we're doing here,' and she rattled away at the man in the same unknown tongue.

Now, of course, there was an exchange of smiles and laughter. The foreigner showed them a gate in the hedge further up the road and insisted they go through and see the horses more closely. Meylisah tried to hang back and wasn't allowed to, but she was soon quite proud of herself when her hand was gently taken and laid on the soft flank of one of the mares - and all the horse did was to turn and look at her with liquid brown eyes, and snort with breath smelling pleasantly of grass. There was more laughter and an almost affectionate leavetaking, with the man leaning over the gate and waving until the carriage was out of sight.

In the carriage there was an excited exchange between mistress and maid.

'I touched it!' cried Meylisah. 'Did you see, madam, I actually touched it! And its coat is as soft as - as your furs. You wait until I tell Hulefa! And what language was that man speaking? Oh, what an adventure!'

Khurrem was strangely subdued. 'Russian,' she said, rather shortly. 'He spoke Russian - he *is* Russian. That's why I could understand him. He's a groom, sent with the horses. You heard what the captain said.' She fell silent.

It took a moment or two for her silence to impinge on Meylisah. Then she asked gently, 'Did seeing the horses make you feel homesick?'

Khurrem frowned, and said, 'I don't think so. It was strange, to see them so suddenly like that, and certainly riding them used to be a wonderful experience - exciting, made you forget everything else - but -' she broke off, lost in memory, and then continued, 'but no, I'm not homesick or regretful in any way. All the wonderful things in my life have happened here, in Turkey, and I don't want to look back. There's just one thing,' she added energetically, 'I realize now what I would like to do - I'd like to learn to ride, properly, I mean.'

Meylisah gaped at her.

And, of course, such an ambition was unheard of among

Turkish ladies. Still, Khurrem achieved it, exercising her by now considerable store of tact and patience. She knew that Hafise, that champion of correct behaviour, would disapprove, but also felt instinctively that Suleiman, whose personal behaviour was ruled by the Law rather than by convention, would not.

The lives of harem ladies were governed by strict rules and little fashions which made the rules bearable. Khurrem started a fashion. 'We need exercise,' she told her younger friends airily; 'dancing and playing catch are not nearly enough.' Soon the stableyard at the Old Palace re-echoed twice a week to the excited little cries and giggles of half a dozen venturesome ladies. Veiled to the eyes and bundled up in shawls and caftans as became virtuous women taking the air, they went round and round under the indulgent eye of the Master of the Stables, mounted on six of his oldest, fattest and most docile horses. He knew they could come to no harm, sitting sideways on pack-saddles equipped with little platforms on which they could put their feet. They looked like countrywomen riding home from market.

Hafise, hearing about the experiment, came to watch them. She smiled a little frostily and raised her eyebrows. But still she had seen and so, tacitly, approved. It was all the rage for quite a month before they got bored with it. After which the Master of the Stables found himself left with one pupil, the Sultana Hasseki herself. Then, he hardly knew how, the tone of the lessons changed and became more businesslike. Before he could look round she had demanded, and got, a proper jineta saddle and was riding astride with short stirrups like a man. Well, too, as if born to it. He was quite proud of her. 'Fearless,' he stated, though only to picked listeners, for he was a discreet man. 'Best pupil I've ever had. A pity she's a woman!'

Of course she told Suleiman all about it in due course after his return, picking her moment. At first he laughed, then warned her to be careful. Presently he gave her a beautiful Moldavian horse for her own and told the Master of the Horse to provide her with a groom. He chose a flat-faced little man from Russia whose name was Kazan, who was kicking his heels about on the stud farm and making no attempt to learn Turkish. Since the Sultana Hasseki came from Russia herself the Master of the Horse felt the arrangement to be an economical one.

BOOK TWO
Ibrahim

13

The cost of Rhodes in life and emotion had been bitter, but it had been won. Suleiman found it difficult to regard it as a victory unless he kept his original aim clearly before him, which had been to clear his seaways of the 'Hellhounds'. He did all the things that convention required of him, even to thanking personally a bevy of female sponge-divers of the island of Symi who had declared for the Turks and helped them by fixing mines under water to the breakwaters, and neglected other things that perhaps he might have done with profit. For instance, after the brief visit with de l'Isle Adam he never again looked at Rhodes' defences and he never talked to Martinengo. But everything he did was done quickly and he left Rhodes on 6 January, never to return.

Suleiman's frame of mind, as the remnants of his army began the long trek back across Anatolia, was not enviable, and his temper uncertain. He was convinced that his own part in the campaign had been weak and indecisive and was shocked to discover that there were whole areas of the art of making war that he still knew too little about. It had been folly, for instance, to bring the feudal cavalry on a campaign where only the janissaries and artillery were needed. There were never enough janissaries, and after this half-year's work there were even fewer. It would be a long time before the army would be ready to take the field again. He half-suspected that the janissary failure had been due to nothing more than the fact that they were not armed with pikes or similar thrusting weapons. Cut off on an island in the driving rain, he had been made to look ridiculous. He wondered what Selim would have thought of the botch he'd made of it. And he thought he knew.

Ibrahim, riding as always immediately behind his Sultan, watched Suleiman's face for any sign of more cheerful thoughts but discerned none. He had tried unsuccessfully to engage him in some kind of conversation, to find something that would stimulate his imagination so that he would slow his horse to a walk, turn in the saddle and talk a little, but to no avail. Suleiman remained aloof, silently brooding, as he had done ever since they had left the island at first light, made the icily cold crossing to Marmarice, and then pushed on for the long road to Kutahia.

It was beginning to get on Ibrahim's nerves. He liked to talk, exchange views and comment, to feel that everyone was in a good humour. He liked to know what was going on. From that it was but a short step to wanting to influence what was going on. At the moment he did not know precisely what was wrong with his master. Of course he knew that the campaign had taken three times as long as it should (he certainly knew that; after the first careless rapture of seeing all those evidences of Greek antiquity, he had soon begun to find the place a bore), he knew that it had been costly in lives and that Suleiman had been baffled by his own dependence on the military wisdom of Ahmed and the others. He knew all these things because Suleiman had discussed them with him freely, and he himself had sincerely tried to keep his master's spirits up and to convince him that his pessimism was ill-founded.

Hitherto he had nearly always been able to influence Suleiman's state of mind. Even on those occasions when he had failed he had always been told what was wrong. Now, suddenly, he was excluded. This was serious on two counts. He was devoted to his master and it was distressing to see him suffer and be unable to assist. Also he was Suleiman's slave, albeit his friend and confidant, and he was well aware (although he never admitted it to himself even in his most private thinking) that his own future depended on Suleiman's continued need of him.

Ibrahim sighed, wrapped his heavy velvet caftan more closely round his body, and peered once more at his master. He could discern no change in his expression and turned his attention to the landscape, but there was nothing much of interest there. The long column wound its way as far ahead as he could see. There was little liveliness among the men who rode for the most part without talking, almost sullen, the only sign of life being the screeching of a half-naked dervish who was running beside the column some way ahead. He was demanding something or other, food or alms, which he would undoubtedly get because the men were superstitious about these fellows, paying a great deal too much attention to their prophecies and their peremptory demands.

Nobody would think this was a victorious army; and certainly no one would think this was a great and victorious Sultan. What was wrong with the army was plain enough. Victory had taken too long, and now that it had come they had been denied their proper share of booty because the Sultan had promised the Rhodians and the Grand Master that their rights should be respected. Naturally the men had looked after themselves as well as they could, and illicit gold cups and silver platters gleamed from under many a cloak and saddle-bag. Suleiman had had to turn a blind eye and hadn't liked it. Too punctilious by half, thought Ibrahim. He experienced a slight tremor of disquiet, and thought suddenly, I'll soon be thirty. How much longer before the great things he promised me materialize? Or are they something else that he'll have to think twice about?

He repressed the thought immediately. Unworthy, he reproved himself, unworthy both of him and of me. I am his only friend, and loyalty is his strongest characteristic. Lulled by the steady motion of the horse, he allowed himself to drift into a reverie.

Ibrahim barely remembered his parents, fisherfolk of Parga on the Ionian Sea, but he did associate them with warmth and affection. He remembered that when he had been carried off by the corsairs who haunted those waters, a little boy of five, he had cried bitterly for his mother. They had stolen him because he was a beautiful child who would grow into a beautiful boy and make somebody a valuable slave. This fact had been impressed on his mind and influenced all his subsequent thinking. In due course he had been taken to the slave market at Izmir where the lady Leila had bought him for his looks, his quick mind and his impudent charm. She had made him. A wealthy widow of Manissa whose only child was married and living in Izmir, she had nobody else to love, dominate, and spend her money on. She had him well educated, to the full extent of his ability, which was great. He loved music and she had him taught the viol which he played to perfection; he also loved the arts and was instructed in them. He learned Turkish quickly. Obviously he had a gift for languages, and must learn more. Whatever he wanted was his to command. Had he been stupid or meretricious he would have been wrecked. As it was the lady Leila very nearly managed to do it, for when he was fifteen and in those climes already a man to all intents and purposes, she fell in love with him. Poor lady, she couldn't help herself. She was lonely and self-indulgent and had done everything for this child, even to correcting his manners and teaching him etiquette herself, and now before her eyes he was becoming a most attractive young man. Who owed her everything.

Possibly Ibrahim realized what was implicit in her eyes and her touch even before she realized it herself. He was not shocked, but he did feel distaste. The lady Leila was his substitute mother, his benefactress, and even though he'd played up to her and extracted as much as he could in the way of gifts, he still looked up to her, was grateful to her, even loved her. Now she was behaving in a way he found grotesque in a lady of her dignity. Besides, she wasn't young and if she had ever been pretty, she wasn't any more. He didn't want her, but it looked as if he might be trapped. Nearly a year went by while Ibrahim allowed himself to be fondled and sighed over. Soon he would not be able any longer to stop it going further. Already the other slaves had got wind of it and were sniggering behind their hands.

But fortune favoured Ibrahim. He was not destined to lighten the last years of the lady Leila, because the young Shahzade Suleiman heard him play his viol and wanted to know who the artist was. Though forbidden to do so the young Crown Prince, newly come to Manissa as a governor of the province of Sarukhan, had taken to wandering the streets at night. He was bored and lonely. The Ottomans took the business of government seriously and Suleiman was a high-minded and industrious boy who worked hard and pleased his tutors. Now, at seventeen, he had been despatched to this most important province to continue to learn the business of governing at first hand. His mother, the Lady Hafise, came too, to control his miniature court and watch over him. But even the most serious of boys get tired of loneliness and constant hard work. So Suleiman kicked over the traces in the mildest possible way, and standing in a quiet street listening to music coming from the upper rooms of a house, he was enchanted.

When Suleiman discovered that the musician was a slave, and a boy of his own age as well, he speedily made his wishes known. 'Buy him,' he said. The purchase was not frowned upon, and the only sufferer was the lady Leila. She behaved with dignity, however, letting it be known that since she was unable to put a price on the boy she hoped his royal highness would accept him as a gift. His royal highness was graciously pleased to do so.

They became inseparable immediately and remained so. Their temperaments were complementary, and besides, neither had ever had a friend before. They talked incessantly, long into the night, and then slept in the same room, at first on separate mattresses and then together. Suleiman's tutors were hardly concerned; they knew that such relationships flared up, became intense, and then wore out. They were partly right in this case. The sexual element wore out, but the friendship remained steadfast. They saw themselves as brothers; or at least Suleiman did. Ibrahim knew better than to presume too much.

Ibrahim knew nothing of sport. Suleiman taught him to shoot with the bow, to wrestle and to ride. Ibrahim knew far more about the arts than his friend, and Suleiman, who had an instinctive love of music and poetry, was happy to follow where he led. If he had to study the arts of war and politics, Ibrahim provided further insights into both because of his passion for history, and if Suleiman learned the business of government, Ibrahim could give him some valuable sidelights on the life of slaves.

So they entered their twenties together, two highly cultured, gifted young Turkish gentlemen. Suleiman, who had to learn to weigh up a man's character and assess his abilities, practised on Ibrahim; and the more he learned of him, the more impressed he became. As for Ibrahim, slavery had taught him to be cooler in his judgements, and Suleiman was both more complex and less articulate than he. He did not always understand his master and could grow impatient with his high-mindedness. There were times when he felt superior to him, conscious of his own quicker understanding and his links with a great civilization. But he loved him, and trusted him as far as he trusted anyone.

Boredom and cold were having a bad effect on Ibrahim's frame of mind and he had several things to worry about. The royal horses were not the least of them. In his humble opinion, too many of the best highly bred horses had been brought to Rhodes, and they had not stood up very well to the inactivity, the cold and the short commons. Ibrahim decided to check them over. It would be something to do, anyway. He spurred his horse forward to attract the Sultan's attention.

Suleiman was still lost in his reverie. But when Ibrahim succeeded in rousing him, he smiled and said, 'If you must. But don't be too long. I've recovered and feel like talking.'

Ibrahim rode off, cursing himself. All I had to do, if I'd known, was ride up and say something – anything at all. Now I've got to look at the confounded horses! It was typical of him that he did look at them, abused a careless groom, and left them the better for his attention.

It was typical of Suleiman that when Ibrahim returned, he apologized for his sullenness. 'I have at last realized that I'm once more on Turkish soil,' he said, and laughed as he looked at the bleak landscape. 'I can't say that it's much of an improvement on Rhodes at present, but it's home. Before the month is out we'll be in Istanbul. I have a new daughter to greet and soon it will be spring. I have much to be thankful for.'

He was talking, Ibrahim noted, as if he had been seeking and finding consolation for something. He felt a little impatient and said robustly, 'You will also be greeted by victory celebrations.'

Suleiman grunted and turned his head to look at his friend, his expression forbidding. Ibrahim refrained from returning the look directly and kept his face straight. After a moment Suleiman grunted again and said, 'It was a bloodstained disaster and you know it as well as I do.' But he did not sound angry, and Ibrahim was encouraged to go on.

'I remember, sir, that when you and Piri Pasha were discussing the janissaries when we first arrived on Rhodes, you said that what they wanted was a romantic mission to fight for, and Piri said something about instant glory. Now, sir, with respect, did you not have some idea that we might find a convenient wicket gate that had been overlooked?'

Suleiman's face darkened, and Ibrahim hurried on, 'Of course you didn't, otherwise why did we take over 100,000 men to Rhodes, as well as that immense armament? You knew it would be hard, perhaps impossible, but you had not visualized it, had not seen it in your imagination.'

'If I had I wouldn't have gone,' said Suleiman gruffly, but Ibrahim could see he was mollified. He hurried to make his point.

'But you did go, and as a result the route to Egypt is safe. You cannot see it as a victory, because when we talk of victory we only think of triumph and cheering and smiling faces.'

'There aren't many smiling faces here, certainly.' The Sultan looked thoughtfully at the column winding its way ahead. He could only see figures huddled in frieze cloaks, the backs of grey sleeve caps with the towering plumes or heavy gold or silver ornaments with which the janissary liked to indicate the length of his service and the campaigns in which he had served. Ibrahim heard him take a deep breath, but he said nothing.

They rode in silence for some while. Presently Suleiman spoke in a totally different tone. 'I suppose you realize there'll be no campaign next year?'

'Europe and no doubt Persia would be relieved to hear you say so, I'm sure,' said Ibrahim demurely.

Suleiman looked into his friend's mischievous dark eyes and laughed suddenly, the first time in days. He said seriously, 'God knows how long it will take to refurbish our losses.' He added, as if to himself, 'Perhaps it's as well. Let the army lick its wounds and heal them; I have something else to think about.' There was another pause, then Suleiman said abruptly, 'Are you devoted to horses then?'

Ibrahim felt a shock of excitement, but managed a laugh. 'To tell the truth, I've always thought them rather stupid animals.'

'Good,' said Suleiman, and Ibrahim was flattered to hear a wealth of satisfaction in his voice. He continued, 'The time has come to do what we have always agreed should be done, and you will play your full part in it, for God knows you are the only man I can trust. When we get to Istanbul, give me time to clear my thoughts, or rather, help me to clear them. Then,' he turned and looked his friend full in the face, 'there will be a new post for you.'

So it had come. It had come when he least expected it, thrown away, like that, from the saddle. He drew a deep breath, but Suleiman forestalled him. 'We'll say no more now. I'm happier than I have been for months. Look, it's growing dark. When we make camp, we'll have supper together and some music.' He turned again to look at Ibrahim. 'Soon you'll have your own establishment and your own harem. It'll make a difference, so we must make the most of the times we have together.' He smiled and leant forward to dig his friend in the ribs, a rare gesture of affection and lightheartedness. He added, 'Still, there'll be plenty of campaigns together, eh? But not, I trust, such another as this has been.'

14

Khurrem had sought to make this room, where they would sit together and sometimes eat a meal, the most beautiful in her new apartments. All the precious things he had given her during the short period of their life together were displayed on the shelves around the walls, and she had added others to them, choosing the loveliest pieces of porcelain, glass and enamel she could find. Even now, when she was so disturbed, she looked around with pleasure. Surely when they were alone together and he saw all that she had done, he would be at ease and become the Suleiman she knew.

Custom had dictated that Hafise must welcome the victorious Sultan on his return to Istanbul and the bosom of his family. So for two hours, dressed in her finest clothes and decked with as many jewels as her maids could load on her, she had stood beside the Sultana Valideh's divan of state, little Mehmed clutching Leila's hand beside her and the wet nurse holding the new baby behind her, and watched her husband go the round of his family and the senior officers of his harem, greeting them punctiliously and saying the things that courtesy demanded. Of course, after kissing his mother's hand he had come next to her. But what sort of welcome could she give him under the scrutiny of all these people, some of whom she barely knew, and what could he say to her while they all stood listening and smiling politely, their eyes hard and curious to see what time and distance might have done to their Sultan's relationship with his wife?

They had learned nothing to titillate that curiosity, that was certain, but Khurrem had been shocked. He was not as she remembered him. He had grown thin, his eyes heavier than ever in the narrow, tanned face. But the real change was deeper and she could not identify it; she felt only that he seemed ill-at-ease and watchful. He had relaxed momentarily when he took little Mihrimah in his arms. The baby had slept blamelessly throughout the ceremony, but when her father took her from the nurse she had roused and opened her large, dark eyes, so like Khurrem's own. Suleiman had looked from daughter to mother, his own eyes momentarily bright and appreciative, and smiled. Mihrimah, sensing that she was still safe, had yawned and gone back to sleep. All the ladies nearby had smiled and laughed a little and said all the fatuous things that are said on such occasions, while Suleiman had handed his daughter back to her nurse and turned to pick up Mehmed and kiss him.

That had been all. Khurrem had stood, her cheeks aching with the effort to maintain a brilliant smile, clutching Mehmed's hand so tightly that he had whimpered a little. Whenever her husband had come within her line of vision she had looked at him, noting anew all the familiar things about his appearance and still thinking that he looked like a stranger. Only, she thought, stranger or not, I still love him however he may have changed. But seven months is a long time and this campaign has done something to him, and I don't know what it is. His letters never prepared me for this, brief and formal as they always were. What can I say to him, now that I no longer know him?

Almost at that moment she had heard his voice behind her. He said softly, 'This charade is nearly over. Go to your rooms. I must talk to my mother for a moment and then I will come.'

His voice had been so low that she could almost believe that she had imagined it, but he was still looking at her. So she had turned, taken her leave of Hafise and, gathering her little entourage around her, had left the room. It had not helped that Hafise, too, had felt that something was wrong. She had grasped Khurrem's hand tightly as the girl bent to kiss her, and whispered, 'Oh, my child!' slightly accenting the last word in a sort of despairing comment on what they both felt but could not name.

Back in her own rooms Khurrem discovered with incredulity that no one else shared her disquiet. As they removed her elaborate headdress and the stiff caftan her maids chattered happily. How splendid his majesty looked, how brown his face, how obviously happy he was to be back with his family! (This from Meylisah, who always confused what she thought people ought to feel with what she actually saw them feeling.) It hadn't comforted Khurrem, who dismissed them a little sharply and sat down to wait.

He is a long time coming, she thought bleakly, and then immediately rejected the idea as unbecoming. Hafise loved him too and must at this very moment be talking to him, delicately probing to discover what was causing his disquiet. Certainly she had every right to a half-hour alone with him after these long uncertain months. And she is his mother! – the thought burst out unbidden – she knows him as I do not and perhaps never can. However loving he is to me, I can never forget that he is Sultan; it colours all our life together, just as the fact that we cannot live together like other folk must colour it. We can only be intimate and alone for such a little part of our lives.

Khurrem got up and went to look out of the lattice, but there was no solace there for her insecurity, only a sullen grey sky. She shook her head at it and sat down again. In an effort to be practical she turned her mind to his letters. They had never been long or informative. She suspected that he was not very good at putting his most intimate thoughts down in writing. Even so he had intimated, often by what he had not said more than by what he had, that something had gone gravely wrong. He had mentioned illness among the men, and bad weather, long periods of waiting and attacks that were called off. How did a man feel in the face of all this, especially if he were Sultan and responsible for it all? But victory had come at last, or so everyone said. Perhaps . . .

There was the faintest of sounds at the door, but her waiting ear caught it. She flew across the room even as the door opened. She had no doubt or hesitation now that he had come at last, and threw herself in his arms. She heard him laugh a little, a choked sound, and he held her away for a moment while he threw off turban and caftan. Presently he said, 'Khurrem, Khurrem!' and then nothing more.

Eventually they drew apart and sat down and looked at each other. Now that she knew he still loved her she thought he looked almost like his old self, and then was ashamed of her selfishness. All I can feel is relief because whatever is distressing him has nothing to do with me. He still loves me.

She despised herself but could not help the happiness she felt.

When they began to talk, however, Khurrem saw that she had not imagined his apparent return to normality. If the physical man was thin and haggard, the inner man was alive with joy at being home again. He kissed her rapturously, held her hand and demanded that the children should be brought in so that he could see how much Mehmed had grown and how much like her mother Mihrimah really was. All this Khurrem watched with delight, and when eventually the children had been kissed and taken away Suleiman turned to her, looked at her attentively, and said, 'And you, my love, how was it with you? I meant to be here when the new baby came, but Allah decreed otherwise.' He frowned ferociously for a moment, and Khurrem, watching his face, wondered why until she realized that the frown masked some other emotion which he did not want her to see.

'I was very well,' she told him, 'And have been all through, never better.' This was true. Except for his absence, her pregnancy had been a happy one and uneventful, and Mihrimah was obviously a healthy and contented little girl. Suleiman looked at her so searchingly, that at last she became a little embarrassed, and said, half-laughing, 'What is it, sir? What do you see there?'

'All my happiness,' he replied abruptly. Then, seeming to wish to talk of other things but still holding her hand, he looked about the room. 'Are you happy here? Do these rooms please you?'

She knew this ploy of his of old. Deeply moved, he could not express his feelings but must take refuge in superficial things. To help him she led him on a tour of her suite, describing everything in great detail so that he did not need to talk, only to murmur in approbation. But when Suleiman saw the wardrobe full of books he became interested. He began taking them from the shelves exclaiming with pleasure when he came upon an old favourite, stopping to read a few sentences aloud and then advising her, 'Read this chapter with care, it is very valuable,' or 'I first read this when I was sixteen, I shall never forget its effect on me.' Suddenly he broke off and exclaimed, 'Khurrem, this is a very hard road you have chosen for yourself. What is its purpose?'

'I am uneducated,' she answered him quickly. 'Oh, I can

read and write in Turkish fluently enough and speak Osmanlija when I am with you and other educated people, but I know nothing of the Ottoman world or of the West.' She stopped and chose her words carefully. 'The more I learn, it seems, the more there is to learn. When you talk to me I want to be able to understand and – and –' she found the words she wanted and brought them out in a triumphant rush, 'play my part in the conversation as your mother does.' She looked at him anxiously. 'When you first talked about Rhodes I had never heard of it. I was ashamed.' She stopped abruptly, angry with herself. She had determined not to mention Rhodes.

Suleiman's reply surprised her. After a moment he said, 'How patient you are! You must want to know about the campaign and you have not said a word. You divined that I did not want to talk about the place and you were right. It has been a bitter experience and one of which I am ashamed. You talk of your ignorance! I have been guilty not only of ignorance but of arrogance in the face of it.' He seized her hand. 'Had I your humility, I would have behaved very differently. As it is thousands have died. Tomorrow,' he finished bitterly, 'the ambassadors of Persia and the Venetian Republic will come in state to congratulate me on a great victory, and it is true the People of the Religion, as they call themselves, have been driven out of Rhodes. But the cost! I don't want to think of the cost, I want only to be at peace and stay with you. And for tonight at least I will.' He took her hand and held it. 'But there is much to be done.'

After their lovemaking was over, both fell asleep very quickly. It seemed to Khurrem indeed that she had never slept so deeply or so dreamlessly. Nobody called her to wake her but there seemed to be a constant monotonous sea of sound and she was afloat on it. It seemed to need a great effort to bring her to her senses so that she could hear the sound consciously and come awake at last. It was dark as pitch; indeed, she was not aware of opening her eyes. All she was aware of was the sound of Suleiman's voice. At first she thought he was speaking to her. She even raised herself on her elbow, saying, 'Yes, yes! What is it?' But when she heard the unearthly quality of his voice and realized the meaning of the disjointed words that poured from him, she was filled with dread. Although she could not see him she knew he was not awake and was not responsible for what he said. Slipping from the mattress, she crept to the room where the children were sleeping and returned with the small pottery lamp that Leila kept burning all night.

It was not so frightening now she had light. Suleiman seemed to be wrapped in deep slumber, but writhed from side to side as if in pain. 'The rain,' he muttered, 'the rain, it never stops, it carries them away, I cannot stop it!' His voice rose to a moan, died away, and then began again, 'The rain, the rain –'

She stared in horror; she literally felt the hair rise on her neck. The next moment she fell on him, shaking him and calling his name. And yet when she eventually succeeded in rousing him he seemed no more than normally drowsy, staring at her with fogged eyes and asking 'What is it, my Khurrem, what has frightened you?'

An automatic desire to preserve him from the fear she herself felt led her to say, 'I'm sorry to disturb you, I had a bad dream,' rather than tell him the truth. Indeed Suleiman fell asleep again almost immediately, and so far as she could tell he passed the rest of the night peacefully, while Khurrem lay beside him wakeful and anxious.

15

After Rhodes nothing was ever to be quite the same again. With Suleiman it was a definite decision, part of the plan he had laid down for the betterment of his empire and the improvement of the lot of its peoples. So far as those around him were concerned, the change was to come, as in the case of Ibrahim, because they had earned it, or, as in the case of Ahmed Pasha, because they thought it was due to them. Khurrem was a different matter; opportunity came to her, as it often does, simply because she was ready for it.

It seemed only a small thing: an invitation from Ayse to visit her. It wasn't even surprising. After her talk with Hafise Khurrem had dutifully begun to entertain and be entertained by some of the ladies of the aristocratic families with connections at court, as well as the wives of the more important court officials and senior army officers who had risen to power after their training at the Pages' Schools. She had been pleasantly surprised. Some of these ladies were interesting people in their own right, and as representatives of their particular strata of the highest Ottoman society they were interesting from a different point of view. Also all of them flattered her, which, even if she was not particularly susceptible, was pleasant.

She soon began to learn that things were not as simple as they appeared on the surface. There were stresses and strains even in the enclosed society of the women which reflected the sharper struggles among their menfolk. The aristocratic ladies looked down on the ladies of the career men, but they had to be polite to them because the career men had the power, and their wives and daughters knew it. Khurrem, her quick wits sharpened by the history she read, watched and listened and kept her own counsel. It helped that she was gay and friendly and approachable, as well as discreet. She noted, among other things, that the recognizable strata of society had, in places, been cut across. Shrewd aristocratic fathers, for instance, had tested the way the wind was blowing and had married a daughter here and there to up-and-coming young Slaves of the Gate, as senior army officers were called.

So she saw nothing sinister or unusual in Ayse's invitation and was even rather pleased to receive it. She had hardly seen Suleiman's elder sister for nearly a year. True, Ayse had courteously visited her along with the other ladies of the royal family after the birth of Mihrimah, but that was all. After all, Ayse had been living a restricted life since Mustafa Pasha had been rather suddenly packed off to govern Egypt direct from Rhodes. If there had been any low-voiced comment about that among the more politically-minded ladies, Khurrem had not heard it, for by that time she had been near her confinement.

She set off in a pleasant flurry of low-keyed excitement. Outings were sufficiently rare even among women of her class to be novel and Khurrem was still young enough to enjoy sweeping out to the courtyard, wrapped to the eyes in a sable-trimmed, quilted velvet caftan, and being ceremoniously assisted into one of the gay, flower-painted carriages reserved for the use of the royal ladies. She had an escort, too, of black eunuchs in their ostrich-feather crowned headdresses, and there was Meylisah, round-eyed with wonder as usual, to carry her handkerchief and her gift of choice sugared apricots.

Her reception was, on the surface at least, all she had expected. That is to say, like a twentieth-century lady going out to tea she was warmly welcomed into a comfortable house. Mustafa Pasha's establishment in the correct fashionable quarter was all that it should be. She was greeted with becoming ceremony and even affection by Ayse, and if Khurrem was a little surprised to see how pale and troubled her hostess looked she naturally refrained from saying so.

Ayse's reception-room was pleasantly warm, the heat coming, in those days of unglazed windows, from numerous ornamental braziers which stood about the room. At her invitation, Khurrem seated herself in a bower of cushions, placed her feet on the tandur filled with lighted charcoal, and drew the quilt which went with it up to her waist. Thus established, both ladies were cosily warm for as long as they remained still and the charcoal lasted.

The exchange of compliments necessary between two well-intentioned ladies who did not know each other very well began. But Ayse's heart clearly was not in it, and when Khurrem remarked politely that she would be delighted to see Ayse's little son, a child a few months older than Mihrimah, she replied shortly, 'His nurse has him in the garden,' and nothing more.

'Oh,' said Khurrem, taken aback. 'Well, perhaps another time!'

'Why not?' replied Ayse listlessly. She rested her head on her hand and sighed deeply.

Khurrem looked at her more attentively. Her face was pasty, her large brown eyes dull and red-rimmed. When last she had seen her, Ayse had been plump, cheerful and embarrassingly talkative; now she was frankly fat, and her frame of mind something to be guessed at since she seemed in no mood to communicate. Although not one to stand on ceremony, Khurrem was aware of a very slight irritation. If she doesn't want to talk why has she asked me here, she wondered. Then she remembered that Hafise had said that Ayse was 'not very happy'. At the time she had taken this to mean that Ayse's marriage was unhappy. Perhaps this was not the case. Perhaps instead her present apparent misery was the natural result of being parted from her husband. If so, thought Khurrem, the reason for my presence here today becomes obvious.

It seemed that she was right. Ayse made no particular effort to be artistic about it. After sitting in troubled silence a little longer, she said abruptly, 'I asked you to come today to ask a favour. I'm sorry if you expected something else. I'm not very good at compliments at the best of times.'

'It doesn't matter,' Khurrem assured her. 'What can I do for you?'

Ayse sniffed. 'I want my husband back. It was shameful to send him off like that! The whole of Istanbul knows he went in disgrace. And yet they did no better on Rhodes after he went.' She groped in the bosom of her crumpled gömlek for a handkerchief and blew her nose.

Khurrem stared. Ayse's whole appearance spoke of emotional

distress but what she said seemed to be dictated less by love than frustrated ambition. Also Khurrem did not care to listen to any criticism, direct or implied, of Suleiman. She remained silent. And presently Ayse, noticing her lack of response, said, 'I see I've offended you. I didn't mean to – I need your help too much.' She sniffed and brought out the handkerchief again.

Khurrem was struggling to be fair. She knew that the devotion which existed between herself and Suleiman was not common, and that there were as many different relationships between husbands and wives in Istanbul as there were marriages. She felt she had no right to adopt a critical attitude towards Ayse because she did not understand her, and she had to admit that Ayse could not be expected to feel very charitable towards her brother. She said gently, therefore, 'What do you want me to do?'

Ayse seized her hand and said feverishly, 'Oh, you will help me! How good you are – I knew you would! All I ask is that you will speak to my brother. He'll listen to you.'

'Won't he listen to you?' Khurrem queried before she could stop herself.

'No, he won't, because if I ask him I'll make a botch of it. You won't understand this, but Suleiman makes me feel inferior. Even when we were all young he was the quiet child who never said much and was always cleverer than the rest of us. Any time I try to talk to him I say stupid things. I hear myself doing it but I can't stop. So, of course, he thinks I'm a fool.'

'I'm sure he doesn't think anything of the sort,' said Khurrem. She did not think she sounded very convincing. She had never heard her husband express an opinion of any of his sisters, but she could well believe that he would have little in common with Ayse, talkative, muddle-headed and self-indulgent as she was. Nevertheless Ayse was sufficiently sensitive to be aware of her own weaknesses and feel herself vulnerable. But she had still given no clue as to her attitude to her husband. Khurrem felt it important to know this; she would feel more sympathetic to Ayse if she could feel that she loved her husband. After a moment's thought she recognized this as the sentimentality it was, but still could not rid herself of it.

She sought the right words and finally asked lamely, 'Do you miss him very much?'

Ayse had been absent-mindedly picking at the beautiful handkerchief in which Khurrem's gift was wrapped. She stopped and asked abruptly, 'Who?'

'Your husband,' said Khurrem, now acutely uncomfortable.

'Oh,' said Ayse almost off-handedly, and went back to picking at the basket of apricots. 'Yes, of course I miss him. He's a man after all and tries his best. He has to, of course.' She smiled sweetly at Khurrem, a smile which invited understanding as from one royal lady to another. But Khurrem did not understand and could no longer help showing it.

'I mean,' continued Ayse bitterly, after a pause which Khurrem had been unable to fill since she did not know what to say, 'that as a Sultan's daughter I have certain rights. I see you do not understand,' she went on impatiently, 'though I would have thought it plain enough. The imperial blood runs in my veins, therefore any man I marry is my inferior. A dagger lies between us, even in the act of love, to remind him of the fact. But I cannot transmit that blood to our children, so he can never hope to see his son as Sultan. On the other hand, he dare do nothing to displease me. There, I think, the advantages end, for certainly, though my husband dare not displease me, I am vulnerable through him. Oh dear me, yes. I suspect you did not know that I have been married twice?'

'No, I did not,' said Khurrem faintly.

'I should like to tell you about it,' said Ayse. 'You, I believe, would understand. My father, the great and indescribable Selim,' her voice was loaded with venom, 'gave me in marriage to one of his viziers. His name was Ahmed Dukaginzade and he came of an ancient and honourable family. He was, himself,' she paused and swallowed, 'everything that a man should be, able, courageous . . . I tell you, Khurrem, from the first night I was with him, no dagger ever fouled our bed! Well, my father allowed us time to know each other and love each other. Then, because my husband failed to put down some miserable janissary uprising, he flew into one of his terrible rages and condemned him to death.'

Ignoring Khurrem's involuntary exclamation of shock and pity, she continued, 'When he was calmer, I begged him for mercy, I was distraught, you cannot imagine . . . Hafise implored him too, but nothing anyone could say had any effect. He had given his word, you see, and would not change. So I was widowed.' She looked at Khurrem and went on calmly, 'I see I have distressed you and I am sorry, but I am glad to have spoken of it to you. The day does not pass when I do not think of him. I believe he was the only person who has ever loved me. Certainly, he was the only one I ever loved. That is a sad admission, is it not? But true.' She nodded sharply, then continued, 'I was allowed to mourn him and live as I wished, that is to say, wasting my time and my life, until two years ago, when my mother and my brother decided it had gone on long enough. Perhaps they were right. Anyway, Suleiman gave me in marriage to Mustafa. He meant well. A woman should be married, I suppose.'

She sighed, and glancing at Khurrem said in a totally different voice, 'I'm forgetting my duty. You're cold.' She clapped her hands, and both ladies sat in silence until the braziers and the tandur were replenished. When the slave had gone, Khurrem said, 'I am so sorry for you. I had no idea you had known so much unhappiness. I thought –'

Ayse broke in a little impatiently, 'I'm not exactly a figure of tragedy, am I? Besides, my brother and my mother were right. I was destroying myself. You can't undo the past and Mustafa is good to me and has given me a son. It is not his fault that I don't love him. I don't even love little Osman very much. He has too much the look of his father. This, of course, is reprehensible of me. Probably I'll like him better when he is older. But all that is beside the point.' She spoke firmly and looked expectantly at Khurrem, who surprised herself by asking, 'What then is the point?'

This directness apparently pleased Ayse. She nodded approvingly and sat up against her cushions. 'To have had two husbands disgraced is more than I should be expected to bear. Mustafa may be a fool in some ways, but he is a brave man and he is mine. I owe him something and I feel that my brother owes me something. Both he and my father disposed of my life for their own purposes. Well, now I want a place in the sun for Mustafa and myself. It is not too much to ask.'

She looked fiercely at Khurrem and suddenly smiled. 'I could not have said any of that to Suleiman. In the first place I could not have put it so well, and in the second place he would have been shocked. Perhaps you don't agree?' She seemed, now that she had put her case, to be almost lighthearted.

Khurrem sat in silence, attempting to match her sister-in-law's cool assessment of her husband's probable reaction to the story she had just heard. She was unable to make up her mind and said so frankly. 'I have never known him to be unjust or dishonest,' she finished, a little desperately.

'Of course he's just and honest,' replied Ayse, almost contemptuously. 'I'll go further, and say he's the only member of our dynasty who's ever attempted to be either, so far as a mere woman can say. But that isn't necessarily enough.' She looked thoughtfully at Khurrem and added, 'I see you're new to this game, but I don't doubt you'll learn to play it well enough in time. I shall leave it to you to decide what to say to him because that's why I asked for your help in the first place.'

16

Suleiman's disquiet had begun to ease. The return to the routines of his life in Istanbul calmed him once the first Friday visit to the mosque was past. That was a painful experience, for the citizens of his capital turned out in their thousands to welcome him home after what they in their innocence saw as a great and glorious victory. That he was young and untried made it somehow all the more glorious. Also, since his accession he had shown himself to be a just, even a generous ruler, who did not see his subjects merely as a continuous source of funds. Full of euphoria, therefore, they blocked the streets and threw themselves to the ground before him. Suleiman, splendidly robed and accoutred in the midst of his escort, had perforce to compel himself to smile and acknowledge their plaudits, feeling himself a bloodstained hypocrite.

He lived through it, however, just as he had lived through the campaign itself. The nightmares which frightened Khurrem and the eternal feeling of weariness and despair began to pass almost without his noticing. Hard work and the routine (much of it dull) of his office, the joy of reunion with Khurrem and the stimulus of thinking about the programme which he intended to put into effect – it was nothing less than a complete reorganization of government – all played their part. Rhodes began to recede into the past. He would never be completely free of it; there would still be nights when his sleep was haunted by bloodstained phantoms and voices that called for release from pain. There would be days when he sat brooding under a sense of guilt and inadequacy until roused by the pressure of his duties. But he had come to terms with it.

That evening, the day of Khurrem's visit to Ayse, he was

aware for the first time of a pleasurable weariness at the end of his working day and active anticipation of a happy evening to be spent with his wife. He remembered that somehow it had never happened that they had listened to the woman singer of whom his mother spoke so highly, and resolved to have her sent for to entertain them after their supper.

In fact, the whole evening proved a memorable experience. Riding to the Old Palace, Suleiman caught himself thinking impersonally about the campaign for the first time. Glancing at his janissary escort, he found the thought coming automatically, they won't be ready to take the field again for at least a year, probably longer. And I must discuss with Ahmed and the others the question of increasing their numbers.

Buoyed up by this new sense of well-being, his thoughts turned inwards and he did not notice anything unusual about Khurrem until they were listening to the singer. That she wore a becoming gown and rather more of her magnificent jewellery than usual was all that he observed. But now, his appetite satisfied by the simple but perfect food Khurrem had set before him and his imagination stimulated by the music, he turned to look at her, to catch her eye and in the exchange of glances to share with her his recaptured happiness.

His drowsy smile was returned by one so brilliant that he was impelled to look at her more closely, and thought that he had never seen her lovelier or more – he sought a word and finally found one to suit him. She is luminous, he thought, she positively glows with life and its enjoyment. My simple Russian girl is changed, he thought, but, thank God, not beyond recognition. She was maturer, quieter, with more dignity and yet, as this evening showed, with no loss of exuberance. She had not been like this on the night of his return. Her joy then had been as real but of a different order. Then she had been tremulous, a little anxious and deeply moved. Now she seemed filled with a vital energy which almost prevented her from sitting still, even to listen to the singer's lovely voice.

Sitting directly opposite her, Suleiman wondered idly about it, for everything about Khurrem concerned him. When the woman had finished her songs and gone, he asked, 'And what have you done today?'

It was the opening Khurrem had been waiting for. On the journey back to the Palace and afterwards while she prepared for

Suleiman's coming, she had devoted a great deal of thought to Ayse's request. While she had sat listening to her sister-in-law she had been puzzled by Ayse's motives and by her own inability to feel at one with her, but at the end when Ayse had talked about 'this game' she had understood suddenly how what she was being asked to do dovetailed with her own disparate plans. Of course! This was how it was done, and how foolish she had been to think that she was alone among women in having ambitions and planning to carry them out. And how naive she had been to imagine that she could do it alone, with the aid of a little knowledge gained from her books! People needed each other, women needed each other, wives and mothers and sisters, each with her little programme or plot (some preposterous no doubt) but all making use of each other, or if you preferred to put it another way, helping each other. And she, Khurrem, would learn to be better at it than any of them because nothing less than her son's life depended on it.

She had gone on thinking about it throughout their supper and heard very little of the singing because of it. She had been busy planning how she would introduce the subject of Mustafa. One thing was certain, she must not make the despicable hash of this project that she had made of her request to Suleiman not to go to Rhodes. Not that the two things had anything in common. That had been foolish, selfish and ill-considered. This was an act of generosity, almost of justice, and since her own feelings were not directly involved she could think clearly about it. She had watched her husband anxiously. If he was tired and low-spirited this evening, as he now so often was, she would not worry him tonight. But if he was reasonably calm she would tell him the whole story honestly. She certainly didn't intend to try to deceive him.

She said, 'I visited your sister, Ayse,' and looked at him with so bright and expectant an expression that she looked positively fierce, causing him to laugh and, misunderstanding the reason for her intensity, to say, 'No wonder you're so ferocious! She has that effect on me too.'

Khurrem looked surprised. 'I was sorry for her. But I still don't think I understand her.'

Suleiman nodded and smiled a little. 'No doubt the story of Ahmed Dukaginzade was aired once again.'

'Oh,' said Khurrem, a little flattened. 'Does she talk about it a lot?'

Suleiman considered, taking his time about replying. He was aware of a quiet enjoyment such as had not visited him in a long time. Easy talk such as this, with someone he trusted - and who more than Khurrem? - delighted him. Also he was uncomfortably aware that his conscience was not entirely clear in the matter of his sister. Since it was a family matter he had no objection whatever to discussing it with Khurrem. She would bring a fresh mind to the business and help him to decide what, if anything, remained to be done about her. He had no doubt that Ayse had attempted to enlist Khurrem's help.

'I hardly know,' he said at last. 'She has few friends. After Ahmed's death she cut herself off from everyone, including those who might have helped her. This I only know from hearsay, since I was not in Istanbul when it all happened. But don't be deceived, Khurrem - Ahmed's failure, or crime if you like, was not so trivial as she has probably told you.'

'She said "a miserable janissary uprising",' quoted Khurrem, realizing that the role of sympathetic friend was less easy than she had led herself to believe.

Suleiman's eyes narrowed. 'Yes, well, it was certainly not on a grand scale, but it occurred at a crucial time and Ahmed's failure to suppress it made it impossible for my father to do something he had set his heart on. Hence his anger.'

Khurrem was silenced for the moment. She wanted very badly to say that even in those circumstances she felt the punishment to have been excessive, but could not bring herself to do so. Suleiman had never spoken to her of his father but she assumed, wrongly as it happened, from her own totally different experience, that he must have loved him. Eventually she said, '*You* only sent Mustafa away.'

The ghost of a smile appeared around Suleiman's mouth and he said, 'And now she wants me to bring him back?'

If Khurrem was dashed she declined to show it. 'Of course she does! And consider how hard her life has been. To have lost a husband she loved so deeply, and now to have the second disgraced! No wonder she feels bitter and lost.'

'Mustafa is not disgraced. I removed him from a command for which he proved to be unsuited and sent him where I hoped he would do better.' Suleiman spoke reasonably in a thoughtful voice which suggested to Khurrem that he was seriously considering what she had said.

Encouraged, she pointed out, 'People thought he was. When I heard about it, I certainly did.'

'Then people – and you – were wrong.' He held out his hand to her and drew her down by his side. 'But it is generous of you to concern yourself about Ayse,' he added, 'particularly as I think (though I may be wrong) that you don't like her very much.'

Khurrem, fitting herself against the curve of his shoulder, made deprecating noises which did not deceive him. After a moment she said, 'When I first met her she irritated me, but I thought I would like her eventually. Only the more I know of her, the less I understand her.' She forced herself to stop there. If I say any more, she told herself, I shall only say things to her discredit. That isn't the way to put a case. She added, 'Will you bring Mustafa home?'

Suleiman did not answer at once; at last he roused and said, 'Yes, but not immediately. That is not possible. But tell her that I will accede to her request. Also, if you think she will believe it, you may tell her that Mustafa is not in disgrace. Will that please you?'

'It would please me more if I could say when he will return,' she said truthfully, adding, 'She lives alone in that great house except for her little boy and her slaves, and has nothing else to think of except her troubles. It would be nice if I could tell her something really definite.'

'But that you cannot do, because I do not know myself,' he told her firmly. 'As for Ayse, do not let your heartstrings be wrung too much. True, she lives alone, but in considerable style. She has her own black eunuchs and a detachment of the Life Guards to guard her. Nor need she remain there alone if she does not wish to. Until Mustafa returns she can live here in her old apartments if she wishes. Then she would have the company of yourself and her mother.' He sighed and frowned slightly. 'I am bound to admit that I sometimes feel a twinge of guilt on her account. But she was not forced to marry Mustafa. Had she refused I should not have insisted. But after seven years of widowhood even she wished for a change, I suppose. It is the misfortune of the sisters and daughters of the Padishah that their status demands that they marry men of high rank. Men of high rank are usually also men of ambition, which means that some of them are bound to come to grief. Ayse has been doubly unfortunate. Had she been more courageous after Ahmed's death, I would have tried harder to help her, I suppose, but we have never been close. She is an irritating woman.' He fell silent for a moment, then added, smiling, 'I find it more difficult to be just to those members of my family whom I dislike than to the rest of my subjects – and even harder to be merciful. I will do my best for Mustafa when he returns, that is a promise.' He turned to look at her, 'Will that also please you?'

Khurrem reached up to kiss him and they were happily silent for a few moments. But her request had started a new train of thought in his mind and presently he said, 'I assume that this is the first time you have been asked to do a favour of this sort.' It was a statement rather than a question, and Khurrem's expression of surprise was enough of a comment. Suleiman said flatly 'It will not be the last.'

'What can you mean?' Khurrem sat up and stared at him apprehensively.

He looked at her with grave tenderness. 'It is not like you to be naive. But perhaps these ladies whose acquaintance you have been making do not yet feel sufficiently confident with you to begin. But you may be very sure they soon will. Indeed they will,' he added, half to himself, 'once I begin to make changes.'

Khurrem sat up on her heels and folded her hands in her lap. It was characteristic, he thought, that she did not find it necessary to ask any more questions about what he meant. Instead she said, 'I think you're warning me against them. It's true, I never thought of such a thing and certainly none of them have ever even hinted at – at –' She shrugged a little helplessly, adding, 'What sort of favours do they ask? Jobs for their husbands and sons I suppose, positions at court, rank in the army. How foolish I am, not to have thought. I shall tell them I never interfere in such things.'

Suleiman laughed. 'Indeed you won't! That isn't the way the game is played at all!'

Khurrem stared. 'That's what Ayse said. She called it a game! Those were her very words. I didn't know what she meant.' It is true that I didn't fully understand, she thought, and certainly I didn't expect Suleiman to concern himself with such petty matters. She looked at him with brilliant eyes. 'Why do you care what they want? You can do as you please. Or can't you? Or is it simply that you want to know what they want and what they are thinking about?'

He spoke much more gravely in reply. 'I was warning you against them. If they think you are weak or naive, they will attempt to use you. On the other hand if they think you are too strong, or perhaps not interested, they won't bother with you. As for my interest, I can do as I like if I hold the balance between the men who serve me. If I know what they want, and, as you say, what they are thinking about, I will know how best to use them. And, Khurrem, using people wisely is the secret of ruling them. I can only be as good as my ministers and officials.'

She had nothing to say to this, but remained staring ahead of her, deep in thought. Her eyes were still bright and expectant, but she also looked troubled. Perhaps I should not have involved her, Suleiman thought – but no, that is foolish. She is involved and cannot help being so. I cannot insulate her from life. It is better to warn her and teach her what I can. I should be grateful to Ayse. At least what she asked was a natural thing and dictated by loyalty. He took her hand and drew her into his embrace. 'Don't be troubled by this, my Khurrem. Your friends are not all calculating intriguers, but ordinary women doing their best to further their men's ambitions. They seek to influence you just as the men try to influence me and there is nothing wrong in what they do so long as you understand what is happening.'

'I'm not frightened,' she assured him, and this was true. What she did not tell him was that, far from being frightened, she was stimulated and excited at the prospect of wielding a little power and influencing the course of events. Had he known the intensity of her response he might have been disconcerted, but some sixth sense warned Khurrem to keep all this to herself. It was not merely that she at last understood how to go about protecting her son but that she instinctively felt in her proper element at last.

Suleiman however was satisfied by what he saw in her brilliant colour and bright eyes. And besides, he was full of his great project and naturally wanted to talk about it. He poured himself a cup of sherbet and re-positioned himself against his cushions.

'My father was a great conqueror,' he began. 'His main interest was the extension of his empire. After the unrest of my grandfather's reign there was a need for internal reform, but he was little interested in that. He cared for the welfare of the army and rebuilt the navy and he saw the ordinary subject as merely the source of the money with which to do these things. He never thought of him as a man with rights.' Suleiman was looking into space, his face grim as he continued.

'I know all this because I too suffered from this indomitable will of his. I too was treated like a piece in some enormous game of chess and moved from place to place as he saw the need. I took the occasion to profit by his example, and resolved that when I was Sultan my Turks should have their personal liberty guaranteed to them by right. It is not something that can be given or taken away by a ruler's whim!' Suleiman heard his own voice ring out in indignation. He was a little abashed at his own vehemence, and added more quietly, 'Ibrahim and I have talked of this, and now I intend to put my resolution into effect.'

'How will you go about it?' asked Khurrem quietly. 'And how do the favours my friends want for their men come into it?'

He glanced at her approvingly. 'First the law must be reformed, in small ways, and gradually. Eventually there must be a whole new code of laws. As to your friends . . . don't you understand, Khurrem, this is not a task I can undertake alone? The changes I want can only come about if I have loyal ministers and officers. Most of the Ruling Class are reliable, but many of the aristocrats, the older Turkish families, are against change of any kind. Others, mostly Devshirme men, young like myself, support me.'

'Now I understand,' said Khurrem thoughtfully. 'I have often noticed that some of the older and grander ladies seem to look down on the wives of your younger officers. I used to think it was just because they were younger and their rank lower. I didn't realize there was anything deeper behind it, though once I heard one of them say, "Oh, but he's Devshirme, my dear!" about somebody else's husband, as if it were a term of reproach.' She shook her head. 'I don't think I've been very clever. I should have realized.' She looked a little sad as she added, 'I shan't see anyone in the same light ever again, shall I?'

'No, my Khurrem, you won't.' Suleiman saw her eyes grow cloudy with thought for a moment and then widen and grow bright again. She leaned forward and touched his thigh almost timidly. 'But,' she added, beginning to smile again, 'it *will* be exciting!'

17

It goes without saying that there were plenty of practical as well as idealistic reasons for Suleiman's programme of reform. He knew, for instance, that many of the sober comfortably-off merchants and members of the guilds of his empire had been alienated by some aspects of his father's government and that he must win their support by showing himself a ruler more concerned with their welfare than Selim had been. He also knew that there would be, to put it mildly, problems in introducing Ibrahim into the administration. That young man was tolerated at court as one of Suleiman's forty gentlemen-in-waiting; but as an officer of government wielding real power he was likely to upset both aristocrats and Slaves of the Gate, as the senior Devshirme men were called.

Fortunately, Ibrahim was never the sort of man to stand in the wings with folded hands waiting to be called to the centre of the stage. He had always taken the trouble to cultivate those he thought likely to be useful. One of these was Iskender Chelebi, an immensely wealthy aristocrat who, by virtue of outstanding ability as well as worldly position, bestrode the rival worlds of the old Turkish families and the ambitious Devshirme. Arnavut Ahmed Pasha was another.

Even before Rhodes, Ibrahim had reasoned that Ahmed was likely to occupy a key position. He was Third Vizier, true, but the Second Vizier was Mustafa Pasha, in whom no one could believe as an administrator and who, after the disaster he had made of his career in Rhodes, seemed likely to stay in Egypt for the rest of his life. Piri Pasha must retire soon, even if he did not die in harness. It seemed likely that Suleiman would choose Ahmed as his next Grand Vizier. His personality may have left a lot to be desired, but he was loyal and regarded as a forward-looking Devshirme man who would do what his master wanted. Suleiman and Ibrahim agreed that with Ahmed as Grand Vizier it would be possible to instal Ibrahim as Third Vizier in his place without too much stress or strain, and then their great work could begin.

So Ibrahim continued to cultivate Ahmed assiduously. It had never been easy to do, for although both men were Greek in origin that was where any similarity ended. Ibrahim found Ahmed distressingly unattractive as an acquaintance. He was as uncultured as it was possible for a man to be who was also a product of the Pages' Schools, seeing himself as a simple bluff soldier and despising all other pretensions. He was also distrustful and moody; and after Rhodes, where he rightly saw himself as having done more than any other single man to make victory possible, he became arrogant as well. Ibrahim, a subtle man, did his best with him, and that best was very good indeed. He had early discovered that Ahmed, unattractive as he was, was a lonely man who felt himself unappreciated. Ibrahim flattered him but this soon became difficult, for Ahmed's appetite for praise, once whetted, became insatiable. However, Ibrahim plodded on, soon coming to enjoy the activity and making bets with himself as to which outrageous lie he could get away with next.

He fell into the habit of visiting Ahmed in the evening, finding him invariably alone, often reflecting on his misfortunes, and always receptive to whatever suggestions his young friend might want to put to him.

One spring evening Ibrahim arrived in the reception-room of Ahmed's selamlik to find his host slumped on a divan, his turban on the floor where it had been thrown and a winecup firmly clasped in one powerful fist. His greeting was noisily affectionate, but Ibrahim, looking at him attentively, was not deceived. He was annoyed about something. Ibrahim sighed. He had spent too many nights listening to recitals of Ahmed's imagined wrongs and they bored him. He was also beginning to have serious doubts about the man himself.

'Will you take some of this splendid stuff, my friend?' Ahmed demanded, flourishing the winecup and lifting the bottle which stood beside him half an inch from the edge of the table.

'I thank you, no,' replied Ibrahim, a trifle remotely. He was himself prepared on occasion to disregard the Muslim prohibition of wine but never to the extent of drinking for the sake of it. Now he thought distastefully, he smells and he's half-cut already. What's upset him this time, I wonder? Ahmed always drank most heavily when he was worried or disturbed, which was one of the reasons why Ibrahim was beginning to doubt him. He was never like this on the battlefield, he thought. Perhaps he's out of his element.

'It's Hungarian, you know. You won't? Oh well, it's your loss.' Ahmed hitched himself upright against the cushions which had been crumpled by his powerful frame and leaned forward to peer at his young friend. 'You look very dapper,' he grunted, staring reproachfully at Ibrahim's gold-embroidered dolman. 'Been in attendance on his majesty, I suppose?'

'Yes,' replied Ibrahim shortly. Ahmed's tone had lit a danger-signal in his mind. He took the bull by the horns and asked, 'Is there something wrong? You are not your usual self.'

'That old fool's ill again,' Ahmed grunted. 'You haven't heard? Yes, well, had some kind of seizure in his garden at home. He won't preside at the Divan tomorrow.'

No need to ask the identity of the 'old fool'. By now Ahmed's hatred of Piri Pasha had become an obsession. 'May I?' asked Ibrahim, and proceeded to strip off caftan and turban, giving himself time to think how to deal with the situation.

Ahmed waved his hand graciously and, reminded of his duties as host, said, 'Will you smoke?' indicating the water-pipe which also stood by his divan. He kept his eyes fixed on Ibrahim's face as if expecting him to perform some kind of conjuring-trick, and when he did not, Ahmed added, 'What's to be done? He doesn't die and he doesn't go. And I'll be doing all the work and getting none of the credit!'

'Well, now, I wouldn't say that's a fair statement of the case. His majesty is not a fool.' Ibrahim strove to speak temperately. 'Of course you're impatient, who wouldn't be? But the Sultan is never ungrateful for good service, as you have reason to know, and in decency he can't retire the old man, if that's what you have in mind, until he's sure he won't recover. In the meantime you've got the opportunity to prove your worth. Give Piri a month or so to lie at death's door while you show yourself irreplaceable, and the thing's done.'

Ahmed listened sombrely, swallowing generous mouthfuls of wine while he did so, but at least he was able to listen and the argument had its effect. He put down the winecup, rubbed his nose, and said, 'Yes, well, I'll say one thing. Our young master's loyal to his friends. He's let that old dodderer lead him by the nose long enough, Allah knows.'

'He has not shown himself ungrateful to you,' said Ibrahim, a shade pointedly. This was true. Suleiman had rewarded Ahmed generously for his part in the Rhodian campaign, but it was perhaps a mistake to say so at this moment. Ahmed's face darkened. He slammed the cup down so violently that it broke and he looked at it curiously for a moment, as if wondering what had happened to it. Then the storm broke.

'You're right, he hasn't! I've been loaded with honours, fur pelisses, robes of honour, all that stuff, and money and land! None of it's any good to me. You know what I want, I want power! Before I'm too old to enjoy it - I'm a lot older than you, you know. Over forty!'

'You're in your prime,' said Ibrahim coldly. But his disapproval was directed to Ahmed's condition rather than to what he said. He too wanted power and thought that Piri had lasted long enough, but he was prepared to be patient and scheme and work for what he wanted, as he was doing now. Ahmed must be prevented from doing anything that would make Suleiman doubt him. Otherwise they would have to look elsewhere for a new Grand Vizier and that would take time, might even be impossible.

Ahmed had the right blend of loyalty and good intentions, bright enough to carry out Suleiman's will and too conventional to have ideas of his own. Ibrahim said, a little more urgently, 'I do beg you to be careful what you say to his majesty on this subject. His affection for the old man is very strong and if you attack him you will alienate the Sultan. By all means make a case for yourself, but perhaps it would be as well to wait until you have shown your quality for a while longer.'

Ahmed grunted and jolted himself back against the cushions. He lifted the bottle, saw that it was nearly empty, and shouted for the slave. Ibrahim watched him warily, rather as a trainer might watch a sulky lion. Not that there was anything lionlike in his appearance. He was a tall man whose army life had kept him thin, but his face with its large, shapeless nose and brutal mouth, which heavy black moustaches failed to conceal, already showed puffiness and red broken veins. Sober, immersed in the work he loved and was eminently fitted to do, he had been an impressive figure on Rhodes. Here, he was impressive no longer. Ibrahim knew a moment of despair. I may not be able to prevent him destroying himself, he thought.

The slave returned with the fresh bottle, was cursed for failing to bring another cup, and was sent to fetch one. While he was gone Ibrahim leaned forward urgently and said, 'You do understand me? You must do everything to gain his majesty's confidence at this time. It would be a gesture he would appreciate if you suggested that the Divan should send a message of good will to Piri while he is ill.'

The slave returned and they were silent, but as soon as he had disappeared Ahmed broke wind noisily and roared with laughter. 'Your pardon!' he howled, lying back and wiping tears of laughter from his eyes with the back of his hand. 'That shows what I think of your message of good will!' He sat up, pulled down his crumpled shirt and busied himself refilling the cup. He seemed suddenly more sober and alert, looking at Ibrahim searchingly over its rim. 'Babes in arms, you two,' he began, 'you and your Sultan. It's about time somebody told him the facts of life. He's never going to reform the law or anything else until he gets rid of that old fool.' He leaned forward and tapped Ibrahim on the knee. 'He ought to cast up the account a little more carefully. Who tried to stop the Rhodes campaign, eh? Good as told him he wasn't up to it. Does he ever think of that, I wonder? Yes, he must,' he added in a low voice almost to himself. 'Thought of it on Rhodes, didn't he? And nearly got rid of the old devil then –'

Ibrahim sighed and wondered if it was any good going on. But tomorrow is Divan day, he thought, and I must get control of this idiot tonight. I'll let him talk on for a while, and perhaps talk himself into a better frame of mind. Then I'll pounce. When he sobers up in the morning he'll remember the last thing said to him. Ibrahim lay back against the cushions, listening with half an ear to Ahmed's wandering diatribe. He looked idly round the room as he listened. It was a slovenly place, insufficiently warmed and lighted, and would have seemed even more untidy if it had been less sparsely furnished. I wonder what women he has, thought Ibrahim, I never heard mention of a wife – but if he has one she doesn't bother to control his household. Or perhaps she doesn't care. What woman could care for this object?

Ahmed rambled on. The shortcomings of Piri Pasha, his devotion to past methods of doing things and outdated policies. 'Still thinks he's working for Selim, still thinks war in Iran and Syria should be the height of our ambitions when anyone can see that any threat we face must come from – from –' he raised a massive, sweaty fist, flourished it aimlessly in an effort to remember what he wanted to say and finished by rubbing his forehead. He looked suddenly old and sick and the fastidious Ibrahim drew away. Ahmed screwed up his eyes, trying to focus them, and said suddenly in a totally new voice, 'Do believe I've had too much of this stuff. Doesn't really suit me, you know. Do apologize.' He forced himself to sit up straight, swaying a little. 'This new feller in Spain and all over the place, what's his name? He's the one to watch.'

Ibrahim's eyes narrowed. 'The Emperor Charles?' he asked.

'Ah,' acknowledged Ahmed in satisfied tones, 'any trouble'll come from him, one way or another.' He picked up his empty winecup, looked at it and set it down again.

'You're very shrewd,' said Ibrahim, and meant it. Just as I was beginning to write him off, he thought. One should never underestimate a man. Give this one a semblance of the power he wants and he'll be transformed, but I must still control him. He continued smoothly, 'Too shrewd to offend the Sultan by presuming to teach him his business. He has forgiven Piri. I do assure you it will be better not to return to the subject.'

'Well,' Ahmed shrugged. 'Our master's too generous, it doesn't do. Where would we all be now if I'd been generous on Rhodes with those rubbishy peasants and Azabs and that rabble, eh?'

'No doubt still there, waiting to win the war,' said Ibrahim patiently. 'But you don't need me to tell you, sir, that that was one situation and this is another.'

'I took your point, young man. I'll lie low. You can stop worrying.' He paused, and added, 'You're a good fellow at that and I won't forget you. I suppose you stand to get something out of it, when the time comes, eh?'

'Out of what?' asked Ibrahim remotely. He had achieved his object and had had enough of Ahmed for the time being, but this was the first time the Pasha had shown the remotest interest in Ibrahim's own motives.

'Give you a word of advice,' Ahmed slurred; 'don't expect too much this time. You're a bright young man but you don't have the right background and you know what these Ottomans are. We Greeks must stand together.'

Ibrahim's nostrils flared, but he remembered his own advice and controlled his anger. In any case, his sense of humour was never far from the surface. I'm being patronized, by God! he thought, and answered evenly, 'Our master is always generous, but I'm grateful for the advice.' He picked up his caftan, saying, 'It's growing late, I must leave you.'

After he had gone Ahmed poured another cupful of wine and leaned back luxuriously against the divan, sipping thoughtfully. When the cup was nearly empty he said aloud, 'Silly young fool! "Our master is always generous," indeed. Well, he'll learn.' He looked into the cup, suddenly sickened, and threw it on the floor where the wine ran out to make yet another stain on the carpet. He rolled over, pulled his legs into a foetal position and began to snore.

18

Ahmed kept his word. He restrained himself before the Divan and even remembered to send compliments to Piri, but circumstances defeated him. Work had to go on, and with only one of the three viziers available this soon became impossible. Piri had partially recovered and, with the obstinacy of an old work horse, maintained that he would soon return to his duties. Suleiman did not believe this but was loath to force the old man to retire. He was fond of him, he was used to him, and he also thought he saw a way to bring about his ultimate wish, something which he had not and would not yet confide to Ibrahim.

'What I must do,' he told his friend a week or so after Piri's collapse, 'is to apppoint a Fourth Vizier immediately. And you know who it will be.'

'I am grateful, sir, my brother,' replied Ibrahim simply. Typical of him, thought Suleiman, he does not hedge or make mock-modest speeches while meaning to accept the post all the time. 'In this way,' he continued, 'we can keep things going while you learn the work of government and the Divan and make yourself known to those who can help you. When eventually Piri goes, Ahmed can take over from him and you from Ahmed with a minimum of disruption.'

Ibrahim was silent and Suleiman watched him curiously. He saw that his friend had opened his mouth as if about to speak a couple of times and had then closed it again. Such indecision was not typical and finally Suleiman said, 'You have something on your mind. Tell me.'

They sat, as they often did in the early evening, in Suleiman's own apartments in the Topkapi. Ibrahim was cross-legged against cushions, flat-backed and flat-thighed as always, but unwontedly thoughful. He was clad in crimson satin and Suleiman smiled secretly to himself at this typical display of magnificence.

Ibrahim took a deep breath and said, 'Ahmed grows impatient, sir.'

Suleiman's eyebrows rose. 'It is only March,' he said, 'and we returned from Rhodes in January. What does he expect? Piri has served my House with distinction for many years. Am I to cast him off simply because his successor decides that he's ready to take over?' He hesitated, and added, 'I still wonder sometimes about Ahmed. I know he's able, but is he discreet? Also, his capacity for making enemies amounts to a talent! He makes no attempt to conciliate the old families and has few friends among his fellows. He dislikes Piri and you will remember he was at odds with Mustafa. This must end somewhere, otherwise –'

What, I wonder, has Ahmed been saying now, thought Ibrahim; has all my patient work with him been in vain? He said aloud, 'I get on well enough with him, sir.'

'That's as well, isn't it? You get on with him – but does he get on with you?'

'He seems to like me, and I know he trusts me,' replied Ibrahim. 'But will he like me so well when I join him in government?'

'Who knows?' There had been an appreciable pause before Suleiman spoke, and when he did there was a certain steeliness in his tone. 'He is his own worst enemy, this we know. But you must be cautious in the early days after I have signed the imperial edict of appointment. A normal man would be glad to see a friend appointed to support him, and see it as evidence of support for his cause. We must pray that Ahmed sees the thing in this light and responds well. But if he does not, Ibrahim, guard your tongue for the moment. When you have established yourself and shown your quality it will not matter what he does; we shall be prepared for it.'

Ibrahim assumed an expression of gravity to match his master's, but he did not feel grave. He was consumed with triumph. Not only would he have a part in government and exercise power as he had always wanted, but he would also have an enormous income – not only from the state but from people who would, legitimately (that being the Ottoman practice), seek to buy favours from him. But to do him justice, he thought first and mainly of what he would be able to achieve. The long hours of enthusiastic talk and discussion and argument between himself and Suleiman were at last about to bear fruit, and it would be sweet. He tried to control, but could not, the smile that rose involuntarily to his lips. Suleiman, watching his friend curiously, saw it and smiled in sympathy. He perceived also that in this first moment of triumph Ibrahim needed to be alone. His customary bearing had deserted him. He stammered a few words of gratitude, looked surprised, and fell into a silence that could only be called sheepish. Suleiman rose to his feet, saying gently, 'The edict will be signed immediately. Now I will leave you and go to the Old Palace.'

Ibrahim sprang to his feet. Suleiman touched his shoulder and said, 'Remain here as long as it pleases you. Good night.' He turned towards the door into his apartments where a flash of cloth-of-gold indicated that his watchful pages had risen to their feet to attend him.

Left to himself Ibrahim took a couple of paces up and down the terrace. The sudden night would fall at any moment. Not very far away he heard the hoarse voices of the officers of Suleiman's escort as they fell in and then the tramp of horses' feet. Then silence closed in. Ibrahim knew that nothing was allowed to interfere with that silence, which was the prerogative of the Sultan. Beyond the Third Court of the Topkapi Palace peace reigned supreme. Tonight Ibrahim suddenly felt he could not stand it. He was a Greek and had something to rejoice over; he needed people around him and excitement. Walking quickly and, from habit, silently, he left the royal selamlik.

Since only the Sultan might ride in the Third Court, he must walk to the First Court where his groom awaited him with his horse. As he walked his mind began to work again. He cursed himself silently for his ineptitude before Suleiman. I behaved like a peasant who has been given a gold piece, he reproached himself. I will need to cultivate quicker wits than that. The old boy (for thus in unbuttoned moods he allowed himself to think of Suleiman) was remarkably tactful. Sometimes I wonder if he doesn't take in more than I think!

He could find his way about the courts of the Topkapi

blindfolded and immediately recognized the shadowy building which now loomed before him. The Divan, he exulted, soon I'll be as accustomed to it as I am to the royal apartments. Not bad for a fisher-lad from Parga! He stopped, he hardly knew why, and strained his eyes to look at the Hall of the Divan more closely, but all he could make out in the deepening gloom was its bulk with the eight domes of the Inner Treasury beyond it. There was nothing to see, and the place for him tonight, he decided, was his pavilion at Kiaghitkhane. Some of the younger Slaves of the Gate would be glad to help him celebrate, though he'd be careful not to say what, of course, and in the modest back quarters of the place there were a couple of docile girls.

Light showed briefly at a door. There was the sound of feet on gravel and voices. Barely curious, Ibrahim turned to look. Someone, several people in fact, were emerging from the Inner Treasury. The light showed him an enormous white turban above a bulky figure, with other smaller turbans in the background; gruff soldierly voices spoke briefly. Ibrahim shrugged and turned to go, uninterested. Someone, a high official obviously since he had an escort, had been working late. Soon, he supposed, he, Ibrahim, would work late too, but tonight he had other fish to fry.

'My young friend!' The voice was thin, the words clearly enunciated, and arms attached to the bulky figure in the high turban were extended. He saw shapely fingers delicately extended to greet him, while he sought furiously to identify the voice. He succeeded, shut his gaping mouth and then opened it again to say respectfully, 'Chelebi Bey, forgive me, sir. I did not recognize you in the gloom.' Silently he cursed his luck. Now that he had decided what to do he wanted to do it as soon as possible, not hang about here exchanging small talk with a man years older than himself. But it behoved him to treat the Treasurer with the greatest respect, especially now.

Iskender Chelebi's escort had now lighted a couple of torches and by their light the two men looked at each other and smiled. 'Walk with me,' the Treasurer said, taking Ibrahim's arm, and perforce he found himself doing so. They proceeded a few yards in silence, and it seemed that the invitation had been issued only in a spirit of common courtesy and nothing more. But then the Treasurer, whom Ibrahim had felt rather than seen to be glancing at him curiously, asked, or rather stated, 'I assume you have been in attendance on his majesty.'

'Yes, sir,' said Ibrahim, unforthcoming.

Iskender Chelebi nodded to himself and was again silent, but only for a moment. He was too well-bred to commit the solecism of cross-questioning Ibrahim on such a subject, but, thought that young man, he seems as though he would like to. What's on his mind, I wonder?

As well as occupying one of the greatest offices in the state, and furthermore, occupying it with distinction, the Treasurer was probably Suleiman's wealthiest subject. Moreover it was inherited wealth which had been augmented into a great fortune by the Treasurer's own undoubted ability. Chelebi came from one of the old feudal families. Altogether then, a powerful man and one to be treated with respect. Furthermore, though the older man had never said anything in particular to instil the idea in his mind, Ibrahim sensed that the Treasurer looked upon him with favour – certainly with more approval than other well-born men about the court could bring themselves to show. When they met Chelebi was always courteous, even gracious, and Ibrahim had noticed that when he was in attendance on grand occasions, the Treasurer always took the opportunity to speak to him even if it was only an exchange of trivialities.

If, however, Chelebi had anything on his mind he took his time about raising it. They walked side by side in silence, and because he was happy Ibrahim unconsciously began to hum one of his favourite airs. Chelebi listened for a moment or two and then observed, 'I perceive you are in good spirits.'

'It's a fine spring night, sir. But I'm sorry if I disturb you,' replied Ibrahim.

'Not at all, it's a favourite song of my own.' Chelebi fell silent again but only for a moment. He said abruptly, 'If you would care to sup with me it would give me great pleasure.'

The surprise was so great that Ibrahim almost stopped dead. Instinct and his feet carried him on while his brain dealt with the situation. He knew that there must be no hesitation; whether yea or nay, the answer must come promptly. He said smoothly, 'You are most kind, sir. I should be delighted.'

'Good,' said Chelebi. He looked up into Ibrahim's face and smiled with the most flattering approval. The shrewd black eyes seemed to range over his face, examining him minutely. Chelebi murmured again, 'Good, good! Let us go, then,' and turned aside to mount his horse.

It was one of the finest meals Ibrahim had ever eaten. Being young and hungry, he did full justice to it, but his brain was not off-duty while he ate. Something was in the air besides a bored and tired man's desire for pleasant company over supper. They talked idly over the meal and found a common interest in poetry and music.

Chelebi possessed a famous collection of Persian manuscripts, and he said, 'I must show them to you after we have eaten.' He himself was eating very little, Ibrahim did not fail to notice, and he observed his young guest minutely throughout the meal. Indeed, his interest would have caused acute discomfort to any young man less self-confident than Ibrahim. He noted also that his host drank a little wine after he had eaten. 'I shall not offer it to you, my friend,' he said, half-filling a winecup, 'knowing as I do his majesty's strictness in this matter. But I have a dispensation. My health is not good at the moment.' Ibrahim murmured appropriately, and could not fail to approve the other's delicacy and contrast it with the blatant vulgarity of Ahmed.

All in all, thought Ibrahim, allowing his eyes to wander round the splendid room in which they were eating, this is a very fine Ottoman gentleman indeed and whatever it is he wants of me I shall strive to accommodate him, because, all this luxury apart, there is something about him that suggests he might be just as effective an enemy as a friend. No doubt I shall learn more when we adjourn to look at these manuscripts.

The manuscripts had another equally splendid room all to themselves where they lived in exquisitely carved cedarwood chests. 'So much beauty deserves to be housed well,' stated Chelebi. He stood still for a moment, grasping the edges of his dolman at chest level with either hand while he apparantly decided which treasure to bring out first. He took his time about opening a chest and extracted an illuminated version of one of the poems of Nejati.

For the next two hours they talked of nothing but poetry, calligraphy and rubrication. Ibrahim's fund of superlatives began to flag; he loved these things, but two hours is a long time. Besides, had Chelebi something to say or hadn't he? He was about to find out. The Treasurer now put into his hands a modest little book of some twenty leaves of vellum. It fell open at an exquisite picture of fruit blossoms against blue sky over green grass, upon which sat a slender youth and a girl. They did not touch, even hands, but just faced each other. Ibrahim took a deep breath and looked. At last he said, 'Is this your dearest possession, sir? It seems the quintessence of spring.'

Chelebi sighed. 'Ah, yes,' he said, without making it plain which comment of Ibrahim's he was answering. 'Spring,' he added and looked Ibrahim straight in the eye; 'a splendid time for the young. At my age, of course –' He shrugged. 'But you feel it, to be sure, all this burgeoning life. My daughter does, also. My eldest daughter, that is – I have several of course. She is a lovely girl,' he finished gently and sighed again.

For the third time that evening Ibrahim collected his scattered wits and just managed to say the right thing – 'You are to be congratulated, sir,' he said in what he hoped was the same throw-away tone his host had used. It seemed to satisfy Chelebi, certainly. He smiled, his eyes as alert as ever, and went on to describe how he had acquired the manuscript. During the process, his arm under the young man's elbow urged him towards the door. Ibrahim took the hint and began to make his graceful farewells. He was pressed to come again, and said he would be only too happy to do so. But at this moment all he wanted to do was get away.

Because Chelebi accompanied him to the door with the most flattering courtesy, Ibrahim had to mount and ride away down the Divan Yolu without hesitation. But once out of sight of the house he stopped abruptly and told his groom to go home. He had to be alone. Once the man had obediently ridden off, Ibrahim remained still for a moment, put his hand over his eyes and said aloud, 'Great God in Heaven!' He said it deliberately, an oath remembered from his Christian childhood and still reserved for times of major stress. He filled his cheeks with breath and expelled it in a great gust to express the same thing, but beyond that he could not go because he had no idea how he felt about this momentous proposal that had so delicately been put to him.

After a minute or two, he began to ride again. 'Can't stay

here,' he murmured to himself mechanically and set course for the Palace, where he had a modest apartment in the selamlik. The motion soothed him and set his mind to work. First of all, had Iskender Chelebi meant what he had said – or to put it another way, had he known what he was saying? No Turk ever mentioned the women of his family even to close friends, let alone to someone who was little more than an acquaintance; and it had better be faced, someone whose status was inferior to his own. Iskender was not a fool either. No man achieved his position in life unless he always knew exactly what he was saying. All of which led to the inescapable conclusion that he had just offered his eldest daughter in marriage to a young man without rank or fortune, unless royal patronage counted as such; for in his shock Ibrahim had almost lost sight of the other thing which had recently happened to him. He was no longer without rank, having just achieved the status of Fourth Vizier. So were the two things related, and had the Treasurer in some way got wind of the Sultan's intentions and decided that he would make a promising son-in-law? It certainly seemed likely. Chelebi was a very subtle man, as he had just demonstrated, and quite capable of detecting a prevailing wind without holding up a wetted finger. Ibrahim nodded to himself. That's the way of it, he thought, but he might have given me a breathing space. I don't even know if I want a wife – in fact, I'm pretty sure I don't. An establishment, yes, by all means; and I had thought of some pretty, well-trained girl to warm my bed. Something biddable from the Place of the Burnt Pillar, perhaps, but a wife – why no, not yet.

But his imagination was already playing around the unidentifiable figure of Iskender Chelebi's eldest daughter. Her father had called her a lovely girl, but fathers are notoriously prejudiced. He really knew nothing about her at all.

Ibrahim had come very near the truth, but the Treasurer's motives were both more generous and more complex than he could possibly guess. He had stood in the torchlight and watched the young man mount and ride away, admiring his grace and controlled strength as he swung himself into the saddle. He's certainly handsome, he thought, and in his Greek way he has dash. All of which appeals to girls. What's more important, he also has brains and is well-placed to use them. Why would his majesty keep him at court all this time unless he intends to do something for him? The other matter was over long ago, and he's certainly gone up the ladder of court appointments fairly fast since then. He made a grunting sound expressive of extreme contentment and turned into the house, pausing only to see that the attendant slave locked and bolted the door properly. Then he returned to his reception-room, thinking, my little Muhsine and her father have much in common. I like the man so why shouldn't she?

What Iskender Chelebi had done was indeed unheard of until one takes into consideration the fact that power and money can do anything. Certainly among the Ottoman Turks marriage was basically a contract arranged between families. A young man's mother found him a wife with the aid of matchmakers and the older women of the family. Girls simply waited to be chosen. But Iskender Chelebi's eldest daughter was a different matter; she was a great heiress and young men worthy of her were few indeed. Her father was bound to take a hand in the business, particularly as he had no wife to help him. He was particularly anxious that her husband should be drawn from the new men, for he was pretty certain that the days of the old aristocracy as a power in the land were limited. True, Ibrahim was not a Devshirme man, but he was certainly a new man and very much in the Sultan's favour. Also, his would-be father-in-law felt he would be grateful.

19

Ahmed ran true to form. When Suleiman sent for him and told him he had appointed Ibrahim Fourth Vizier, he controlled himself pretty well. The Sultan was a reasonable man, but his manner this morning did not encourage Ahmed to feel he would welcome argument. Indeed at first, Ahmed, who had, as was now becoming his usual practice, drunk himself to sleep the previous night, could feel no particular reaction except a vague disappointment. He didn't mind young Ibrahim who seemed to know which side his bread was buttered on and obviously looked up to him. As of course he should.

It was not a Divan day, of which there were four in the week. Suleiman, instinctively distrusting his Third Vizier's reactions to the news, had deliberately chosen that day to give Ahmed time to come to terms with it, and watched him calmly and in silence. Ahmed stood glowering before him, conscious principally of a bad headache and a growing atmosphere of royal disapproval. Aware that he must say something, he barked in the soldierly tones he liked and always used to impress people, 'Grateful to your majesty. Work piles up. With your permission I'll return to it.'

Suleiman bowed and, suddenly moved to pity though he hardly knew why, said, 'Your devotion pleases me, Ahmed.'

Ahmed raised slightly bloodshot eyes in surprise, but gratified none the less he marched out, and the Sultan, watching him go, shook his head and wondered at the change in him. Ahmed on Rhodes had been in his element, but here in Istanbul he was moody and difficult. It was all very well to reflect that jealousy of Piri was weighing him down. Grand Vizier material should not be so obviously corrodible.

Ahmed swung out of the royal selamlik, heading for the Hall of the Divan only a short distance away. Suddenly he felt the need of fresh air and stopped irresolutely. His head throbbed as if there was a battering-ram inside it and he was conscious of a great tide of anger rising in his chest, so that he felt he might stifle if he didn't get relief from it. He sniffed the air loudly and swung off again in the direction of Seraglio Point, ploughing along with his head down and his arms going like pistons. There was practically no one to see him except a few gardeners intent on their work. Besides, the Pasha always marched about like a bull at a gate, his eyes bursting out of his head. Anyone who looked at him would notice nothing out of the ordinary.

He took refuge in a small pavilion built long ago for the pleasure of one of the past sultans, and now ruined and deserted. He planted himself squarely on an old divan and stared angrily at nothing. So this is how great Selim's son treats his worthiest servants – he clings to an old ruin who is no use to himself or anyone else and gives me nothing! Where would he be without me? Still on Rhodes as young what's-his-name said the other night. He went over it all again, savouring his self-pity and hatred of the Sultan and Piri. After a while, when he had time to think of it, he spared some of his fury for Ibrahim. He'd taken care of himself, all right! He had never given any hint of what he expected to get for his devoted and continuous services, and he, Ahmed, had been too trusting, straightforward soldier as he was, to wonder about him. He should have known better, though the fellow was only a trumpery musician at best.

Because he was as big and strong as a bull Ahmed had always got along pretty well in the disciplined society in which he lived without ever making much effort to master his emotions, which were turbulent. Anger and suspicion were his constant companions. He knew his weakness and when he considered it important, honestly tried to overcome it. As now. He tramped backwards and forwards across the sagging floor of the little pavilion reminding himself of Suleiman's justness, his obvious gratitude after Rhodes and his devotion to Piri, which explained everything. Another thought was more effective: once Ibrahim appeared in the Divan he would show himself up for the ignorant nonentity he was and he, Ahmed, would shine by contrast. This pleased him. He stopped in his tracks and said aloud, 'It's make or break for you, my lad!' Outside, the sun shone and birds were beginning to sing. He marched out and went back to his office.

Perhaps it was unfortunate that Ibrahim chose that afternoon to call on him, a courtesy visit due to the acting Grand Vizier from a newly appointed colleague. Ibrahim, who had thought the matter over carefully in the light of Ahmed's difficult temperament, felt that the sooner the visit was made the sooner the Pasha would be reassured. He was wrong; in the fragile state of Ahmed's emotions the sight of the handsome young man, gaily dressed and exuding self-confidence and well-being, was an offence. It said much for his self-control that he did not roar abuse at him. Instead he leaned back against the divan on which he sat and impatiently waved away the clerk to whom he had been dictating, raising his full, dark eyes to Ibrahim's face in an expression of cold enquiry.

Ibrahim perceived his error immediately; also that there was nothing to be done about it. He smiled, therefore, and said, 'I fear, Ahmed Pasha, that I am precipitate. I should perhaps have sent beforehand to see if you were able to receive me.'

'It is usual,' growled Ahmed. He sat stretched out upon his divan, enormous hands resting on his thighs and his eyes still steady on Ibrahim's face. In this place, sombrely but sumptuously clad and wearing his high, white turban, he was impressive, even daunting.

Ibrahim's eyes narrowed, but he said gently, 'Then I apologize for disturbing you. Zeal must be my defence, and a desire to be of service to you, sir.'

Ahmed grunted, but relaxed enough to fold one hand over the other. He couldn't find fault with what Ibrahim said or the manner of its saying, but he noted that the fellow stood his ground and was pointedly making no suggestion that he should withdraw. He considered telling him to go. It would have been a small victory which he would have enjoyed, but then what? A complaint of discourtesy to his majesty very possibly. This upstart would be likely to hide behind the Sultan's robes and that couldn't be afforded. He growled, 'Since you've come, we'll dispense with ceremony. Be seated.'

Silently, Ibrahim sat down on the divan indicated. Better not speak until spoken to since that seems to be the way he wants it, he thought. His cool reception and the formal greeting had told him all he needed to know about Ahmed's attitude to his appointment but he was not yet prepared to accept it. He had spent too much of his time soothing the Pasha into accepting him as a friend to give up now.

Ahmed meanwhile had made his own decision. He had to put up with this incubus until he made a fool of himself. In the meantime cautious civility would do no harm. He said pointedly, 'You have taken us all by surprise, sir.'

Ibrahim smiled. 'Let us both consent to be surprised, then. His majesty certainly surprised me.'

Ahmed's heavy lids drooped over his eyes while he considered the next line of attack. Ibrahim leant forward and took the bull by the horns. 'Come, sir,' he said, 'I had thought we were friends, but it seems I have displeased you. Be open with me and tell me what is wrong. Is there someone else you would prefer to see in my place?'

'You mistake me,' Ahmed grunted. 'I am simply somewhat taken aback. But not displeased, no, no, by no means. To be sure, you'll have a lot to learn. I'll warrant you'll find the work of the Divan and the administration a change from anything you've met up to now.' The thought of this sweet-smelling courtier wrestling with finance, the law and foreign policy delighted him. He produced a grim smile.

The smile he received in return was radiant. 'Sir, I am at your service. You have only to try me.'

Ahmed examined him thoughtfully. Normally a reasonable judge of character, he had been blinded in Ibrahim's case, first by contempt and then by fear and prejudice. He looked at the smooth, olive-skinned face and saw only a handsome puppet. The bright intelligence and sensitivity eluded him. 'Well, fortunately you have three days to prepare yourself for your first appearance before the Divan. Today is Wednesday, but by Saturday you must be ready. Presumably you have some notion of the function of the Council and the part you will have to play.' He nodded carelessly and added, 'I will tell you what I can now and, of course, ask any questions that occur to you. After that I shall hand you over to the senior chancery secretary who will instruct you further and in detail. If there is anything you do not understand,' he allowed himself to sneer openly, 'you can always come back to me and I will do my best to enlighten you.'

A faint flush appeared on Ibrahim's cheeks. 'You are, as always, the soul of consideration, sir. I shall do my utmost to avoid troubling you again, burdened as you are.' If it comes to insult, he thought, I have been trained in a better school than you, my friend. But he had no intention of quarrelling with the Pasha if he could avoid it.

Ibrahim Pasha, for such he now was on his elevation to the rank of Fourth Vizier, made his first appearance in the Divan on the following Saturday. So far as he was concerned nothing was required of him on the occasion beyond being present, sitting where he was told, and conducting himself with becoming decorum. This caused him no difficulty. He had even, after due consideration, dressed himself in unwontedly simple and sombre clothes.

At this time Suleiman still presided over the Divan at its meetings on Saturdays, Sundays, Mondays and Tuesdays. They were solemn occasions, distinguished both for the rigid ceremony with which they were conducted and the amount of work the councillors managed to get through. The Divan was a purely administrative and judicial body and not to be confused with a Western parliament, since it had no law-making function. But as the principal court of the empire and its administrative council, its importance was immense.

Shortly after dawn Ibrahim found himself outside the Hall of the Divan accompanied by a couple of chancery secretaries, a bodyguard and several slaves about whose function he was not clear. He and his little retinue were surrounded, indeed hemmed in, by a crush of other distinguished persons and their retinues, all apparently intent on being at the right place at the right time, though from their excited milling about it was not clear precisely what the order of precedence was. Ibrahim, who enjoyed a great occasion, would have been happy enough to stand by for a moment or two and watch, but his senior secretary would not allow this. A fussy little man, overshadowed by his turban, he plucked at Ibrahim's sleeve and murmured, 'Sir, do not allow yourself to be pushed to the front – you are to take your place in inverse order on each side of the door! These people do not know you. To be sure, this pushing is very unseemly –' he stopped to glare at an inoffensive Beylerbey from some distant province, and then returned to his ineffectual pulling at Ibrahim's dress. 'Tell me where you wish me to stand and I will see that I get there,' suggested Ibrahim patiently at last. He took ceremony seriously, indeed enjoyed it, but the man's fidgeting was getting on his nerves. Eventually the councillors arranged themselves in two long lines on each side of the doors of the Hall of the Divan, meticulously disposing themselves in correct order of precedence. As the only vizier, since Ahmed was to occupy the position of Grand Vizier, Ibrahim found himself the subject of furtive glances of enquiry from his fellows. He quite frankly enjoyed this, but was impatient for the proceedings to start.

It was apparent that Ahmed, when he arrived, was enjoying his lofty position too. He strode between the ranks of officials wearing an important frown. He avoided looking at Ibrahim.

The Hall of the Divan was sombrely magnificent, its most noticeable feature being a broad sofa which extended round three sides. Ahmed, according to custom, established himself at its centre with Ibrahim on his right. To his left sat the judges of the army, the Kaziaskers, and beyond them the Treasurers, with Chelebi Bey much in evidence. He bowed to Ibrahim and smiled, his eyes twinkling. This compelled Ahmed to turn to his right and, apparently for the first time, to discover him too, but his bow was perfunctory and his face unwelcoming. Ibrahim, easier now, bowed back with unimpeachable courtesy.

He was aware of curious and appraising glances on all sides, but with typically Ottoman regard for solemnity and ceremony the members of the Divan kept their curiosity well in check; after a furtive glance or two, they ignored the new man in their midst. Indeed, there was little time for speculation. After a minute or two Ibrahim found himself on his feet, head bowed to receive the Sultan. Prayers followed immediately and the day's business began.

Ibrahim was soon conscious of disappointment. He had known what to expect, of course; he knew that matters of law and of high policy rested in the hands of the Sultan alone and were only a subject for debate, that the Divan was basically an administrative body and a court of law. But he had expected something more than the Beylerbey of Anatolia prosing on about his difficulties in the collection of taxes, and few seemed to be listening to him, except possibly Suleiman and Ahmed who sat impassive, his heavy features inscrutable. Indeed, there was a certain amount of coming and going, little knots of councillors gathering, turbans together, hands folded within sleeves, for individual discussions on other subjects. It was all orderly, dignified and, so far as he was concerned, incomprehensible. Still, Rome was not built in a day. He set himself to listen to the Beylerbey. The man certainly was a bore, did not know how to present his material, was bogged down by detail. Ibrahim frowned, concentrating on the man's problem, becoming interested and involved as he began to understand the difficulty. Presently an idea shaped itself in his mind. Why not a tax farm? And if the Beylerbey collected any more than the sum stipulated it would be his. That would stimulate his zeal! Ah, but the poor must be protected from extortion. His eyes narrowed as he thought deeply about that related problem.

The morning passed in a flash. After the Governor of Anatolia's tax difficulties there had been more talk of internal affairs, and then the Divan had become a court of law with the presentation of lawsuits by the Chaush-bashi, the Grand Marshal of the Court. Some of these had been fascinating! Ibrahim roused, startled, to find that the simple midday meal of bread, meat, rice and fruit was about to be served. He'd been there for six solid hours and it had seemed like half an hour. He scrambled to his feet as everyone rose and Suleiman, looking withdrawn and dignified, withdrew to eat his own lunch in stately seclusion. He certainly never knew that Suleiman had glanced at him once or twice during the course of the morning and smiled privately to himself at his friend's rapt expression. He was aware of one thing only. The Divan's work was not dull, but absorbing and of the first importance, and he, Ibrahim Pasha (how he liked the sound of that!), intended to master every last detail. He approved of the order and discipline of the proceedings, the silence with which each speaker was greeted, the constant arrival and departure of officials, each in his distinctive robes or uniform (and he certainly approved of those), as they were needed to give opinions on whatever was in hand. Before he was much older he would know who they all were. In short, he was in his element.

During the brief interval while the meal was served, eaten and cleared away, Iskender Chelebi came over to congratulate him. He spoke kindly, made a few remarks about the morning's business and moved away without referring at all to their previous meeting. But Ibrahim knew that it must be on the Treasurer's mind. It was certainly on his own. Courtesy demanded some sort of answer without delay and he had been worrying about the decision he must now make. But this morning, in all the excitement of his new status and absorption in his new work, he found that he felt quite differently about it. It was not something to worry about but another new and stimulating opportunity, something to be examined from every angle, certainly, but not to be met with fear and trembling.

As if following the example of Iskender Chelebi, or perhaps because they knew of their Sultan's interest in the new Fourth Vizier, several more high-ranking personages now took the opportunity of coming over to compliment Ibrahim. He made full use of these exchanges, presenting himself as a modest young man overwhelmed by his new position and anxious not to make a fool of himself. He received offers of advice and information from all sides, all of which he was firmly determined to take up. When, turning to sit down again as the afternoon's session began, he met Ahmed's baleful eye, he returned the look coldly and squarely, thinking, if it's a battle you want, my friend, I reckon I'm in a fair way to win it.

20

Ibrahim's appointment had sparked off a great deal of emotion, most of it jealousy or aggression. Of the people concerned, Ahmed was naturally the most implacable. But the person who felt most alarm was Hafise. As Sultana Valideh she was entitled to express a certain amount of interest in political affairs, but she was certain that downright condemnation, which was what she felt, would serve no useful purpose.

There was only one course she could take, and the next time her son visited her she pursued it with her usual energy.

'The appointment of the Fourth Vizier has caused some comment, my son,' she began carefully.

'It was necessary.' Suleiman's voice was a trifle sharp and Hafise wondered if he might be feeling himself on the defensive. 'I doubt if Piri will ever work again. Thus from three viziers I was reduced to one. The need for a trustworthy and able man was imperative, and Ibrahim is the ablest man I have, mother.'

This certainly did not sound like a defence; it was more like a declaration of war. Hafise thought carefully and said, 'There are many among your rising men who might consider themselves to have a claim to a viziership.'

Suleiman looked amused. 'A greater claim than Ibrahim, no doubt? I'm sure that's being said. To which I can only reply that in my judgement, which is the only one that counts, they are wrong.'

Hafise was dismayed and unwillingly impressed. His calm incisive way of speaking, the words he used, his very manner, were those of a ruler who knew his own mind. He was certainly growing, this son of hers and Selim's, beyond all knowing.

Suleiman, noticing her discomfiture, smiled at her reassuringly and then said seriously, 'Dear mother, listen to me and answer me this. Why is it that you and some of my oldest and most trusted servants believe that I should be ashamed of my friendship for Ibrahim? He is my oldest and closest friend, and I have learned more from him than from anyone else. He is as a brother to me, and I know him like a brother. If he were in any way unworthy, do you think I should not know it by now?'

Hafise pressed her clenched fingers against her mouth, near to tears. He had cut the ground from under her feet and what he said was unanswerable. But all the same she said passionately, 'I cannot bear to think that your actions are questioned, especially when those that question them may have a certain amount of justification.'

Suleiman laughed gently. 'There is no need to be gloomy, mother, or dramatic either. Ibrahim has already made his mark on the administration, I'm told. In a few days he will make his first address to the Divan, and then his quality will be seen by all. Moreover, my impatient young friends seem to have overlooked the fact that I have yet to appoint another vizier – if Piri retires, two more. They will have their chance.'

'Well, I only hope you are right, but don't say I didn't warn you.' She was ashamed of this gem as soon as it was spoken, and that Suleiman only smiled and kissed her tenderly before taking leave only made it worse.

Ibrahim addressed the Divan a week after taking office. The subject he chose was modern methods of tax-collection, and he had, of course, taken the subject from the speech he had heard on his first morning, just a week ago. He was modest, lucid and not too radical. He also avoided the mistake of being too brilliant, so that his speech was widely applauded, even by some of the most reactionary of his listeners. So wise a head on young shoulders, they said, to have chosen a subject of such basic importance to the empire and to have dealt with it with such a depth of knowledge and understanding. His majesty had been right all along, as of course they all knew he would be, in choosing his protégé for this all-important post.

Ahmed, stony-faced, listened to them buzzing like bees around him. When Defterdar Iskender Chelebi rose in his turn and praised 'his young friend's' sound financial thinking it became almost more than he could bear. The Defterdar, of whose wealth and ability he was jealous, never did more than exchange a few chilly words of conventional greeting with himself. Yet this upstart, this mountebank, was already on friendly terms with him! He hardly heard the rest of Chelebi Bey's short speech, being busy assembling his raging thoughts for his own. As soon as the Treasurer sat down, he lurched to his feet and into the attack.

A young courtier, he said, alert in the ways of the palace and the stable but hardly anything else, one week in his post, presuming to lecture them – his majesty's councillors – on one of the most complex aspects of their work! And where did these advanced ideas on tax farms and such come from and who had tried them out? It was all very well to pick ideas out of the air and show off a little knowledge, but if, as he shrewdly suspected, Ibrahim Pasha had borrowed his ideas from Europe, hadn't he better wait and see what sort of mess the Europeans were making of it? A certain amount of murmuring in the background assured him that some of his listeners were with him, but he lingered too long over his rhetorical question, and there was Ibrahim, who was not a Greek for nothing, back on his feet, face like a thundercloud, and being (of course!) recognized by his majesty.

Ahmed slumped back on the divan behind him and listened glumly while Ibrahim smartly demolished him. Ibrahim liked making speeches and was good at it. He had been furious when he rose to his feet but soon talked himself out of his rage, even beginning to enjoy himself as he cast scorn over Ahmed's diatribe. He referred to him once as 'his aged friend and mentor', and the councillors, while not eactly giving way to belly laughter, were certainly on his side.

When the long day ended at last and they were free to disperse to their homes, the members of the Divan talked it over quietly as they walked or rode away and came to the conclusion that it had emphatically been Ibrahim's day and that there was a great deal more to the new Fourth Vizier than they had been prepared to believe. Some of them wondered how long Ahmed could survive after his ill-advised attack on his new colleague, while the shrewder Sultan-watchers among them opined that his majesty had intended it to happen that way all along.

In that they were wrong, for Suleiman was no manipulator

of men. But even when they were still in their early twenties, he had dreamed of the day when he and Ibrahim would rule together. Now suddenly it was all working out as he had always wanted. Ibrahim had scored a personal triumph, Ahmed had covered himself with shame (and that Suleiman had not wanted, for he believed that if he were ever to achieve his heart's desire, it would have to come gradually), and most important of all, he had observed that morning a current of feeling in the Divan which suggested that Ibrahim might be acceptable as more than Fourth Vizier. Only it could not be brought about at once.

Restlessly he prowled his rooms in the Topkapi, considering what to do next. It did not take him long to decide what that must be. He summoned Ahmed and talked plainly to him.

'Your intransigence could cost you the Grand Viziership,' he told him roundly. 'What have you against Ibrahim Pasha that you should attack him in such terms? Let me tell you that you did not have the sympathy of the Council with you this morning!'

Ahmed stared. Suleiman watched him with distaste, tinged with the same obscure pity he had felt for him on a previous occasion. The man seemed to be going to pieces, red-eyed and rumpled as he was. But when he spoke his manner was as abrupt and decisive as ever. 'With respect, your majesty, that's as may be. Some of us don't believe in change for the sake of change.'

Incensed, Suleiman sat down, taking his time and controlling his anger. 'But, Ahmed,' he said reasonably, 'we are all agreed on the need for change. I have looked to you to initiate it, and so far without success. Yes, I know that at the moment the pressure of ordinary work is very great, but already Ibrahim has cut out a lot of old-fashioned and unnecessary work.' He said this deliberately, hoping to sting Ahmed into self-defence.

It was useless. Ahmed stared at the wall and sneered. 'I am not a paper-merchant, your majesty. My training has been on the field of battle.'

Suleiman compressed his lips and stood up. 'Very well, Ahmed Pasha. I note that you have nothing useful to say to me. You will therefore listen to me and do as I say. You will avoid quarrelling with Ibrahim Pasha and you will cease to interfere with him. He will organize the work of his office as he sees fit. Nor will you make personal attacks in the Divan on him or anyone else. Since all my instructions to you today seem to have been negatives, here is a positive one. Make an effort to master your jealousy and spleen before it is too late, and work with him.'

When Suleiman arrived at the old Palace, much earlier than usual and unexpected, he saw a new dimension of Khurrem's life. She had been visiting one of her new friends and came to greet him still clad in her outdoor clothes, excited by being out and about in the city and delighted because he had come to see her unexpectedly. It was Suleiman's turn to wonder if it would not be pleasanter if they lived together, and how much he missed because he only saw her and his children when he came as an honoured and expected guest. But, being used to dealing practically with problems all his life, he could only conclude that the Topkapi could not house a whole new family of women, slaves and children. It was, after all, not just his home but a seat of government, a place sacred to men and their work. Women and children would disrupt things. As quickly as the idea had come into his mind he dismissed it, and said only, 'How very elegant you look! Where have you been?' And you, thought Khurrem anxiously, look exhausted and strained. But she sat down beside him and prepared to divert him, telling him the gossip of the city she had picked up from the ladies with whom she had spent the day. He leaned back against the cushions, relaxed and half-listening, until Piri's name intruded itself. Suleiman opened his eyes. 'What about Piri?' he asked.

Khurrem looked across the room, taking her time while she arranged her recollections of what had been said. Finally she replied, 'The ladies have decided that he will not recover and should retire. Gulnus is of the opinion that his majesty has been very kind to wait so long to replace him, but that was for my – and your – benefit, of course.' Suleiman smiled, admiring her new incisiveness. 'She dislikes Piri's wife, therefore she would like to see him eclipsed.'

Gulnus, it now emerged, was the elderly, wealthy widow of a former court chamberlain, a mischievous gossip who still kept up her court connections, and Khurrem, it was plain, had accurately assessed the lady's capabilities.

Adopting the same light tone in which Khurrem had spoken, Suleiman asked, 'And have Gulnus and her friends decided who the new Grand Vizier is likely to be?'

'No, but Gulnus disapproves of Ahmed Pasha, who, she says, drinks too much.'

Suleiman made a small sound of disgust. 'How can she know such a thing? These women will say anything!'

'Ye-e-s,' said Khurrem doubtfully. Suleiman sat up and looked at her, demanding, 'Well, how could she know?'

'The slaves,' explained Khurrem, half-apologetic in the face of his vehemence. 'Gulnus's body-maid is half-sister to Ahmed's cook. I *think* that's it. These things are so complex, aren't they? What are you laughing at?'

Later, after they had eaten and were soothed and refreshed, he returned to the subject. He did not attach any great importance to the opinions of the Istanbul gossips, but they were capable of suprising him from time to time. The matter of Ahmed's tippling, for instance, was not something of great importance, but now he could see that there were those who would regard it as a very real shortcoming.

'It was always my intention,' he said, 'to replace Piri with Ahmed, but he disappoints me more and more. Now he is jealous of Ibrahim and made an ugly scene this morning in the Divan when Ibrahim made his first address.'

'I thought they were friends,' said Khurrem in surprise; 'I remember your telling me so.'

'Not since Ibrahim's appointment. I should have appointed him in any case, but I congratulated myself that it would please Ahmed to have a friend to work with. I was wrong. He only sees Ibrahim as a rival, and it is impossible to reason with him.' Suleiman sat back against his cushions with a sense of comfort and relaxation. The problem was still as serious and no nearer solution but it was in perspective.

'Do you think,' asked Khurrem, 'that Ahmed would do better if you made him Grand Vizier? It seems to me that he has waited a long time for his ambitions to be fulfilled and now feels himself thwarted.' She looked at him anxiously, wondering if he would think her presumptuous.

Presently Suleiman raised his head and smiled at her. 'Yes! You are right to make me look at this, for I see that all my hesitations have come from a sense of guilt, rather than from the desire to be sure I have chosen the right man. Now that I think about the matter clearly, the first thing I perceive is Ahmed's jealousy. He has never been free of it, first of Piri, and now of Ibrahim – even of my poor, ineffectual brother-in-law! It corrodes all his thinking and I cannot believe he will ever free himself of it. But it has destroyed his judgement! How can I make such a man responsible for the empire?'

He got up and began to pace the room, speaking thoughtfully as he walked. 'I have felt guilt because Ibrahim is my friend and I would rather see him occupy the position of supreme power than Ahmed or anyone else, and because I shall be accused of favouritism if I appoint him. But in one week he has done more to reform the Divan's work than Ahmed or anyone else has attempted in six months. And his address this morning was brilliant! I would be a fool and a coward to ignore all this simply because of misplaced loyalty to the products of the system. I had faith in his ability and I was right. Now I must back my faith and appoint him.' He swung round suddenly to face Khurrem and asked abruptly, 'Well, is my reasoning sound?'

She smiled and said formally, 'I cannot fault it, your majesty.' And indeed she felt nothing but pleasure. Although she had never met him, she felt she knew Ibrahim well. Suleiman talked of him often and she had seen him more than once riding in procession with her husband. She liked the look of him – he seemed a buoyant, cheerful man who laughed easily and could raise the introspective Suleiman's spirits when he was worried. Then, too, she felt much in common with him. He knew what it was to be a humble slave, looked down on by his fellows and seeking a place in the sun for himself, just like her. Now, by his own intelligence and character, he'd finally achieved it. She wished him well with all her heart. At the back of her mind was also the thought, he could be a good friend to little Mehmed. I must cultivate him. She too had travelled a long way since Rhodes.

21

In the midst of the excitement and personal fulfilment of his new office Ibrahim had something equally disturbing to think about in the matter of Iskender Chelebi's daughter. Disturbing but on the whole pleasurable. His first reaction had been that the suggestion was a gross imposition on his personal liberty. He did not want a wife, did not want to be tied down, with all the implications of property settlements (what property had he, as yet, anyway?), of children, of family responsibility. He wasn't prepared for any of it, had never thought of it, and besides had his way to make in this exciting new world his Sultan had pushed him into, and which he knew to be his natural home.

Still, for some time now he had felt that he needed someone, a girl who would be familiar, whose interests would be his, who would be warm and gentle and there when he wanted her, as opposed to the girls he had now when he needed them, infinitely docile and obliging but quite uninteresting on any level except the physical. There was also the matter of speed, too. He must make up his mind quickly or risk offending the Treasurer. If it came to that, any answer except 'yes' was likely to offend him. Ibrahim felt himself caught in a cleft stick, taken advantage of, and yet . . . He found himself thinking about this unknown girl more and more, and the process was entirely gratifying.

He knew that the real Muhsine might easily prove to be a disappointment after all this imagination, but still he did not stop. For one thing, it was a relief. He could hardly bear to think about his own future prospects because they seemed so exciting as to be impossible. That Suleiman had said nothing to him on the subject meant nothing. He knew how his master's mind worked. He either said everything or nothing at all. So Ibrahim dreamed about a girl whom he had never met and gained comfort.

When he finally made his decision, conveying it to his prospective father-in-law was the simplest part of the thing. Ibrahim marvelled at the ease with which it was accomplished. After the Divan one April morning, he found himself beside Chelebi Bey as the councillors left the building. He met the older man's eyes and smiled. The Treasurer bowed, and said smoothly, 'My young friend, good day to you,' and they began to walk together in silence until they had outstripped their fellows. Then Ibrahim remarked, 'It is a fine spring morning, sir. On such a day my thoughts turn with pleasure to a certain Persian manuscript.' Once said, he thought his words pompous, even fatuous, but they seemed to please the Treasurer, who, after a moment, murmured, 'So glad to hear it, so very glad,' and after another pause added abruptly, 'If, as I believe, you have no female relative to act for you, I know of a discreet elderly lady who will undertake your part of the arrangements.'

That was all that was said on that occasion. Ibrahim could hardly believe he had taken the momentous step.

Nevertheless, two days later, a respectable elderly male slave called on him at his office and invited him in the name of his mistress, the Widow Halima, to call upon her that evening at her house in the Eyub Road.

Outwardly calm, but inwardly aware of excitement, Ibrahim dressed himself with enough splendour to impress a well-bred elderly lady and presented himself at the specified time. The Widow Halima's house, though small, was in a good quarter of the city, overlooking water, and well-maintained. Obviously the property of a retired lady in good circumstances, and just what he would expect from anyone as careful and discreet as the Treasurer.

At first sight, however, the lady proved to be disconcerting. She was extremely small, wrapped from head to foot in draperies of sombre silk and tightly veiled. Nor was she alone, for two female slaves were in attendance and almost equally anonymous. Taken aback, Ibrahim bowed and offered the customary greeting, 'Peace be on you,' and after a moment's hesitation a rusty voice piped up from behind the widow's veil with the response, 'On you be peace and the mercy of God and His blessings.' There was another pause and he was invited to sit down. Ibrahim did so and silence fell, apparently for good.

After a moment's slight panic, during which he wondered if he had perhaps come to the wrong house, his sense of humour came to the rescue. What kind of fool do I look, he asked himself, shut in a small room with three female statues? No doubt this lady is examining me carefully to see if I'm suitable before she takes me on as a surrogate aunt or whatever she's supposed to be, but equally I'll be damned if I'm prepared to discuss anything so momentous as my marriage with a bale of silk. I must have a look at her face – she may be mad for all I know.

He was rescued by the appearance of two more slaves bringing refreshments of sherbet and small cakes, which they proceeded to serve with an elaboration which would not have disgraced the Old Palace. This helped a little but not much; obviously his hostess was not going to eat and drink with him. However, thought Ibrahim, when I've tasted this stuff, which I don't want, I'll thank her. Then she must speak; plainly, I was expected and preparations were made for my reception. He disposed of a small dry cake and sipped a little sherbet, dipped his fingers in water and had them dried by one of the slaves, and then sat back. To his surprise Halima matter-of-factly pulled aside her veil and said, 'So. Now we will talk. You,' she added to the slaves, 'may go.'

The face she presented to him was wrinkled like a nut and very heavily made-up. Indeed, it took him a moment or two to attempt to imagine what she looked like behind the display of kohl and rouge, but he noted that the black eyes below the eyebrows which had been painted into one thick black line, in keeping with the Turkish idea of feminine beauty, were bright and knowing. She began to talk immediately.

'It's a pity you have no family, but of course at a time like this they can be a hindrance. I like a man to know his own mind and it seems you do.' She nodded to emphasize her words. The more she talked, the more decisive her manner became. 'You're a little old to be marrying for the first time, but no harm in that, either. So. I understand you have no establishment as yet. That is the first thing to take care of. A house and slaves. Money?

Ibrahim smiled. 'That is no object,' he told her and enjoyed the experience.

'Ah,' said Halima caressingly. 'To be sure. Well . . . I suppose you will want to live somewhere in the area around Divan Yolu? Yes? If you wish, and I understand you're a very busy man, I will undertake to find a house or houses for you to examine. And slaves, of course? But I assume you are already supplied with the basis of a household.' She smiled at him, her eyes very searching, one tiny hand held up like the paw of a cat in a delicate gesture of enquiry. Ibrahim hardly knew whether he was more attracted by her efficiency than repelled by her appearance.

'I shall be grateful for anything you can do in that direction,' he said. 'But I beg you will not spare money or effort. I want the best of everything.'

'I never spare money. In the long run it's wasteful. As for the effort, well, it is a pleasure to be of service to one's – h'm – nephew, shall we say? And of course I'm always curious.'

This last, down-to-earth and truthful statement made him warm to her. He smiled and she smiled back, then coughed and resumed, 'I suppose if we are lucky and everyone works hard we should have the establishment set up in a month. Is that satisfactory? Very well, I shall aim for that. Now.'

She crossed her little cat paws in her lap and was silent for a moment, obviously considering what to say next. But Ibrahim was relaxing, getting used to her. While she thought, he looked curiously round her reception room, noting that while furnishings were sparse, the carpet was a splendid Uşak and the cushions and hangings of the finest damask. Obviously Halima was a lady who knew what was what, and Chelebi Bey had not failed him. Involuntarily he expelled a sigh of relief and the widow heard him and misinterpreted it.

'Marriage is a serious step,' she chirped, 'but necessary. What do the Traditions tell us? "When the servant of Allah marries he perfects half of his religion", and of course you are aware of the Prophet's other sayings on the subject.'

'To be sure,' responded Ibrahim, poker-faced.

'However, to continue, we have much ground to cover. Have you thought about your presents to the bride?'

Apart from jewellery he had not, and said so.

'Ah, jewellery,' said Halima approvingly. 'Well, to be sure, that's up to you, as much or as little as, er –' she coughed.

Having established that he was well-supplied with funds she now reserved the right to be delicate about the matter, Ibrahim saw.

'But,' she continued rapidly, 'first things first. An exchange of gifts opens the procedure. A silver jewel-box is a suitable item, and also perhaps toilet articles,' she glanced at him brightly.

'I should like to select them myself.'

'A very proper attitude,' she approved. 'I shall continue. After the exchange of gifts, I shall call upon the bride-to-be and give her a mother's blessing. I shall take with me a basket of sweetmeats, one of which she will bite in two, and give one half back to me to convey to you as a token of her willingness to accept you. A most charming ceremony, I always think.' She raised her voice oratorically and hurried on, 'A few days later you will be required to send the aghalik, which is your contribution to the cost of the wedding festivities, to Chelebi Bey. A week later comes the civil marriage at the home of the bride, when the contract of marriage will be drawn up and signed. And then, after a suitable interval, we come to the dughun, the period of social functions which finally bring you together as man and wife. This lasts for a week. It begins with –'

But Ibrahim had ceased to listen. The European in him was dismayed, even outraged. He said desperately, 'Is all this necessary? Surely –' he stopped as an expression of amazed hauteur spread across Halima's face.

'Necessary!' she repeated, and again, 'Necessary? My dear sir! Ah, but you're eager! As is only right and proper. But you must remember that her marriage is the climax of a young girl's life. She and her family have prepared for it ever since she was born. Surely you would not deprive her of the greatest moments of her life?'

I shall never make a good Ottoman, Ibrahim told himself, but at least I can keep quiet about it. 'My bride must have everything that will make her happy,' he stated firmly. 'That comes before all else.'

'To be sure,' replied the widow, not quite persuaded. She coughed. 'Shall I go on?'

'Pray do. You were quite right. I was carried away by impatience.'

Mollified, she began to describe the activities which would lead up to the bride's arrival at her new home and the consummation of the marriage. Ibrahim's house, when he acquired it, would, he learned, be invaded by the bride's female relatives three days before this happy event. They would proceed to decorate the rooms set aside for the bride's use with a display of the wedding gifts, her jewellery and trousseau and household goods. 'But apart from that,' said Halima encouragingly, 'most of the ceremonies will not involve you, only the bride. One day she will spend at the bath, of course, the following day there will be a great reception for all female relatives at her home, with the ceremony of Henna Night in the evening. And the day after that she will take leave of her father and leave his house for ever.' She sighed sentimentally. 'Really most affecting! That reminds me, I shall have to see about a go-between. I know the very woman, no problem there. Now, sir, have you any questions for me at this stage?'

'I'm overwhelmed with your grasp of the subject, madam,' said Ibrahim truthfully. 'Two things: do you need any money at the moment? And is there anything I have to do now?'

'Such tact and practicality! One perceives immediately how you have risen to your present eminence,' cooed the widow, raising her paw once again. Ibrahim noted that one claw was decorated with a superb emerald ring. 'Time enough for money when we begin to spend it,' she told him; 'and I will send Asraf to you when I have news of houses for you to see.'

She rose with her usual abruptness, terminating the conversation; bowed to him, saying the customary words of farewell, and waited for him to take his leave.

By the end of April Ibrahim was the owner of a handsome house in one of the streets bordering the At-Meydan, the Hippodrome of the Byzantines and still the central square of the city, favoured because of its nearness to the Topkapi. Ibrahim, the lover of antiquity, liked it because of its links with the past. He could look from his windows at the Serpent Column which had once graced the Temple of Apollo at Delphi, and the house was charming, sufficiently large, and with two enchanting rooms panelled in carved wood. These he naturally allocated to the use of Muhsine. For the rest, he took up residence there as soon as he conveniently could. At first he found the house so large that he had difficulty in finding his way around it; by the end of a week he had decided that after a few years he would have to find something larger, so easily did he slip into the ways of grandeur.

His first task, and one which he had dreaded without quite knowing why, was to tell Suleiman of his impending marriage. He had been less than fair to his royal master; Suleiman was unaffectedly delighted. 'I have waited for this, sometimes blaming myself that I made so many demands on you that you had no time for what must become the mainspring of your life. You will be very happy, I know it.' After a moment's thought, he smiled and added, 'And of course it will do you no harm to have chosen so wisely. In the great future I see for you, Iskender will be a good friend.'

Now what does he mean by that? Ibrahim asked himself, and could not bring himself to dwell on the question. Certainly Ahmed was deteriorating rapidly. There had been another ugly scene in the Divan the previous day, and Ibrahim had to exercise all his fund of urbanity and good humour to prevent its becoming something worse. But happiness made this easy to do, Ibrahim was happy. Why shouldn't he be? He was on the threshold of great things. Only sometimes, when he was tired at the end of a long day's work, he found himself wondering about his bride with a little apprehension. Romantic dreams were all very well, but time was growing short. Soon she would be in this house, living intimately with him, using the exquisite things he was buying for her - the jade mirror inlaid with gold, with its battery of toilet jars, the gold comb, the ivory jewel-casket. What would she really be like? Beautiful, certainly, but suppose she was stupid, or talked too much? There was no earthly way of knowing, and perhaps he had been a fool. When such thoughts as these visited him Ibrahim set his jaw and spent more money. Why not? It was there to spend, not only his princely salary but the bribes which poured in legitimately (since that was the system) from those who wanted favours or jobs from him.

The expenditure of money on such a scale and his own demonic energy got everything done by the last week in May. He had paid the aghalik, purchased and despatched with all due ceremony the wedding-dress - and no wedding-dress had ever been like it; even Halima's eyes had grown as round as saucers when she first saw the confection of embroidery and silver and rose brocade. 'My dear sir!' she had gasped and said no more. Legally, they were now man and wife, for the civil marriage ceremony had been solemnized over two weeks before at his father-in-law's house. Oddly, he had rather enjoyed it, although he had not seen so much as an eyelash of the bride. But he enjoyed negotiations, even when no one, certainly not himself, was taking them very seriously. Generosity was the keynote of the proceedings, both on his part and that of Chelebi Bey. But it was plain to Ibrahim that his father-in-law was feeling the coming separation, and this impelled him to try to raise the older man's spirits. He succeeded only two well and Chelebi Bey went to bed that night more than a little fuddled, while Ibrahim succeeded in forgetting his own growing fearfulness for a few hours.

Now the day, so long awaited and so meticulously prepared for, had come and nearly gone. His house had been full to bursting from first light. Muhsine's younger sisters, her cousins and friends and aunts, had arrived early. He had heard them chattering and laughing and the rustle of their wedding finery as they made their way to the harem to await the coming of the bride. She came at last, carried in a chair beneath a baldachin of rich brocade so that she still remained invisible, and accompanied by a noisy procession of musicians and male relatives and hangers-on. Even then he wasn't allowed to see her. He had perforce to go to the neighbourhood mosque with his friends – and what a lot of friends he suddenly found he had! And what a fool he felt, although normally no one enjoyed being the centre of attention more than he. But at last, on his return, he had been escorted, with a great deal of good-humoured pushing and shoving, to the door of his harem. Some woman (he had no idea who she was) had taken his hand and led him up to a motionless figure draped in rose brocade which looked vaguely familiar to his bemused eyes.

Later, when he thought about it, he was compelled to admit that all he had felt at that moment had been impatience to get the whole thing over. He was tired, he had expended too much emotion on – what? He didn't know, but he did know that it had not been attended by fulfilment or anything like it. Afterwards he remembered her hand, small, olive-skinned, perfect, with its oval fingernails and henna-tinted palm. It emerged from the draperies and rose to her head and drew back the silk veil. Well, she was beautiful, no doubt about that, but she was also a complete stranger. While she took his hand and kissed it and murmured something, he didn't hear what, he thought about that. The perfect face that had been revealed to him was empty of meaning for him, except that he thought he could detect signs of strain around the large, black eyes. Well, he could sympathize there; and suddenly he remembered that something was expected of him. He fumbled in the folds of his sash (gold brocade, of course, and covered by a dolman of emerald Bursa velvet; finery was not to be confined to the bride when Ibrahim was the groom), and finally brought out his 'face-see' gift of one perfect pear-shaped pearl. Since she seemed as bewildered as he, he pressed it into her hand.

Then it was all over and he had to return to the selamlik, there to endure curious or sly glances from his friends, and to remember that in his confusion he had forgotten that he should have embraced his wife when he gave her the pearl. Now, no doubt, she must think him a complete boor. He felt embarrassment rise, and took out his handkerchief and mopped his brow. Ibrahim, my friend, he admonished himself, control yourself. Remember who you are, and never let it be said you were demoralized by a woman. You've known quite a few in your time and never been at a disadvantage before.

He forced himself to remember his duties as host, to say the right things and respond to the robust leg-pulling that his guests began to inflict upon him. The noise of their chatter and the endless wailing and braying of the professional musicians was intolerable, but he put a good face on it, while his mind was busy with the problem of the imaginary woman who had comforted his dreams for over three months and who had now finally fled, exorcized by a black-eyed stranger. His sense of loss was ridiculous and totally his own fault.

The wedding feast, of which he could eat little, seemed to last forever and he longed to escape from it, even if it meant making himself agreeable to this strange girl and eventually making love to her. He thought about that now as a duty. This elaborately dressed and painted doll standing on the threshold of her equally ridiculously decorated rooms meant nothing to him at all.

He noticed a lull in the racket going on about him, and looked up to see that the friends nearest to him were looking at him expectantly. He turned mutely questioning to the man sitting beside him, an older, married man who laughed in reply to his look and then said gravely, 'Yes, my friend, time you were about your duties.'

So now, here was Ibrahim the married man, standing obediently, as he had been instructed, on her crimson silk bridal veil, which had been laid carefully over the floor just inside her room, while Muhsine, unveiled and with her black hair streaming over her shoulders, stood on the edge of it, hands folded in front of her. A very grave girl, this, he thought looking at her coolly, and found that this pleased him. He then remembered the prayer which he was supposed to repeat, knelt down and, infected by her seriousness, said the prayer through with unwonted solemnity.

It became easier after that. For one thing, the women were no longer in charge. Their preposterous customs and injunctions were done with and he was master in his own house for the first time – a pleasing thought – and pleasing, too, now that it occurred to him, was the fact that Muhsine was silent before him, hands still linked in front of her, looking up into his face expectantly and smiling a little now; a smile, moreover (now that he looked at her carefully), that had a touch of mischief about it, as if she was not going to be overwhelmed by the situation however it might turn out.

'I see you're wearing your pearl. Do you like it?' It was all he could think of to say, but he supposed it would do as well as any other opening.

She glanced down at the jewel and said, once more grave, 'It's very beautiful, but then all the things you have given me are beautiful. I knew they would be.'

'How did you know?'

She seemed to be disconcerted, as if she had said more than she had meant to say. But perhaps he imagined it, for she answered readily, 'But everyone knows how fastidious you are, and how much you know about things like jewellery and – and art objects. My father says so.' She said this as if her father's dicta had the authority of natural law. Ibrahim found himself thinking how pleasant it would be to hear her say, 'my husband says so' in the same tone of voice. He only just remembered to instruct himself not to be fatuous.

'Shall we sit down? Perhaps you are tired, but I should like to talk for a while,' he continued, and took her hand. And if that's not fatuous, I don't know what is, he thought, despairing of himself. But Muhsine seemed to notice nothing wrong, and allowed him to draw her down on to a small divan. He chose it deliberately, for it was on the same side of the room as the alcove in which his wife's friends had laid out all her splendid new jewellery. 'If we sit here,' he said, 'we can't see all the display which hurts my eyes.' He said it seriously but meant it as a joke, and was delighted by her hearty and easy laughter. 'It's vulgar, isn't it? But it will have to stay there tomorrow. We'll be on show to the whole neighbourhood.' She shook her head over the folly of it all, or so it seemed, and fell silent.

So far, so good; she was charming, and not, it seemed, a slave of feminine convention, which dictated that she should not even speak to him without prolonged persuasion; her hand still lay warmly in his and she made no effort to draw it away. He looked at her, noting the fine, curving nose and generous mouth, and when she looked up and caught him staring he was able to say, without embarrassment, 'You must forgive me, but, after all, I never saw you before.'

She laughed at this, too, and did not make any silly, coquettish remarks. 'Of course,' she said matter-of-factly and added warmly, 'How difficult it must have been for you.'

'And for you, too, I should have thought,' said Ibrahim.

'Well, it's different for girls. I mean, we have to do as we're told. And, of course, I have seen you before. More than once.'

She saw his stare, and explained, 'You often ride past our house, I mean my father's house, and one day I asked who you were. That's all.'

Ibrahim absorbed the implications of this in astonished silence. Those who believe that man is the eternal hunter are only partly right. He also likes to be flattered; Ibrahim certainly was. Muhsine said no more on the subject and he did not press her. Later, at his leisure, he wondered whether she had influenced Iskender Chelebi to approach him and decided that she was too well-bred and delicate-minded a girl for that. After all, Iskender was a very sensitive man and devoted to his child. The very enquiry would of itself be enough.

22

At the end of June Ibrahim became Grand Vizier. No one in government circles was particularly surprised by then. The rows in the Divan had become a scandal and most reasonable men were prepared to agree that Ahmed was almost always the aggressor. Then again, Ibrahim demonstrated more clearly every day that he had been born for the job. Problems that seemed insoluble to lesser men he analysed brilliantly and disposed of, seemingly without effort. And then he was so vital and friendly and good to look at. Only the most crabbed old stick-in-the-mud of a councillor could find anything to complain about in him. Under his influence the younger men began to see that, far from being their rival, he was their ally. 'We are all young men together,' he would tell them confidentially. 'We have a young Sultan and look at what he has already achieved! This is the time to bring young minds to old problems. Only stand by us and there is nothing we cannot accomplish.'

Before Suleiman could proclaim his friend as Grand Vizier, however, he had several duties to carry out. The most painful was to tell Piri Pasha that he must retire. He had known this most faithful servant nearly all his life, and could hardly imagine what it would be like to work without him. Piri had been his first tutor and his first Grand Vizier, and his advice had been invaluable until this last year when things had soured considerably. But now that the parting of the ways had come Suleiman was prepared to forgive the old man for his unpalatable advice, even to admit privately to himself that Piri's greatest sin had perhaps been to be right once too often.

He admitted this sense of guilt to no one, of course, but it certainly influenced the enormous pension of two hundred thousand aspers which he resolved to pay the old man; and their last interview, when Suleiman had Piri brought to the Topkapi to hear what his Sultan proposed to do for him, was painful, more painful for Suleiman than for Piri indeed, for the Grand Vizier, sick and old as he was, seemed bewildered and unable to understand what his master was telling him.

Suleiman had been distressed enough by his appearance. He seemed to have shrunk so that his robes were too big for him, and the eyes that Suleiman remembered to be as keen and fierce as a falcon's glanced vaguely at him and slid away almost without recognition, although he attempted his old, punctilious greeting. He was so frail that his master intercepted his attempt at a low bow and tried to persuade him to sit down. He would have none of it, however, but stood, bracing himself against a divan, head down, waiting to hear his fate.

Suleiman judged it best to get it over as soon as possible. 'You are not regaining your strength as you should, Piri,' he told him. 'Your doctor and your family worry about you, while you worry about the empire, and so you do not recover. You used to tell me about the wonderful tulips you hoped to breed when you retired. I think the time for that has come. Work in your garden in the sun and get strong again.' He felt the worst kind of hypocrite as he spoke, for it was plain that Piri would never be well or even clear-headed again. But he talked on, telling his old servant about his pension and thanking him for his years of devotion. He spoke stiltedly for he knew that he could never find words strong enough to acknowledge such single-minded service. He soon saw that it hardly mattered what he said, for Piri could not take it in. He only stared at Suleiman as if his faded eyes could hardly see him and murmured confused thanks for his majesty's many kindnesses. The Grand Vizier who had always known the right thing to do, and had done it with style, had been transformed into a trembling wreck of a man who did not even know when to take his leave but had to be taken by the hand and led away by his servants.

Suleiman watched him go with guilty relief. That night he disturbed Khurrem, dreaming of Rhodes and crying out hoarsely about the men dying in the mud.

A pleasanter task, and one he delegated to his wife, was to tell his sister Ayse that her husband was returning from Egypt immediately to resume his post as Second Vizier. Then he sent for Ibrahim.

It was a matter for pleasure to have to send for him. It was two weeks since his friend's marriage, and except in the Divan and when his presence was required on matters of business Ibrahim had been conspicuous by his absence from the Palace, which, the Sultan felt, was as it should be. That his friend was now married and, it seemed, as happy as he was himself was another bond between them, another experience shared.

Ibrahim was nervous when he came. Suleiman, knowing him so well, saw that immediately, although the Fourth Vizier was outwardly as calm and cheerful as usual. Suleiman considered for a moment and then dismissed the attendant courtiers so that he and his friend were alone. It had been his intention to make a formal announcement of Ibrahim's appointment in their presence but something in his friend's manner, in the way he looked almost imploringly into his face as if trying to convey something, warned him that it was not going to be quite as simple as that. He wondered if Ibrahim had failed to understand the implications of the events of the past two weeks, of his own silence on the subject, and knew that it could not be that. They had always understood each other, and he understood now that Ibrahim had something on his mind so important that it must be disposed of before all else.

As soon as they were alone, therefore, he sat down, looked up at Ibrahim and said simply, 'You know that the moment has come. So why are you –' he paused, seeking words, 'looking both ways?'

Ibrahim took a quick step forward and then down on one knee before him. This demonstration of respect, or possibly of entreaty, was so unexpected that Suleiman was taken by surprise. Ibrahim the relaxed, the humorous and unceremonious, behaving like the most punctilious of all his court! He stared, and asked mildly, 'In Allah's name, what is it?'

For his part, Ibrahim had thought long and earnestly about what he should say and how he should conduct himself during this interview; to this extent his behaviour was not spontaneous, but it was quite sincere. He said simply, 'What I am about to ask will not please you, sir.'

'Let me be the judge of that. Come to the point.'

'Yes, sir. Sir, I am not making a joke.'

Suleiman noted the beads of sweat on his friend's upper lip and believed him. He said neutrally, 'Go on.'

'Sir, I have been your servant for ten years, and it is true that during that time you have never raised your voice to me in anger. But we have been companions and friends, and I have been honoured by your confidence and trust. In such circumstances, how could I do other than respond totally? In everything you sought to do I have supported you, and indeed, have always been in agreement with you. Now, a change is coming.' He stopped abruptly, and Suleiman saw his throat move convulsively as he swallowed.

Suleiman said mildly, 'That change can only be for the better,' but he was only uttering soothing sounds, giving Ibrahim a breathing space, and Ibrahim showed that he understood this by hurrying on, ignoring his Sultan's words.

'If I become Grand Vizier our relationship must change. Or rather I shall change. I must. I can't foresee exactly how this will be, but I know it must be. And so – forgive me, sir – do you.'

Suleiman interrupted him peremptorily. 'I don't accept that. We are like brothers, or more like twins! On what do we disagree? Nothing of importance. We have discussed everything and have one mind between us. But I understand your feelings.' He smiled suddenly and extended his hand to Ibrahim. 'You're about to take a most momentous step. Naturally, you are nervous and ask yourself if you can succeed, if I shall be satisfied with everything you do. I understand all this. You must remember that I underwent something of the sort when I became Sultan.'

Ibrahim was sufficiently recovered to smile in his turn, but he was not satisfied. 'With respect, sir, there is one important difference. You had not, and have not now, a master.' He perceived that a change of tack might help matters, and continued, 'Sir, consider your forebears.'

'What about them?'

Ibrahim held up a finger. 'The great Mehmed dismissed his first Grand Vizier, Jandarli Halil, confiscated his goods and imprisoned him.' His ever-ready tact had prompted the choice of this example; Selim had executed seven or eight of his Grand Viziers.

'I see your drift. Do you really think I would do the same to you?'

Ibrahim hesitated and then said, 'I beg you to consider, sir. Who knows the future? Circumstances could arise when you might want to. Ruling an empire is a serious matter, and sometimes leads to bloodshed.'

Suleiman frowned. 'What in Heaven's name is disturbing you, and at such a time? I thought you would be as full of confidence and joy as I am –'

'I wouldn't dare to say any of this, sir, if I didn't believe that now is the time, at the beginning of everything, to understand clearly what can happen between us in the future and prepare for it.'

It was a toss-up whether Suleiman was going to lose his temper. It could be seen in his restless movements and the sudden brightness of his eyes. Normally, he allowed Ibrahim to argue freely with him and enjoyed the exchange, even when it got rough, but today was different. Today was the great day, the culmination of all their planning and effort, and now, it seemed, Ibrahim must choose to back away from their enterprise and look sideways at it. Nevertheless, in spite of himself he was impressed by his friend's desperate sincerity; and also suddenly perceived the danger, the catch. To give way to anger now would be to prove Ibrahim right before they had even begun.

'Very well,' he said, almost humbly. 'I understand you. What do you want me to do?'

'Only to give me your word, which is your bond as all the world knows. If you tell me that you will never dismiss me in anger, then I am satisfied. More, I am happy.'

'Then it's gladly given,' Suleiman told him. 'On my head, I swear I will never dismiss you in anger or disgrace. That's my solemn word, and not lightly given, either, though for the life of me I'm unable to imagine the circumstances in which you'll ever need to invoke it.' He laughed, embarrassed by their unwonted formality, and said, 'Will you stand up now and summon my pages? We must send for the nishanji and discuss arrangements for your appointment.'

The gist of that conversation passed into legend and later came to be invoked as evidence of Ibrahim Pasha's surpassing wisdom. Certainly, a man is entitled to protect himself if he can.

So, on 26 June 1523, the imperial edict was signed which made Ibrahim Pasha Grand Vizier of the Ottoman Empire in the thirtieth year of his age. There was less stir and gossip on the subject than there might have been because of the skill with which the thing was managed. It was not until it was too late that the Sultan's loyal servants came to realize the extent of the change, for Ibrahim became Grand Vizier with widely extended powers. It was the natural thing to do, to share the burden of the government of the ever-extending empire. Mehmed II, that invaluable example of wise statecraft, had done it, after all. That same Jandarli Halil, who was so much on Ibrahim's mind at this time, had been succeeded by Zaganos Pasha, like Ibrahim a new man who was given greater responsibilities. Now it was to be done again, and about time too. After all, the responsibility for everything, from deciding the pension of the keeper of garrison stables in Mosul to declaring war or peace, still rested on the Sultan himself; it was time to share the load.

So Ibrahim received the imperial ring from the hands of Suleiman as a symbol of his new power and set about the task of ruling.

As Grand Vizier he was commander of all armies in time of war, and was the only one apart from the Sultan with the right of life and death over the subjects of the Sultan. He was the promulgator of all new laws and was responsible for putting them into effect.

These powers were impressive enough, but Suleiman went further: Ibrahim was given exalted military rank as well and made Beylerbey of Roumelia, Commander of the Army in Europe, Beylerbey of Anatolia, or governor of European Turkey. More impressive in the eyes of the man in the street and the soldiers were the visible dignities heaped upon him. The bunchuk, the old horsetail standard which had come down from Ottoman nomad days as a sign of a man's rank in war and his fitness to bear it, was revered and recognized by all as an emblem of dignity in office. Four horsetails were usually granted to a Grand Vizier. Six were conferred on Ibrahim, only one less than the Sultan himself. His salary was increased over that of his predecessor by half as much again. He had eight guards of honour and twelve led horses, the finest that could be found. His state barge had twelve pairs of oars and a green awning, and when he appeared in public, his guards cried, 'Peace unto you and divine mercy', and 'May the Almighty protect the days of our sovereign and of the Pasha, our master'. Only the Sheikh-ul-Islam equalled his dignity, and his power was not temporal.

Ibrahim accepted all this magnificence with frank enjoyment. His master might have his mind set on higher things and crave seclusion, but not he. He liked beautiful things about him, to look at and touch; he liked gorgeous clothes and knew he wore them well. He had a sense of style and occasion, his entertainments were superb, with splendid food and exquisite music, and when he rode out in public on ceremonial occasions he acknowledged the acclamations of the crowds with the same gaiety and gusto he brought to everything else – in particular, to work. He was meticulous and dashing at the same time, but above all he enjoyed watching the effect on other men when he attacked some weighty problem and resolved it with ease, to the wonder of those about him.

Admiration is strong stuff and Ibrahim could have drowned in it had he been susceptible. It was readily available in the Divan and at the Palace. At home, love and admiration were lavished on him. To Muhsine he was the sun, the moon and the stars. In return he loved her to the extent of his capacity, lightheartedly and uncritically, revelling in her loveliness and elegance, constantly surprised by her quick wits and depth of feeling. The last sometimes bothered him. He was on the crest of the wave, and reserved his deepest emotion for his work; at home he wanted a light touch. But they were very happy from the outset, when they had come together as easily and readily as a pair of handsome young animals.

There was no cloud on Ibrahim's horizon; and no irritant in the foreground, either, for Ahmed departed almost immediately. As soon as it became plain that the Grand Viziership was not for him, he sought audience of Suleiman. He had heard, he said, standing in front of his Sultan as stiff and militarily correct as ever, the very picture of a splendid Slave of the Gate, that Choban Mustafa Pasha was returning from Egypt.

Suleiman, equally solemn, agreed that this was so, and waited, hopefully, for what was to come.

'If your majesty has no one in mind for the governorship of that province, he began, and stopped. Ungenerous himself, he found it hard to ask a favour, particularly when he felt he deserved it.

Suleiman made it easy for them both. He was becoming increasingly concerned about what to do with Ahmed, who deserved some reward for Rhodes. If Egypt was what he wanted, Egypt he should have. He told him so, and wished him well with a warmth that held considerable relief. Thinking about it afterwards he decided that it was a good appointment; Ahmed would have a free hand and the ever-present chance of the action which he craved, for Egypt was by no means as settled as he could have wished. When he heard about it, Ibrahim agreed with him. They were both wrong.

BOOK THREE

'May Your Sword Keep Its Edge'

23

The janissaries always had grievances; they were soldiers, after all. They hadn't wanted to go to Rhodes, and after they had taken the place for their Sultan (and at what a cost in lives!) he had reneged on his promise and refused them the right to take booty. Now, back in barracks, re-equipped, and their numbers in process of being restored, they had to see their Pashas passed over and an outsider named Grand Vizier. This fellow, Ibrahim, wasn't any kind of a soldier, not a product of the Devshirme or even of the Schools. True, he had been on Rhodes with them but only because the Sultan made him go, couldn't get along without him, so they heard. But he hadn't been in evidence on the field of battle, had he? Frenk Ibrahim, they called him, Ibrahim the European, by which they really meant Ibrahim the outsider. Now here he was, the second most important man in the Empire, with his twenty-four thousand gold pieces a year, while their own Ahmed Pasha, who'd really pulled the chestnuts out of the fire on Rhodes, was bundled off to Egypt. It was true he was a right bastard, but he was a good soldier. And that was how they liked their commanders, and their viziers.

It wasn't an issue with them, as the loss of booty could be. Politics wasn't their business, they weren't interested, but all the same it rankled. When they counted over their grievances, as soldiers will, they remembered to add in the matter of Ibrahim Pasha, Grand Vizier.

Suleiman heard none of this, but he knew his janissaries. Knowing the janissaries and keeping one jump ahead of them – more if possible – was one of the marks of a successful Sultan. They had even caught Selim napping once, but only once.

Now that Ibrahim had taken over the day-to-day work of government he had time to reflect on many things, one of which was the corps of janissaries. There would be no war this spring, and possibly not next spring, either, which was something else they might not care for.

That evening, as he now usually did, Ibrahim had come to supper and to report on the day's business in the Divan, and Suleiman took him to walk in the Palace garden before the light failed. Ibrahim was full of his own affairs, taxes in Roumelia, a fascinating law case. Having to apply his mind to those troublesome fellows in barracks did not please him; in fact he found himself getting a mite impatient with his majesty sometimes, but was careful not to show it. He gave Suleiman credit for a sixth sense where some aspects of government were concerned - after all he'd been brought up to it. But where in God's name had this particular worry come from? The janissaries were as quiet as lambs, had to be, after the tousing they'd taken on Rhodes.

'They've got plenty to keep them occupied,' he pointed out. 'All the new recruits to train, new equipment, the best they've ever had, to break in - the new firelocks, for instance -'

'They don't like firelocks,' grunted Suleiman, marching along, tall and thin and obstinate, hands locked behind his back. 'They always preferred cold steel and still do. They like the new pikes, for instance. But that's beside the point. As you've just pointed out, they've had a bad time, there's not going to be a war this spring, and if you think they're pleased about your appointment, you're wrong.'

Ibrahim raised his eyebrows and was silenced for a moment. It was news to him that what soldiers felt on such a subject was of any importance. He said, 'Their commanders are behind me, sir. I don't have to remind you how many of them have been promoted or are about to get new posts.'

Suleiman stopped abruptly and turned to put an arm round his friend's shoulders, as if he realized he had given some slight offence. 'Of course they are,' he said heartily. 'They see the reasons behind what is done and know we have not betrayed them. But I'm thinking about the rank and file, who only see what they want to see, because it's not their business to know the motives behind events. We're changing things and they don't like change. It makes them nervous. We have to think of something.' He stopped speaking and walked quickly on, clenching his hands.

Bursting with energy to do something, but not sure what, thought Ibrahim. Nevertheless, he was puzzled. He hurried after Suleiman, demanding, 'With respect, sir, how do you know they feel like this? Have you heard rumours, complaints?'

'I haven't heard anything, no, it's not that.' Suleiman slowed his brisk walk once again. His expression changed to one almost of baffled fury as he sought the right words and could not find them. Ibrahim, ever tactful, made meaningless remarks about the beauty of the evening and the splendour of the trees until his master burst out, 'Don't ask me how I know what they feel because I can't tell you! But I'm one of them. They've dominated my life ever since I was a child, and rightly. My father knew better than to ignore them even though they loved him, and – and, yes, there is something else. A small thing, but something. You know I go to take my pay as a non-commissioned officer in the corps?'

Ibrahim did know. He had more than once been present at the ceremony when the Sultan lined up with the janissaries of the guard to get his handful of aspers, and so underline his link with them. He admired the seriousness that Suleiman always brought to the occasion. He himself would have felt an idiot.

'The last few times I have done it, there has been a feeling – an atmosphere. There's never much said, there can't be, it's all cut and dried and doesn't last long, but usually they're full of smiles. It's a great joke to see the Sultan lining up with them, but they like it, you know what I mean, there's a warmth. But not recently.' He shook his head, his expression absorbed and grim.

'No, sir?' prompted Ibrahim softly.

'No. It's been correct and cold and totally meaningless. I'm not imagining it.'

'I'm sure you're not,' agreed Ibrahim, and meant it. His Sultan might not have his brains (it is amazing what a little success will do for you; he wouldn't have expressed that opinion, even to himself, a short while ago), but no one could doubt his sensitivity. 'There might be something else behind it, sir.'

'Such as?' Suleiman gave a little grunt of a laugh. 'Of course there's something else, all the grievances they've ever had – low pay, poor food, their officers, Rhodes.' He said the last word with a weight of meaning which made Ibrahim glance sharply at him. Here's someone else who's never recovered from Rhodes, he thought, and sighed. Suleiman had succeeded in dispelling his own effervescent mood. Still, if the matter's serious (or if he thinks it is, which comes to the same thing), we had better consider it. He looked at the velvet sky and asked, 'Shall we return, sir? It's dark.'

In the selamlik there was the light of a hundred oil lamps, the comforting smell of savoury food. They went to table, and Ibrahim, who enjoyed fine food as he enjoyed everything which appealed to the senses, was restored. Besides, the short walk back to the Palace had given him time to get his wits to work. He looked at Suleiman on the other side of the table, silently rolling rice into balls which he obviously never intended to eat, and suggested, 'We need a gesture.'

Suleiman looked up. 'Exactly. Something of their own which no one else can share. You've thought of something?'

Ibrahim smiled tentatively, his lips red and moist from the rich pilaff he was eating. 'I *am* thinking, sir. Do you remember Sinan?'

'The engineer-architect? Of course I do, he's not the sort of fellow anyone forgets. Do you know what became of him?'

Ibrahim wiped his lips and pushed away the flap of fine bread which had served him as a plate. Then he folded his arms and leant on the low table. 'I noticed your interest and kept track of him, sir. He has served his apprenticeship. When you saw him he was, as you know, a cadet still in training. Well, he served on Rhodes, meritoriously, as you'd expect. Now he's recommended to become a janissary of your household. The ceremony of investiture will be held at the end of the month. As a senior member of your slave household I have undertaken to be his sponsor.' He stopped and looked at Suleiman, his eyes sharp and expectant.

The Sultan flung down his napkin. 'But this is splendid news!' He leaned forward and clapped Ibrahim's shoulder. 'This is the very thing! The ceremony of Passing through the Gate is something that I've never seen, but this year –' he broke off while he thought, and then went on decisively, 'It shall be held in the Hippodrome and I will preside. You will be present as the sponsor of one of the cadets, which in itself will be enough to show your interest in the corps. We'll re-create their legend for them.' He fell silent again for several moments, and added, 'Yes, that's what we'll do.'

Ibrahim watched him curiously for a moment. Not for the first time he was a little disconcerted by Suleiman's capacity for seizing on an idea and expanding it or converting it until it became something else again. Now he was not quite sure what Suleiman had meant.

'What legend are we to re-create, sir?'

Suleiman was playing with the goblet fashioned from a single emerald whose miraculous powers were supposed to preserve him from poisoning. He frowned at it and then swallowed the last of the water it contained. 'My ancestor, Orhan Khan, is supposed to have founded the janissaries, aided by Kara Halil, his great general. Of course, I don't believe he did anything of the sort.' His sudden smile was shyly mischievous. 'But that doesn't matter, *they* believe it. Now, they also believe that when he raised his first company of tribute lads and brought them to Anatolia, Orhan the Golden – he was called that because of his golden beard, you know – marched them to Haji Bektash, the great missionary and warrior who founded the dervish order, so that he could bless them.'

Ibrahim stirred a little uncomfortably and said, 'I believe I've heard something of the story.'

Suleiman chuckled. 'If you're going to have much to do with janissaries, you'll need to know more than "something of the story". Now, the saint came out of his grotto to meet them, and Orhan drew up his troops in front of him. Haji Bektash called the very youngest recruit to him. When the boy knelt at his feet, he put his hand on his head and blessed him; then he lifted his arms to call down Allah's blessing on him. But his long, trailing sleeve caught in some way, probably on the buckle of the boy's belt, and the sleeve was torn free of his garment. The Haji choose to treat this as an omen. He ripped out the sleeve and fitted the armhole edge on the young soldier's bare head as a cap. The rest of the sleeve fell down his back. You see that cap every day of your life. Those two legends, myths if you like, are the articles of faith of the janissaries, and whether you like it or not, they believe them implicitly as they are entitled to do. Everyone must have something to believe in.' He stopped and drew a deep breath. 'I can't offer them another saint, but I am their Sultan, and you are a general. We will make it a great ceremony for them, something to remember all their lives and something to reassure them about the present.'

He went on in a totally different tone, 'I'm delighted about Sinan. I shall enjoy seeing him again. In fact, I shall enjoy the whole thing.' He slightly accented the 'I' and Ibrahim, ever alert for such nuances, noted the fact, just as he had noted it when Suleiman had said earlier, 'whether *you* like it or not'. I always underestimate him, he thought, he knows the military mystique means little to me, but how? I'm always careful about what I say.

He did not remember that only a few months ago such differences of outlook and temperament would not have troubled either of them.

It is to be supposed that Christian parents in Anatolia and other provinces dreaded the coming of the Devshirme to deprive them of their most promising sons. Yet perhaps not always; certainly, bribes were sometimes pouched by the collectors from fathers of likely Muslim lads who knew their boys stood a better chance of the good life, such as it was, if they could only get a foothold in the Sultan's army. With reason: what was there for them, Christian or Muslim, in their home villages, except hard work and poverty? Whereas with the army a boy could wind up anywhere. Even if he didn't make the grade and remained a janissary all his life, still, that was something! Even to get into the corps the tests were rigorous enough.

'The mark of a slave suitable for arms-bearing is that his hair is thick, his body tall and erect, his build powerful, his flesh hard, his bones thick, his skin coarse, his limbs straight, and his joints firm – Shoulders must be broad, the chest deep, the neck thick and the head round . . . the belly must be concave, the buttocks drawn in and the legs in walking well extended.' So read the manual that the collectors of tribute boys knew by heart, and this was just the beginning. By the time they had finished with a boy there was little they did not know about him, physically at least. They stripped him, though not quite naked (being Ottomans and particular about modesty), laid him on a table and went over him inch by inch, looking for signs of disease and weakness. They even had their own means of assessing intelligence by what they called 'physiognomy, a branch of prophecy' and were by no means indifferent to physical beauty.

Physical perfection and mental alertness were not the whole story of the janissaries although it is said that the very look of them, as they loped into battle at the jog-trot which characterized them, struck terror into the hearts of their enemies. There was still the business of training. By the time their sergeants and their traditions and their loyalty to each other had done with them, they were indeed terrible.

On that fine July day, however, when they poured into the Hippodrome in their thousands, it was their splendour as men, as drilled and disciplined fighting machines that was most in evidence. These qualities displayed themselves only in the carriage of heads, the flash of eyes, the precision of movement. Out of the thousands who came together that day, several hundred of them, cadets who had honourably served their time, were to 'pass through the gate' and be invested as full-fledged members of the Sultan's slave household.

The Sultan decreed that day was to be distinguished by every possible mark of honour, and to that end he brought together the highest officials in the land to see them parade, but not to take part in the ceremony; the ceremony was for the janissaries alone. The guests, powerful and important as they might be in other walks of life, were there to see and admire.

At dawn, though, when the first companies marched into position they had the Hippodrome to themselves. The first arrivals had made an early start, for Suleiman, determined to have the ceremony remembered by as many as possible, had brought them in from the garrisons of Davudpasha and Uskudar as well as the barracks of Istanbul itself.

These first-comers said their prayers and ate their frugal breakfast of bread, vegetables, an olive or two perhaps, and water, and then took up their positions. There was no loud talking, no laughing, no pushing and shoving. Their training did not allow it.

By the time their Aga arrived, heralded by his three-horse-tail banner, the Hippodrome was a sea of orderly colour, wave upon wave of it, the grey of caps, scarlet and blue of jackets, the white and gold of banners and plumes. The smartest of the lot, of course, were the companies of cadets who had been drawn up before the tribune soon to be occupied by the Sultan. The Aga of Janissaries narrowed his eyes and examined them thoughtfully. When he was satisfied he barked an order and white-plumed officers moved in smartly to select representative youths from each company. These fortunate few fell in immediately before the tribune, closed ranks and came to attention.

Silently the distinguished visitors began to arrive and take up their positions on each side of the Sultan's platform. They too were sober and orderly and knew where to go with a minimum of fuss. Like the janissaries, too, they carried their splendour on their backs and on their heads; on their backs, because they were rich and could afford it, and on their heads, because the colour of a man's turban and the way it was wound or draped indicated his office and status. Only one man was simply robed in white and wore a plain white headdress, and he was almost the most powerful there; certainly he was venerated as no one else, except the Sultan himself. This was the Grand Mufti, the Sheikh-ul-Islam himself, who interpreted the Sacred Law and represented the Kingdom of God on earth. No doubt the young soldiers looked at him with suitable respect, but any affection they had for men of religion they reserved for their own chaplains; each company had one, a member of the Bektashi dervish sect. They weren't part of the army and had no status; officialdom frowned on them, but the janissaries clung to them. They were part of the tradition.

Ibrahim, meticulous as ever, had arrived and taken up his position just before the Sheikh-ul-Islam, for their rank was equal and he felt it proper to show respect for the faith. He had also felt it proper to play down his usual magnificence. Suleiman had not said but had implied that his bearing was rather less than soldierly. It was a mild joke and did not rankle, but all the same . . .

A stir that became a murmur and then a cheer made itself felt on the far side of the Hippodrome. It died away and was replaced by complete silence as Suleiman made his appearance riding a splendid Arab stallion at the walk. He chose to ride across the Hippodrome, right through their ranks and alone.

The escort skirted the square and took up their positions beside the tribune. They were all there today, Solaks in gilded helmets and plumes, the halberdiers with their artificial tresses hanging before their cheeks, the Royals, red-clad and armed with two-edged swords. Not that they got much attention. All eyes that were free to look anywhere except straight ahead were on the Sultan as his horse carried him silently towards his station. Today he wore the helmet of victory he had rejected on Rhodes. It was lofty, studded with pearls and diamonds and crowned with a white plume. He carried its weight easily, and glanced from side to side as he rode, eyes bright with anticipation, a slight smile on the moustachioed upper lip.

The ceremony was very simple. As soon as his majesty was ready he lifted his hand and the Aga of Janissaries moved forward to present his cadets. He spoke briefly and bowed and the Sultan bowed in his turn. He dismounted and descended the steps of the tribune and stood for a moment looking along the ranks of serious young faces, very much like his own in some ways, except that his was dark, hook-nosed and Asiatic and theirs were mostly fair-skinned, wide-eyed and European, but all wearing, Sultan and cadets alike, the same expression of grave concentration.

When he had looked his fill, he walked along their ranks and spoke to as many of them as he could, but especially those who had served on Rhodes. These he cross-questioned pretty thoroughly, frowning at much that they told him. Naturally, their number included Sinan, six foot four of sinew and competence in the uniform of the Engineers, and thirty-four years old, for he had been older than most when first taken up by the Devshirme.

At last the Sultan returned to his dais and watched the rest of the inauguration. When all was over he re-mounted, rode down the ramp and prepared to return to his Palace as quietly as he had come. Except that as he rode through their ranks the second time the cry rose from thousands of eager young throats, so deafeningly that what they were shouting was not at first very clear – 'Padishahim chok yashur!' which means 'Long live our Padishah!' It rang round the Hippodrome and was taken up by other voices among the watching citizens, and reverberated until long after Suleiman had disappeared.

Was it a success? Among those who were present, undoubtedly, if emotional impact was anything to judge by. Even Ibrahim was moved and the Aga of Janissaries was hoarse with emotion. The cheering cadets would, as Suleiman had hoped, remember it all their lives. But emotion is tricky stuff and has a way of backfiring. There were plenty among the older men, tough and disillusioned veterans of Selim's wars, to whom one ceremony was much like another. These were the men whose caps sported fantastic plumed and jewelled ornaments to prove their service in many wars and many lands, and who knew that all a soldier had to come back to at the end of the day was a pallet in a barrack room and a mess of vegetables for his supper. Money, which bought the things that made life worth living, came from booty. And they knew they must wait for their Sultan to lead them out in another war before they could get a crack at any. It was easier for some; Frenk Ibrahim had sponsored one of today's cadets, very nice of him, to be sure, and he could afford it. Wasn't it rumoured that that great palace being restored in the very Hippodrome itself was to be his new home?

24

For the first time foreign ambassadors took an interest in one of the inmates of Suleiman's harem. They wrote home to their masters that there was a new woman in the Sultan's life whose position seemed to be impregnable. They knew nothing else about her, not even her name, except that she was Russian-born, and for that reason they called her Roxelana or Roxana. Had she known, Khurrem would no doubt have felt flattered and have laughed heartily at the same time. A year earlier she might have felt surprise, but now she was more assured. She was a success, after all. She had outlasted Gulbehar, her only rival, and she was the Sultan's wife, not merely his favourite. Above all, she had fitted in, taking her place as a well-bred, well-educated lady of undoubted character. Beautiful, to be sure, why else would the Sultan be interested in her? And adept in arts that the harem had to teach. Above all, a favourite with the Sultana Valideh. The ladies who gossiped about her over julep and sweetmeats agreed that if Hafise Hatun had set her face against her it would have been a different story.

Khurrem had changed, of course. Self-confidence and success are not won without cost. The early joy of her love for Suleiman had passed and she was not aware of it. Too many new considerations crowded her life, above all the need to make Mehmed's position impregnable. To this end everything was subordinate, and the changes that Suleiman was making in the political scene gave her opportunities that she was eventually to make full use of.

Only Hafise was aware of the extent of Khurrem's development. Suleiman certainly noticed nothing; he was as devoted as ever. For Khurrem what had been a wonder had become a comfortable pleasure, and she thought carefully about how to please him. Now that she had such extensive and luxurious quarters she made sure that when he came to the Old Palace to see her, he saw no one else. True, she was his wife and could not be supplanted, but she was not going to be rivalled, either. This was not yet a conscious policy so much as healthy instinct. She still loved him and was not going to share him, but above all, she was going to protect Mehmed.

She had learned to play politics along with the other ladies of Istanbul society. Gradually, her household extended. The young woman who had not known how to make use of all her slaves now had a small secretariat, a devoted little band of eunuchs who wrote her letters and brought her news from the Divan, the markets and the streets. They were headed by an odd-looking, pale-faced white eunuch of immense dignity and apparently limitless knowledge named Macar.

All this activity and the care of her growing family kept Khurrem fully occupied, but she still made time to ride whenever she could. She was sure the exercise was good for her and she never felt more vigorous and alive than after a long afternoon in the fresh air. And she was always discreet about it.

Hafise watched all this development with interest and approval. One day, if all went as she hoped, Khurrem herself would take her place as Sultana Valideh, mother of the Sultan, and the most powerful woman in the empire. She even approved the fact that Khurrem's relationship with her had become a little guarded although it saddened her. She has to go her own way, she thought. I'm growing older and I suppose some of my friends must seem stiff and passé to her. Certainly, they differed on one very important subject: Ibrahim.

Not that they discussed him. Hafise felt that Ibrahim was a subject she could hardly bring up with Suleiman's wife, for confidences on the subject might lead to embarrassments. As for Khurrem, she felt by instinct that the Sultana Valideh must dislike him because she never mentioned him, thus arriving at the right conclusion by the wrong route. This was a matter for regret but could not be helped. The old Khurrem would, perhaps, have cross-questioned Hafise on the subject, seeking to understand or persuade. The new Sultana Hasseki had learned discretion. One thing she was determined on, in fact elementary good manners demanded she do it: she must receive Ibrahim

Pasha's wife on the occasion of her marriage.

Now that Khurrem's life was so much more complex it was essential to take thought, to weigh what she said and to control herself. It was not always easy and she certainly did not enjoy it. The enjoyment now was of a different calibre. When she succeeded in getting a job for the husband of a friend, or influencing a councillor to think in a certain way on a certain project, then it was triumph, the pleasure of feeling that she could induce people to act as she wanted. And there was nothing wrong with what she did. It was all for the benefit of others that she helped set up charitable institutions, schools and hospitals. She did not interfere in matters of policy, except when Suleiman asked her advice.

The matter of Muhsine was going to be a little ticklish, she felt. Superficially only a pleasure, she told herself, glancing at the hand-mirror she was holding to see how Meylisah was getting on with braiding her hair. Goodness she was taking her time!

'At this rate we'll be here all day,' she grumbled. 'What's the trouble?'

'It's a very elaborate style and your hair is very thick,' Meylisah told her mildly.

'H'm,' grumbled Khurrem, holding the glass over her head in a vain attempt to see what was happening behind her, 'I don't know, I'm sure. I don't want to sit still this morning, I'm nervous. Can't think why. Is this really going to suit me when it's finished?'

'It suited you all right at the Queen Mother's reception three days ago,' said Meylisah patiently round a mouthful of tortoiseshell pins.

'I suppose it did,' sighed Khurrem. 'But all the same –' Meylisah put down the comb, extracted the pins from her mouth, and folded her hands at her waist. 'What are you stopping for?' demanded her mistress, turning right round to look at her.

'For you to make up your mind, mistress.' Timid as she was, Meylisah had learned from Hulefa's example that it was sometimes a good idea to be firm with Khurrem.

'I haven't –' began Khurrem indignantly, and stopped. Funny, she thought, what a lot we can say to each other without words, and how nice it is to be understood. Sometimes.

Aloud, she said, 'You're right. I'm not sure about it. I don't want to be dressed up like – like the empress of China just to receive one lady. If she's that sort of person she might think I'm trying to impress her. I think, on the whole, brush it out, Meylisah, and start again.'

'How?'

'Oh, don't be difficult! My usual style, of course, and quickly.'

Meylisah took up the hairbrush, and Khurrem sat and fidgeted. What is the matter with me, she asked herself, why am I so concerned about this wretched young woman? She will probably be charming, she ought to be, she's had all the advantages. She sat staring into space, remembering that even Suleiman had noted that she was to receive Muhsine today, and earlier that morning as they parted from each other had said gently, 'I hope you will like Ibrahim's wife.'

That was the trouble; everybody hoped they would be friends, and so the very weight of these hopes and expectations were against them. It's like a marriage, thought Khurrem bleakly, except that we're not going to have to live together, which is probably just as well. She had ineradicable memories of the reactions of some of the ladies she had met two years ago when, shy and insecure, newly married and conscious of her slave background, she had been presented to the wives of Suleiman's courtiers. Some of them, daughters of old Turkish families and conscious of their status had, in the nicest possible way, set out to make her miserable and had succeeded. She did not think Muhsine would be so misguided as to attempt such a thing, but she might very possibly feel the sort of resentment which had led them to behave in such a fashion. And if she does, Khurrem told herself, I shall be aware of it, no matter how she conceals it. In fact, I shall imagine it's there anyway.

She sighed gustily, and tried to feel ill. A sudden bad headache would solve things for the moment. The visit would have to be deferred until she was calmer. It was useless, however. The mirror showed a face glowing with rude health, and anyway she was not the sort of woman who backed away from problems. I have got to meet her today, she instructed herself, and no matter what she is like I have got to try to like her. Not only for Suleiman's sake, but also for my own and Mehmed's. Through her I can reach her husband. Which is really why I'm in this state; so much depends on this relationship.

There was argument over an arrangement of flowers beside Khurrem's divan. 'Take that thing away, I'll knock it over, it's too big,' instructed Khurrem, sweeping into her reception-room, a vision in yellow damask, ten minutes before the all-important visitor was due.

'I spent an hour arranging that this morning,' objected Hulefa.

'Put it somewhere else, then. But not near me, the lilies smell so strong,' snapped the Sultana Hasseki.

In a way it was as well that baby Mihrimah chose that moment to be sick.

It would be pleasant to record that despite all the tension the first meeting between Khurrem and Muhsine went as merrily as a wedding-bell, but it did not. Khurrem, ruffled, overreacted, while Muhsine was shy. Ibrahim like Suleiman wanted the girls to be friends, but did not content himself with expressing a hope. He loved to shine in Muhsine's eyes and loved giving instructions anyway, so he had burdened her with a word-portrait of Khurrem which was doomed to be misleading, since he had never met the original. 'Let her do all the talking, my darling,' he directed. 'From what I hear she likes to be the centre of attention. You're so lovely she won't want you to do much more than be looked at, I'm sure. But pay her all due respect, she's a very powerful young woman and his majesty's devoted to her.' Having said enough to paralyse any new wife with fright, he added gaily, 'Don't be shy, I'm sure everything will go very well,' and went off to the Divan, surrounded by his slaves and certain that he had paved the way to a lasting friendship for his wife.

So Muhsine spoke when she was spoken to, and Khurrem chattered feverishly, looking at her visitor's pure profile and thinking her proud and self-important in the extreme. Muhsine, for her part, studied Khurrem's lively countenance and expressive hands and decided that the Sultana Hasseki talked too much and was inclined to show off. Still, she thought, I suppose it's very difficult to have to meet so many different people and make conversation with all of them. No wonder she chatters. Since she was not required to say much herself, she was the more observant. Khurrem, having exhausted her greetings and felicitations, was silent, preparing for another flurry of conversation. It did not help that, now it was too late, she felt the beginnings of a headache. She said brightly, 'How hot it is, even for July! May I offer you sherbet?'

'You're very kind. That would be delicious.'

Khurrem drew a deep breath and expelled it in an inaudible sigh. She's not even trying, she thought indignantly. She just sits there and looks superior. I have to admit that it probably comes quite naturally to her, for she's one of the loveliest girls I've ever seen. She looks so calm and pure it's hardly natural, yet I'm sure those black eyes can flash when she's ruffled! Oh, what can I talk about next – 'I beg your pardon?'

She said this so fiercely that Muhsine, who had ventured a low-voiced comment on Hulefa's flowers, was quite taken aback.

'I was admiring your lilies,' she muttered and could not dredge up another word.

Khurrem clapped her hands and grimly ordered the refreshments from Hulefa, who came and took in the situation at a glance.

'Would the lady care to see the children, mistress?' she demanded, poker-faced.

'Oh, yes!' cried Muhsine, coming to life and forgetting all Ibrahim's instructions. 'Oh, if I may, that is. I love children!'

'Do you?' asked Khurrem, sitting up and looking at her more kindly. 'Well, then, send Leila in with them. That is to say –' she suddenly remembered Mihrimah's indiscretion, but Hulefa had already gone.

The sherbet came first and was consumed, still in comparative silence. But if silence can be said to have quality, it was a more friendly one. Both ladies felt more comfortable anyway, and Khurrem, still observing her duty as hostess, noticed Muhsine's 'face-see' gift hanging on a chain at her throat and commented on its beauty.

Muhsine flushed, and said shyly, 'It was a gift from my husband.'

Khurrem noted the flush and thought, she's capable of emotion anyway. I really shouldn't jump to conclusions quite so quickly.

Leila brought back the children. Mehmed was shy with strange ladies, he saw rather a lot of them and had learned to be wary, clinging to Khurrem's knees and staring hard at the visitor. Muhsine noticed how his mother's arm went instinctively round him, and how lovingly her other hand smoothed his soft, reddish hair. She smiled with sudden sweetness and said, 'May I hold the little one? Is it a girl?'

Khurrem looked doubtfully at Leila, who nodded and said, 'She's all right, mistress. She's sound asleep, just look at her,' and went over and plumped Mihrimah on Muhsine's knee.

Things went much better now, of course. There were all the natural questions to be asked and answered and enlarged on. Muhsine, it emerged, had had to be something of a mother to her younger sisters, despite all her father's money and innumerable slaves. 'Children get lonely,' she commented, so matter-of-factly and naturally that Khurrem quite warmed to her, and was stimulated to describe certain memories of her own childhood which she would never have expected to share with a high-born Turkish lady.

It was all Mehmed's fault, if indeed fault it was subsequently declared to be. He stood quite happily by his mother while she talked to the new lady who was nursing his sister. Since she wasn't worrying him with silly questions he couldn't yet answer, or stroking him which he hated, he began to take a good look at her and finally decided that she was all right. Presently he detached himself from Khurrem and crawled and toddled his way to her, confident of a kind reception. He got a smile and a finger to hold, which was fun for a minute, but they went on talking. He lost interest in the finger and began to tickle Mihrimah, who woke up and was sick all over again.

'Oh, your beautiful caftan!' cried Khurrem, jumping to her feet. 'Here, Leila, take her, she – oh, dear!'

'It's perfectly all right,' said Muhsine, looking up and actually laughing. 'It's the heat, I expect, and waking up so quickly. My youngest sister was always the same.'

A crowded half-hour later it was established beyond a doubt that her delicate pink caftan, one of the glories of her trousseau (though of course she did not say so), would never be the same again. Khurrem was mortified. It was bad enough that the thing should happen, but she thought her slaves behaved badly too, running excitedly about and exlaiming, 'Vah! Vah!' and spilling water on the carpet. She later admitted to herself that this was transferring her bad temper from Muhsine to them. She had to confess to herself that her first impressions of Muhsine had been wildly wrong. Muhsine herself, although far from understanding Khurrem as yet, was very ready to admit that exotic as the Sultana Hasseki appeared at first sight there was much about her that was likeable. They parted cordially, were prepared to meet again without dreading the experience, and felt that the friendship that everyone saw as so desirable was at least a possibility.

25

Suleiman had believed that as soon as he was free to follow his own inclinations, he would be as happy and fulfilled as he now saw Ibrahim and Khurrem to be. For two or three days this was so. With his usual energy he arranged for some of the most distinguished jurists of the day to come to the Topkapi and talk to him on the subject which he believed to be closest to his heart – the reform of the law. They came, and he welcomed them eagerly, some of them men whom he had known all his life, like Kasim, one of his early tutors, and others like the great Kemal, who had fallen out of favour with Selim and been sent away from court, whom he knew by reputation and now met for the first time.

He set them to debating, and listened eagerly at first as they expounded and argued. But after a while he became disillusioned; he was a young man, eager and impatient for achievement, while they were philosophers and lawyers to whom debate itself was all-important. They had grown grey in the pursuit of pure truth and knew no other way to reach it. Haste in any case was fatal, they seemed to be telling him, and you are young and have plenty of time ahead of you.

Suleiman stirred uneasily and dropped his head forward a little, resting his chin on his hand. Ibn Kemal, distracted by the movement of his Sultan's hand, looked at him thoughtfully. His return to Istanbul, summoned by the new Sultan, was something of a triumph for him and, basically a simple man, he accepted it as such and was grateful. He found his new master an interesting study and at this moment wondered what had caused him suddenly to become restless and look so – he sought a word and was only satisfied with 'haunted'. He considered this for a moment or two and concluded that the great should not be burdened by sensitivity in addition to their other responsibilities. He had liked this young man on sight, had felt a bond with him even before they had exchanged many words, and had seen that Suleiman responded to him in the same way.

Ibn Kemal glanced happily round the magnificent room, its windows shaded against the sun and the marble fountain giving an illusion of coolness. Really, his majesty had offered them the most splendid hospitality and was treating them as if they were his most distinguished subjects, instead of being, as they all knew only too well, among the humblest. Which brought him back where he had started, to sensitivity again. In his youth he had known Bayezid, and in his prime, Selim. Now, in his old age – well, late middle age (he was only in his fifties, after all) – he was encountering Suleiman, who looked as if he might unite the virtues of both, the sensitivity of the introspective man and the vigour of the tyrant.

Scholarly and tidy-minded, Ibn Kemal smiled at his conclusion and turned his attention back to the current speaker who stood by the fountain, one hand grasping his beard, the other extended in the air as he made a point.

Suleiman forced himself to listen and was attentive for the rest of the day, even contributing to the discussion himself. But he found his mind constantly going back to the subject of war, and the disaster of Rhodes. A year later it still occupied his thoughts. He determined to discuss it with Ibrahim.

He found himself a little wary of approaching the subject directly, although he knew that Ibrahim was as open-minded as any of these philosophers, perhaps more so because of his European background. But just at the moment Ibrahim was overwhelmed with the practicalities of his new office. Suleiman felt instinctively that his friend might not altogether understand or sympathize with his desire to probe into a subject which might strike at the roots of the empire. I don't even know whether I want to alter anything, he concluded, only to understand why I must do what I do. This was not quite honest. One thing he did not want to do, and that was to make war again – to smell the mud of earthworks or to see men suffering and trembling with fever or torn apart by bullets.

When Ibrahim came that evening, therefore, Suleiman was silent on the subject closest to his heart. They talked at first about the conference itself. 'It is splendid talk,' said Suleiman carefully. 'I can see that I have much to learn.'

Ibrahim looked at him attentively. He thought his majesty looked ever so slightly hunted, as if the learned men had worried him in some way. He said, 'They are teachers above everything else, sir. However, a little experience of actual decision-making might alter their ideas considerably.'

Suleiman rose to his feet. 'Let us walk out,' he said. 'I'm dispirited.' The heat of the day had passed, but the air was heavy and the clouds low. Ibrahim observed that Suleiman walked slowly as if drained of energy.

'It's true,' Suleiman said at last. 'They disappointed me, and you just put your finger on it. With a few exceptions, such as Kemal who has an independent mind, they are all teachers and the things they are saying to me are the same things they say to their pupils, day after day, year in, year out. That's not what I want.'

He plodded on in silence for a while, hands clasped as usual behind his back, the arrogant nose seeming to smell out the way in front of him. Presently he said, 'I thought it would be easy. I have a course set out before me and time at last to follow it, but now I'm not sure where the path leads. And it's the same with everything. For instance, I would like to do something to beautify this city, to make it a pleasanter place for those who live in it. But how?'

Ibrahim's large black eyes became even larger as he stared at his Sultan in astonishment. 'But that's easy! Better roads, hostels for travellers, gardens with water –'

Suleiman grunted fiercely, but could not help smiling at his recollection of what had been said to him. 'I sent for my architects. Hostels they can manage – but roads, such as the Romans built, good roads?' He shook his head. 'It seems we've lost the art. As for the garden haven I had in mind, all they can do is copy the gardens of the Serai. I want something different. But I can't design a water-garden, I don't know how.' He looked fiercely at Ibrahim, who could not help laughing.

'Sir, sir, the way of the innovator is hard, and you are in a hurry. We must find better architects, better designers, young men like ourselves. You have already said this, sir, in another connection, have you not?'

Suleiman grunted again, but he was mollified. But Ibrahim had his own preoccupations. He went on, 'By your leave, sir, speaking of new men: does your majesty remember the Venetian fellow, Luigi Gritti?'

'I have every reason to,' replied Suleiman; 'a man of great perspicacity, Gritti,' he chuckled. 'When I assumed the Sword of Osman, Gritti wrote home to the Venetians and warned them that I was something more than the gentle lamb the Pope in Rome said I was. Nobody took any notice of him at the time. What about him?'

'Only that I am considering making him my Dragoman of the Gate, if your majesty approves the choice.'

Suleiman remained silent, his face expressionless. But he continued to stroll along the little winding path they had chosen because of the splendid view over the Golden Horn at the end of it. Ibrahim knew that if Suleiman had been annoyed by what he had said, his pace would have quickened.

'It is an important post, sir. I believe, as things are, it will become more so. We need someone who understands the western powers, knows how they think.' He hesitated, noting that Suleiman's gaze was still benign. 'I believe that sometimes diplomacy might serve our ends as well as threats, or even better.'

'Selim would not have agreed with you.'

'The world is already less simple than it was in your father's heyday, sir. The time may come when we will have to decide who threatens us most, Persia, or –' he shrugged, 'Hungary, Austria. This new Emperor Charles is a different breed of man, and we need to understand him and the others. There are new young rulers throughout Europe.'

'And Gritti will be a key to their thinking, you hope?'

Ibrahim glanced at his master thoughtfully. Suleiman's tone was cool, almost bantering. The suggestion that a Westerner should occupy a post which really amounted to liaison officer with foreign countries was totally revolutionary. There would be trouble with the old guard over it, he was sure, unless Suleiman was prepared to back it.

'Tell me about Gritti.'

That's more like it, thought Ibrahim. He began to expound, telling how Luigi Gritti was a son of the former Doge of Venice, Andreas Gritti, a great man who had served his city well, and how the son Luigi was, so far as brains went, a worthy son of his father. Unfortunately, though, Luigi was a bastard. Not only could he not inherit his father's estates, he could not serve the city of Venice either. A disappointed man, he had come to Istanbul where what counted was a man's quality, not the accident of his birth. And in Istanbul he had done very well for himself, amassing a fortune by astute trading and the sale of information. He got on well with the Ottomans, taking the trouble to learn their language and to understand their point of view. He had been right about a lot of things, Ibrahim said, and not only about the quality of their new Sultan.

'He has the freedom of the *Magnifica Comunita*, the Venetian settlement in Galata. Messer Marco Memmo, the Venetian ambassador, relies upon him for information and is led by the nose. So too are the envoys of Ragusa and Genoa, as well as the Polish king's agent. They don't like him, but they can't get along without him.'

'Indeed,' murmured Suleiman; 'and does he lead you around by the nose, my friend?'

'I thought you would ask me that, sir. No. He and I are old friends. If you consider it for a moment,' Ibrahim hesitated, and then decided to take the plunge, 'he and I have a lot in common. It happens that his mother was Greek, but it's more than that. We are both acquainted with the seamy side of life and can't forget it. Such good fortune as he's had he got here, in Turkey, and he doesn't forget that. So far as the West is concerned, he's got a chip on his shoulder a mile long.' He nodded in satisfaction and added, 'And I can control him.'

They had come to the end of the path. The sun was low and obscured by cloud. Sky and water were a dirty white, with no colour or movement anywhere. Suleiman grunted at it. 'Nothing to see,' he complained. 'We'll go and eat.' He swung back the way they had come, Ibrahim at his heels.

They walked in silence for some minutes, Ibrahim's eyes bright and questioning on his master's face.

'Your Venetian, is he a Muslim?' Suleiman asked at last.

'No, sir, he retains his faith.'

'Employ him then.'

Ibrahim looked surprised, and Suleiman said, 'If he had become more Ottoman than the Ottomans I think he would not be much use to us. But it sounds as if he has kept his balance.'

They were nearly back to the selamlik when Suleiman asked, 'How would your friend react if we told him to go to the princes of the West and seek their friendship?'

Ibrahim did not hesitate. 'No doubt he would be surprised, but he would attempt the task and achieve a measure of success. The Sultan of the Ottoman Empire can always have friendship from lesser rulers.'

Suleiman grunted. 'Perhaps I have not made myself plain. I'm not talking about friendship as a diplomatic device – we use it so already. I mean absolute friendship, agreement not to make war on each other. What do you say to that?'

Ibrahim laughed. 'The idea has first to be conceived, and not only by one ruler alone. It is useless to proffer the hand of friendship to the Emperor Charles, for instance. He would no doubt grasp it and then tear it off at the wrist. But as an idea to be developed gradually, over the years – over the centuries more likely – why, it has untold possibilities. Smaller and weaker countries would undoubtedly seek the favour and help of any great power that was prepared to befriend them, and offer their vasselage in return.' His voice was respectful as he said, 'You have outstripped me, sir. You are pursuing what I said earlier about the use of diplomacy and taking it to its logical conclusion.'

'No, I'm not,' replied Suleiman roundly, but he was not prepared to elucidate. He saw that Ibrahim was right. A world without war was unthinkable. What they could pursue in philosophical debate as an absolute good for a problematical future was one thing, and his unavoidable course was another.

26

Nothing would do but that Ibrahim must have a splendid new residence; more than a residence, indeed, for he must have his own offices, a chancellery where he could conduct all business other than that of the Divan. It went without saying that the new home must be as splendid as possible in keeping with his new status. There was a palace on the At-Meydan, overlooking the Hippodrome, which had been built by one of Selim's last Grand Viziers. Now, of course, it had reverted to the Sultan, as did all the property of such officers at their death. It was the perfect place for Ibrahim, and Suleiman was very happy to hand it over to him, for he wanted the world to see the trust and reliance he placed in this splendid friend of his. Nothing could be too good for him. Indeed, at this time he began to understand something of Ibrahim's passion for splendour, and ceased to laugh at his friend when he appeared in sumptuous clothes, attended by numerous slaves as splendidly clad as himself. The lesson had at last got through to him that magnificence was an attribute of power.

So Ibrahim took over what had been the Jandarli palace and proceeded to make it his own. This included, of course, extensive rebuilding and total redecoration. The lofty, well-proportioned public rooms were stripped and filled with beautiful things - polychrome tiles, cast bronze grilles, jade mirrors inlaid with gold, and wood-carvings set with mother-of-pearl. He sent to Persia for enamels and porcelain and decorated the walls and ceilings with paintings in relief. Everybody talked about what he was doing, on the whole with approval, until he bought two ancient Greek statues and had them shipped to Istanbul and set up in his palace. They were superb nudes and this was felt to be going a bit too far, although they went into his private rooms and were seen by nobody who might be offended by them. Ibrahim did not notice, or perhaps did not care, what was said about this. Truth to tell, he was getting just a little too big for his elegant leather boots, was very conscious of his European origins and inclined to see the Ottoman way of life as static, not to say provincial.

He had always been aware that his wits were quicker than his royal master's, but affection and gratitude had kept the balance more than steady, for he had always admired Suleiman's strength of character and remembered never to underestimate his intelligence. But now he was aware of a welling-up within himself of sheer ability, and confidence in that ability. There was nothing, it seemed, that he couldn't undertake and make a success of. With that feeling came impatience with those who did not keep up with him, and he saw Suleiman as one of that number. Of course, he was aware that the Sultan was actually having trouble adapting to the new order of things he himself had brought about. But Ibrahim was careful to hide his own feelings and made no effort to identify with Suleiman's – there wasn't time for all this introspection.

The most splendid apartments in the new palace were to be set aside for the harem, that went without saying. Everything revolved around Muhsine; he could no longer imagine how he had lived without her. Indeed, he wished she was more enthusiastic about the magnificence he was planning for her, but supposed that a girl with her background took this sort of thing in her stride. Although her father seemed sufficiently impressed for both of them.

One afternoon in September, he had made a point of coming home early so that he could take her on the Bosphorus. In the few hours of daylight left to them, he planned to take her as far as they could go in the general direction of the Sweet Waters of Europe, using his official barge, of course. But she wasn't ready, not even dressed! The windows of her room were shuttered against the midday sun, but even so he could see there was something wrong.

'Muhsine! What's wrong – I thought you would be ready and waiting by now. You've never forgotten?'

She was lying with her face hidden in her cushions. He saw her sit up hastily and brush the hanging sleeve of her bodice across her eyes. He hurried to sit beside her, thoroughly disturbed.

Her voice came thick and choked, 'I'm sorry, I had a headache, and I – I fell asleep –'

'You don't sound as if you've been asleep, more as if you've been crying. Muhsine! What's wrong?'

'There's nothing wrong.'

He put his hand under her chin and tried to turn her face so that he could look at her, but she resisted, repeating, 'It's nothing, really. I'll get dressed. I'm sorry to keep you waiting.'

'I don't mind waiting, just tell me what's wrong.' He put his arm round her shoulders and kissed her cheek, which he found to be wet. 'I knew you were crying! Now tell me – something has upset you, I've never seen you like this before! Muhsine!'

She leaned against him and put her head on his shoulder, shaken by sobs. Ibrahim held her tight and stared across the shadowy room, completely out of his depth. He had always made the most of any opportunities that came his way with women; there had been flirtation, giggling and lovemaking, but never anything like this. He wasn't prepared for it, was even a little resentful of the depth of feeling her tears roused in him. He sat, helpless and worried, until the sobs lessened and she raised her head and sniffed a little.

'Come now,' he said, assuming an authority he was far from feeling. 'Whatever it is, I'll deal with it. Trust me.'

'How I wish you could! Oh, Ibrahim, do you know how long we've been married?'

'It only seems about a week,' he told her sincerely. 'What of it?'

She smiled a little and rubbed her cheek against his brocade-covered shoulder, but she was a direct girl and never beat about the bush. 'It's four months, but I don't conceive – I'm so terribly worried.'

Ibrahim's first impulse was to make light of it and comfort her and he gave way to it wholeheartedly. 'Four months? A lifetime! Aren't you allowing yourself to get carried away? In any case, what does it matter?'

He wished immediately that he had not uttered that last sentence, for she said reproachfully, 'Oh, Ibrahim, you know it matters! And besides, I want your child, I want it desperately. Suppose –'

'Then why not see a midwife?' He felt quite uncertain, but supposed this was the right thing to say.

It was. 'My aunt knows a reliable woman.'

'And did your aunt put the whole thing into your head, by any chance?' He thought grimly that if he was right he knew just which aunt it was. A small, brisk woman, always wrapped like a mummy in her draperies. Her snapping dark eyes had followed his every move at the wedding ceremonies.

'Oh, no! Not entirely – I had thought, myself – but when I saw her the other day, she asked. Oh, Ibrahim, you know how elderly ladies are!'

'Look, Muhsine, you're a beautiful, healthy girl and I love you. I don't care if we never have children except that it would make you miserable. Go and see a midwife – go and see a wise woman if you like, though what she could do for you beyond muttering mumbo-jumbo, I don't know. But, above all, don't worry!' He sat up. 'Does that make you feel better?'

She sat beside him, her hands quiet in her lap, and muttered, 'Yes, yes, much better. How kind you are!'

'Well, now, we still have time. Dress yourself, and we'll go on the water – it will cheer you up and give you something else to think about.' He clapped his hands, and said, 'There! I've summoned your maids. I'm not giving you time to sit and brood.'

He was right, it did cheer her. In later years when he had occasion to think kindly of Muhsine it was always this evening he remembered.

Because she had no time for the elaborate toilette beloved of Ottoman ladies she had put on the first things that came to hand, dressed her hair in two simple plaits and wore no jewellery except her 'face-see' pearl. Her large eyes were mild and limpid after the shedding of so many tears, and because she was relieved and happy to be with him after so much private and feverish distress, she seemed especially gentle and anxious to please.

It was a beautiful afternoon in late September with a little breeze ruffling the water, a benign sun declining over them turning everything they saw to gold. There was really no need for words, even Ibrahim saw that; besides he had plenty to think about – he always had. Most of it was pleasurable, for at the moment everything he touched turned to gold, quite often literally: bribes for dropping a word into this one's ear, or for confirming that one in the post he wanted, fell into his lap for the very minimum expenditure of effort, it seemed. But it didn't do to become careless. It was necessary to be vigilant just to preserve the status quo, especially when everything depended on the whim of one man.

Though in the case of Suleiman, he thought, 'whim' is hardly the right word. No one was ever less likely to act on a whim than his master. Indeed, he might be happier if he sometimes did, Ibrahim decided robustly, and frowned suddenly, wondering if there was more he could have done recently to raise Suleiman's spirits. If only I knew what was behind all this dejection and restlessness I could act, he decided. Perhaps . . .

He raised himself on his elbow, for he had been lying on his back beneath the barge's light canopy, staring out at the cloudless sky, and asked, 'Muhsine, have you seen any more of Khurrem Hasseki?'

'Oh yes,' she told him eagerly. 'How wrong I was about her! She is really the most unaffected of women. Ibrahim, I do so like her. Of all the women I know she is the only one it is possible to talk to without wondering what lies behind her words. She is never spiteful or envious.'

'That's just as well. I mean it's desirable that the Hasseki Sultana should be as you say she is. I suppose what you're really telling me is that she likes you too.'

'I hope so, I believe so.'

'I merely wondered what she says about his majesty.'

'She never talks about him! That is to say, she doesn't discuss him. But she wouldn't, of course.'

He laughed, teasing her, 'I thought you women talked of nothing else . . . Muhsine, you haven't said anything to her about not having children, have you?'

She frowned. 'It's not a subject I want to talk about to

anyone, and I certainly don't know Khurrem Hasseki well enough to discuss it with her. Why do you ask?' He saw anxiety clouding the happiness in her eyes.

He clasped her in his arms, saying urgently, 'No reason at all, and indeed I don't know why I asked. Confide in her by all means if you wish.'

He felt her relax against him, and held her close while he asked himself why indeed he had panicked suddenly about her possible childlessness. The answer was very simple. He didn't, for some reason, want Suleiman to know. He considered this discovery with something like incredulity. To think that Suleiman, that most steadfast of friends, would regard such a personal misfortune (for as such he would surely see it) with anything but compassion and sympathy was unthinkable. So why was he worrying? The answer came readily, for Ibrahim could usually be honest with himself if the matter involved was not to his discredit – he didn't want anyone else to know. It was unacceptable to him that he, Ibrahim, the successful, the brilliant, the admired and envied, should prove to be subject to the same misfortunes as lesser men. And he found he didn't like himself for feeling it. You're a scoundrelly sort of fellow at bottom, he told himself, caressing Muhsine's slender back and feeling her soft hair against his face. It's not as if you want to become some sort of patriarch, surrounded by your descendants. That's not your style at all; you don't even share the average, honest Ottoman's desire to beget sons to the glory of God and to carry on the family business. Your glory's in the here and now and you know it. Be honest, there isn't an ounce of fatherly feeling in you. When Suleiman so far forgets himself as to enlarge on young Mustafa's strong limbs or Mehmed's probable intelligence all you feel is a strong desire to puke. Be grateful you're not being saddled with any of that. So far.

Still, when they reached home, he followed Muhsine to her room and said teasingly, 'Come here, and let's see what we can manage this time!'

She came into his arms very readily, but there was a feverishness in her response to his lovemaking which rather dimmed his own pleasure.

The next morning she seemed happier, saying firmly that she would take his advice and in the meanwhile forget all about it. The trouble was that he couldn't forget all about it now that she had told him. A child, a son preferably, would show an envious world that there was absolutely nothing that Ibrahim could possibly want that he could not have.

27

Ibrahim was not alone in finding Suleiman difficult to handle at this time. Khurrem worried about him too. But at least she had a clue to the cause of his trouble because he was sleeping badly again, tossing from side to side and sometimes getting up and pacing the room. She knew his habit of hammering away at something in his mind until it yielded up its own solution. This had certainly not happened over Rhodes, and Khurrem, ever practical, could see no way in which it might. War is war, she told herself, and people and things get destroyed; there's no way to alter it. If he could only stop blaming himself, or even talk to me about it, he'd be happier.

Suleiman certainly was not going to do that. If he could not bring himself to discuss the matter with Ibrahim, who was a man and his closest friend, his brother in spirit, how much less likely was he to talk to a woman about it? But her loving sympathy made itself felt so strongly that he was prepared to talk to her freely about practically everything else. 'I'm restless,' he admitted to her one evening. 'I miss the routine, perhaps, though when I was tied to it I chafed against it. How I hated those long days in the Divan, with nothing productive at the end of the day! But now I feel I'm missing something, which is ridiculous, because Ibrahim tells me all that is done.'

Khurrem looked at him closely, noting that he had grown thinner of late. The beak of a nose seemed more prominent and the wide, grey eyes more sunken. She sought something to say, knowing that what mattered was instant response rather than a display of wisdom. She thought of suggesting a few days' hunting, and rejected the idea at once. Insulting, she thought, like telling him to go away and stop worrying. On impulse she said, 'Perhaps you need a new routine.'

He was pacing the room, padding up and down like some large restless cat. But not the comfortable sort of pet cat the Prophet was so fond of, she thought, more like a leopard in a cage.

He stopped and turned to look at her and was momentarily deflected from his course, thinking how lovely she looked in her thin turquoise muslin – lovely, and at the same time satisfying and easy. I can never do without her, he reminded himself, not for the first time. How fortunate I am in this, at least. But she was looking at him expectantly, was even a little apprehensive, as if what she had said (what was it?) might annoy him. He remembered her remark and found it stimulating.

'Yes! There may be something in that. Perhaps I have tried – tried –' He sought words impatiently as usual, failed, and made do with others, '– too hard.' He began to pace again, but this time, thought Khurrem, with an appearance of greater purpose. 'Yes, that's it,' he went on. 'I've been too frantic, expected too much, looked for an absolute where probably there isn't one.'

Khurrem's eyes narrowed. She hadn't the remotest idea what he was talking about, but had no intention of admitting it. She had made a random, but, she hoped, practical suggestion. Now look how excited he was getting! And what was an absolute? But at least he was happier. In fact he was coming towards her, hands outstretched and saying, 'How profound you are! Things are always so much simpler than I think.'

She accepted the kiss he awarded her very readily, thinking that any profundity was undoubtedly within himself, and set herself to discover what she had achieved. She could not think of any way to manage this except by a direct question. 'What will you do?' she prompted.

'I will tell you what I won't do. I will no longer waste time in pointless anxiety about whether my decisions are the right ones. I never used to. At Manissa,' his eyes became remote as he looked back to his carefree days as Crown Prince and governor of Sarukhan, 'I gave judgement as I saw fit, and was sometimes even proud of what I had decided. Of course, it was simpler then and I was younger –'

'It was only three years ago,' interjected Khurrem.

'I know, but it sometimes seems like three centuries. I have allowed myself to be overtaken by anxiety, I think. This conference of learned men has unsettled me, too. Simply, I had forgotten that it is the nature of philosophers to philosophize and of teachers to teach, but not to make decisions. I expected them to tell me what to do.'

'You have never needed anyone to tell you what to do,' Khurrem interjected firmly. 'I have never known anyone so definite once he's made up his mind, except perhaps my father.'

The compliment pleased him, also the comparison with her father, who had been a priest of the Russian Orthodox Church and, if his daughter's recital of his sayings was to be relied upon, a very remarkable man. Khurrem never mentioned her family except when she was happy and self-confident, so that this fact also was a cause for rejoicing.

Suleiman sat down beside her and took her hand in his, as if he could at last allow himself to rest. 'Ibrahim said much the same thing a while ago, but I was in such a ferment that it passed me by. What was it? Something to the effect that the experience of making decisions would benefit the philosophers. You are both right, of course. I will digest what they have told me, bring my own mind to bear on it, and start the great work of restating the moral law without more ado.' He laughed exultantly. 'And there, if I'm not much mistaken, is my new routine. It should only last me for the rest of my life.'

Khurrem was suddenly a prey to indecision. It was the mention of the moral law which had done it. Sooner or later, she thought, her heart beating fast at the realization, he must come to consider the Law of Fratricide. Would it not be a good thing, now, while he's suddenly so happy and confident, and so pleased with me, to ask him to change it?

It was on the tip of her tongue; a very few words would do it. She raised her hand to her lips, saw how it trembled, and was warned. Not now, she counselled herself, you've not had time to prepare, you could spoil everything. You could destroy his euphoria and make him distrust you, perhaps forever. Besides, this is one subject on which he will take advice, from the philosophers, the Grand Mufti, Ibrahim . . . No, much better to wait – after all, you haven't yet got Ibrahim on your side, you haven't even succeeded in approaching him.

She dropped her hand to her lap, clenching it to stop the

telltale trembling. How I wish this was not necessary, she thought. It's changing me, I'm becoming hard and scheming. If I'm not careful I'll come to see Suleiman only as a means to an end, instead of the generous, loving man that he is.

'I'll tell you something else I will do, too,' Suleiman said. 'You know that the Grand Mufti is growing old and increasingly feeble? Well, I've decided on his successor.' He laughed jubilantly. 'This will surprise them, the entrenched fathers of the church and the law; I'm going to bring in a younger man, someone with some blood in his veins and ideas in his head! Ibn Kemal, he's my man - not only learned but alive!'

Khurrem thought hard. He had told her about the conference of jurists when he convened it, but truth to tell, she had not been much interested. But the Grand Mufti, the Sheikh-ul-Islam, was a different matter, for he too could influence Mehmed's future. His advice was always sought in matters of truth and justice and never ignored. He amounted to the keeper of the Sultan's conscience. Fortunately her memory was good, even for items only half-heard. She said, 'He is the man your father sent away from Istanbul.' I can always remember the activities of the great Selim, she thought, a little bitterly. He could be relied upon to exile a worthy man - when he didn't execute him.

'The very same,' agreed Suleiman. 'He's a man in his fifties, able, vigorous and open-minded, very different from the present incumbent who is old and saintly and no longer quite of this world.'

'Well,' said Khurrem honestly, 'then I'm sure I wish Ibn Kemal a great future. Will -' she hesitated, and added boldly, 'Ibrahim also be pleased with your decision?'

He stared at her in surprise for a moment, but then he burst out laughing, a sound so unaccustomed of late that she also began to laugh without knowing what she was laughing at.

'Ibrahim,' said Suleiman eventually, 'will be so relieved that I have at last brought myself to make a decision of any kind on any subject at all, that he will be delighted. I have led the poor fellow a dance lately. One of the pleasures of this period of - of - mental sloth, but the only one, has been to watch my poor old friend being patient with me and trying not to show it. You, my lovely Khurrem, have been much better at hiding your feelings, and have at last led me out of it. For which

I am more grateful than I can tell you.'

She stared at him in genuine amazement. 'But I have not had to hide my feelings! I haven't felt impatient, only worried for you because –' She let the sentence trail off deliberately. If he had forgotten Rhodes, only for a short time, she was not going to bring it back into his mind.

It seemed that he had, for he suddenly declared himself to be hungry, and asked, meek as a schoolboy, if she could find him something to eat. 'I supped with Ibrahim earlier,' he said, 'but truth to tell, I wasn't interested in food. Or anything else, if it comes to that. Poor Ibrahim! He is always hungry, but he was hard put to it to get enough to eat in the intervals between starting subjects for conversation and watching me ignore them. He laughed again, a little shamefacedly, then burst out suddenly, 'How pleasant this is! Just to be with you and feel happy again, as we used to be.'

When eventually their supper came, they were so light-hearted over it that even Hulefa was compelled to laugh and later confided to Meylisah that she wouldn't have believed his majesty capable of such gaiety had she not seen it with her own eyes. To which Meylisah, who after all had been Khurrem's oldest friend in the harem, replied in as superior a tone as she dared use to Hulefa that it was all the influence of Khurrem Hasseki. 'When first his majesty took an interest in us,' she said, 'he was very serious indeed, and seldom smiled and never laughed. But our mistress has changed him beyond belief.'

Suleiman, had he heard this dictum, would have agreed wholeheartedly. Later that night, lying satisfied and at peace beside the sleeping Khurrem, he reflected on his good fortune. He had an enchanting wife, healthy children and a good friend, which was more than some men who were not sultans ever achieved. He had, he hoped, already shown Khurrem how deep were his feelings for her. In a little while, say a few months, it would be time to signal in some way his gratitude and affection to Ibrahim. He would have to plan what form that honour should take. Having decided this, he returned to designing in his mind a magnificent jewel for Khurrem. Emeralds, he thought, I've never given her emeralds. It shall be a necklace, and perhaps also earrings, though not too heavy, she's only a little thing . . . He yawned and slept.

So the year drew to its close more happily for Suleiman than it had begun. He began to work on his canon of the law and found it hard going at first, but he persevered. His remembrance of the nightmare of Rhodes did not leave him entirely and his hatred of war remained with him, but he learned to live with them as necessary evils. Some day, he promised himself, he would come to grips with the problem of war. At the moment, however, it was a problem in abeyance, for the Turkish performance on Rhodes, whatever the Turkish Sultan might think of it, had impressed the rest of world sufficiently for them to want to give the Turks a wide berth. Even Persia, that ancient enemy, was quiescent.

With time to spare, Suleiman looked around his empire with a questioning eye and began to take an interest in its many peoples. It was noted that, just as he turned away from older, traditional advisers in favour of younger men, now he began to talk to men of the European empire, to Serbs and Croats, and in their own languages too. It was all tentative; he was pursuing no definite policy, just turning a thoughtful and enquiring mind towards the outside world to see what he could learn from it.

There was pleasure as well. The greatest, undoubtedly, was to learn as autumn drew on that Khurrem was pregnant again. She, too, was happy, for children and childbirth were no problem to her, as healthy a girl as ever drew breath. The particular happiness for Khurrem this time was that Suleiman was at home with her. Not that he remained in Istanbul the whole time; it was not to be expected that a young and vigorous man was going to hang about the city and the harem forever. He wanted exercise and sport, and there had been precious little opportunity for either during the last two crowded years. So, this autumn, he decreed a prolonged hunting expedition to Edirne. Nobody objected. The senior Slaves of the Gate certainly did not, for they went too, as well as the Divan, the Grand Vizier, and the whole kit and caboodle of government. It was the usual arrangement, and convenient. A man could do his job and enjoy himself at the same time.

Nobody consulted the janissaries, naturally, but for once even they had no comment to make. It stood to reason there could be no war this year and they'd had their great parade earlier on. Not that parades put silver into a man's pocket or meat into his mouth, but it was nice to be appreciated, and they noted with satisfaction that recruitment was continuing. The magic promise of twenty thousand by 1530 was being bandied around. It portended much, and for the moment they were content.

28

Khurrem and Muhsine had become firm friends at last, each finding a great deal to admire in the very different personality of the other. Muhsine wished she had Khurrem's sturdy strength and basic lightness of heart; Khurrem sighed after Muhsine's dignity and serenity, especially in her sorrow over her childlessness about which, of course, the ladies of their circle were becoming curious. Khurrem, when the whisper reached her, snapped at the news-carrier with such viciousness that it was tacitly agreed that Ibrahim Pasha's wife was not a subject for comment. But that didn't help Muhsine. Nothing did.

It was not a subject that Muhsine wanted to talk about and Khurrem, divining that this was so, respected her new friend's wishes. But gradually a few words were said, now and again, that expressed the yearning of one and the sympathy of the other. And Khurrem took the earliest opportunity to open a tentative relationship with Muhsine's husband. What could be more natural, for instance, than her saying, as she did one late autumn afternoon when the two girls sat cosily together, hands folded inside the sleeves of heavy caftans and feet on the tandur, 'How grateful I am to your husband! He has brought so much peace and happiness into our lives by releasing the Sultan from the Divan. And I hear his wisdom acclaimed on all sides. Please tell him I said this.' There, she thought, with the irony that was becoming a feature of her dealings with the people she wanted to make use of, that should be enough to please him.

She waited long enough to see Muhsine flush with pleasure and say 'How kind you are!' and then changed the subject. When they met next, a few days later, Muhsine reported shyly that Ibrahim had indeed been pleased, and added that he wished Khurrem Hasseki to know that he was at her service at any time. He had not, in fact, been deceived, although he had been flattered. This lady, he thought drily, wants something from me and presently I shall find out what it is. He was quite willing to accomodate the Sultan's wife if it was humanly possible. Apart from everything else, she had been kind to Muhsine and he was grateful.

As winter softened into spring, however, those around her began to worry about Khurrem. She was pale and drawn, could not eat, and was increasingly nervous. She could think only of one thing: that the new baby would be another boy, that he would die, and that it would be her fault for not begging Suleiman to change the Law of Fratricide the night she had almost found the courage to do so. Unable to confide in those who served her, she grew so feverish and distressed that her maids confided in Hafise who sent for the midwife. She in turn reported that she could find nothing physically wrong with her patient. 'But,' she said, 'I have never seen her in this state before. She has always been a model patient. Perhaps she has something on her mind.'

Hafise thanked her, sighed, and went to see Khurrem who was still abed after a restless night. She looked down at her gravely, noting the heavy eyes and flushed cheeks.

'Are you ill, my child, are you in pain?'

Khurrem slumped down into her bed and shook her head. Presently she looked up and said weakly, 'My head aches and I haven't slept.' She made an effort to sit up, but decided against it. 'I'm sorry, dear madam, I'm not good company this morning.'

Hafise said to Hulefa, 'Bring rosewater to cool her cheeks, and some julep would be nice, perhaps.'

'I don't think I could manage julep.'

'Nevertheless I think you should try it,' said Hafise kindly but firmly. She sat down by the bed and waited for the slaves to leave them alone.

It did not take the Sultana Valideh very long to get the truth out of Khurrem. Indeed, once the girl had made the decision to confide in her the words tumbled out almost incoherently, and she cried heartily and with considerable relief after she had finished. Hafise shook her head. 'You can no longer contain yourself,' she told her daughter-in-law sadly, 'and there is no reason why you should. You must tell Suleiman how you feel and what you want him to do. You have delayed too long for your own good.'

'I shrink from it,' cried Khurrem wildly. 'I couldn't bear it if he were angry with me again! I simply could not bear it, I believe I should die.'

A bitter little smile played round Hafise's lips when she heard this, but Khurrem, lost in her own troubles, did not notice it. Hafise said, 'Neither you nor I is the kind to die of sorrow.' She sighed, and seemed for the moment to have lost the thread of what she wanted to say, but went on at last, 'Besides, Suleiman is a different kind of man from – He is not the sort of man to bully a sick woman. And you are sick, you have made yourself so. What do you think will happen to you and the baby if you don't get some relief? Does it not also occur to you that this matter is a source of misery for him as well as you? He cannot make things worse for you than you have made them for yourself.'

When the maids returned with rosewater and julep, Hafise had gone and Khurrem was sitting up in bed, red-eyed but noticeably more cheerful.

She was in a pitiable enough state that evening, though, when Suleiman came to see her. It is one thing to understand what has to be done and another actually to do it. The battle was largely won for her, however, for Hafise had seen her son beforehand. She told him the truth. Like Khurrem, she enjoyed manipulating people, taking an impersonal pleasure in watching them react to the skill with which she could put her case. However, this was a matter both too serious and, for her, too sorrowful to be the subject of a game. She also thought she knew her son's own feelings in the matter. She told him that Khurrem had made herself ill because she could not bring herself to tell him how she felt. She ended, 'This monstrous law has been a nightmare for too long. It poisoned my life and now bids fair to ruin Khurrem's.'

Forewarned as he was, Suleiman was still shocked at his wife's appearance. Her eyes were enormous in her pale face and she seemed unable to remember the thread of what she had started to say, staring at him in despair, her eyes bright with tears.

He was filled with remorse, for he knew that this was a subject with which he should have dealt long ago. 'Your son will be safe,' he promised her urgently. 'I will never invoke this law against him, or his brothers if we are fortunate enough to have more boys. I will find a way to do away with it – this I promise you on my head.'

It distressed him to see how long it took her to get used to the idea that at last she could be at peace. But if eventually it did penetrate her feverish mind that she had nothing more to worry about, it seemed to Suleiman that his own worries had just begun. The Law of Fratricide had all the weight of the Sheri, the Sacred Law; Mehmed II had given it legal sanction, supported by the authority of the Ulema and the sanction of the Koran. How did one get past that, even if convinced it was desirable? After all, even before the Conqueror, the killing of inconvenient brothers had been found necessary from time to time, and had not Prince Djem brought about civil war by proposing to share the empire with Bayezid II? The time might well come when the name of Suleiman would be cursed because he had presumed to betray the wisdom of his ancestors.

He sent for Ibrahim and put the problem before him, and Ibrahim brought the full weight of his intellect as well as the subtlety of his character to bear upon it. He believed that success in office depended on working to a principle, and so far as his Sultan was concerned the principle he had formulated for himself was first to find out what Suleiman wanted to do, and then if humanly possible to arrange to do it.

'When I consider the heritage my illustrious ancestors have left me,' said Suleiman, 'I wonder whether they inhabited the same world as we do. And yet it is only about ten years since this abominable law was last invoked.'

Standing gravely before Suleiman, Ibrahim grasped the fronts of his gorgeous dolman with both hands at chest level in the judicial attitude he had sometimes seen Iskender Chelebi adopt, and bowed his head, knowing that no comment was expected or indeed possible. Seven years before his own death Selim had had Suleiman's three younger brothers put to the bowstring, thus leaving the way clear for Suleiman's succession.

To Ibrahim the European this seemed, and had always seemed, the height of barbarism. But all he said at last was, 'It is true we now consider ourselves more civilized, but it is to be remembered that your grandfather Bayezid would have annulled the law had it not been for Prince Djem's rebellion.'

'Is that supposed to be an argument in favour of its annulment?' demanded Suleiman drily. 'Because if so, I don't think much of it. Djem brought the empire to the greatest state of unrest it has ever known.'

Ibrahim smiled. 'I have failed to make my meaning plain, sir. It is, in fact, an argument which can be used against or in favour, just as you will. If you wish it, it is a precedent that can be quoted. Bayezid *did* intend to annul it, whatever intervened to change his mind, and other Sultans *did* ignore it. We have to think of practicalities. If you wish to end this anachronism, now is the time; for the authority of the Sheikh-ul-Islam is what can make or break such a change. The new incumbent, Ibn Kemal, would have reason to be grateful to your majesty, and therefore to look with favour on something so close to your majesty's heart.'

Suleiman stared at him doubtfully. 'You are offering me the means to do what I want, for which I thank you from my heart. But what I really want you to do is to present me with an argument weighty enough to convince me that what I want to do is right.'

Ibrahim only just prevented himself from shaking his head in amazement. What a fellow he is! he thought; no wonder he loves the law!

'This law amounts to the destruction of family life, the warping of each generation through fear and distrust,' he said flatly. 'Consider only what this means, sir. Do *you* believe that "the death of a prince is more desirable than the loss of a province" as was said when the law was first made?'

Suleiman looked at him and then away, his wide grey eyes shadowed and remote. At last he said, 'I can't answer that question. What is a province? A piece of land merely? No, you know better than that! Conquest and loss mean death and misery for thousands of people. But then, to condemn a son or a brother – no, there must be another solution! But I am always aware that we are in the hands of Allah. Ultimately the choice is His and we are only His instruments.'

Ibrahim inclined his head, saying smoothly, 'We are always resigned to His will.' But he was conscious, not for the first time, of a vast impatience with the massive conservatism of the religious law which bound even so well-intentioned and intelligent a ruler as Suleiman. 'But even so, you must make such dispositions as seem good to you, always guided by Him as you are. Let us consider a different approach. For instance, your majesty might name a successor now.'

Suleiman sat down and looked moodily up at him. 'I know, I know. But it is too soon for that. My eldest son is still a child and the second only a baby. Until we can know their quality we cannot decide.'

'Not necessarily,' said Ibrahim. 'In the West, as your majesty knows, a ruler is relieved of this choice. The sword or the throne passes automatically to the eldest son.' He watched Suleiman closely as he said this. As a European he naturally considered the law of primogeniture the most natural and reasonable way of selecting an heir and would have been glad to see his Sultan adopt it.

But after a moment or two of deep thought Suleiman said firmly, 'We see only too plainly to what that principle can lead. We have only to consider my European adversaries. For instance, the King of France, a poltroon whose word no man can trust. The Emperor Charles? Well, perhaps. The Hungarian? Weak and pleasure-loving. Need I go on? No, Ibrahim, I do not propose to evade my responsibility, and when the time comes I will choose as my successor whichever of my sons shows himself the most suitable to rule. And I will be guided by Allah in this as in all things.' He expelled a deep breath. 'And in a little while, whenever we have a new Sheikh-ul-Islam, I will follow your advice and get rid of this infamous law which has caused so much suffering in the past.'

Impulsively he held out his hand to Ibrahim. 'How grateful I am to you, my always reliable friend, for giving me that advice!'

Ibrahim bowed modestly and his smile was wry. Suleiman would have been amazed had he known what was in his Grand Vizier's mind as he rode away from the Palace. A very clever lady, he was thinking; she must have done her work well for his majesty is quite unwilling to consider a succession which does not give her son a chance at the Sword of Osman. And who knows how many more sons she may bear? I must find a way to cultivate this woman.

The daughters and sisters of Sultans were usually married off to senior officers of the army or court, men sufficiently able and advanced in their careers to be able to afford the honour of supporting a royal lady and all the caprice and self-importance with which she might be endowed. But the lucky bridegroom need never flatter himself that he might sire a ruler. The blood royal was not transferable through the female line. If there were those irreverent enough to see the honour as a dubious one, they were silent on the subject. Certainly when, in the spring of the year, Suleiman had to turn his mind to the matter of finding a husband for his younger sister, Kadija, his sole purpose was to confer benefit on the lucky man whoever he might be.

Kadija had quite a lot to recommend her apart from her royal blood. She was pretty, for one thing, which Suleiman's other sisters were not, and she was lively, good-tempered and, above all, biddable. It was therefore with a gratifying sense of conferring honour and pleasure on both parties that he decided to give her in marriage to his good friend Ibrahim.

It seemed to him the perfect solution to more than one problem; he had learned from Khurrem that Ibrahim's first lady was childless and, happy in his own growing family, he grieved for his friend. Naturally, in that heavily male-dominated society, he communicated his decision to Ibrahim before anyone else – to whom it came in the nature of a thunderbolt.

Since he always thought well on his feet he was able to procrastinate long enough to give himself time to weigh up the proposal. His first impulse had been to refuse outright, an impulse which was strangled at birth. He said carefully, 'Sir, I'm overwhelmed and lost for words.' This was more than true. But he was thinking, Muhsine. Great God in Heaven, Muhsine!

Suleiman, almost innocently happy in his sense of doing a good thing for all concerned, smiled at his friend's amazement, which he was sure arose only from a deep sense of gratitude and perhaps a feeling of unworthiness at so profound an honour. He said, 'I'm happy to have deprived you of the use of your tongue for once! But since we have long been brothers in spirit, it seems good to me to make the link a fact recognizable to all.'

Ibrahim bowed automatically. Then it occurred to him that the less he said the less there would be to unsay when he could bring himself to repudiate this unheard-of proposal.

Suleiman went on, still calm, still smiling, 'Kadija is a charming girl. Even I can recognize the fact, and I'm her brother! She's good-tempered, too –' He went on at some length, and Ibrahim, lost in his own tumultuous thoughts, heard very little of it. It seemed to him incredible that anyone so close to him in spirit as Suleiman had always been could sit there and talk this nonsense, remaining unaware of the ferment going on in his own brain. Stop it! he silently implored him, look at me, get me out of this nightmare! But Suleiman was looking at him, and saw nothing except what he expected to see, his normal sensitivity blunted by a very satisfactory sense of doing good. And now Ibrahim's mind was whispering to him, getting to work, calculating the advantages. Ibrahim Pasha Damat, son-in-law of Sultan Selim, brother-in-law of Sultan Suleiman! It was a fitting reward . . .

He heard Suleiman's voice again over the mental and emotional tumult – 'I have thought that the marriage might take place early in the summer. In that way it will mark the end of your first successful year as Grand Vizier.' He rose to his feet and, advancing on his old and faithful friend, embraced him. Ibrahim, paralysed by indecision, looked up into his face and saw that he was deeply moved. He was suddenly intolerable to himself and Suleiman saw his friend's expression change in a way he could not understand. As if he were in agony, he thought wonderingly, as if the simple thing I am doing for him is more than he can bear. What a good fellow he is!

'No doubt you will wish to be alone to come to terms with the new situation. You will have much to do during the next few months, so go now, and we will speak again on the subject in a few days,' he told Ibrahim kindly, and dismissed him.

The Sultan had naturally not expected opposition from Ibrahim and it went without saying that he did not expect it from his own harem either. True, he knew his mother's feelings on the subject of the Grand Vizier, but he also knew that she alone of the senior ladies would be aware of the difficulties involved in finding husbands for imperial princesses. He did not foresee any difficulty from Hafise. He was right in this. True, the interview was not a comfortable or warm one, but she raised no major objections to the match.

Sitting upright, as carefully dressed as ever, she nevertheless looked a little pinched and (did he imagine it?) yellow as she listened to him, nodding her head in a resigned fashion when he had finished. The only thing she said which could be seen as opposition was, 'You realize, my son, that once Kadija is married to – to your friend, her total loyalty will belong to him.'

Suleiman raised his eyebrows. 'But naturally, mother, I would not have it otherwise. Loyalty to Ibrahim is loyalty to me.'

Hafise folded her hands within her sleeves as if she were cold, and said, 'We must see about clothes and jewels for her.'

But Suleiman was not as happy about this as he felt he deserved to be. He would have preferred to see her fly into a rage and smash porcelain as she had been known to do in the past. He did not care to think of his mother's growing old.

Unpredictably, the opposition came from Khurrem. She had recovered satisfactorily from her fever and Hafise and the midwives were pleased with her, but she was not so far gone in dreamy anticipation of childbirth that she did not sit up and stare at him in amazement, crying, 'I never heard of such a thing!'

The old Khurrem would have shouted, 'Have you taken leave of your senses?' but she now had an unsleeping censor in her mind to guard against such outbursts. Even so, it was emphatic enough. Suleiman, sitting at his ease on a divan opposite to her, drew himself up and asked coldly, 'Why not?'

'It would be so cruel to Muhsine! She loves him devotedly!'

Suleiman's expression changed. 'I know,' he said simply; 'I'm not a fool. Some of life's laws are hard for women to bear. She will understand that – better, perhaps, than you can. It is not fitting that a man of Ibrahim's quality should not have children. This is not a subject upon which you and I should quarrel, my Khurrem.'

She saw the danger, but felt there must be something she could do for Muhsine. How could I bear it in her place? she asked herself. She did not know what rules might exist in this sort of situation but feared the worst. 'But what will become of her?' she demanded, and knew when he stiffened and sat silent that she had lighted on something that Suleiman himself found hard to justify. She leaned forward. 'She wouldn't be sent away – he couldn't repudiate her! Oh no, that would be –' She stopped, unable to find words.

'The rule is that a man who marries an imperial princess must put away his other wives,' he told her bluntly.

There was a moment's silence before she said in a small, wondering voice, 'But that is monstrous.' He watched her small face grow tight and pinched with suppressed anger. 'I wouldn't have believed it possible. Her father, how will he feel? It's not as if she were just a slave or anything. She's well-born.'

'That doesn't affect the issue,' Suleiman said patiently; 'or shouldn't.'

Khurrem was wondering what more she could do. Tears, she asked herself, or a show of illness? She wisely decided against either.

The last person to be told, but not consulted, about the Sultan's arrangement was the prospective bride. She was wholeheartedly delighted – the only person, apart from her brother, who was. She had, of course, heard all about Ibrahim Pasha, his brilliance, his good looks, his luxury. She thought complacently that she was doing very much better for herself than any of her sisters.

In the meantime Ibrahim was fighting his own battle. He had left the Topkapi in a daze and had automatically made for his office in the Divan. Before he got there he had found a formula that satisfied him. Like Khurrem, he soon lighted on the problem of Muhsine's future. If he tries to make me put her away, I'll refuse, he told himself. That would be the ultimate barbarity, and I won't do it. He felt great relief as soon as he had formulated this idea, as if the greater betrayal could be cancelled out by refusing to countenance the lesser.

As he sat in his room alone he found himself able to adduce any number of reasons why he should obey Suleiman's command, the first and simplest being precisely that it was the Sultan's command, which could not be questioned or refused, especially when it took the form of a signal honour. He was not very satisfied with that, for he knew perfectly well that Suleiman, his friend, would have understood (or at least accepted) a refusal from him if it had been offered as soon as the proposal was put. The trouble was, he had hesitated too long.

He loved Muhsine devotedly, but things had been getting difficult between them since she had discovered her childlessness. This was not his fault, he told himself. She had become over-sensitive, brooding over the shame and disappointment, and nothing he could say or do made any difference. He supposed there were things he could have done, like forbidding her rabble of elderly female relatives the house; but now it was too late.

He had been totally sincere when he had told her that he was not anxious for children, but the situation was a bit different now. Whatever his private views might be, the fact remained that he was an Ottoman, and Ottomans valued progeny. Even the Sultan had noticed their failure to produce that valuable commodity and was tacitly giving him the opportunity to put the matter right. The more he thought about it, the more he realized how impossible it was to refuse.

He got up and paced. I didn't want to marry, he reminded himself. It had never occurred to me. Why couldn't Iskender – He checked that thought; it was just a little too dastardly. But the sense of grievance, of having been made use of, was still there.

It went into abeyance when he went home and faced Muhsine. Then he felt himself the most miserable and cowardly dog alive and could not bring himself to tell her what he had brought upon them. But he lay awake beside her that night, staring into the darkness, wondering, not how to get out of it, but merely how to tell her. He had opted again for what he could get.

29

If Khurrem had shown unwonted self-control in front of Suleiman, she gave full rein to her anger and concern on Muhsine's account as soon as she was alone. She was appalled at what seemed to her the cruelty and unfairness of the fate that had befallen her friend. At first she gave way to anger against Suleiman for bringing it about, but eventually it became clear to her that the culprit was not her husband but Muhsine's. He had been compliant when he should have been resolute, and so consigned a loving and beloved wife to a lifetime of misery. And no one could do anything about it.

This thought gave her pause. Always practical and resourceful, she now found herself completely baffled. All her frustration was channelled into a flood of love and pity for the victim and she never stopped to think how best to express it, only that it must be expressed, and that as soon as possible.

A message imploring Muhsine to come to the Old Palace was countered by a sad, prim little note saying that she regretted that she was 'too unwell' to visit or receive visitors. 'I should think so, indeed!' stormed Khurrem and ordered her carriage. She descended on Ibrahim's harem like an avenging fury, and the well-trained eunuch kiaya who received her was swept out of her path, although he did his best. The Sultana Hasseki simply said, 'I will announce myself – I know the way.'

Thus it was that she walked into her friend's luxurious reception-room to be confronted by a scene she would never forget.

Muhsine, hands decorously folded in her lap, sat bolt upright on a divan. She had taken care over her dress and her make-up. Indeed, so pale was she that the small amount of rouge and kohl which she normally allowed herself stood out lividly on her cheeks and around her eyes. She was looking at no one but down at her clasped hands, and her long, curling lashes showed very black against her white skin.

Around her were grouped her aunts. There were only four of them, but it seemed to Khurrem's gaze that the room was full of small, shrouded figures, all with their eyes – black like currants, some sly, some malicious – fixed on Muhsine. It looked as if they had been there for some time and were settled for a long stay, for Khurrem saw that they had been provided with refreshments. Indeed, the lady nearest the door, hearing Khurrem's somewhat headlong entrance, had raised her head from the cup of sherbet she was sipping and was staring in surprise at the new arrival.

Muhsine had seen her too and came forward to make her curtsey and lead Khurrem to sit beside her on the divan. The old ladies rose to make their bows and curtseys to the Sultana Hasseki, but seeing her enter immediately into a low-voiced conversation with their niece, felt themselves at liberty to talk to each other. This they did with such freedom that Khurrem, whose hearing was excellent, had no difficulty in picking up snatches here and there.

'My dear, she should never have married him. I knew, the moment I set eyes on him at the wedding –'

'Well, you really can't blame *him*, you know. After all, the honour is very great –'

'Resignation is what she must try for now. What else is there left for a woman in her situation?'

'– devote herself to good works. I know of a sisterhood –'

Khurrem heard all this and more with increasing anger and incredulity while she spoke words of comfort to Muhsine. When she could stand it no more, she whispered to the girl, 'How long have they been here?'

Muhsine pushed the heavy hair away from her face. She said listlessly, 'They came quite early this morning. The aunts haven't much else to do but visit. I don't mind them really, you know. They mean well.'

'No, they don't,' replied Khurrem sharply. She rose to her feet and stood facing the little assembly. She really looked very impressive, and they looked up at her and fell silent quite quickly, fidgeting a little as the Sultana Hasseki's flashing, angry eyes roved over them.

'I think you should leave now, ladies,' she said, with customary directness. 'There's nothing here for you. It is too early for the vultures to gather.'

It took them a moment or two to believe that they had actually heard correctly. Then, Khurrem noted with satisfaction, their going was more like a flight than a departure.

The room was suddenly silent. But after a moment or two Muhsine raised her head and looked around as if she had never seen it before. She said, apparently at random, 'They helped to bring me up, you know.'

'Oh,' said Khurrem. 'Did they? Well, they haven't been much help to you, have they?'

Muhsine flushed. 'If I'd had more courage I'd have broken away from them when –' she swallowed, 'when I was married. I know Ibrahim doesn't – didn't like them coming here so often. I've been foolish in many ways.'

'I shouldn't be so ready to blame myself for misfortune if I were you,' said Khurrem, but felt that that was as far as she could allow herself to go in the face of the girl's manifest misery. She changed the subject. 'Do you think you could sleep a little? You look very tired.'

Muhsine nodded in a lacklustre fashion. 'I am tired. I didn't sleep last night and they were here first thing this morning. Tomorrow –'

'Tomorrow I shall be here,' Khurrem told her vigorously, 'and I shall see to it that they aren't. And I'll stay all day, every day, so long as you need me.'

She was as good as her word, arriving first thing in the morning and leaving just before sunset. Her little victory over the aunts was her easiest task during this unhappy period, during which Muhsine oscillated between periods of icy and unnatural calm and moods of black despair, when she wept bitterly and remembered the happier, early days of her marriage. Indeed, it seemed to Khurrem at these moments as if she was determined to torment herself as much as possible and at first she tried to silence her, until it occurred to her that there was purpose in Muhsine's painful reminiscences. As if she's seeking something, or trying to remember something, she thought wonderingly. I don't understand what she's seeking, but if it helps her that's all that matters.

She was not altogether happy with this facile explanation, however, and arriving one morning to find Muhsine looking rested and brighter in spirits than she had been since the nightmare had begun, Khurrem ventured to probe a little.

'I hope you don't think any more about the things your aunts said,' she began carefully.

'About what?' asked Muhsine. She had a little watering-can in her hand and had been attending to her flowers and plants for the first time in many days.

'About resignation and guilt,' said Khurrem boldly.

'Oh,' said Muhsine and looked away. Presently she said, 'Why do you ask?'

'Because I want to know. It's important for you to put it out of your mind. I want to know that you don't believe any of that nonsense.'

Muhsine turned to look at her. She had gone very pale. After a moment she said softly, 'I try not to, but it's hard to do. I'm barren, and that's something you can't ignore.'

'But that's not your fault!'

'I try to believe it isn't, certainly.' She hesitated, and added deliberately, 'Let me tell you something that may shock you.'

She folded her hands in her lap and proceeded to recount how she had seen Ibrahim riding past her father's house and had fallen in love with him, and how Iskender Chelebi had gone about getting this desirable young man for his daughter's husband.

Khurrem listened with interest, and when she had finished, demanded robustly, 'Well, what's wrong with that?'

Muhsine took a deep breath and said, 'I fight against it, but I can't help believing – I can't forget that if I hadn't – hadn't wanted him, this misfortune wouldn't have fallen on him, well, on both of us. I try, truly I do, but I was brought up to believe –' She burst into tears.

Khurrem seized her by the shoulder, shaking her vigorously. 'You stupid girl,' she cried, 'you are corroded by guilt! Implanted in you by those awful old women and their stupid beliefs. God knows you have trouble enough without believing you brought it on yourself!' For a moment or two Muhsine continued to sob hysterically, but then she controlled herself and, with an obvious effort of will, stopped crying and dried her eyes.

Now Khurrem put her arms around her and began to talk to her as sensibly and sympathetically as she could about the folly of cruel and old-fashioned beliefs, using every argument she was capable of in an all-out effort to rid Muhsine's mind of the varied guilts the old women had implanted in it. Late in the afternoon she had the satisfaction of seeing Muhsine fall quite naturally and peacefully asleep, and decided that she could go home a little earlier than usual. She had come to a rather important decision.

She was in her carriage, waiting to drive out of the palace courtyard, when she noticed a solitary man on horseback, richly dressed and attended by a Spahi escort, waiting in the avenue outside to enter through the gate. A hurried glance told her that this was Ibrahim, and she was glad that he could not see her. As the carriage passed, she noted his air of dejection. When she had last seen him, riding in one of the great processions of the past three years, he had been smiling and gay, bowing and waving to the watching crowds, on the crest of the wave. He looked very different tonight in this unguarded moment at the gate of his splendid palace, so different that she could almost have found it in her heart to pity him; but not quite.

That evening, Khurrem made ready for Suleiman's coming with more than usual care, seeing to it that his favourite dishes were prepared for him and wearing her most becoming robe and jewels. He had done full justice to his supper and was sitting back against his cushions apparently at peace, when he disconcerted her somewhat by saying, 'You're tired, my dear one, and a little strained. Shall we have the musicians?'

'I would rather tell you a story,' she replied.

He looked at her thoughtfully for a moment, and asked, 'Is it a sad story?'

'Very,' said Khurrem steadily, wishing he was sometimes less perceptive.

'I wish you hadn't involved yourself in the Lady Muhsine's affair,' he said after a moment. 'I don't care for you to be distressed in this way, especially in your present condition.' He looked at her serious, determined expression and sighed. 'Well,' he said, holding out his hand to her, 'come and sit by me and tell me what you want me to know.'

Khurrem started at the beginning. She told him how she had

gone to Ibrahim's palace day after day, sometimes finding the unhappy girl in tears, sometimes calm and talking about her former happiness. She told him how, in her total loss of security, Muhsine had wondered aloud whether her father would welcome her back to live with him, or whether he would regard her, as she said, 'as an embarrassment'.

She could see that Suleiman did not like hearing any of this, but he listened nonetheless, without interruption, looking grimmer by the minute. Khurrem, watching his face carefully, went on to tell him how, at the beginning, there had been moments when Muhsine had begged to be told that it was all a nightmare, that Ibrahim was not taking another wife, and that everything would be the same again, 'as it used to be'.

Then Suleiman did stop her, rising to his feet and pacing the room in agitation. 'But this is terrible!' he cried. 'What can be done for her? She is not disgraced – but it did not occur to me –' Presently he added, stopping in his pacing, 'She is guilty of nothing!'

Khurrem did not tell him that she had spent hours attempting to get that fact home to Muhsine. Instead she said patiently, 'Since she is childless, it is nevertheless natural that she should feel so.'

He turned quickly to face her, saying, 'I know, I know! This is the principal reason – but it never occurred to me that it would cause such misery.' He continued his restless prowl, adding, 'Iskender came to see me, too. He is greatly distressed for his daughter. She need not fear that she has lost his love. He will welcome her back to his house with every tenderness.' He continued, with apparent irrelevance, 'He is an old and valued friend and servant. And now you –' He turned round and said gruffly, 'I have to admit I have been somewhat precipitate in this matter.'

To have induced Suleiman to admit to an error in judgement was indeed a victory, but Khurrem was very careful not to show, even by a change in expression, that she was aware of what she had achieved. She said matter-of-factly, 'What will you do?'

He put his hands behind his back and faced her. 'What can I do? It is impossible to recall my word. Indeed, it would be most unfair to Ibrahim to do so. I have conferred a great honour on him, which he well deserves. The marriage must go forward.' He stood still, frowning, and thought. Eventually, he said, 'The Lady Muhsine must retain her status as Ibrahim's principal wife. I am aware,' he added, meeting his wife's eye, 'that that will do little to restore her happiness, but at least it will protect her dignity and satisfy her father. No doubt, also, it will please Ibrahim.'

Khurrem's lips tightened slightly. Let us by all means consider Ibrahim's feelings, she thought bitterly, but did not say so. She suddenly felt very tired, a weariness, she could not help thinking, which proceeded as much from what she had refrained from saying as from what she had actually said in Muhsine's behalf. She had every right to congratulate herself on her victory, but did not feel jubilant.

As for Muhsine herself, Suleiman was right when he said that his decision would not bring back her happiness. He was also right when he said that Muhsine would understand the situation better than Khurrem could. After all, Khurrem was still a European in the secret depths of her emotions, as Ibrahim was still a European just under the skin. Muhsine was grateful to Khurrem for her advice and support, and possibly even strengthened by it. Certainly she behaved with matchless dignity and made things easy for Ibrahim and his new wife. That young lady's happiness was tempered quite a bit when she learned that she, a royal princess, was not to be First Lady of his harem, for she was a fierce young woman with a healthy sense of her own importance. However, on reflection, she decided that to have charge of a harem was really beneath the dignity of a daughter of Selim, and that the arrangement she had was the best one after all.

Ibrahim was deeply relieved when he learned that Muhsine would retain her status in his harem. He did not want to lose her; most certainly he did not want to be put to the test of refusing to marry Kadija if Muhsine were to be put away. Now that the danger was eliminated he never asked himself whether he would have had the strength to refuse the great honour after all. What was the point? After a while he succeeded in persuading himself that probably Muhsine would settle down and accept the situation quite happily after a while. After a few more weeks he began to wonder what the Princess Kadija was like.

Iskender Chelebi, who was a complex man, oscillated

between, as he said, complete understanding of Ibrahim's difficult position, and black hatred of the man who had ruined his daughter's life. As a good Ottoman he disapproved of the latter emotion and tried to repress it, but not with any success.

30

Istanbul in the spring of 1524 was a fitting setting for a royal wedding. It was already a cosmopolitan city; indeed, nearly half the population were foreigners, for when Mehmed the Conqueror took Constantinople from the last Byzantine emperor he entered the city to find it deserted. A city is not a city without people to live in it, so Mehmed took care of the problem by offering 'houses, vineyards and gardens in Istanbul' to anyone who was prepared to come and live there, and had families sent from every province of his empire to settle the place. Many Greeks who had left came back, bringing their Church with them. Later, there were refugee Jews and Moors from Spain, Armenians, and the Serbs whose gallant defence of Belgrade had so impressed Suleiman that, having destroyed one home for them, he had brought them back to Istanbul where they had built themselves another and called it Belgrade. Down by the harbour lived Berbers from Africa and Arabs from the Red Sea, who traded in the luxuries the all-conquering Turks were beginning to regard as necessities – spices, ivory, silks and pearls.

Most of these outland people were as energetic as the Ottomans themselves, working at handicrafts and shopkeeping, and rebuilding, if only with wood and clay, the streets destroyed during the Conquest. But the new city that rose in the midst of the older, Byzantine one was beginning to be beautiful too. Mehmed built two mosques, as well as schools, hospices and a hospital. He tidied up Aya Sophia too and added a minaret. And, of course, he had to have a palace – two, in fact. His establishment grew too big for the Old Palace, so he built the Topkapi.

The city that Suleiman inherited, then, was big and vigorous, with nearly half a million people, the worthy centre of an empire, outward-looking and still hospitable to foreigners, allowing them to follow their barbarous customs so long as these did not conflict with the Ottoman's more demure way of life – and, of course, to trade, since trade was the life-blood of the city. And where in the world was there a splendid covered market like Istanbul's?

Suleiman loved the place, looking upon it as his home. Later, when he found a worthy instrument, a gifted engineer officer named Sinan, he was going to beautify it with more mosques and schools and foundations of all kinds. So far all he had done in this respect was to start the building of a new aqueduct to bring fresh water into the city. He wanted to do a great deal more; in particular in the early summer of this year he wanted to celebrate his sister's marriage to Ibrahim Pasha. He decided to include the city in the wedding festivities, and for nine days all comers would be his guests.

The festival would be held in the Hippodrome and the Sultan himself would be there to welcome his people on each of the nine days. Such festivities were not unknown to Istanbul. Every year, for instance, the guilds put on a spectacle, each guild marching in procession to the house of the Chief Mullah of Istanbul to display specimens of their wares. But the Sultan's spectacle was to outdo everything that had been seen before. Each day was to be given over to a different section of the community, from the Beylerbeys and Sanjak Beys, the governors of provinces and districts, down to the humble army scouts. The Istanbul guilds naturally took part. There were a bewildering number of them, from stonecutters, scavengers and executioners (a prominent and very busy professional body) to salt-beef merchants, horse-jobbers, snow and ice-merchants and the purveyors of slaves. All marched in their characteristic garments and carrying the tools of their trade, to the wild and barbaric music of a multitude of bands. The noise and confusion was incredible. Only one guild did not put on a show for his majesty; they weren't officially recognized anyway, except when they paid a discreet tribute to the chiefs of police. This was the guild of thieves and pickpockets who regarded the festival as a gift from Allah to the furtherance of their business. Although not marching, they were active.

Suleiman presided over all this, sitting in state on a gold divan beneath a silken pavilion. But he did not enjoy his own part very much. It was necessary for him to open proceedings on the first day with a speech, which he did as briefly as possible, speaking in praise of the new Grand Vizier in whose honour, after all, the whole performance had been put on. Then he handed out gifts to representatives of his peoples and sat down gratefully to watch the spectacle, while thousands of his citizens jammed the approaches to the Hippodrome and climbed the trees in order to enjoy, in respectful silence of course, this unusual view of their ruler.

Suleiman was used to being looked at when he rode through the streets about his lawful occasions or when he presided over the Divan or some gathering of learned men. However, the sight of masses of ordinary people, the details of whose lives and thoughts he could only guess at, unnerved him. He sincerely wished them well, did more for their well-being than any other of his house, but could not feel comfortable in their midst. His ruffianly father, who was wont to express his contempt for the common people in the most bloodthirsty terms, would have enjoyed this occasion much more than Suleiman did.

Fortunately for Suleiman, on most days there was something to watch that he could enjoy. Below his magnificent silken pavilion an arena had been laid out where exhibitions of various sports had been arranged to accord with the natural taste of the organization whose day it was. Thus the provincial governors amused his majesty and his guests with a display of that pastime known as the *jirit* or the javelin-chase, which had become so popular as to displace polo as the national sport, while at the other end of the scale the scouts, the akinji, staged a series of horse-races so exciting that the populace forgot themselves and cheered on their favourites with as much enthusiasm as if his majesty had not been present. Not that it mattered; Suleiman enjoyed this exhibition of horsemanship as much as anyone else. Were not his scouts a byword throughout Europe for the speed of their light, Tartar horses and their devastating horsemanship? The French and the Hungarians knew all about that. There were other sports, too, archery and wrestling for instance, which reminded them (if they needed reminding) that their origins lay among the nomads of Central Asia.

There was also food for the mind. The writers and the poets had not been forgotten when it came to arranging the various celebrations. When the arena was not full of horses and their riders or wrestlers or jugglers, there were grey-bearded sages or nervous young men reading their poems in aesthetic competition. Some of these must have been hard for Suleiman to bear, for his own taste was excellent. But he took it all in his stride, presenting prizes of horses from his own stables to some of the lucky winners, as well as silver-mounted saddles and purses of gold pieces. And bearing in mind that he was host to his people, he had ordered that cold fruit drinks should be served to all comers by his own household staff, which delighted the family parties, even if some of the elegant young pages shuddered a little as they pressed snow-cooled cups into eager, grubby fists.

The highlight of the last day was the fighting of mock battles by the janissaries. Not only would this delight the citizens, it was felt, but it would be salutary for the foreign ambassadors who were present, too. The only jarring note was that after it was all over and the Sultan's pavilion was deserted, its gay silk walls rustling in the evening breeze, and all the ambassadors and distinguished guests had ridden off to attend Ibrahim's wedding dinner if they were lucky enough to be invited, the janissaries proved difficult to get rid of. Their Aga ordered them back to barracks as usual, but not all of them went. There was a tendency to hang about the At-Meydan in little groups, murmuring and scowling. All they had to look forward to was another summer of exercises and routine duties. They were getting bored with all that.

Why did Suleiman do it? It was by no means his usual style, and although there were subsequent royal spectacles he never again opted to play such a prominent part in any of them. It was a good idea, certainly, to play host to his fellow-citizens, if only once in his life, and of course it impressed the foreign representatives. If nobody wanted war just at the moment it was perhaps as well to remind all concerned of the slumbering might of the Ottomans.

On the third hill, of course, very different ceremonies and displays were going forward. A wedding was enough, but a royal wedding which was also the wedding of Ibrahim Pasha was something else again. Hafise bestirred herself. She found it difficult to approve of the bridegroom, but he was certainly a desirable husband from the point of view of status and wealth, and Kadija was in raptures. Silly girl, thought her mother, and then controlled her irritation. The girl was entitled to such happiness as she could snatch. After all, the fate of royal daughters was dreary enough. Being a lady of the older generation, one thing she did not hold against Ibrahim was his attitude to Muhsine. The poor woman was barren, therefore a second marriage was fitting – that was the way she summed it up.

So the Sultana Valideh organized the whole thing herself, with the help only of the Kislar Agasi, her own efficient kiaya and a whole regiment of slaves. After a couple of days she began to enjoy the business for its own sake and became lighter of heart than she had been for some time.

As for the bridegroom, his state of mind would have given Khurrem considerable satisfaction had she known about it. He had made his choice, having most carefully weighed the pros and cons, and now expected to be happy. He was anything but. Muhsine had accepted the situation, she was still there in his harem where she belonged, but he was not happy and he did not know why. Clearly, nobody could help him, certainly not his new bride, whatever she might be like. At least, not yet.

Two days before the end of the week of wedding celebrations, Suleiman went to see Khurrem. He was tired after the unaccustomed strain of being in public, 'on exhibition like one of the wrestlers or jugglers' as he put it to himself, but he was not unhappy, was even slightly amused at himself. He found that Khurrem had been established on a wide divan just under an open lattice looking out into the Palace garden. He looked at her searchingly as was his habit, and saw that she was in good spirits, presiding over the comings and goings of her slaves as they laid out the opening courses of a simple meal on a low table.

'Why are you here? What is going on in the garden?' he asked, sitting down without ceremony and seizing a bunch of grapes. 'I'm hungry,' he added, as if this were not self-evident. 'The whole of Istanbul brought its food into the streets today, but I got none of it.'

'It's Henna Night,' said Khurrem. 'All the girls will come

into the garden as soon as it's dark. Look! The slaves are lighting the lamps already.'

It was indeed suddenly dark, except for the glow-worms of light from the lamps the black slaves had brought out and hung in the trees. Presently they heard the music of guitar, flute and drum, though the musicians were invisible as they were sitting on the terrace below Khurrem's lattice. It was a simple ceremony that was about to be enacted, one of those legacies from the remote past whose meaning had been forgotten. Now the bride, her girl friends and younger female relatives were coming out into the garden. At first the sound of their clear, excited young voices was all that indicated their presence, and husband and wife smiled sympathetically at each other in the dim light from their own lamps.

Now the girls began to move away from the Palace along the garden paths, and it could be seen that each girl carried a taper as the trail of tiny flickering points of flame marked their progress through the garden. They were unveiled, each girl dressed in her best, and it seemed to the hidden watchers that, half-seen as they were, their faces – gayly smiling, half-frightened or gravely intent, glimpsed for a moment and then disappearing into the blackness of the night – were lovelier than they would ever appear in full daylight.

The bride led the long, straggling procession as it fluttered and swooped along paths and over grass. They saw the gleam of the jewels at her breast and in her ears, the graceful sweep of her arm as she raised her taper over her head for one moment and called excitedly to those who followed immediately behind her. Then she disappeared, and there was only the pale blur and flutter of silk and muslin, the pinpoints of light from the tapers, to show where she led.

'Peris in paradise indeed,' said Suleiman, half-laughing. He rose to his feet and crossed to the lattice for a better view. But the laughing rustling train of shadowy figures had passed out of sight and out of earshot; the musicians had followed them. Except for the lamps and lanterns in the trees the garden below was now dark and deserted.

'Will they come back?' he asked.

'Presently. They will go all round the whole garden first. Afterwards Kadija will have to go into your mother's reception-room and have her left hand smeared with henna paste, and everyone will give her a gold coin –'

He interrupted her. 'Don't tell me any more. I prefer to remember her and them as I have just seen them. Anything that follows must be an anti-climax.'

Two nights later, Suleiman was present on a very different occasion and in a very unusual guise, for he attended Ibrahim's wedding-feast as a guest; a most unusual honour. There was nothing simple or shadowy about this function. Ibrahim's palace gleamed with gold and precious stones; everything that was not old and priceless was new and superb. Curtains of gold brocade sheathed one side of the entrance-hall, splendid silk of all colours of the rainbow the other. The guests ate from gold dishes. But the greatest magnificence radiated from the host himself. Ibrahim had indeed made his choice, and this evening he was sure it had been the right one. Who else, he asked himself, was honoured by the presence of the Sultan at his wedding-feast? Who else had so splendid a palace in which to do him honour, or so distinguished a train of guests to welcome him? Even the Venetian ambassador himself had openly sought an invitation! Luxury, splendour, and himself a worthy centre for it all. A man must make his choices and be prepared to sacrifice something to achieve them. It was all a question of knowing what one wanted and driving straight to the goal.

Certainly this night saw Ibrahim at his zenith. It delighted him to see his guests both enjoy his hospitality and wonder at it. Offering Suleiman sherbet in a cup cut from a single turquoise, he said laughing, 'Your feasts will never be able to compare with mine!'

Suleiman looked at him, half-smiling, but surprised none the less. 'Why so?' he asked.

'Because I alone of living men have the Lord of Two Worlds as my guest,' Ibrahim pronounced, and laughed delightedly as those within earshot applauded the delicate flattery.

31

While Ibrahim was achieving his ambitions in Istanbul, his rival, Ahmed, was preparing the way to taking power in Egypt, and so, he hoped, settling scores with Suleiman. He had arrived in Cairo in August 1523, still burning with resentment and having learned nothing from the experiences of the past few months. Truculent and arrogant as ever, he was determined that Egypt should provide him with the opportunities denied him in Istanbul, and it has to be admitted that Egypt in 1523 was ripe for the activities of a man looking for power and trouble.

Seven years earlier, Selim the Grim had conquered Egypt, not as part of a deliberate policy of annexation but almost incidentally. At war with his perennial enemy, Shah Ismail of Persia, Selim found himself threatened by Ismail's ally, al-Ghawri, the Mamluk Sultan of Syria and Egypt. No one attacked Selim without regretting it, and in a few months al-Ghawri was dead and Selim was master of Syria and Egypt. After the prolonged campaign of 1516–17, Selim was anxious to return home, but he was not prepared to abandon Egypt which he saw as a bulwark against the Portuguese, who threatened the Red Sea. Having destroyed the Mamluk sultanate Selim decided enough was enough; he was not prepared yet to embark on a programme of Ottomanization. Besides, the Mamluks were a body of tough fighting men who had originated as slave soldiers in the early middle ages, and he may have felt a certain kinship with them. They certainly regarded him, almost with veneration, as a folk-hero. Whatever the reasons, he appointed as viceroy Khair Bey, a Mamluk of the old school and his most trusted collaborator, who served him faithfully (though not without profit to himself) until his death in 1522. While he lived there was no revolt against Turkish authority, but it was questioned soon enough after he died. For this reason Suleiman had decided that the next viceroy should be an Ottoman and had sent Mustafa Pasha to Egypt. Revolt, headed by two Mamluk provincial governors, flared up almost as soon as he got there.

Their reason for rejecting Ottoman rule was interesting; members of the old Mamluk military élite, they relied entirely on their own prowess as fighting men and contemptuously rejected the new military techniques like artillery, which Selim had used to defeat them with such conspicuous success. 'We will not leave the kingdom to these Turcomans,' they said, 'who don't understand cavalry warfare.'

Mustafa, whatever his faults, understood all kinds of warfare well enough to defeat them soundly. But then he was replaced by Ahmed.

The ordinary people of Egypt, the fellahin and the merchants, had no say in the government and, in fact, nothing to do with it except to pay their taxes. The Mamluks governed the country in the name of the Ottoman Sultan, just as they had done since the thirteenth century in the name of the Mamluk Sultans. True, they were not left entirely to their own devices. Selim had left some Turkish troops in Egypt to form a permanent garrison and act as a check on the Mamluks. There were two corps of janissary infantry and two of Sipahis, the élite Ottoman cavalry armed with guns.

To an ambitious and able man Egypt offered a unique opportunity. If he was prepared to accept the status of viceroy of the Sultan in Istanbul his position was demanding and responsible, and if he made a success of it the rewards from a grateful ruler would undoubtedly be great. On the other hand, if he elected to declare himself Sultan of Egypt, he might rise to the heights or meet a swift and nasty death. Ahmed, whose judgement of himself at any time was optimistic, had no doubt of his ability to succeed in the latter role. Indeed, he went to Egypt with no other object in mind.

Suleiman had not allowed him to set out for Egypt alone. He had sent with him Janin al-Hamzawi, a loyal and gifted Mamluk officer who had already had a distinguished career as liaison officer between the court of the Sultan in Istanbul and that of the viceroy in Cairo. Ahmed regarded him with undisguised hostility and suspicion. He had counted on doing as he pleased in Cairo. This inquisitive stranger had obviously been sent to spy on him by the Sultan! It was useless to expostulate with him, or to point out that a man of Janin's wide experience, with his unrivalled knowledge of the complex political relationships of the Egyptian capital, would be invaluable to Ahmed. What did he want with advice on how to treat the Mamluks? If they didn't like what he intended to do, he'd soon deal with them! They were old-fashioned soldiers, were they? So was he! In an access of rage he yelled at the unfortunate Janin that he knew very well what he'd come to Cairo for, and clapped him in jail.

Indeed, once he arrived in the capital, Ahmed's behaviour became increasingly unstable. He had never conducted himself like an ordinary man, was not interested in anything except fighting and gaining power, and had never even thought what he would do with it when he got it. Now, shut away in a foreign country for whose ways he felt contempt, he found himself isolated and forgotten, and yet observed at every turn. He became convinced that Suleiman had sent him away to have him assassinated and that Janin was the chosen instrument of the Sultan's revenge.

Consequently, when the commander of the janissaries of the garrison called upon him, very stiff and correct in his red and blue uniform with the white ostrich plume rising from his turban, and took issue with him about Janin's arrest, Ahmed slumped on his divan of state and regarded him with lacklustre eyes until he realized that this upstart, a mere colonel of janissaries, was actually daring to express disapproval of his actions. At this point he reared up, roared at the janissary commander in a voice which could be heard echoing around the empty state rooms of the viceroy's palace, and then summarily ordered his execution.

Ahmed came briefly to his senses after that sentence of death had been carried out. He knew very well that it would create a scandal and probably get back to Istanbul, but he was beyond caring. He had not come to Egypt to rule the place for anyone's benefit but his own, and there were some among the provincial governors, brutal opportunists like himself, whom he thought he could rely upon. There was also Qadizade Zahir al-Din, a fierce, black-bearded member of the Safawiyya Order. This man was a bit of a mystery. His origins were obscure and he professed strong Sunni religious convictions – that is to say, adherence to the same branch of Islamic belief that was current in the Ottoman empire. But his talk, once he had established relations with Ahmed, began cautiously to reveal something quite different. He talked much, and with approval, of Shah Ismail. When he sensed that Ahmed was not reacting with proper Ottoman horror to these openings, he went further. Shah Ismail would never prove ungrateful for any help that would throw the Turks out of Egypt. The man who achieved that goal for him could expect to be confirmed as Sultan of Egypt. And there was Syria as well to be considered.

Ahmed had burnt his boats with the murder of the janissary commander, whom he now decided had been designated by Suleiman to be his own executioner. More and more of the Mamluks rallied to him, for Ahmed still had a fairly firm grasp of essentials. The land tax revenue had been administered by Ottoman tax-collectors and remitted to the central Treasury in Istanbul. Ahmed turned the tax-collection into fiefs and gave them to his supporters, of whom the most notable was an Arab chief, Abd al-Daim, who ruled the province to the east of the Nile Delta. All this time, too, he had been building up a private army, mostly of Mamluks. Now, dramatically, he went into open rebellion and proclaimed himself Sultan of Egypt by having himself named in the bidding-prayer in all the mosques, and even had his name stamped on the coinage.

There were setbacks right from the outset. The Jewish master of the Cairo mint, Abraham Castro, a faithful servant of the Sultan who knew he had everything to lose at the hands of the Mamluks, fled to Istanbul and informed Suleiman of this open treason; and the janissaries of the garrison, roused to fury by the brutal murder of their commander, entrenched themselves in the Cairo citadel. This impressive fortress, built by Saladin on a spur of Mount Mukattam, appeared impregnable, but there was a subterranean passage leading into the dungeons which was known to some of Ahmed's useful followers and the citadel fell to him.

His most dangerous opponents routed, Ahmed felt that he could afford to give his régime a veneer of legitimacy and called upon the four chief judges of Egypt to recognize him by an oath of allegiance.

At first Ahmed could count upon a certain amount of popular support, since the people could expect more effective government from a Sultan on the spot than from one in Istanbul, but Ahmed had all the qualities of a born tyrant. When the country people failed to pay their taxes, he found other ways of raising money which quickly undermined his rule. He confiscated the property of wealthy merchants and practised wholesale extortion on minorities like the Jews and Christians.

His judgement, never his strongest attribute, had led him to release Janin al-Hamzawi from prison after the murder of the janissary commander, and Janin lost no time in organizing opposition to Ahmed with the support of an Ottoman officer and a loyalist Mamluk grandee. During the last week of February, just six months after his arrival in Egypt, their troops caught up with Ahmed in a bath-house. While Ahmed's few faithful supporters struggled with them, Ahmed, his beard half-shaved and gibbering with rage and fear, fled across the roofs of Cairo.

He was not finished, however. He had always been a good man in a crisis even when it was of his own making, and now, deserted by all except a few faithful followers whose loyalty deserved a better cause, he still managed to escape from the capital and make his way to Sheikh Abd al-Daim in the lands between the Delta and Syria. There, incredibly, he managed to build up a following of Arabs, Circassian Mamluk troops and even some renegade Ottomans. The inducements he offered were brutally direct: freedom to loot Cairo, and, for the Arabs, three years' freedom from taxes.

Meanwhile in Cairo, Janin al-Hamzawi and his supporters had taken over the administration and the command of the army. A general mobilization was proclaimed against Ahmed, who was described as a supporter of Shah Ismail and an infidel (that is to say, whether or not Ahmed had become a Shi'ite it was now safe to call him one). A small task-force was sent to arrest him and failed, so Janin led out a force of 2000 troops equipped with eight cannon against the rebels. Now, at last, came the dramatic news that a thousand janissaries had landed at Alexandria to prove that the news coming from Cairo over the last six months had not gone unheeded in Istanbul. The father and brothers of Sheikh Abd al-Daim urged him to give up Ahmed; a government in faraway Istanbul was one thing, but janissaries on the doorstep were very emphatically another. He did not need much persuasion, but in any case Ahmed's forces were already melting away. Ahmed was caught and put to death. He had succeeded in bringing revolution and disorder to Egypt and death to himself in little over six months. He was the first of several viceroys of Egypt named Ahmed, but he was the only one who earned the additional title of al-Kha'in, 'the traitor'.

The janissaries whose arrival in Alexandria had caused such dismay were commanded by Ahmed's old rival, Mustafa Pasha, who was beginning to know Egypt pretty well by now. He cleared up what Janin and his adherents had left unfinished and returned to Istanbul with Ahmed's head pickled in brine, but his remit had not included bringing order out of the chaos into which the government and administration had fallen. It needed a genius to do that.

32

On the whole, the summer of 1524 was a very happy one in Istanbul. Ibrahim, having married the princess Kadija, found himself very well satisfied with her. She was, he decided, very much his type of girl, small and pretty rather than beautiful, stylish in her dress, about which she thought a great deal, and much addicted to the smooth elegance of silks. She was as ignorant as most well-born ladies, but a mistress of the small-talk of the city. Above all, she delighted in Ibrahim. They speedily came to understand each other very well indeed. And Muhsine? Muhsine fitted in. Whatever agonies she went through when Ibrahim first broke the news to her that he was taking a second wife she had kept to herself after the first anguished outburst of rejected love. For one thing she could not bear to see Ibrahim's own pain when he was confronted with hers. For another, what else was there for her to do, or for that matter, for either of them to do?

As first lady, she directed the household. This suited Kadija once she thought about it. It was all very well to be indignant that she, an imperial princess, daughter of one Sultan and sister of another, should have to rank second to anyone, but assuming responsibility for anything so boring as the discipline of slaves and the choice of food was a different matter. So long as Ibrahim put her first, which he so obviously did, she was not going to complain. So Muhsine went quietly about running the vast palace and bottled up her emotion; over the years it withered, as emotion not used is likely to do. She began to busy herself with charitable matters, endowing a small hospital for women and overseeing much of its work herself. And presently, in response to steadily repeated appeals from Khurrem, she resumed her friendship with the Hasseki Sultana again and found more comfort in it than she had imagined possible. But the lovely blooming girl who had been married to Ibrahim had gone for good and in her place was a grave young matron with watchful eyes and a face already marred by lines and angles where once had been only rounded curves.

The birth of Khurrem's second son was an occasion of considerable rejoicing in the city as a whole, but in court circles it was felt that the Sultan's wife had very definitely become a power in the land. Not only had she done her duty brilliantly by producing three children in as many years, two of them sons, but it was plain to all that her grasp on his majesty's affection was, if possible, stronger than ever. Suleiman's emotion when, as head of the imperial household, he named the new baby Selim after his father was very plain to be seen. And that wasn't all; those in close touch with his majesty had long noted how much time he spent with the Hasseki Sultana, and not just in making love to her, which would be totally understandable since she was said to be a very handsome woman, and a man, especially a Sultan, is entitled to his pleasures. But no, there was more to it than that; much of the time he did no more than talk to her, on all kinds of subjects, just as if she were a man!

Some of the older Slaves of the Gate found this difficult to understand and therefore reprehensible. Here was their Sultan, with access to the most beautiful women in the world, lusty, healthy girls no doubt (and what would some of them not give to have their pick of his majesty's harem!) and all he did was to spend his time talking to his wife!

It was at this time that the whispering about Khurrem began. In an age when good health was always precarious and childbirth fraught with dangers, it was enough for a royal lady to produce three healthy children in a row (and look as if she was capable of going on doing so) for her to be looked at a little askance. What supernatural powers might she possibly have to enable her to do this? When she also triumphantly retained her husband's love at the same time, why, she must be a witch! The men shook their heads and looked knowing, while their wives whispered about the Evil Eye and love potions. Since neither Suleiman nor Khurrem knew anything about this jealous chatter, it did them no harm. But Khurrem's reputation in the West and over the centuries suffered irreparable damage.

That summer, for the first time in his reign, Suleiman allowed himself some relaxation. The only cloud on the horizon was the trouble Arnavut Ahmed Pasha has stirred up in Egypt, but he judged that its seeds had been there already. 'If not Ahmed,' he told Ibrahim sombrely, 'then someone else. My father did not complete the task of pacifying that unfortunate country and hardly made any attempt to provide for its proper administration. Now the people suffer accordingly. Once Mustafa has completed his task there, someone must go out and finish the job.'

Ibrahim agreed wholeheartedly, having a strong suspicion as to who that someone would be. A visit to Egypt would fit in very nicely, he thought complacently. In the spring perhaps, because at the moment he was enjoying himself. There was a good deal of brilliant entertaining that summer, and also there was his new wife. She had whispered that she thought she might be pregnant; in which case a trip abroad early in the new year might be just the thing, because he did not really see himself in the role of devoted husband to an enceinte royal lady. Kadija was enchanting, but occasionally showed signs of that hauteur which distinguished all her family, and he judged it might become hard to put up with in the later stages of pregnancy. It would be a pity to mar their relationship when all he had to do was arrange to be out of the way. Muhsine was the one to deal with all that; no doubt she would enjoy it, and so far as he could judge the two women got on well together.

These were only some of the thoughts on the subject of Egypt that visited Ibrahim's mind after he heard what Suleiman had to say about it. His own interest always came first with him, but that is true of most of us, and the matter of Cairo was one of the first importance. He longed to come to grips with it, and in this he was totally altruistic, except that he wanted to show once more the ease with which he could bring order out of chaos.

However, in the end, despite all Ibrahim's speculations, it was Suleiman who made the final decision, insisting that Iskender Chelebi should accompany him. 'His experience in fiscal matters is unrivalled,' he said firmly. It cast a shadow over Ibrahim's pleasure. He respected his father-in-law, even liked him, was certainly grateful for his help when he had been taking his first tentative steps as Fourth Vizier, but somehow the Defterdar made him feel uncomfortable. It surely couldn't be that the older man resented the business over Muhsine; after all, they were both men of the world and his majesty's edict could not be gainsaid. It wasn't as if he had repudiated Muhsine! No doubt he was imagining things, for Iskender was a very dignified man and did not unbend easily. Also, it had to be faced, they were now to a certain extent rivals for the Sultan's confidence, though that was not a consideration which Ibrahim needed to take too seriously.

At the start of their journey they had Suleiman's company, for as an unrivalled compliment he accompanied their vessel in his flagship from the Golden Horn as far as Buyuk Ada, the Great Island, the largest of the Princes' Islands in the Sea of Marmara. After all, their mission was of tremendous importance, not only to the empire's revenues but also as an earnest of the importance the Sultan placed on the safety and freedom of his Egyptian subjects. Let it fail and Egypt could still be lost. And it was Ibrahim's first independent enterprise, therefore his majesty's full support for this most brilliant of his servants must be seen.

Escorted by five thousand janissaries, they travelled without undue haste; pressing though Egypt's need might be, they had other duties as well. Ibrahim visited Aleppo and Damascus and stopped to spread a little fear among the governors of these cities, who had, as was the way of governors when they could get away with it, been poaching the Sultan's revenues and neglecting his justice.

At last, on 24 March 1525, Ibrahim rode into Cairo. The occasion being what it was, he chose to ride a splendid Cappadocian horse from Suleiman's own stables, saddled and bridled with gold-inlaid leatherwork worth 150,000 Venetian gold ducats, Suleiman's parting gift. He rode alone, surrounded by his pages who were clad like the Sultan's in cloth-of-gold, with a detachment of Sipahi cavalry carrying his house banners, blue and white in colour (the colours of Greece, proudly flaunted; no wonder they called him Frenk Ibrahim). Among the five thousand janissaries who followed in his train was Sinan the Spearhead.

Iskender watched all the ceremonies, the fetes and the bestowal of robes of honour with narrowed eyes and a heart full of hate. Let him go wrong, he prayed, let him waste his time in this senseless extravagance and everlasting exchange of compliments. This place could be the end of him; one little thing would be enough to start the blaze. But Iskender was soon compelled to admit to himself that not only did Ibrahim know what he was about, he was prepared to give unsparingly of his time, of his undoubted ability and his powers of persuasion. Indeed, it seemed that his personal magnetism might be, after all, his greatest gift. Apart from his good looks, the way his black eyes smouldered and his body tensed eagerly under the superb brocade robes (and how Iskender hated those robes and the long fingers loaded with rings!) when he emphasized a point in argument, seemed to be irresistible. Iskender even felt it himself. And talk! There was certainly no one like him for that. In no time he had the Arabs and the Mamluks in the hollow of his hand.

Ibrahim was not soft, either; he knew how to put first things first. And the first thing was to catch those traitors who had aided Ahmed and had slipped through Mustafa's net when he descended on the country like a whirlwind. Several Mamluk and Arab chiefs were caught and publicly hanged, putting the fear of God into the Egyptians. But having frightened them he then soothed them, receiving petitioners in person. Three hundred debtors were released from prison at one fell swoop and their debts paid by the Treasury. Nothing, it seemed, escaped Ibrahim's inquisitive, probing eye, not even the education and upbringing of orphans, of whom there were, after all the recent troubles, an inordinate number in Cairo. So he drew up a body of rules for their care. Bearing in mind the preoccupation of Suleiman his master, he took care about the re-establishment of the law, both local and Koranic, but with a sensitivity most unusual for his time he varied and moderated them to suit local needs and prejudices. In this way he underlined the rule that the Sultan's justice was equal in all parts of his empire.

But of all the work done in that crowded three months in Egypt the most important was that undertaken jointly by Ibrahim and Iskender to reform the tax system. Iskender first worked out the value of the revenue which the province could afford to pay over to Istanbul, then he and Ibrahim worked out the means of collecting it.

Ibrahim, the leader, the talker, persuaded and cajoled the

local officials into accepting their findings. He was totally happy and fulfilled in the work he was doing and totally unaware of the black malignity which filled the heart of the quiet man who shared the task with him. Indeed, egotist that he was, he felt nothing but admiration and gratitude for his able father-in-law.

There was generosity as well as good business. Tax concessions were made to encourage the farmers who had fled in the wake of violence to return to their land; and buildings and irrigation systems destroyed at the time of Selim's conquest and during Ahmed's revolt were rebuilt or repaired. Every effort was to be made to restore normal life.

In particular Ibrahim was absorbed by the restoration of some of the historic buildings of Cairo which had been allowed to fall into disrepair. He also built new ones at his own expense, for the erection of mosques and schools was, after all, an act of piety, and while Ibrahim might find piety itself beyond him he had no objection to being seen to obey the letter of the law. Indefatigable as ever, he filled such spare time as he had with sight-seeing. He only wished he could persuade his father-in-law to unbend a little and join him. But it was useless; Iskender would go nowhere with him. He smiled his tight smile and shook his head, saying only, 'My young friend, I am older than you and my pace slower. This heat exhausts me.'

On a visit to the citadel, Ibrahim was pleased to see engineer janissaries at work repairing the place, restoring the walls and fortifications. Quite apart from military prudence it was good public relations; they must never miss an opportunity to underline the benefits to be gained from Ottoman rule. He made a point of saying as much to the high-ranking Mamluk officer who was his guide.

His party passed on and came at last to the council chamber of the Mamluk Sultans, the Divan-i-Kebir. There were more engineers at work here, and obviously this was a slower operation involving more skill and patience than the heavy work on the walls. Ibrahim was delighted, assuming his most charming smile and prepared to enlarge on this further evidence of Ottoman efficiency and care. The smile became broad and sincere when he recognized the huge back and shoulders of the janissary sergeant in charge of proceedings.

'Sinan abdur Mennan! My dear fellow, how very pleased I am to see you again!'

The giant turned slowly, stiffening to attention as he saw the large gathering of distinguished persons, high-turbaned and gorgeously robed, behind him. It may be that his face assumed the slightly dogged expression of the true professional about to be harried by important amateurs when he first looked at them, but it cleared when he recognized Ibrahim. He smiled broadly and bowed with real reverence.

'And what goes forward here? I see that the walls are stripped to the plaster.' Ibrahim stepped forward and stared upwards. 'What were the walls faced with, and what are you doing to them?'

Sinan's vast hand swept up to his moustache and he twisted it. Finally he said, non-committally, 'I cannot tell your excellency what the original facings were; I'd guess they were fine marble, but they're gone now - looted, I suppose.' His eyes sought the ceiling.

Ibrahim's fine dark eyes narrowed thoughtfully. He glanced at his guide and observed that his face wore a somewhat bitter-sweet expression. Finally he said carefully, 'Alas, yes. Much that was beautiful has disappeared from our city and will never be seen again.' Ibrahim quickly changed the subject. 'And have you been able to visit some of the mosques and public buildings? What do you say to the domes, eh, Sinan? They'll teach our builders something, will they not?'

'Yes, sir, they will.' Sinan still seemed to be labouring under a constraint. He evidently felt that his response had been inadequate and added, 'Architecture depends on surroundings. What looks fine here might not seem so well in Istanbul. A bit more discipline does better there, I fancy. With respect, sir.' He gave a sideways glance at the Mamluk officer.

'I shall tell his majesty that I have had this unexpected pleasure, Sinan,' Ibrahim said in farewell, and glanced at his secretary to make sure that that overworked personage made a note. He went thoughtfully on his way. Who would have thought that his enormous protégé united so much tact with his other attributes?

The time came when Ibrahim saw the missing marbles from the citadel. They had been removed at the command of the great Selim when he entered Cairo in 1517, and they reappeared in the walls of the Pavilion of the Prophet's Mantle in the Inner Courtyard of the Topkapi when it was built a couple of years later.

The mission left Cairo in June, their work triumphantly completed. Ibrahim's last act in the city was to appoint a governor, selecting for the post the candidate who seemed to have the most economical turn of mind. Generosity was needful at times, but prudence has its points, too. He took with him a large sum in gold to be paid into the imperial Treasury. The journey back was intended to be as carefree and leisurely as had been the outward voyage, but the mood of triumph and holiday was rudely shattered by an urgent message from Suleiman. There was trouble in Istanbul; they were to come with all speed.

33

'Each man files past the Aga holding the tail of the tunic of the man in front of him. The Aga gives each one a blow in the face and pulls his ears,' Hulefa's janissary brother paused, not for breath, but to take aboard a huge mouthful of pilaff. He masticated stolidly while Hulefa ladled more food on to his flap of bread and produced that small grunt of contempt with which women of all lands and all ages have been wont to greet what they regard as evidence of masculine stupidity.

'What on earth for?'

'To teach them obedience, woman,' growled Kasim. He cocked a hungry eye at the bountiful pot she held between her hands. 'Some more rice and a few of those peppers perhaps. Your lady spreads a good table.'

'My lady would have my throat cut and my body thrown into the Bosphorus if she knew where her food was going at this moment,' responded his sister, vigorously serving rice and peppers as directed. 'No, she wouldn't, she'd look the other way and pretend she hadn't seen a thing. That seems an idiotic way to teach anybody anything. Why not just tell them?' she added, reverting to her previous remark.

'Because recruits are recruits the world over, and each lot is dimmer than the lot before. They have to be shown before they can be told. Besides, at the moment there are so many of them there literally isn't time to lecture them. The barracks is bursting with country bumpkins in new tunics getting their first look at the big city. Nothing but misdirected energy and silly questions! "What shall I do with this, corporal? When do we get paid, corporal?" I ask you! Done nothing yet but cost his majesty money and they want to know when they're getting ıd!' He tidily swallowed the last of his bread, and sat back eplete. 'Ah-h! Best meal I've had in days, sister.'

Brother and sister occupied a small kitchen, intended for the preparation of light refreshments for the senior ladies of the harem by their own slaves. At this time of the day as Hulefa well knew it was deserted, and a very useful place to which one could bring a pot of food for a hungry brother and reheat it. Hulefa did it quite often, for Kasim was quartered in At-Meydan and could slip in to see his sister whenever he was free. His presence in the Old Palace was highly illegal and could, in theory, lead to disgrace or death for both Hulefa and Kasim should it be reported. But then Hulefa was an institution; a bit of a bully and ready with a quick slap if a girl didn't do her work properly, and equally ready to stand by her with a quick excuse to the kiaya or a kind word if she got into trouble. She was influential, too, as Khurrem Hasseki's personal slave, but this hadn't made her forget her origins. So the harem as an entity approved of Hulefa and her smart, well-set-up janissary brother and said nothing about these visits. Some of the younger girls thought Kasim very good-looking and managed to be hanging about the corridors when he slipped in and out – which amused him, but did not go to his head. As he said, but not to Hulefa, 'A fellow knows when he's on to a good thing and doesn't spoil it. Besides, when I want a bit of muslin I know where to go.'

Today he seemed in no hurry to go anywhere. It was a cold afternoon with a wind straight from the steppes of Siberia raging across the city. Hulefa glanced at her brother unsmiling, felt in the folds of her wide belt and produced a small paper-wrapped packet which she dropped into his lap. He unwrapped it eagerly. 'Halva!' he exclaimed with delight, and bit into the crisp, rich sweetmeat. 'Good!' he commented when he had finished it, 'and a very nice end to a very nice meal.' He nodded approvingly at his sister. Characteristically, neither smiled. They were not demonstrative. The strong, bold features which were good looks in Kasim, and only heavily striking in Hulefa, proclaimed their relationship, as did the down-to-earth plain speaking in which they both indulged. Hulefa said, 'Good! I should think it is, made in our kitchen for his majesty no less. He's very partial to it.'

'Glad we've got something in common, then.'

Hulefa frowned and glanced quickly at him. 'Something wrong?'

'No. Should there be?'

'I thought you sounded a bit fed-up just then, that's all.'

Kasim rubbed a large capable hand around his impeccably shaven chin. 'I don't know,' he said, glanced round the room, sighed, rubbed his chin again, and repeated, 'I don't know, I'm sure.'

'Well, if you don't know, I'm sure I don't.' His sister stacked crockery vigorously. She looked at him again and added, 'Come on, something's worrying you.'

Kasim rearranged his legs in search of a more comfortable position. When he finally did speak, the words came out with a rush. 'I wish we could get a bit of action, that's all!'

Hulefa put down a pot and looked at him carefully.

'There are thousands of these kids, trained up to the ears, in barracks all over the city. We don't know what to do with them, they don't know what to do with themselves! They've got no money, the weather's bloody, they've been promised the earth, and what do they get? Barrack life in Istanbul, that's what!'

Hulefa scratched her head through her veil. 'I thought you always said recruits are all the better for being dissatisfied. Gives them a bit of steel.'

'So I did, and so it does, and it's good when they've got a campaign to look forward to. But have they? That's what I want to know, that's what we all want to know! And the only person who does know is his majesty and he isn't saying. Suppose he's waiting for that Greek so-and-so to come back from Egypt and tell him!'

'That will be enough of that sort of talk,' Hulefa told him crisply. 'If you knew his majesty you'd know nobody tells him what to do.'

'Yes, I suppose so. But I tell you I'm worried! The men grumble. Of course they do; if nothing happens this spring it'll be three years since Rhodes, and we got nothing out of that. It's not what we're used to.' He looked up at her, his manner as reasonable as if he were explaining a point to one of the recruits, and this very calmness was more worrying than his previous vehemence. 'The chaps talk openly about what they'd like to do if there isn't a war. That would be bad enough, but with all these youngsters about, not dry behind the ears yet – I tell you, sister, I don't like it.'

Hulefa could not disguise her concern. 'What are you talking about? You sound as if you really expect trouble! How bad is it?'

Kasim cursed his ready tongue. 'I don't *expect* anything. I don't *know* anything! It's simply a bad atmosphere. The men are discontented and they talk too much in front of these kids who're all dying for an opportunity to prove they're men. The rest of us have been cooped up too long doing nothing. We want action and we want money. Now, as like as not, the really unstable characters will work themselves up one of these nights, loot a shop or two, beat up the watch and anyone else who gets in the way, and that'll be their lot for the time being.'

He thought about it for a moment and added, 'With any luck.'

'And without any luck?'

He shrugged. 'It hasn't happened for a long time, not since I joined the corps anyway. One night when they can't take any more, they'll upset the cooking-pots over the fire – you've seen 'em, sister – let their food run to waste or burn. Then, as you know, that's a signal to the Sultan and each other that they've had enough. Then they go on the rampage – riot, pillage, murder!' He broke off when he saw her expression. 'Look, I'm frightening you, and for no good reason. Anyway, if anything were to happen you'd be all right, guarded like you are in this place!'

'I can see that'd be a help,' replied his sister stonily. 'And what will his majesty be doing while they're doing all that?'

'Well, there you are, you see, we don't know,' responded Kasim in the same tone. 'We don't know this Sultan like we knew the old one. Keeps himself more to himself.' He lapsed into thought for a moment and then came to his feet, his wide leather belt creaking. He picked up his wicked-looking dagger and thrust it into place through the belt, stretched, and pulled down his tunic. Hulefa, watching, suddenly saw him as a stranger for a moment – a dangerous, heavily-armed stranger. If she felt any impulse to shudder she easily repressed it, but Kasim, picking up his dark blue woollen cloak, looked at her uneasily. 'Now you're not to worry about what I've said,' he told her, roughly protective. 'I thought it right to warn you, but just because I warn you it doesn't mean anything's going to happen, right? See you three days from now, same time?'

Hulefa, having opened a small inconspicuous door and watched Kasim slip quickly and quietly through the heavy shrubs on that side of the Palace garden, gathered up her pots and spoons and made her way swiftly through the corridors to a small room at the front of the building, from whose window she could survey the main gate. This was her invariable practice, to make sure that he got away without being stopped and questioned by the guard. Presently she saw the smart, well-knit figure of a janissary corporal of the 67th orta appear outside the gate, stop as if he had all the time in the world and exchange a few words with the sergeant of the guard. She saw the two men laugh, watched the janissary step aside and swing his heavy cloak around him, and then walk off twirling his moustaches. 'Impudence!' muttered Hulefa to herself and permitted herself an affectionate smile.

Back in the apartments of Khurrem Hasseki Sultana, however, she relapsed into more than her accustomed gravity as she thought about all her brother had said. Grave news it certainly was, if it was to be believed. Kasim was not the sort of man to indulge in drama for the sake of impressing his womenfolk. She wondered what she ought to do. The possibility of danger was hard for her to visualize. Although a slave, she was protected, well-cared-for and happy; the worries of everyday life for ordinary citizens hardly touched her. Even if there was trouble, she thought, it would hardly reach us here, so well guarded as we are, and not by janissaries either but by his majesty's Spahis outside and the black eunuchs inside. The idea that danger threatened Khurrem Hasseki and the Sultana Valideh was unthinkable and she expelled a sigh of relief. Besides, there was his majesty. Would he be planning to go off to Edirne again for the hunting if he thought there was the slightest danger? To anybody who knew him the idea was impossible. Hulefa, always practical, spotted Khurrem's robe on the mattress where she had carelessly thrown it, and began automatically smoothing and folding. Suddenly she said aloud, 'All the same it wouldn't do any harm just to say a word in passing. I'd feel easier.'

Suleiman was indeed planning to go hunting, was in fact ready to go. He loved the chase, loved being in the open air in the company of like-minded men, free for a while from the day-to-day worries which were his constant companions while he remained in the city. Hunting was always followed by deep, dreamless sleep and for a while he would be totally carefree. He couldn't wait to get away. But he was not irresponsible. He knew that this spring would be the last for some time when the war-drums would not sound, and he determined to make the most of it. He had talked to the Aga of the Janissaries, cross-questioning him about morale and the state of recruitment, and had received reassuring answers. A more experienced Sultan might have preferred to rely on his own judgement, for the present Aga was a sanguine man who was looking forward to retirement. Of course the men were a little restless, he told his Sultan, but he had taken care of all that. He had organized a really gruelling programme of training for the spring, and that would give them no time to worry about imagined grievances. He smoothed his grey moustache and his eyes glistened in anticipation as he thought of the month of good hunting in front of him. For of course, like last year, the Divan and all the chief officers of state were also going on the expedition.

'You are sure?' Suleiman pressed him.

'Sir, would I leave the city myself if I thought there was the slightest danger?' The reply had been prompt and confident and Suleiman had been satisfied.

Now Suleiman found himself in a carefree holiday mood. At first after Ibrahim's departure he had missed his friend and the nightly informal exchange of confidences. But the absence of even the most beloved friend and companion tends to have its compensations. Ibrahim was brilliant, no mistake about it; he was also restless, vigorous, and always in a hurry to get things done. He quite often went a bit too fast for his royal master who liked to take his time about decisions, and as he grew older was increasingly given to introspection. Suleiman found that he rather enjoyed taking up again some of the governmental tasks which he had delegated to his Grand Vizier and dealing with them at his own pace and in his own way.

There was also the fact that he could see more of Khurrem, returning to his old custom of having supper with her at the Old Palace and finding it a wholly delightful experience. Moreover, he had fallen easily into the habit of discussing affairs of state with her; it soon became a perfectly natural process.

He did not (it would never have occurred to him) compare her with Ibrahim. But during these few months he became aware that the quality of her mind did in some way complement his own as Ibrahim's did not. Which, he thought, is quite right and proper. Ibrahim is a highly gifted man, decisive and bold in all he does. He is nobody's complement, and I begin to be aware that he and I could on occasion be at cross-purposes. Which, indeed, is right and healthy. But Khurrem is an extension of myself, and my thinking is reinforced and deepened by hers. This, in addition to everything else she gives me.

So the six months of Ibrahim's absence had been remarkably peaceful and happy, and it was in Suleiman's mind to do something - something simple and unpremeditated - which would please his wife and at the same time show the reliance he placed upon her. He did not have to strain after an idea; it came to him easily when he remembered how she had sometimes expressed a wish to visit the Topkapi again. She had only been to his quarters there on one occasion: the night, never to be forgotten, when she had been brought there four years ago for his imperial pleasure for the first time. Well, she should come there again. His hunting-party was to leave the royal stables in two days time, and Khurrem should come to the New Palace and watch their departure. Moreover, there was something else he wished her to see.

Thus it was that on the morning of Suleiman's departure, Khurrem was in a state of high and pleasurable excitement as her maids dressed her and not really in the mood to be receptive of sombre warnings about the future.

Hulefa, too, had taken her time about things. Deliberate as always, she did not rush to confide in Khurrem. The opportunity must be right, and she had to be very careful what she said. Too much would get Kasim into trouble; not enough and her mistress would think she had taken leave of her senses. So she allowed a whole day to go by and suddenly found herself confronted with the news that his majesty was leaving the very next morning and that Khurrem Hasseki required to be called and dressed two hours earlier than usual so that she could go to the Topkapi to see the hunting-party depart.

Angry with herself, all the more because her usual prompt

efficiency had deserted her, Hulefa resolved to come out with her story without further delay. Her mistress's good-humoured drowsiness was no help. She sat on the edge of her mattress brushing the heavy red-gold hair from her eyes and yawning. 'I always promised myself,' she said between gapes, 'that when I was a kiaya I would never rise early again. Well, here I am Hasseki, and still doing it!'

'But not very often,' murmured Meylisah, slipping a warm shawl round Khurrem's shoulders.

Khurrem blinked and rubbed her eyes. 'Just think,' she said, 'his majesty says they rise even earlier when they're in the hunting-field. How odd men can be, to be sure!'

Hulefa looked at her. She had made a quick recovery after the birth of Selim and had never seemed more vital or more lovely. It was unthinkable that anyone so much loved and so triumphantly herself should be put at risk. She repressed an impulse to fling herself at Khurrem's feet, pour out her story and burst into tears. Stony-eyed, she stood in front of her mistress and stared ahead.

'I'll have my tray now,' said Khurrem, 'then perhaps I'll feel warmer. Hulefa! I said I'd have my – Hulefa, is something wrong?'

Recalled to herself, Hulefa automatically knelt down and laid the tray of rolls, olives and jam across her knees.

'How lovely, hot soup!' murmured Khurrem. Then she raised her eyes and looked closely at her maid. 'Hulefa, something *is* wrong. Tell me!'

Hulefa clenched her fists and came out with it, baldly, 'I want to warn you, madam. There is trouble on the way – the janissaries are discontented, they might –'

Khurrem put aside the tray and said, more sharply than she intended, 'Did your brother tell you this?'

'Oh no, madam!' She managed to say it so positively that Khurrem, after a quick glance at her, was satisfied. Hulefa never lied, and besides, why should she? She can rely on me not to give her brother away, reasoned Khurrem, who had forgotten or perhaps never known that ultimately slaves never really trusted their owners; especially not when the life of someone beloved was in the balance. Thus Hulefa's judgement was tragically at fault. Khurrem would have taken her warning very seriously had she known its origin.

As it was, she said, 'Where did you hear about this?'

'In the Spice Market, madam, the other day when you sent me for ambergris.' Hulefa listened to the lies rolling off her tongue in something like despair. I've ruined everything, she thought.

Khurrem's eyes narrowed, but she picked up her tray again and began sipping soup. Then she said, 'Well, but all rumours start in the bazaars, everyone knows that. Are you sure your brother hasn't heard anything? He'd be the man to know what's going on.'

Too late Hulefa realized her mistake and tried desperately to rectify it. She began, 'Well, he did say something –'

Wheels crunched in the courtyard below and there was the sound of hooves. Khurrem flew across to look out of the window. 'Allah askma!' she gasped. 'Here's the carriage and the escort and I'm not even dressed. Hulefa, we'll have to talk about this when I come back!'

34

Khurrem was getting quite blasé about taking to the streets. Why, sometimes she left the Old Palace as often as twice a week! But this, of course, was an unusual occasion; except for two rooms, she had never seen any part of the Topkapi, and she had been far too emotionally concerned and excited on that previous occasion to look about her. Still, she remembered her dignity. She certainly stared as she was driven through the Bab-i-Humayun, the Imperial Gate, and across the wide First Court, but was careful to sit well back against the seat with her veil carefully adjusted. Anyone so ill-mannered as to glance into the carriage as it passed would see nothing but the shadowy figure of a lady well wrapped up against prying eyes and the cold.

The Second Court was something else again. Once through the Ortakapi, the Central Gate, Khurrem simply had to crane forward and gasp. She had an impression of fountains, their water crystal against the pure early morning sky, of slender cypresses and a golden roof barred with turquoise and topped with a gilt crescent. Then the carriage passed under a portico and stopped. A moment later she was walking through an imposing doorway in the wake of a personage whose vast turban seemed to extinguish such face and features as he might have. He preceded her, bowing low and walking nimbly backwards, into the most impressive room she had ever seen in her life. She had only a moment in which to get an impression of jewel-set gold enamel, of a wide red divan extending all round the walls, before Suleiman appeared from behind a screen and advanced swiftly towards her, smiling in welcome, his low turban and plain hunting-dress providing an odd contrast to the splendid surroundings. Except for her guide, rapidly effacing himself backwards through a door on the right, they were alone.

Khurrem made a deep reverence. She felt that not only her husband's rank but this place demanded it of her, and as she looked up she saw that Suleiman had understood her motive and approved her action. He took her hand, saying, 'I thought you would like to see the Hall of the Divan. My quarters you can visit any time, but the Divan is seldom empty as you see it this morning.'

Khurrem was a little disappointed. She had always wanted desperately to be able to identify herself with his life when he was away from her and it would have pleased her to see his rooms and be able to visualize him against his background. But he had said, or implied, that she might come to the Topkapi again, and he never did anything without a motive even if he was not always very good at expressing himself in words. So he had brought her here with a purpose. She looked round the splendid place, admiring its beauty but both daunted and disappointed by the quiet and emptiness. She said suddenly, 'It must be very different when all the councillors and officers are here. How I should like to see that!'

That was not the right thing to say, she divined at once. A woman to see the Divan in session, whatever next! But to her surprise he neither laughed nor quelled her with a cold look, he only said seriously, 'Why not? Some day. See, this is where I sit,' and he pointed to a gold-covered divan segregated behind an imposing gilt screen. Khurrem dutifully looked but could think of nothing to say although she tried desperately. It was beautiful but only a room.

Incurably truthful, she said, 'It doesn't feel like the seat of power.'

She saw him glance at her quickly but it was a moment before he replied, 'It isn't. I am the seat of power. You know, that is what I hoped you would say. I think that sometimes you feel you are excluded from what is important in my life and that the time I spend with you is merely an interlude. This is not so.' He glanced up at walls for a moment almost disparagingly – almost, thought Khurrem, as if he despised the place – and went on, 'Important work is done here, yes, all the administration, and law suits are heard and money granted – but the power, the real power which sets it all in motion, which decides on peace or war, life or death, is mine and mine alone. And I am only what those whom I love and trust make of me. Of those you are paramount, my Khurrem.'

She was lost for words, wanted to cry and clamped her jaw against the tears, finally looking up at him with wide but dry eyes.

He took her hand and she thought he was going to lead her out of the Divan building, his purpose accomplished, but instead he led her out of the Hall and through an inconspicuous door at the rear. She found herself facing a tiny flight of marble stairs. Suleiman's hand under her elbow impelled her forward, and in the dim light she heard him say, 'Come, there is something else for you to see.' His voice was different now, matter-of-fact and carefree. The stairs were narrow but easily climbable. They gave on to a tiny room whose only light came from a small window on the far side. 'Go and look out,' said Suleiman. She did so, and found herself looking down into the Hall of the Divan. She could see everything. Anyone who sat or stood where she was would have an unparalleled view of everything happening below.

She turned to him and asked, 'And can you hear as well as you can see?'

Suleiman laughed and said, 'That's my practical Khurrem! Yes, you can. Moreover, anyone sitting at this window is invisible from below. My great-grandfather, who always thought of everything, built this. He, too, seems to have tired of the interminable sessions of the Divan and did not want always to waste time on it. So he had this little place built. His idea was that he could slip in here occasionally and watch what went on without anyone knowing he was here. Only he took care to let the Council know that he intended to do this from time to time. In that way, he reasoned, they would be impelled always to conduct themselves as if he were present!'

Khurrem considered this and said, 'I can see they would. Do you ever come here?'

'I have never done so, so far. And with Ibrahim as Grand Vizier it really is not necessary. But –' he paused thoughtfully, 'who knows? I do not intend to cut myself off entirely, that would not be right.'

Khurrem bent forward and looked down into the Hall

again. Suddenly the thought of the wily Mehmed craning down to watch his viziers and councillors seemed to bring the Divan to life for her. She imagined the pompous gentlemen on the red divans discussing and gesticulating, each with one eye on the little window. Suleiman watched her, smiling. He said suddenly, 'You would like to see it, wouldn't you?'

She stared at him, and he added, 'Well, why not? You are part of it, after all.'

Outside, he said, 'The time has come for me to leave you. Will you take me in your carriage to the stables? It is only a short distance, and you will be able to see everything.'

She sat silent beside him on the short journey, and when the noise of baying hounds, the shouting of commands and the sound of hooves told her they were nearing the stables all too soon, she said suddenly, 'I had so much I should have said to you and now it's too late, but thank you for bringing me here and – and –' Something perilously like a sniff escaped her and she stopped. Suleiman pressed her hand firmly and warmly and said, 'I shall be back in a month, my Khurrem, and this is only your first visit. If I stop the carriage here you will be able to see the cortege ride off. Look! There go the hunting leopards – aren't they splendid?'

She knew that he was talking to give her a chance to control herself. With an effort of will she checked her tears for the second time that morning and stared dutifully out of the window at the handsome spotted cats as they passed, straining at the leashes held by the huntsmen and almost dragging them along. And there was, she saw, so much more to look at. Superb horses, and the falconers with the hunting-eagles that Suleiman loved, and all the gay, colourful crowd of courtiers and soldiers, all talking and laughing (for there was here none of the silent respect accorded a Sultan on ordinary occasions) and all impatient to be off! And she was happy, happier than she had ever been before in her life, so why was she keeping him beside her when he ought to be gone, when, if she was honest, she could see he was as eager to set out on his holiday as the rest of them? 'You mustn't make them wait any longer, and oh, I hope it will be splendid hunting!'

As she smiled so did he. He waited long enough to say, 'I will bring you an egret's plumes,' and then was gone.

He had thought of everything. Her carriage had been

discreetly positioned in the stableyard so that she would be able to see the whole brilliant company move off without herself being too much in evidence. But although she dutifully stared out at the horses, hounds and men, all she saw was Suleiman. She watched him mount with typical lithe control and turn in the saddle, laughing, to speak to one of his companions. She thought she had seldom seen him so high-spirited. He looked well-rested, younger, than at any time since Rhodes. The harsh lines that experience had etched from nose to mouth, and the grim set of his mouth itself, were all relaxed. She smiled involuntarily and watched him until he disappeared in the direction of the stable gate. When he had gone she relapsed into her own thoughts and barely noticed anything else.

It seemed to her that she had done none of the things she had so confidently promised herself to do to fit herself for her position, or what she saw as her position. She had not studied hard, she had not even been successful in her attempts to influence Ibrahim Pasha or any of the other influential men in government. She'd had her little successes, but really she had to face the fact that she wasn't much of a schemer; she wasn't cold-blooded or unscrupulous enough. But still, thanks to Suleiman's generous love, she and her little family had come through so far. She had much to be grateful for.

She was roused by the consciousness of silence where there had been so much noise and bustle and looked out of her window to see that the stableyard was deserted except for a couple of grooms who were already casting covert glances at her carriage. Whatever was she thinking about on a cold morning like this to keep her horses standing and her escort waiting in the First Court! Urgently, she gave the signal to move off and settled back to enjoy her return journey to the Old Palace.

While the carriage waited in the First Court for her escort of Life Guards to take up their positions, Khurrem's mood of dreamy contentment was roughly shaken. There was always a lot of coming and going in the First Court. All visitors to the Palace complex must pass through it, for one thing, and in any case the Palace Hospital was there and the fuel store. So she had been watching everything with mild interest when out of the corner of her eye she spotted three janissaries. There was nothing amiss with their appearance; no soldiers had ever been more smartly turned out or had proceeded on their way with more dignity. What caused her heart to miss a beat, or seem to, was the thing that two of them carried on a yoke across their shoulders: a shining copper cauldron, a magnificent cauldron, obviously new and perhaps on its way to be blessed by the dervish chaplain and received into the oda to which it now belonged. In common with everyone else in Istanbul she knew all about the dreaded preliminary to a janissary uprising and stared at it in horrified fascination, then determinedly sat back against the seat. She would not look at it, it was only a cooking-pot and that evening it would be sitting on a fire somewhere, already stained with soot and containing enough rice for the supper of twenty hungry men.

The carriage jerked and moved on. When it came abreast of the little trio Khurrem could not resist the temptation to peer out at them. Three bland young men, their faces cleanly shaved and devoid of expression. Two privates carrying the cauldron, very new privates at that for they had nothing in the front of their caps except their obligatory spoons, led by a non-commissioned officer of some sort, carrying ceremonially the great copper spoon which went with the cauldron. He was very dapper, from his spotless turban to his yellow boots. There was not a thing in the appearance of any of them to frighten anyone, and she really ought to be ashamed of herself. It was the sight of the cauldron that had done it, so soon after Hulefa's disjointed, and really (when she came to think of it) rather pointless warning, based on nothing but rumour as it seemed to be.

She gave herself a determined little shake and sat upright. If she wanted to see for herself what the mood of the janissaries was like, now was her opportunity. In a very few moments some of them would be presenting arms as her carriage drove through the Imperial Gate. But she saw nothing whatever to justify her sudden lapse into panic. The janissary guard were a model of alertness as they saluted her carriage when it passed through the gate, and a little knot of off-duty soldiers lounging in the shade of their famous tree were a picture of good-humoured relaxation. There were even a couple of officers, plume-crowned and red-booted, standing together engaged in serious conversation. She saw one of them, a handsome creature with knowing eyes, twirl his splendid moustachios and glance at her carriage as it passed. Nothing could have been more normal. I'm glad I didn't tell Suleiman, she thought.

Back in the Old Palace, Khurrem spent the rest of the morning enjoyably engaged in choosing materials for new caftans and chatting with Fatma, the kiaya of the Silk Room, a lady of formidable character and a great one for knowing all the latest gossip. She remembered this fact when, in a lull in the serious business of the morning, she stopped to refresh herself with a little junket.

'What do you hear from the merchants?' she asked casually, as Fatma, breathing heavily (for she was remarkably fat), re-rolled a heavy bolt of silk.

'About what?' demanded Fatma, always direct and not particularly civil. But she had had charge of Khurrem during her early days as a slave, and had proved herself a good and loyal friend.

'Nothing in particular, just wondering if there was any news?' replied Khurrem airily.

'Don't crease that silk, girl,' snapped Fatma sotto-voce to the timid novice who had accompanied her into Khurrem's rooms, and then added aloud, 'Nothing much, except poor old Korkud in the Covered Market was broken into last night. Cleaned him out, they did, all his best stock gone and the rest ruined. Sick all over the place, disgusting.'

Khurrem's eyes widened. 'What does he sell?'

'Velvets, plushes, tissues, that sort of thing.'

'Poor man! I'm so sorry. Who could do such a thing?'

'Who ever does anything like that? Janissaries, of course. Police caught one of them, drunk as a lord, lying in his own vomit, the dirty beast. There's nobody worse than soldiers on the rampage.'

Khurrem's heart lurched and she was careful not to look at Hulefa, whitefaced in the background. After a moment she asked carefully, 'Do they often do that sort of thing?'

Fatma grunted. 'There's rotten apples in every barrel and they're always short of money. Materials are easy to sell and no questions asked. This lot must already have got money from somewhere or they wouldn't have been drunk to start with. Well, now, lady, about that silver tissue – do you want it embroidered or left plain?'

'Whatever you think best,' said Khurrem, elaborately careless.

'It's all the fault of the police,' grumbled Fatma. 'They're only soldiers themselves, after all, so what do they care? Slack, that's what they are.' She had plenty of friends among the merchants and was reproducing their grievances. But Khurrem listened to her with a sinking heart. Later in the afternoon Hulefa, her face whiter than ever, appeared in her reception-room and said, 'Oh, madam, may I speak to you?' Her hands were clasped against her breasts and Khurrem saw that they were shaking.

'What is it?' she demanded.

Hulefa seemed to have difficulty in finding words and couldn't meet Khurrem's eye. 'First of all, madam,' she said, speaking carefully, 'I lied to you this morning. You see, I was afraid I might get Kasim into trouble if I told the truth. Janissaries don't go against each other. I mean, he did warn me, it wasn't just a rumour.'

Her face was woe-begone. The hard-bitten Hulefa seemed on the verge of tears, and Khurrem instinctively clasped her hand in both her own.

'I'm glad you've told me,' she said, 'though I have to admit I did guess. But even so, what is there for us to do? Except for an isolated incident last night, nothing's happened. The city's quiet and so are the soldiers.'

Hulefa did her best, nodding her head and saying, 'Yes, madam. I'm sure you're right, madam,' and obviously not meaning a word of it.

'Even if you had told me about Kasim I couldn't have told his majesty. What would he have thought? We haven't anything to go on.'

Hulefa had gone back to twisting her hands against her bosom. She stared at her mistress with wide, worried eyes. 'There's something else, madam. Kasim was to have come here today –'

'Here? Literally into the Palace?'

'Yes, madam, here. We've nowhere else to meet and he's all I've got. I give him a meal sometimes, that's all. I know it's against all the rules but really there's nothing wrong about it. You could trust my brother anywhere. Anyway, I'm very sorry to cause you trouble, madam. I suppose the Aga of the

Girls will have me –'

'The Aga of the Girls will do nothing to you. You're *mine*!' snapped Khurrem. 'What else were you going to say?'

'Only that Kasim never came, madam. And I'm worried to death.'

Khurrem sat down to give herself time to think. Hulefa's worry was infectious, all the more because she was normally so calm, so full of strong common sense. In the past it was Hulefa who had given good advice and kept Khurrem from making a fool of herself. But this was different, and if it was based on fact, much more serious than anything they had ever faced before. 'When should Kasim have been here?'

'At the noon hour, madam.'

Khurrem glanced through the window. 'It's not yet sunset, and there could be all kinds of explanations for his absence. Well, couldn't there be?'

'I suppose so, madam.'

After over five years, thought Khurrem, I find I don't really know her very well. And I would never have believed her capable of lying to me. We're all vulnerable through those we love. Poor Hulefa. She got to her feet and said as calmly as she could, 'I believe the best thing would be for you to go to the barracks and try to see Kasim. Could you do that?'

She realized that what she suggested was far from simple. Janissaries were not allowed to marry and were discouraged from contact with their families. It would not simply be a question of presenting herself at the barracks and asking to see her brother.

'I'll go.' The interruption came from Meylisah, kneeling in her usual place in one corner of the room. It had not occurred to either Khurrem or Hulefa to exclude her from their talk, why should they? She was one of them, one of the family, and with all her giggling, silly ways, as much a part of them as little Mehmed himself.

'Meylisah!' exclaimed Khurrem, 'but you can't –'

'Why not? I'm little and nobody notices me particularly. Please let me, it's something I can do.'

It was true, nobody did notice Meylisah because she was so small and self-effacing. And really, her silliness proceeded more from talking without thinking than from any lack of intelligence.

'All right,' said Khurrem decisively, 'go at once. But if you see anything that frightens you, any disturbance of any sort, you're to come straight back, do you understand? And Hulefa, you go and fetch me a caftan and something for my head, I'm going to see the Sultana Valideh.'

35

It was a cosy, intimate scene she was breaking into; Hafise was warmly wrapped in a padded silk caftan, enriched with Chinese embroidery, her toes on the tandur. On the edge of the carpet on which her divan stood sat the harem story-teller. Sirhane, Hafise's other maid, occupied a stool nearby. All three ladies blinked at her a little drowsily. But Hafise saw the expression on her daughter-in-law's face, cleared her throat, and said calmly to the story-teller, 'I will hear the rest another time. Sirhane, bring sherbet for Khurrem Hasseki.'

When they were alone, she continued, still calm, 'Well, child, what has gone wrong?'

Khurrem took a deep breath, and said clearly, 'Nothing necessarily, but I thought you should know.' Her head was quite clear, she found, and she embarked on her story soberly, leaving out only the details about Kasim which she knew would anger Hafise.

When she had finished there was silence while the Queen Mother sat pondering. Presently she asked, 'Has anything been done to find out why this man did not meet his sister today?'

'Meylisah has gone to the barracks,' said Khurrem. Her voice sounded weak in her ears and she felt suddenly inadequate in the face of Hafise's unmoving, stately presence. It did not help that she said, 'My child! It's nearly dark! It would have been better to send one of your secretaries.'

Khurrem felt herself shrinking, and could hardly believe it when Hafise added calmly, 'But you have done absolutely right. I think we will now send for the Chief of Police. As it happens, I have heard something that you have not. A gang of these brutes broke into a house in the Armenian district and terrorized the family last night. Plainly, we must have an explanation if there is one. Don't look so distressed, my dear; see, here comes Sirhane with your drink. Sirhane, I want a messenger to go to army headquarters. Ask the Aga of the Women to send someone responsible. Now, I must write a note –'

She rose stiffly to her feet, and Khurrem, like Suleiman a short while before, was aware for the first time that Hafise was beginning to feel her age. But it only showed in her gait and a certain lack of buoyancy in her manner. Her mind was as clear and her determination as strong as ever.

As the acting Chief of Police discovered when he entered her presence more than two hours later. He had been at his supper when the messenger arrived and not best pleased to be called out at this hour of the night at the behest of a woman, even if she was Sultana Valideh. So he finished what was left of his köfte and rice before he left and rode the short distance to the Old Palace at the regulation speed.

In the meantime, Meylisah still had not returned, and now they were worrying about her as well as everything else. All in all, the acting Chief of Police got a poor welcome from the two stony-eyed ladies who received him when he did arrive. Still, he was an able man and once he understood what the trouble was, set about reassuring them. Yes, it was true that there had been a bit of janissary trouble the night before, but they had trouble most nights of one sort or another. This was nothing to worry about.

'So you think there is no dissatisfaction in the corps?' asked Hafise quietly. Instead of sitting on her divan of state, she was standing up, very straight and dignified, in front of it, with her hands behind her back.

'There's always discontent in the ranks, especially in peacetime, lady. Nothing we cannot handle.' Since he meant it, he sounded absolutely convincing.

'Very well,' said Hafise shortly. She was tired, and it did begin to seem as if she and Khurrem were making a mountain out of a molehill.

'As to the slave who has gone missing from here, I'll have her found and brought home,' he promised, sounding very masculine and comforting. 'You'll probably find, ladies, that she wandered into one of the bazaars. You know what slaves are.'

'I know what my slaves are,' interjected Khurrem. Hafise's fingers pressed hard into her shoulder and she was silent, her face burning with shame as she listened to Hafise courteously bidding the man goodnight and thanking him for his civility. When he had gone she said miserably, 'I caused all this trouble, I'm so sorry, but really –'

'You have nothing to apologize for,' Hafise told her firmly. 'Even if what that man says is right, you still acted wisely in coming to me. In any case, I am not satisfied that we have heard the last of this. And your maid has still not come back.'

But Meylisah appeared half an hour later, tired, hungry, and bearing only good news. Kasim had been sent to escort a detail of new recruits to Uskudar barracks. She was sorry she had been so long but it had taken all this time to find anyone who knew anything about him. So there it was, and they could all sleep easily. They all did, except for Hulefa and Khurrem who could not sleep for shame.

On the following night, the janissaries rioted in the city. They broke open the gates of the barracks on the Third Hill and streamed out intent on destruction, carrying their javelins, firelocks and sabres. Some stopped to break into the splendid houses on the Divan Yolu, among them Iskender Chelebi's, carrying off gold and silver plate, jewels and brocaded robes. Others made for the Jewish workshops, looting them and burning houses for warmth, their young, fair faces wolfish in the light of the red flames. In the deserted barracks their cooking-pots lay in the ashes of the fires, the Sultan's food spilt and burned in token of their rejection of it and him. The city trembled, helpless, as they raged across it, leaving death and destruction in their path.

The acting Chief of Police went back to the Old Palace in the early morning to see if the Sultan's ladies were safe and to report on what he had done, though this he kept to a minimum. However exalted, women were women and the taking of decisions was the business of men. The previous night's activities had shaken him but not to the extent of making him question his own certainty that he was right. Besides, he was ambitious; the Aga of the Janissaries was not going to thank him if he sent messengers after him demanding help as soon as his back was turned. On the other hand, when he had quelled these tiresome young troops and put the fear of God into them, both the Aga and the Sultan too would be grateful and impressed. At the same time he was conscientious, and after delivering his brief report, hesitated a moment.

Hafise misunderstood his hesitation. 'You must not worry about us,' she told him gently. 'We are well guarded here by the Life Guards. And as you say, the janissaries are no longer interested in the Third Hill, they've got all they wanted –'

'What about the ladies in Ibrahim Pasha's palace, will they be safe?' Khurrem asked.

'They should be, madam. You can rely on me to do my utmost and the Lady Kadija has her own detachment of Life Guards.' He was not going to say any more. He knew very well that the janissaries hated Ibrahim Pasha. There was not the slightest possibility that they would spare his home, but he thought they would leave his imperial wife alone. Anyway he was not going to dwell on horrors. He thought he had handled a ticklish situation pretty well so far, and touched up his heavy moustache with his forefinger. Perhaps that self-satisfied gesture was what did it. The next moment he heard, from the younger lady, of course, the very question he had been dreading. 'Don't you think you should send for the Sultan?'

Shaken for the second time that morning, he temporized, 'My dear lady! There's no need for alarm, I promise you. His majesty would not thank me –'

She broke in on what he was about to say – she really was a most ill-mannered young woman and not one he would tolerate in his own harem – 'But that's exactly what he would do! If we delay too long who knows what they will do or where they will go next? Do you think you know?' she finished, glaring in a way he could only describe to himself as unwomanly. It did not help that he did not know how to answer her.

Hafise rescued him. 'You will leave this to me, Khurrem.' And turning to the Chief of Police, the Sultana Valideh proceeded to cross-question him – on what had happened, on the arrangements he had made, on what he thought would happen next. She listened to his answers without comment and then dismissed him. 'I shall expect you to report to me again at dusk,' was all she said to him before he marched out.

He was glad to go; those two made him uncomfortable and

besides, he had a million things to do. Now the die was cast he felt quite buoyant. Now it was all in his hands he would show them the stuff he was made of. He had plenty of men and could rely on them absolutely. (In this he was only half right – there were plenty of them, but most of them were itching to be emulating their fellows. Before evening fell they had been infected by the prevailing hysteria and were busy contributing to the general mayhem.) He would have it all under control, he reckoned, by tomorrow's dawn. After that, of course, there'd be no stopping him. His eye caught what appeared to be a bundle of rags lying by the roadside. He barked an order and three of his little escort detached themselves and picked up the body of a girl caught on the street after dark by the marauding young troops, raped, and left for dead.

The Chief of Police left silence behind him and in the case of Khurrem, ever-increasing conviction of disaster. 'He's wrong!' she burst out to Hafise. 'I'm sure he's wrong! I don't think we can rely on him – he doesn't believe anything really bad can happen because it never has before! Oh, dear madam, can't *you* send a messenger to Suleiman?'

Hafise said wearily, 'It is too soon, my child. I cannot judge, and I am afraid of acting too hastily. When he comes back this evening we'll see better what to do.'

'Yes,' said Khurrem readily. 'Yes, very well, dear madam, I'll leave you to – to think about it. Come, children,' and she went quietly out of the presence-chamber.

She went quietly because she had made up her mind what to do, and there is no need to make a fuss when one is determined. She led her little family back to their nursery and handed them over to Leila and the nursery-maids, giving Leila clear, crisp instructions to cover the next few hours. Before she left she kissed the children and hugged them all. The maids saw nothing unusual in this; she was a very affectionate mother.

Back in her own rooms, she sat down and thought for a while before rising and going to the small room which served her as an office. She was relieved to see that it was deserted except for her principal secretary, Macar. He rose to his feet when he saw who it was and remained, expressionless as ever, quietly waiting for her instructions.

'Macar,' said Khurrem and stopped, not knowing quite what to say to him. She usually had no difficulty in coming to terms with her slaves, but Macar was still as much of an enigma as he had been when he had first come to her. Silent and efficient, carrying out her instructions to the letter (when he did not anticipate them), she still had no clue as to what or how he thought. She supposed that this must be because he was a man and a eunuch at that. Anyway he was essential to her plan. Please God I'm not wrong about him, she thought, and repeated his name.

He responded in his own way. 'The news from the city is very bad, lady,' he said and waited for her instructions to continue. Of course! If anybody knew what was going on it was Macar. Gathering information was his trade, and it had never once occurred to her in her confusion to send for him this morning and pump him of all he knew!

Now she listened with increasing dismay as he unfolded a catalogue of violence which seemed to embrace the whole city, and certainly only confirmed her in her determination. 'What do you think we should do, Macar?' she demanded forthrightly.

He did not waste time uttering disclaimers that he was only a slave, without the right to an opinion, but said firmly, 'Send for his majesty. Only his presence can end this.'

Khurrem expelled a deep breath. 'That is exactly what I intended to do. Can you ride?'

Instead of giving a direct answer he drew himself up and said, as if in reproof to a foolish question, 'Madam, I am a Hungarian. That is what my name means.'

'Oh, of course,' said Khurrem hastily.

Macar, having begun to talk, allowed himself to be carried away and actually asked a question, 'Do you require me to go to Edirne and bring his majesty back, lady?'

'No,' said Khurrem firmly; 'the responsibility is mine, therefore I require you to escort me to Edirne. I must go myself, so that I can tell him exactly what has happened. Will you do this?'

Everything depended on his answer. No one knew better than Khurrem that as a white eunuch he was not her slave but Suleiman's and could refuse to carry out even her commands. And if he did, who else could she find to help her in this most desperate of undertakings?

'I will, lady.' The answer came, as usual, unhurriedly, even tranquilly from the colourless lips. Only this time, having spoken, he permitted himself the smallest of smiles. Or perhaps she only imagined it.

'Thank you, Macar.' The relief was so great she found herself gabbling. 'You see, the acting Chief of Police refuses to send for him, he's quite sure he can do it all by himself, and the Sultana Valideh wants to wait, but I'm sure, *sure*, we should act now, but I have no authority –' she stopped, ashamed of this relapse into what sounded perilously like hysteria. But Macar only nodded his head, his long, white face expressionless, and said, 'You have the right of it, lady. But consider this: speed is essential. Do you think you have the stamina for such a journey? Remember, it is a hundred and fifty miles to Edirne.'

At least he did not tell her that she was only a woman! Gratefully, she replied truthfully, 'I can only try. I think I can manage. After all, I'm quite young and very strong. And I have been well-taught.'

'That I know.' He raised a large, pale hand and caressed his upper lip thoughtfully. 'We will need plenty of gold, for we shall have to buy horses for the journey, and replacements on the road. Also food and weapons –'

'Weapons?' repeated Khurrem faintly, but he ignored the interruption as if she had not spoken and went on unhurriedly with his shopping-list.

'Harness and saddles and all the usual requirements for a journey. We do not want to draw attention to ourselves, madam, but another companion would be prudent. Can you trust that groom of yours? That he does not speak Turkish is an advantage.'

'An excellent idea,' said Khurrem, and pulled herself together. She had begun to have second thoughts. Whoever heard of a Sultana taking to the road like a common gipsy? And what would Suleiman think of her, if, after all, she was ultimately proved to be wrong? But that was something she was not prepared to think about. She took a deep breath and asked matter-of-factly, 'I hope you know the road to Edirne, Macar, because I don't.'

This time he looked as if he might be going to laugh, but

only said, 'Yes, lady, I know the road well. In the time of Sultan Bayezid, I had occasion to make the journey more than once.' He became serious immediately. 'Lady, there is much to be done. We must be out of the city before the gates are locked at sunset, and I cannot be sure how long my preparations will take. Therefore, with your permission I will take my leave. Have you warm, dark clothes?'

Khurrem roused herself. 'Tell me what money you need and I will bring it to you.' That at least was no problem; she had money, and jewels, too, if necessary. 'I thought it would be wise if I disguised myself as a boy –'

He nodded. 'That would be prudent. The road to Edirne is well-used and we do not want to be the object of comment of any kind.'

'How long will it take us?'

'That will depend on you,' he told her bluntly. 'The Sultan's messengers can do it in less than twenty-four hours, but they are seasoned horsemen and stop for nothing. When I was younger –' He shook his head. 'The only one of us who is up to their standard is possibly Kazan. But you, lady, will be the pacemaker. I am compelled to speak bluntly so that you know where you stand.'

She took a deep breath. 'Then I'll just have to do my best, won't I?'

Khurrem sat alone in her bedroom, trousered and booted, the neat turban that Hulefa had managed to contrive hiding her hair. She had inspected herself carefully in the mirror and had to admit she didn't look bad. Nobody would give this insignificant, thin-faced boy a second glance, which was just as it should be. Downstairs Kazan, carefully coached, lurked in some cubbyhole known only to himself. Smiling broadly, as if he had been invited to accompany his mistress on a pleasure-trip, he had told her that he would be ready whenever she was.

'Where shall I find you?' asked Khurrem.

'I will find you,' responded Kazan, grinning away. 'When you come down, I will know.'

Satisfied, she had sat down and quickly written a note to Hafise. This was, of all the preparations, the most painful. There was nothing she could say that would not hurt and outrage the Sultana Valideh, so that after several false starts she contented herself with a simple statement of fact, and after sealing the note, handed it to Hulefa before she could change her mind. 'Wait half an hour after we are gone, then take it to the Sultana Valideh. And, Hulefa, you know nothing. It's best that way. Do you understand?'

Sitting on her bed, tightly clasped hands gripped between her knees, Khurrem waited. She didn't know what had happened to Macar. Perhaps, after all, she was not as clever as she thought, and he was no more than a common thief – had taken her gold never meaning to return. Or perhaps the janissaries had got him. Soon it would be sunset. If he didn't come in another half-hour, she and Kazan would steal horses from the Old Palace stable and set off alone. She didn't know the road to Edirne, but it must start from the Edirne Gate, that was common sense. After that, she told herself, I've got a tongue in my head, I can ask.

Hearing low voices and hasty footsteps in the corridor, she hurried out. Macar was there with Hulefa, looking tired and rather dirty, but very much master of himself.

'What happened?' demanded Khurrem.

But he would not wait to explain, nor to eat or rest. All he said was, 'We must go now, lady, there is no more time.'

It was much better once they were in the dark, deserted streets, although the news Macar delivered in a low voice as they rode was grim enough. Everything had taken him much longer than he expected, because the city, in the grip of fear, was paralysed. The markets were closed, and he had had to go out of Istanbul to find horses, all the time keeping a wary eye out for rampaging bands of troops. Khurrem, glancing up at the lean figure, dressed now in a rakish-looking sheepskin coat, swaying so easily in the saddle beside her, was filled with new respect for her secretary.

'We must get out of the city as fast as we can,' he was saying; 'this is the quiet time, but once the darkness falls, they will have slept off their debauch and be ready for a new one. It would be better to give the Topkapi and its neighbourhood a wide berth, but to reach the Edirne Gate we have to pass very near.' He shrugged. 'We must keep a close watch, that is all we can do. If we cannot take the Edirne Gate we must make for the Silivri or the Yedikule – Yedikule will be better, I believe.'

The streets they rode through were deserted. Perched on the

hard-bitten roan which was the best of the three mounts Macar had been able to find, Khurrem felt dangerously exposed, while at the same time keyed-up and excited. At all events it was better to be on the move, doing something! Why, just about now the Chief of Police would be calling on Hafise for another pointless discussion, while she was already on her way. The very thought exhilarated her. She had two reliable companions and money in her belt. Nothing could stop her now!

Unfortunately, something only too palpably could. It was dark now, but even so they could sense a movement ahead. Kazan hissed suddenly behind her.

'What –' began Khurrem, and stopped her horse too quickly. Feeling him slip on the greasy cobbles, she gave way to panic. She was alone, her companions had melted away, she did not know which way to turn! A cry rose in her throat and she managed to choke it down just as she saw a white hand descend on her bridle and jerk her mount away to the left. Apparently there was a turning which she had not seen and Macar and Kazan had. Oh, she must do better than this, and the noise she'd made! These janissaries, if janissaries they were, must have heard her, might even be at their heels.

'The place is swarming with them. We must abandon the Edirne Gate,' whispered Macar. 'This way now.'

'I can't see!' gasped Khurrem.

He had no comfort for her. 'Your eyes will grow accustomed to the darkness; we dare not risk a torch.'

There was nothing for it but to ride on, peering into the blackness and hoping that it contained no obstacles. There was no sound except for the clatter of their horses' hooves. How on earth did Macar know where he was going, if in fact he did? And how much longer before they left the city behind? They seemed to have been in the saddle for hours already. She took a deep breath and tried to swallow her growing hysteria. She hated the dark; if she'd thought about it before she set out, she might never have started. But it was shameful that a grown woman should give way to a child's terror in this way. She sniffed, feeling tears of misery start from her eyes. Well, let them come, perhaps she would feel better for them, and certainly they wouldn't bother her companions since they couldn't see them. All the while they were moving forward and there was no sign of life. But now Macar's hand descended on her bridle again and she reined in, managing better this time.

'Yedikule,' he whispered; 'can't you see the towers?'

Well, yes, there certainly was a difference in quality in the darkness where the sky should be. There were supposed to be seven towers. She would take his word for it that they were all there.

'We are in luck.' Macar spoke calmly and in his normal voice. 'There is no guard here – I did not think there would be, for as you know, this is only used on ceremonial occasions. But splendid as it is, it has its deficiencies. Now we must wait for the moon to rise.' So saying, he dismounted and began calmly groping in his saddlebags. Kazan did the same, and came to Khurrem to help her from the saddle. Macar waited while she slid to the ground, and then said, 'With respect, you must not let him do that again. If you are a boy, you must dismount like a boy. If you do that in the wrong company, it might cause comment. Will you eat something?' He held out a hunk of bread.

Khurrem took it meekly, though she had never felt less like food. Nor could she be quiet or still. 'How shall we get through this gate?' she demanded. 'If it is not guarded it must be securely locked – what can we do?'

'I cannot show you until the moon rises, which will not be long now,' said Macar patiently. He spoke from the ground where he had seated himself, leaning against the massive, ancient wall.

She said contritely, 'Of course. You have done wonders, Macar. I'll wait until you're ready.' She forced herself to sit down, to lean against the crumbling stones, even to take a mouthful of bread. She'd never be able to rest, she had too much on her mind.

When Macar woke her, the moon was bright and clear. She started up, and then relapsed against the wall as she remembered where she was. She could see everything just as if it were broad daylight. There was Kazan, silently grinning from ear to ear as usual, standing by the little group of horses, and here was Macar with his hands folded in front of him, his normal stance when waiting for instructions, saying in his solemn way, 'Come, lady, time we were on our way.'

She sat up and stretched, saying, 'I've never been asleep!

Oh, you shouldn't have let me –'

'We had to wait for moonlight,' he reminded her gently, 'but now there need be no more delay. Come!'

She needed no further bidding. She was rested, she could see. She felt wonderful. But how on earth were they to pass this great mass of masonry, these towers in the old wall, not to mention the great gate which was so obviously chained up? She looked anxiously after Macar, who had walked past the gate as if it was of no account and had turned south along the wall . . . She saw him nod to himself as if satisfied, and now he came back and said, almost gaily, 'Lead your horse, lady, our path lies this way.'

Well, it was quite easy, after all. To the south of the towers and the great gate was another gate, much smaller and just as obviously locked. But beside that was a great gap in the masonry of the wall. Clearly repairs were intended, for tidily stacked to one side was the rubble, mortar and sand the workmen would use whenever they came back to do the job, once the janissaries had stopped running amok and allowed decent people to get on with their lives and work as Allah intended. In the meantime, this merciful gap was just large enough to lead a horse through.

By midnight they had passed through Silivri on the Marmara coast.

36

They still followed the coast once they were through the dreaming cluster of small houses which was all they ever saw of Silivri, and when they were clear of it, Macar slowed his tired horse to a walk and said, 'We may take things more quietly now. The animals are weary, and as you see, the going is rougher.'

It was. Silivri lay on the eastern side of a long bend or bight in the coast. Now they could see to their left the long, sandy shore of the Sea of Marmara; and low, steep cliffs, a denser black against the black sky, rose on their right. The road was narrower now, uneven and pebble-strewn.

'When do we leave the coast?' asked Khurrem, suddenly conscious of aching back and thighs, though still buoyed up by the urgency of her mission. Only once had she looked back after passing the Yedikule Gate, and that glance had shown her the angry red glow of fire against the night sky. After that, she had kept her eyes on the road ahead. Now it was wonderful to slow down, to hear the peaceful sound of running water from the numerous little streams that abounded here.

Macar looked at her thoughtfully, accurately assessing her state of mind. He said firmly, 'In about an hour we shall reach the village of Eregli. It is small, but there is an inn –'

'No!' cried Khurrem. 'We can't stop to rest, we can't!'

'We must.' The tone was, as usual, tranquil, but also definite. 'We cannot travel this stretch of the road without light of some sort, and soon the moon will set. Also, there will be fresh horses at Eregli if Allah wills. If not, these animals must be rested. So, if you please, lady, at Eregli we stop until sunrise.'

He heard the sharply uttered 'Oh!' of frustration, but gave more attention to the sob on which it ended, saying gently, 'A journey has its rhythm like everything else. Darkness and weariness must be served.'

She said bleakly, 'That's no comfort,' but offered him no more arguments.

The keeper of the inn at Eregli, roused from sleep, regarded them with disfavour – he thought at first they were brigands – until comforted with a gold piece and the promise of a good price for his best horses at dawn. Then he became helpful and brought them milk and barley bread, apologizing for having nothing hot to offer them, and showed them where they could sleep.

It was only a tiny place, mud-built. Most travellers went on to the state-run caravanserai at Corlu before stopping to rest, but, as Macar said, the place was adequate and its keeper seemed both honest and willing. Anyway, they had no choice.

Now that she was settled down against her saddlebag on the close-packed dirt floor, Khurrem was willing to admit that an hour or two's rest was welcome. She felt less feverish, more relaxed. And she was released from one nagging worry. Now she knew she could keep up with her seasoned companions, and neither of them made any bones about being glad of food and sleep. Why, there was Kazan, curled up like a vast black cat in his serviceable black felt jacket, already snoring like a bubbling stewpot!

Perhaps it was the noise that he and their fellow guests made, all snoring on different notes as they lay companionably round the walls of the large, dingy room, that kept her awake, or perhaps it was the effort not to think about her many worries. Still, she didn't mind too much, it was pleasant enough lying here, once she got used to it. Even the snores were mildly comforting. It was smelly, of course, not much like her rooms in the Old Palace! But a haven, none the less.

Beside her, Macar did not seem to be sleeping, either, for she heard a bump and a rustle as he furtively rearranged his long legs more comfortably. Now her eyes were getting more accustomed to the darkness, she could see his outline as he lay on his back, hands behind his head, his shoulders supported on his saddle.

Of course she had wondered about him idly from time to time as she wondered about all her slaves until her friendly curiosity got their stories out of them. But Macar's self-sufficiency, his self-effacing dignity, had always resisted her efforts and she had eventually found it easier to take him at his face value. But now a few hours had changed all that. He was no longer merely a competent slave but a valued, resourceful companion. She had to know more about him.

So the next time she heard him move, Khurrem whispered 'Macar?' and was immediately rewarded by an answering whisper.

'Can't you sleep, either?' she asked him.

'I seldom sleep on a journey. It is enough to rest and perhaps doze a little.'

'Oh. Have you travelled a lot?'

'I was a soldier, and soldiers go where they are sent.'

Feeling snubbed and disappointed, she said, 'I'm sorry, I didn't mean to pry.'

There was silence for a little longer, then she heard him sigh. 'There is no mystery about me, but my –' he hesitated, choosing his words carefully, 'my active life ended a long time ago. And most of my memories are painful. For the past thirty years I have been a eunuch, a slave in the Sultan's service. Resignation is hard to learn when you're young, but I achieved it at last. Now I have peace, can even take pleasure in my work, particularly when I have the opportunity to make use of such skills as I have, half-forgotten as they may be.'

He sighed again, but .went on without prompting. 'My home was Atany, a village in northern Hungary, famous for horse-breeding. My family described themselves as landed gentry – it would have been more accurate to say prosperous farmers and be done with it. It hardly matters, for I'm the last of them, and as you see, neither the one or the other.

'It had been my ambition to become a soldier, like my older brothers, and serve the great Matthias Corvinus against the Austrians. When I was sixteen and burning with ambition, I entered the army. Alas, he died almost at once. I saw a little service, but my first action was almost my last, for I was taken prisoner at Belgrade, fighting the Turks under the Sultan Bayezid. Since the Turks like Hungarians rather less than most of their numerous enemies, they made me what I now am.'

He broke off, while a harsh voice from the other side of the room cursed him, bidding him 'be quiet and let others get a bit of sleep!'

Khurrem lay still, abashed, and rather glad that she was not called upon for any comment.

They set out again at dawn. And if Khurrem and her secretary were both a little oppressed in spirit, they really had no reason for dissatisfaction. True to his word, the inn-keeper provided them with three reliable if unexciting hacks, and a hot breakfast of barley-porridge and stewed mutton. He also gave them advice which later proved to be disastrous.

'Don't wait to get fresh mounts at Babaeski or any of the towns,' he told them kindly. 'You'll meet gipsies and other nomads on the road who'll charge you less. Of course, you'll have to look sharp after them, look out for animals with ginger up the back passage and that sort of thing, but,' he finished winningly to Macar, 'you look like a gentleman who knows what's what and you should manage.'

It was a fine, clear morning, and as they followed the road inland to Corlu Khurrem felt the first telltale breath of colder air on her cheeks that told her they were emerging onto the great central European plain. Her spirits rose. Even Macar allowed a frosty smile to stray across his fine-boned face, while Kazan, who apparently asked nothing more of life than a horse under him and a destination as distant as possible, varied his eternal, enigmatic grin with snatches of song delivered in a voice as harsh as a Russian winter.

They slowed down perforce to jog through Corlu, saw other travellers leaving its caravanserai ('Sluggards,' commented Macar, looking down his nose), and a great caravan of waggons laden with fruit and grain for the markets of Istanbul. Then suddenly, it seemed, they were away from the head-waters of the Ergene River and on the fine road leading over countless bridges, through vineyards and orchards, to Edirne.

Now there was nothing to do but ride; no problems, but no excuses either. It was nearly midday when Khurrem began to be aware again of an aching back and tired wrists, while Macar, after distributing bread and meat from his store, remarked thoughtfully that at the next opportunity they should think about remounts.

They had already seen plenty of nomads on the road, lean, hard-bitten-looking men, clad in dirty sheepskins. Their women sat at the roadside, careless about veiling themselves if they were gipsies, and always knee-deep in starved-looking children. The animals their men offered for sale were staked out by the road, too. 'Trash for the most part,' said Macar contemptuously, and it was not until just after midday that, coming upon another small encampment by the road, he cast an expert eye over its gaggle of horses and reined in.

It was a lonely stretch of road, tree-shaded on one side, rocky on the other, and there were no other travellers about except the three men, two sitting idly by the roadside and one mounted. They had no women or children with them, there were no cooking-pots, none of the saddlery and other impedimenta which had distinguished the vagabonds they'd seen before. As Macar and Kazan dismounted, Khurrem took a comprehensive look at the threesome and decided to remain in the saddle, hardly knowing why. She just felt safer that way. But Macar was looking at the horses, the best he'd seen. No one could blame him if his sixth sense was a bit late in operating. He had a lot on his mind. So he strolled over to the nearest of the three and asked the cautious question that should start the bargaining.

Meanwhile Khurrem sat her horse and wondered why she felt frightened. She was used to seeing outlandish and aggressive men by now. Indeed, in her short life she'd had quite considerable experience of rogues. Now, looking again at the three of them she couldn't quite make up her mind. Her first instinct had said 'beware', but they did seem to be reacting quite normally to Macar. They were roughly civil, ready with their sales-talk, telling him that their animals were the best he would see on that or any road, and one of them, small, dirty and completely anonymous, rose to his feet and accompanied him across the thin grass to look at them. And Macar was going with him, talking in his unhurried fashion and apparently noticing nothing.

She looked uneasily around. It did not help to see that Kazan had dismounted and disappeared. Where to, for heaven's sake? She turned round to see that the mounted man had moved up closer to her. He seemed to be the group's leader, although he had so far done none of the talking. He was a burly fellow, full-fleshed, seeming to burst out of his flashy clothing. He had a great beard, like the tight, curly coat of a black lamb, which spread across the lower part of his face and half his chest, and he caressed it lovingly as he sat there, looking, not at Macar, but at her. She felt the bold eyes, black like the beard, seek hers and was afraid to look at him. She turned away, affected to examine the countryside around, suppressed a yawn with a hand that shook no matter how hard she tried to control it, and looked resolutely into the middle distance, while all the while she felt his eyes on her face, compelling her attention.

Oh, dear God, she thought, suppose he's guessed about me?

Behind her, Macar prosed on, extolling the performance of the animals they would be leaving in part exchange, while the other two nomads stood by, showing little interest now in what he said, their busy eyes darting everywhere, over their clothes, their saddlebags, their mounts. That's what's wrong with them, she realized suddenly. They're looking us over. Like victims. And I'm sure their leader has guessed I'm a woman. She drew a deep breath, and, hardly knowing what she did, put her hand on her girdle. Through the folds of thin silk she felt the outline of the knife Macar had given her before they left, and which she had forgotten immediately. It was no comfort. She had no idea how to use it.

The bargaining had grown animated again, and black-beard seemed to have lost interest in her. He'd moved up the road again, and now sat, arms folded, as if bored with the proceedings. She expelled a trembling breath and wiped her sweating fingers furtively on her trousers. Perhaps, after all, she was wrong. I'm new to all this, she thought, and there's no doubt they all look furtive.

Deadlock seemed to be reached suddenly. She saw Macar raise his hand in a gesture of negation, saw the heads of the two nomads turn with one accord to black-beard, and heard him say, in a voice both rich and high-pitched, 'Tell the gentleman I'm not difficult to please. He can take the horses and leave me the boy.' And he followed that pronouncement with a breathless giggle.

There was silence. In Khurrem's case the silence of complete incomprehension, while she thought, stunned – boy, what boy? Then – Oh God, he means me! While she wrestled with the thought she heard Macar say coolly, 'Completely unacceptable.' And the two ruffians moved purposefully closer to him.

After that several things happened simultaneously. Sunlight

glinted on steel as Macar's scimitar cut through the air, while there was a crump! as something whizzed through the air and took one of them on the back of the head. He crumpled up in the road so suddenly she could have laughed had not all this satisfying activity left her with the black-bearded man for her own opponent. After it was all over, she remembered feeling quite aggrieved by this because he did seem the most dangerous of the three. As it was, she had little time to think about it, having only one weapon. He was still some ten feet off but coming for her fast when she threw the knife.

'I don't know how you managed it, it isn't a throwing-knife,' said Macar respectfully, rising to his feet after inspecting the body, 'but you got him through the windpipe for all that. Tell me,' he added curiously, 'why didn't you just ride off?'

'It never occurred to me,' said Khurrem faintly. She felt sick, but fought off the sensation, not wanting to lose her dignity. She would have liked to dismount but felt any activity to be beyond her at the moment. So she sat still, pale-faced, while Kazan emerged from the bushes where he had been hidden, carefully coiled up his sling, and went to help Macar tidy up. One of the ruffians lay unconscious in the road with a bump on his head, while his companion, bleeding copiously from the wound in his arm inflicted by Macar's scimitar, sat beside him and cursed them roundly.

It only took Macar and Kazan a few minutes after that to collect the three best horses and saddle two of them. Then Macar turned questioningly to Khurrem who was compelled to say, 'I'm afraid I can't quite manage –' They lifted her gently from the saddle and sat her down by the roadside while they dealt with the third. When they returned to her she was still pale and listless, but brightened up and even laughed a little at some incomprehensible remark from Kazan.

'What does he say?' asked Macar, helping her to mount.

'That he hasn't had so much fun since he left Russia,' she told him shakily.

'H'm,' said Macar primly, 'I have always thought Russians were barbarians. 'I beg your pardon, lady,' he added, after further thought, 'but you are not really a Russian, are you?'

After that dramatic half-hour the rest of the journey could

only be anti-climax. If Macar glanced anxiously at his mistress from time to time, he said nothing, feeling that she could best come to terms with her experience if left to herself. As for Khurrem, her mind was in a turmoil. Any effort at self-control and rational thought was impossible, so after a while she abandoned herself to numbed shock. The rhythm of riding helped, so did weariness. By the time, late in the afternoon, that Macar raised his whip and pointed silently at the first towers and domes of Edirne on the skyline, she had sufficiently recovered to be irritable and unduly worried about minutiae.

'How will we get to his majesty?' she fretted. 'And what will he say when he sees us – we look terrible! And oh! I never thought, his gentlemen mustn't see me like this. Oh, why didn't I think –'

'You may safely leave all that to me, lady,' Macar soothed her. 'It can all be accomplished without difficulty, I promise you.'

And so it was. It was still light, but only just, when they reached the Sultan's camp on the edge of the Maritsa marshes on the European side of Edirne. Suleiman was about to sit down to his supper when he was told that the Sultana Hasseki's secretary and two companions sought urgent and private audience with him. The gentleman-in-waiting who brought this request had raised his eyebrows somewhat when he saw the three bedraggled travellers, but knew Macar by sight.

Suleiman recognized his wife straight away. His eyes travelled over her stained and dusty person in amazement and he looked about to embark on one of his famous rages. One glance at her stricken face, however, inspired him to control himself. Instead, he took her hand and said simply, 'Tell me.'

With a little help from Macar, she did. He listened, expressionless, while they told him what was happening to his capital city, and if his eyes narrowed and his face darkened while they talked, that was all. Then he thought for a moment. When he spoke it seemed that he was calm and prepared for anything.

'I cannot linger to tell you what I think of all you have done,' he said to Khurrem. He still held her hand. 'I must leave you now; there is no time to be lost. In the meantime, you must remain here until I send for you. These are your quarters now.' He kissed the hand he held, bowed to her and left the tent. They heard his voice outside in a moment as he issued brief orders.

A small party of the younger Slaves of the Gate were to ride with him, as well as a detachment of his personal guard. The best and fastest horses were to be prepared immediately for the journey back to Istanbul, and the rest of the hunting party, including the Aga of the Janissaries (Suleiman mentioned him specifically), were to follow, making the best time they could. When his party was ready to leave, the Sultan spoke briefly to them, outlining the route they should take. They could not rely on getting into the city by the direct road; instead they should ride to the Sweet Waters of Europe, at the point of the Golden Horn, where there was a small kushk. There they would take stock of the situation as they found it and get into the city as best they could. They were impressed by his calmness and clear thinking, which was no index to the turmoil which raged within him.

On this day, while Khurrem rode north, the janissaries contemptuously pushed back the ring of police which surrounded them and broke into the palace of Ibrahim Pasha Damat. They enjoyed themselves there, went into an ecstasy of destruction in the selamlik, carrying off the beautiful things, gold plate, jade and jewels, which it had given Ibrahim such pleasure to own, but smashing his nude Greek statues to smithereens, for they were an abomination in the sight of Allah. Then they set fire to the place. In the harem, Ibrahim's two ladies listened in helpless terror to the crashes and yells, the crackling of the flames. But they were safe, surrounded by their black eunuchs and ringed in steel by the Life Guards. In any case, the troops had exhausted their rage for the time being in Ibrahim's part of the palace. They reckoned they'd given him enough to remember them by. And anyway, they did not attack women except when they were drunk.

They stormed through the city again that night, the Jewish quarter and the Covered Market being their favourite targets, as usual, taking time for an orgy of eating and drinking in the cookshops and the houses they broke into. They didn't forget to demand 'tooth rent' from the terrified householders whose food they took, for the wear and tear on their teeth while they ate. This ferocious joke was perennial with them whenever they went on the rampage. And of course they found more wine, they could always be relied upon for that. That day was the climax of their 'gaudy'; after it was over some of the recruits and younger men were notably less enthusiastic. With their bellies full and some nice little souvenirs tucked away for the rainy days that were sure to come, they began looking over their shoulders, wondering what authority would do when it caught up with them. But the ringleaders, the grim old sergeants with nothing much to look forward to, hadn't finished yet.

At the mid-afternoon of the following day, Suleiman sat a tired horse in a meadow and watched flames and smoke rising from the ruins of his Customs House. He was deathly tired, but buoyed up by the emotion which possessed him, and had possessed him all through the intolerable journey – shame at his own incompetence, anger at the performance of his disorderly slave soldiers, and humble gratitude and admiration for Khurrem.

He passed a hand over his dust-grimed face and thought about the next move. If they had not already overrun the Topkapi they would get there sooner or later because it was their headquarters as well as his. So that was where he must go, turning inland from the sea-walls of the Golden Horn and entering his Palace by the Gate of Felicity. He turned to pick a handful of trusted Pashas and, with them and his Life Guards, mounted a fresh horse and rode off.

The first Court, the so-called Court of the Janissaries, was deserted when he got there. There were no sentries, no men at all, but under their famous tree a cauldron lay on its side, soot-blackened, in the ashes of a dead fire. Suleiman looked at it, his face expressionless, but the pace at which he rode perceptibly increased. He led his little troop to the Hall of Audience near the janissary barracks. This too was deserted, but there were men lounging about outside, men in dirty tunics with tired, brutish faces. Suleiman looked at the state of them and felt the life-giving rage boil up inside him. His hands trembled and clenched on the reins, he snarled an order for the regimental officers to come to him and marched into the hall.

He did not have to wait long. The word ran like lightning through the courts, 'the Padishah is come!' and the ringleaders, who had been waiting for this, pressed into the hall, bitter, angry men brandishing swords and screaming at him to do his holy duty and lead them against the infidel. More men pushed in behind them and most of the officers were left outside, unable to get in.

Suleiman drew his sword and stood watchful, grateful to them for the opportunity to let loose his rage. As the first man pressed up to him, screaming, senselessly brandishing a javelin, he lunged and took him in the throat with his sword-point and saw him crash to the carpet. The noise he made seemed deafening against the hysterical gabble of his fellows. They saw and heard, too, and momentarily were silenced. But the second man's momentum carried him on, sword flourished in a freckled fat paw, and his Sultan looked him in the face and cut him down. A third he wounded in the shoulder and spared.

There was silence now. They had seen a lot of blood on carpets during the last couple of days, but had not exactly expected that any of it would be their own. They watched, uncertain for the most part. But at the back were still plenty of angry, determined older men, watching with narrowed eyes. There was a sudden sound in the new silence, a small sound but menacing, as a dozen bows were drawn back, arrows fitted and aimed deliberately at their Sultan's heart. All eyes turned back to him to see how he would take it, and so far as they could see, it made no impression on him at all. He just stood there, sword dripping blood on the carpet, coolly looking at a fourth man who might, or might not, have been menacing him. This fellow was a cool one, too. A little chap, his uniform still neat and dapper, he held a sabre in a capable hand and was obviously well able to use it, except that he smiled suddenly, shook his head ruefully and sheathed it. There was a sound then like an enormous sigh, as several hundred men let go their breath. Only then did Suleiman raise his eyes to the drawn bowstrings. His eyes narrowed, but there was no hesitation about him. Quite deliberately he glanced over his shoulder, taking his time about it, apparently to see if the doorway was clear. It was. In fact, the regimental officers were in now, their swords drawn. Suleiman took one step back, paused to sheath his sword, and then calmly continued his backward progress, stepping lightly and silently in his soft, dusty boots.

As soon as he was outside, he heard words of command ring out as the officers took over, and if the smile that crossed his lips beneath his moustache was at all ironic, he made no comment to his Pashas when he rejoined them.

It was stalemate, after all. They could quite easily have killed him if they had been determined enough. Equally, he had shown them his courage and his contempt for soldiers who behaved like ruffians. From then onwards they lived in fear of each other. They had shown their Sultan that he had failed in his duty towards them, and in his duty as the bearer of the Sword of Osman against the infidel whom he had sworn to eradicate from the face of the earth. Their philosophy was a rough and ready one with very little about it that was noble, but they could enforce it and Suleiman never forgot it. Next spring he would be ready to lead them against the Hungarians, or anyone else who might offer him an excuse. But in the meantime there would have to be a reckoning. The ringleaders of the uprising were court-martialled and executed and many of the field officers and company commanders reduced in rank. After this severity, Suleiman thought about the harshness of the life of the janissaries and distributed 200,000 gold pieces among them as a sweetener. He wasn't prepared to do more. Soldiers were not supposed to be pampered.

Suleiman's own courage gained him a kudos which he knew, secretly, he didn't deserve. He had learned a lot from the experience and hadn't enjoyed any of it. He supposed that there might one day be a world in which people did not make war on each other, but it emphatically was not a world which contained janissaries. He and they were inextricably bound together for the rest of his life, and that life would have to follow the pattern they dictated.

It was several days before husband and wife were reunited. An anonymous vagabond boy riding to Edirne in a day and a night was one thing, but it was the Sultana Hasseki who had to come back to Istanbul, properly dressed and veiled and driven in a carriage with an escort, as a royal lady should be.

Once their affectionate greetings were over, Suleiman demanded and got the full story of her adventures. He was silent so long after she had finished that she looked anxiously up at him, thinking he was angry with her.

'It wasn't a very dignified performance, I suppose,' she said at last, penitent.

He turned to look at her in amazement and then said quietly, 'You humble me, my Khurrem.'

Abashed, she could think of nothing to say or do, at first. Much later, thinking to amuse him, she said, 'Macar told me the most difficult part of the whole operation was buying women's clothes for me at Edirne. They were very suspicious of him at the market there.'

Suleiman laughed. 'Ah, yes,' he said, 'I have not forgotten Macar. I'm afraid you must prepare yourself to find a new secretary, my Khurrem.'

'Oh no! That's not fair,' she cried.

'To you, or to him?' He took her hand again. 'Haven't you thought, now that you know him better, that so mettlesome and courageous a horse deserves a wider field than he has at the moment? The post of Emir al Akhor is vacant.'

She was impressed by the high-sounding title. 'What does he do?'

He laughed. 'Something that should be child's play to Macar. He has charge of all my and the army's horses. After this week's experiences he should find it a restful occupation.'

However unwilling, she had to agree. The post might have been created for him and Macar deserved it.

She felt suddenly tired and a little sad. For all the risk and fear and, she had to admit, lack of dignity, it had been a great adventure and she had enjoyed nearly all of it. It would take a little while to settle down to ordinary life again.

She caught Suleiman's eye. He was smiling at her as if he understood exactly how she felt. Khurrem smiled back uncertainly. But then she suddenly realized that just over a week ago none of it had happened. If she looked back over the past five years, why, what a lifetime of experience she had packed into it. With her little family growing up, and a great Sultan for her husband, the future would be just as exciting.

Suleiman sent urgently for Ibrahim to come back and help clear up the confusion the janissaries had created. When he heard what had happened the Grand Vizier clothed himself in mourning (his dramatic instinct was always very sure) and came hotfoot. He got a tremendous welcome home, but he was badly shocked when he saw the state of his palace and the destruction of his treasures. Still, he recovered quickly enough once he embarked on the task of replacing them.

Glossary of Turkish Words

Aga	A general officer
Aghalik	An Aga's office or post
Akinji	The irregular cavalry
Asper	A silver coin of low value (100 to a piastre)
Azabs	The irregular infantry
Beylerbey	A general of feudal cavalry and governor of an important province or group of provinces
Bunchuk	The horsetail standard
Caravanserai	A kind of oriental inn where caravans put up
Chaush-bashi	A chief usher or marshal; a grand official
Damat	Imperial son-in-law. Strictly, only given to husbands of daughters married while their fathers were alive
Defterdar	Financial minister or treasurer
Dervish	A Muslim 'friar' who has taken vows of poverty and austere life
Devshirme	A gathering or collecting of tribute boys
Divan	The Ottoman council of state
Dolman	A long robe with tight sleeves worn by men under the caftan
Gömlek	A woman's chemise or underblouse
Halva	A sweet based on semolina and almonds
Hanim	Lady

Harem	That part of the Muslim house occupied by the women
Hasseki	'Chosen'. The title of the sultan's favourite lady of the Harem
Hatun	Lady
Ikbal	'Fortunate'. The first rank for advancement in the harem
Jineta	Simply a light-weight saddle used for riding astride with short stirrups. *Not* a Turkish word but Spanish
Kadi	A judge
Kadin	A woman of the harem receiving the sultan's special favour
Kapu Aga	The white eunuch in charge of the Topkapi Saray
Kaziasker	Judge of the Army; one of the two chief judges of the Ottoman Empire
Kiaya	Steward; lieutenant; housekeeper
Kizlar Agasi	General of the Girls; the black eunuch in charge of the harem, i.e. the Old Palace
Köfte	Rissole or meatball, usually of minced lamb
Kushk (ang. kiosk)	A light open pavilion or summerhouse
Mamluk	A member of the military body which seized the Eygptian throne in 1254 and remained the ruling class until 1811
Mufti	A Muslim legal authority. The Grand Mufti is Head of the Muslim Institution
Mullah	One learned in theology and the sacred law of Islam
Nishanji	A chancellor; the keeper of the Sultan's seal affixed to all documents issued by the Divan
Oda	(Lit., a room) A company of janissaries, later, a regiment or division

Orta	See *Oda* above
Padishah	'Sovereign'. A title of Persian origin. It indicated the highest possible rank and was applied only to the sultan
Pasha	A very high-ranking official
Peik	A member of the Sultan's bodyguard of halberdiers
Piyade	Infantryman; foot-soldier
Sanjak	A district
Sanjak bey	A high officer of feudal cavalry, and governor of a district
Selamlik	The men's quarters in any house. Lit. 'The place of greeting', i.e. the one place where visitors can be received, as opposed to the harem, which is sacred to the women
Seraskier	A commander-in-chief
Shahzade	'Son of the Emperor'; title given to the Sultan's son
Sheikh-ul-Islam	The Mufti of Constantinople and Head of the Muslim Institution
Sherbet	A cooling drink made of fruit juice and sweetened water
Sheri	A sacred law, not subject to amendment, but capable of modification
Shi'ite	A member of the Shia, a Muslim sect which regards Mohammed's cousin, Ali, the fourth Caliph, as the Prophet's true successor
Sipahi or Spahi	A cavalry soldier; a member of either the standing or feudal cavalry
Solak	A janissary bowman of the Sultan's personal guard
Sultana Valideh	Queen Mother
Sunni	The orthodox Muslims who accept the traditions as well as the Koran

Ulema — The whole body of Muslims learned in the Sacred Law; the council of wise men presided over by the Sheikh-ul-Islam

Select Bibliography

Admiralty (Great Britain), Naval Intelligence Division, *Turkey*, 2 vols. (London, 1942–3)

Alderson, A.D., *The Structure of the Ottoman Dynasty* (Oxford, 1956)

Aslanapa, Oktay, *Turkish Art and Architecture* (London, 1971)

Bradford, Ernle, *The Shield and the Sword: the Knights of St John* (London, 1972)

Brockman, Eric, *The Two Sieges of Rhodes, 1480–1522* (London, 1969)

Coles, Paul, *The Ottoman Impact on Europe* (London, 1968)

Corrie, Jean, *The Travellers' Guide to Rhodes* (London, 1970)

Cragg, Kenneth, *History of the Ottoman Turks* (London, 1878)

Downey, Fairfax, *The Grande Turke: Suleyman the Magnificent* (London, 1929)

Durrell, Lawrence, *Reflections on a Marine Venus* (London, 1953)

Forster, C.T. and Daniell, F.H.B., *The Life and Letters of Ogier Ghiselin de Busbecq*, 2 vols. (London, 1881)

Goodwin, Godfrey, *A History of Ottoman Architecture* (London, 1971)

Hasluck, F.W., *Christianity and Islam under the Sultans*, 2 vols. (Oxford, 1929)

Holt, P.M., *Egypt and the Fertile Crescent, 1516–1922* (London, 1966)

Inalcik, Halil, *The Ottoman Empire: the Classical Age, 1300–1600* (London, 1973)

Jenkins, Hester, *Ibrahim Pasha*, Studies in History, Economics and Public Law, (New York, 1911)

Lamb, Harold, *Suleiman the Magnificent: Sultan of the East*

(London, 1952)
Lapidus, I.M., *Muslim Cities in the Later Middle Ages* (Cambridge, Mass., 1967)
Lewis, Bernard, *Istanbul and the Civilization of the Ottoman Empire* (Norman, Oklahoma, 1963)
Lewis, Raphaela, *Everyday Life in Ottoman Turkey* (London, 1971)
Lybyer, Albert Howe, *The Government of the Ottoman Empire in the Time of Suleiman the Magnificent* (New York, 1966)
Merriman, Roger Bigelow, *Suleiman the Magnificent, 1522–1566* (New York, 1966)
Pallis, Alexander, *In the Days of the Janissaries: Old Turkish Life as Depicted in the 'Travel-Book' of Evliya Chelebi* (London, 1951)
Penzer, N.M., *The Harem* (London, 1930)
Seward, Desmond, *The Monks of War* (London, 1972)
Shaw, Stanford, J., *History of the Ottoman Empire and Modern Turkey*, Vol. 1, *Empire of the Ghazis, 1280–1808* (London, 1976)
Stratton, Arthur, *Sinan* (London, 1972)
Sumner-Boyd, Hilary and John Freely, *Strolling through Istanbul: a Guide to the City* (Istanbul, 1972)